MW00908564

Abused children often create imagin‍ with an impossible reality. But what if the imaginary friend became real and the secret worlds could be visited? *Beyond the Horse's Eye – a Fantasy Out of Time* is a book built around a fascinating concept: empathy for all living things can be channeled into a powerful energy force. A period of rich ferment—the 1960s in the U.S.– with opposition to the Vietnam War, the civil rights movement, the movement for sexual liberation, revisited, as species beyond humans, join forces with young earthlings, now with empath power, and cooperate to change history. Worlds, energy forms and loves collide with unexpected results. An exciting read that is wise and full of intuitions on pain, survival, rehabilitation and change.

Sara Flounders, Co-Director, International Action Center

By employing the thoroughness of an architect's layered blueprint, the savvy of a scientist's research, the imagination of a painter's universe-scape, Janet Rose has constructed a fascinating intergalactic setting inhabited with larger-than-life extraterrestrial gurus and their earthling protégés, a trio of multi-talented, street-smart avengers. The wise Imari from Galern II train the threesome, who have overcome abusive childhoods, as Travel Monitors to engage in high-stakes interplanetary drama to save the universe from repeating horrific devastations by present-day intergalactic and earthling imperialists. In this breathtaking adventure we witness LGBTQ sensibilities expand as we travel with J and her comrades through Earth's transition from the Atomic to Empath Age. Fasten your space-belts as we, the readers, are challenged and inspired by these unique characters' impassioned struggles (from beyond our galaxy, to Jupiter's Europa and New Jersey), along with their extraterrestrial allies, to save humanity, universal harmony and egalitarianism.

Jeri Hilderley, Author, *Mari* and *Rune Seeker*

Janet Rose has written an intriguing intergalactic mystery, thriller, love story. If you want to be transported from Earth's harsh realities to a far more evolved place of compassion and connection, read this book!

Susan Elizabeth Davis, Author, *Love Means Second Chances*

Take me some place I've never been before. Take me to a place that is new and yet is part of my earliest dreams of what could be. Janet Rose blends the yearnings and nightmares we remember from childhood with the sophistication of political awareness in the present, but never lets us forget the intensity of our earliest memories. In a complex amalgam of past and present, she allows us to unite the personal and political in a fascinating journey from the end of World War II to the uncertain present. This odd combination of fantasy and political commentary is a must-read for anyone interested in the fate of the human race.

Sue Harris, Ph.D., Psychologist; Director, *Poison Dust: A New Look at U.S. Radioactive Weapons*; Co-Director, Peoples Video Network; Harry Potter aficionado.

3/29/14
To Nicolai
Enjoy !
Janet

Beyond the Horse's Eye

A Fantasy Out of Time

Janet Rose

word space PUBLICATIONS

Beyond the Horse's Eye—A Fantasy Out of Time
Copyright © 2012 Janet Rose

WordSpace Publications: WordSpace@WordSpacePublications.com

Library of Congress Control Number: 2012953580

International Standard Book Numbers

Trade paperback: ISBN-10: 0988539705

E-book: ISBN-13: 978-0-9885397-0-9

Text set in Minion Pro and Myriad Pro
Designed by Lallan Schoenstein

Printed in the United States of America

Copyright © 2003 Mumia Abu-Jamal from *Death Blossoms*, reprinted by permission of the Frances Goldin Literary Agency.

From *Trail of Tears: The Rise and Fall of the Cherokee Nation* by John Ehle, copyright © 1988 by John Ehle. Used by permission of Doubleday, a division of Random House, Inc.

From "Power." Copyright © 1978 by Audre Lorde, from *The Collected Poems of Audre Lorde* by Audre Lorde. Used by permission of W.W. Norton & Company, Inc. and Charlotte Sheedy Literary Agency (UK rights).

From *Foundations of the New South Africa* by John Pampallis, copyright © 1991, by John Pampallis. Used by permission of Zed Books.

From "Ballad of Birmingham" in *Roses and Revolutions: The Selected Writings of Dudley Randall ed.* by Melba Joyce Boyd, copyright © 2009, by Wayne State Press. Used by permission of Melba Joyce Boyd.

From *Hiroshima: Breaking the Silence* by Howard Zinn, in Open Magazine Pamphlet Series, copyright © 1995. Used by permission of Myla Kabat-Zinn.

The photograph of the Horsehead Nebula on the cover is incorporated into the design with the kind permission of the astrophotographer David Malin, © Australian Astronomical Observatory/David Malin Images (http://www.aao.gov.au/images/captions/aat036.html).

The photograph of the Warsaw Jewish Ghetto Uprising, April-May 1943, on the cover of the booklet *Save the Children*, by permission of the United States Holocaust Memorial Museum. Credit: National Archives and Records Administration, College Park Instytut Pamieci Narodowej Panstwowe Muzeum Auschwitz-Birkenau w Oswiecimiu.

Cover and text design: Lallan Schoenstein; Initial cover design: Felix Serrano

To all who have struggled, do struggle,
and will struggle with tender revolutionary
solidarity for a humane and just world.

History is a clock that people use to tell the political and cultural time of day. It is also a compass that people use to find themselves on the map of human geography. History tells a people where they have been and what they have been, where they are and what they are; most important history tells a people where they still must go and what they still must be.

Dr John Henrik Clarke

Still, many of these children don't give up. Perhaps the best thing we can do for them is to nurture their hope— give them reason for new hopes and feed the hope already within them so it can grow into something strong that will sustain them through life. ... Children do not only have an innate hope. They are hope. And more than that: they are our future. ... They carry their hope with them to a future we can't see.

Mumia Abu-Jamal, from "Children" in
Death Blossoms: Reflections from a Prisoner of Conscience

We are an army of lovers who cannot be defeated. We are laying the groundwork for another world.

Occupy Wall Street, from
"First Communiqué; Invisible Army"

CONTENTS

PROLOGUE

1947

A dim ovular vehicle, gently shimmering in reds, greens and yellows, float-ed silently down the Hudson River Valley, honing in on the red and green rotating beacon on top of the George Washington Bridge. It hovered briefly over the beacon, merging with its beams. They brightened. Then it looped and glided north-eastward, unnoticed by the pair of lovers on Riverside Drive, or by the overnight truckers making their way across the bridge from New Jersey. Slowly it dipped toward the dark tarpapered roof of a six-story tenement in Washington Heights.

Within minutes a thin shimmering figure emerged from the vehicle. At first glance, one might say it was human, with its two arms and legs, loosely adorned with soft vibrant multicolored silks. But it was disproportionately thin for its almost seven feet, so thin one would expect it to struggle against the swift October winds. Instead, it stood without effort in the shadow of the vehicle, listening. Then it walked slowly toward the edge, stepped out onto a fire escape ladder and glided down to a fifth floor window without touching a step. At the same time, two other almost identical figures emerged from the vehicle, and, turning their heads toward their disappearing comrade, stood perfectly still in the shadow of their craft.

❋ ❋ ❋

J held her breath and listened for every tiny sound. Had she fallen asleep by mistake? She must mind-protect Mommy. She must stay awake to grab Daddy's mind and put him to sleep before he grabbed at Mommy and gave her those big black bruises. Sometimes his dizzy gasoline stink filled her nose and made her carsick, so she couldn't send her mind into the living room way down the hall. If she could hear him coming, she could sometimes make Mommy not feel before his stink made her too vomity to do that mind-pro-tecting thing.

When he did come home early and just went to bed, well, then she would just be able to sleep. But first Mommy had to check the room. Under the bed for bears. Push the door flat against the wall so nothing could hide behind it. Close the shade of the fire escape window because shadows from the light outside could become bouncing goblins on the walls. So many things to check. "Okay, J, I checked under the bed. No bears. See? No bears. Now close your eyes." If her singsong voice had that slight "hurry up already" in it, J's throat would tighten. When Mommy's voice sounded like that, there'd be no goodnight hug.

Sometimes she fell asleep by mistake, and later in the night she would wake up to Mommy crying softly in the bathroom, right next to J's room. Sometimes she'd brave the bears and tiptoe (can't wake up Daddy!) into the bathroom and hold on to Mommy's back going up and down with her crying. Mommy would be sitting on the bathroom floor next to the tub, her head buried in her arms. She'd just hold Mommy a little bit because Mommy didn't like hugging, and then she'd tiptoe back to bed before Mommy shooed her away. Sometimes Mommy got really mad right away. That was worse. Sometimes she tried sending her mind-kisses instead; other times she'd just squeezed Mommy's crying out of her brain.

Once she decided to be really brave. She scampered down the hall to the living room. "Stop! Stop! Stop it!" she screamed, pulling at Daddy's pea jacket from behind with all her might. Maybe she dreamed she was so very brave. She didn't remember what happened next. She was back in bed, sobbing under her pillow so she couldn't hear them any more. That's when she decided to do that mind-protecting and mind-kissing thing.

Once Daddy's yelling and thumping had been so loud, the policemen came. J pretended she was asleep when they came into her room, her cheeks burning hot when one of them called Mommy "ma'am" and said what a cute little girl she had. Another time, somebody knocked on the pipes. Daddy's yelling suddenly hushed. Then he was crashing pots in the kitchen. "I'll show you who to bang at!" as he smashed them against the pipes. Maybe that's when the policemen came.

Now Daddy was coming home late again.

If only her lady would come to her now, before he smashed into the apartment. She imagined her lady's strong and loving hand and placed it on her back. She heard her lady's fairy angel words in her ear. Her loving hand on her back spilled into her throat, a silent crying ecstasy. She made her lady disappear so that she could make her come to her again. In her head she made her lady say, "My poor little baby girl. Everything's going to be okay now. You'll see." Then she made her lady just hold her tight so she could silently cry herself to sleep in her lady's loving arms.

No, a better idea. Maybe she could pretend her lady helps her get onto the fire escape, and helps her brave the goblins, and then she could dangle her feet through the bars of the fire escape like she always did during the day.

And it would feel so good, hanging her legs between the fire escape bars, pee-pee and tummy pressed against the bars, real hard, five stories up. Falling without falling. A good dizzy, rushing from her toes to her throat. The night goblins will kill her. That's okay. Mommy and Daddy will really miss her and love her oh so much. And Mommy and Daddy will cry like they did when Bubba died, and love each other again. She won't have to mind-protect anymore, ever.

She thought up her lady for one last time. Her lady will make her braver. She put her lady's hand on her back, and scooted barefoot past the bears (waiting under her bed to grab her ankles) toward the nightmare shadows at the window, very quickly and quietly, so Mommy and Daddy wouldn't hear. She climbed out on the fire escape, sat down, and eased her tushy toward the bars. She pushed each leg out through separate openings until they swayed freely over the alleyway five stories down. Falling without falling.

She shut her eyes tight to hide from the goblins that were surely creeping toward her.

Maybe it was very late or very early, because the George Washington Bridge trucks were not humm humm humming. Maybe she just didn't hear them.

This time, when her cry rippled from her spine into her neck and into her throat, while she was falling without falling from the fire escape, her lady's hand (not goblins!) felt really warm and strong. Like it was stroking, pressing against her back for real. J's eyes were wet. Her chin was wet. Her cheeks burned hot. And she very much wanted to open her eyes. She didn't dare. She didn't want her make-believe, maybe real live angel lady to go away.

She allowed herself to be lifted. She walked with her lady, her eyes squeezed tight, like she was asleep but awake.

* * *

The tall, thin shimmering figure guided the tiny child up the ladder to the roof, where the dim ovular vehicle glowing in reds, greens and yellows sat in silence, and two tall thin figures stood along side.

* * *

The winking yellow and white lights of the city formed a soft backdrop that night for the iridescent tableau in the center of the tarpaper roof where I met my future.

The familiar, strong and tender hand on my back, the other on my shoulder, guided me toward the center of the roof. My hugging angel lady for real! I decided that this real live lady wouldn't go away if I opened my eyes. So I did. I couldn't quite see my lady. Everything was wispy and blurry, but I did make out many shadows, and two long, thin wavering goblins vaguely lit by the moon glow and vibrating in rainbow colors brighter than the colors in my Crayola box. The air smelled like burnt toast, or maybe burnt chocolate pudding. I didn't feel scared at all.

The lady on the roof said there wasn't much time. There was some faint murmuring all around her. So these were the fire-escape goblins, I thought. It would be just fine to be kidnapped by them, just as long as my angel lady came along with me.

I think it was ten years later, when I was fifteen, I admitted to Telmx just how much I cherished her hand on my back that night. We called it "the roof moment." She said, "When I said there wasn't much time, we knew you had no concept of time as a dimension. Then we felt you struggling to understand our deeper meaning. It took us by surprise, and we giggled with delight. I was also very tense. You were my first recruit."

I learned that Telmx had been a new mentor, so talented and dedicated that her research earned her the honor of being the youngest Travel Scout graduate ever assigned mission recruitment duty on a primitive planet. Because I was her first recruit, Telmx held me as special. I still feel that tingly glow when I think about our "roof moment."*

*My life-partner Scotty crafted our recollections into Beyond the Horse's Eye by visiting and recording the Virtual-Empath (V.E.)-dream-memories of everyone involved in the Mission. In the tradition of the Imari, she then invited each "character" to use a V.E.-viewer to enter and review the manuscript residing in one of her empath chambers (she printed out hard copies for the earthlings who weren't yet empathically capable of entering someone else's chambers). My friend Katie was inspired to write her own chapter; and we pushed Scotty (who meticulously had kept her personal point of view out of the book) to do the same. Everyone else tweaked a fact here and there but approved the work as is. As I revisited those times (I am almost 70), particularly the early years, I too was moved to add my reflections, which Scotty interspersed throughout. We decided to call her book science fiction, because if it were characterized as historical truth, all of us— and the work itself—would be retro-swept into oblivion. —J

PART I

1947-1957

CHAPTER ONE

Telmx

The Sub-Committee on Intergalactic Security and Recruitment held hearings in the northeast spoke of the sprawling Council complex on Locur Centrex. The Sub-Committee consisted of eighty-two representatives from the full 2,867-member Intergalactic Council, which in turn represented the 300 billion different species from thirty—soon to be thirty-one—galaxies. Telmx squatted among a handful of sentients in the reception area, an immense comfortable chamber tastefully decorated with miniature tapestries, frescos and holograms from every part of the known universe. Soft out-loud music, along with their appropriate aromas, competed with her anxious anticipation of the hearing. Goshing, her mentor and a permanent member of the Sub-Committee, was probably at that very moment sponsor-presenting Telmx's petition for monitor recruitment right behind the huge closed doors on the far side of the reception area.

No way of knowing what was going on. In the Intergalactic Council complex, shielding was so tight, even Goshing and Telmx, highly evolved Imari empaths, could not empath to each other across even the thinnest of barriers. She couldn't even read others in the reception area, squatting, sitting, lying down, standing, swimming (in huge portable tanks), hovering around her. Every time she visited Locur Centrex, there were more varieties of sentient life forms to learn about. This time, a pair of round, floppy-eared gray beings hovered far above her, near the top of the domed ceiling. Their noses resembled the elephants she had recently encountered scanning the Earth's jungles, except, like most sentients who agreed to join the council, they had huge sapien hands—four of them, in this case. Some day she would read up on studies about the correlation between the rate of planetary industrialization and the number of thumbs the dominant species possessed. Near her, two Orangas were chattering in a language she vaguely understood. They were small furry creatures with long shingled tails, whose dramatic gestures punctuated their loud vibrant conversation.

Her petition was going to be tricky. By accident, responding to the distress of the little earthling child, she had entered her mind too completely. J was now a Level I empath, without the express consent of the Council. She needed that consent without letting on that she had already inadvertently recruited. If they found out she had superseded her authority, she would lose all she had trained for and ever wanted to be. Old Gir and Goshing had been great about it, but the Council would certainly expel her from the Order of Empath Travel Scouts, not to mention the censures that Goshing and Gir would have to endure. Better if this little detail were just kind of left out—which made her all the more grateful no one in these chambers could listen to each other's minds.

"Telmx Galencia Eja-K'arika?"

A sinewy calico Gorrime standing before her broke her reverie. It still startled her that in this place of empath silence she could not anticipate someone intent on addressing her. She knew this receptionist from last time—a distinguished Imari-like sentient, except he was much shorter, and possessed overlapping tufts of long wafting cilia along his forehead and the sides of his face.

"Yes." Her mouth went dry and her cilia began to ache. So it's time, she thought.

"Please follow me."

She felt for her V.E.-disks, now shoved deep into the front pocket folds of her ceremonial wishaptha, and stood to her full height, dwarfing most of the sentients around her.

✳ ✳ ✳

Asmurbari greeted Telmx at the chamber entrance. She eagerly absorbed his soothing aura as he leaned over and warmly squeezed her hand. He was almost twice her size, with those chiseled sapien features characteristic of his rainforest homeworld. From under his emerald tunic, black and gray fur emitted the same tranquil aroma her travel teammate Old Gir had once given her for her Name Day. He led her to a small dais, where a soft mat faced the multi-tiered semicircles of intergalactic delegates in their individualized species comfort zones, on pillows, chairs, lean-backs, mats, or floating in tanks. He squeezed her hand again, and lumbered slowly across the floor to his lean-back among the delegates.

The huge chamber was colorfully decorated with intricate tapestries and frescos. Its dome was divided into sectors, and within each one hovered a muted hologram of a galaxy, some spiral, some spherical, others elongated and still others, various unique shapes. Rising and setting within each galaxy floated smaller holograms of land and cityscapes, natural and architectural treasures from the homeworlds of the representative species. Every few minutes, each galaxy hologram rotated slightly within its sector to form a fresh background for newly materializing treasures.

Telmx squatted awkwardly on the mat, pulled her V.E.-disks from her pocket and laid them on the viewing console hovering on her left. She wasn't used to speaking in public. She hated all the attention focused on her, and wished she didn't have to sit so alone, separated from those she loved and depended upon. She most dreaded the cross-examination without having Goshing's mind in her mind. She felt like an awkward rebellious adolescent, defending her right to participate in empath circles or to drink bot before her Ascension date.

The murmuring in the chamber was deafening. Being an empath did not prepare her for this part of her work. How did Goshing do it so easily? She spotted her on the third tier, talking animatedly to an Oranga squatting behind her. She wondered if Goshing knew she had entered and was playing diplomatic dumb. Perhaps she was drumming up more support. What if she says something Goshing doesn't approve of? It's one thing to be supervised after the fact. It's another when your mentor observes you right on the spot. On the spot—that's what it was. If only Goshing would turn around, just to say hello.

On the first tier, almost directly below Goshing, sat, or rather dozed, two Pomdos, black and white bear-like sentients, strikingly similar to Earth's pandas. The elder delegate had been devastating and disarming during his cross-examinations the previous time. The younger, a newcomer, a middle-aged female Pomdos, must be his non-voting apprentice and his eventual replacement she had heard about. Between them was a large bin of bamboo shards. Nearby, several smaller species of Pomdos-like sentients were also dozing, some hovering, some squatting, and one bobbing peacefully in a portable tank. Their block was large and formidable. They half listened, but they vigorously objected to almost everything the Imari proposed, and their faction was growing in numbers.

The Imari, the Imari-like, and their allies, those who paid attention to the lessons of history and insisted on maintaining vigilance, were probably still the plurality, but their supremacy was precarious. If only Goshing would turn around.

A series of bells signaled five minutes to deliberations. People were taking their places. Some were fiddling with their V.E.-viewers and headphones. Another Asmurbari squeeze would be great just about now. Goshing reached for Telmx's eyes, smiled broadly and raised her head high, revealing her long throbbing neck veins, the traditional Imari gesture of support and strength.

Telmx slowly let her breath out, raised her own head and nodded in acceptance. She searched deep into the side pocket of her formal wishaptha for the gift Goshing had pressed into her hand at the café that morning, a smooth jade carving of Kro'an'ot, the legendary founder of Modern Imari Empath. She fingered its intricate curves. "Wise awareness and foresight in the midst of adversity," Goshing empath-whispered as she left Telmx for the morning session. "See you soon, my dearest. Let Kro'an'ot in your heart find her own way to your tongue."

She reached for a small steaming cup of chi from the cart as it floated by. Now the second set of bells. Murmurings gave way to softer stirrings, as people settled in with their tea and adjusted their earphones. The elder Pomdos was alert now, shifting his great weight forward in order to poke at his sleeping apprentice.

The dome lights faded slightly, and a hover-glow illuminated a small, stout sapien, speaking in a tongue Telmx could not decipher. She rotated the dial on her earphones.

"... just returned from C42, in the R-345 system within the G'uw spiral galaxy. Her graduate simulations of its future, presented last year, detected troublesome signs of primitive empath travel by an ethically immature species residing on that minuscule minor planet they call 'Earth.' At that time, the General Council authorized her Imari Travel Scout team to perform a limited close-in scan.

"In amplification and clarification of Councilmember Goshing's sponsoring petition before the break, we now turn our attention to her student, Telmx Galencia Eja-K'arika of the Order of Empath Travel Scouts, who will present to this Sub-Committee her triad team's close-in scan data and petition."

The formal language was too loud, too cumbersome. She fingered the Kro'an'ot stone.

"... she seeks this Sub-Committee's approval of her team's petition for additional allocations from the central empath energy reserves to continue their work and for a revised mandate of their Mission on C42, to be submitted to the General Council body, which convenes at secondary sunrise tomorrow."

Murmurs.

"Telmx Galencia Eja-K'arika, welcome to the formal deliberations of the Sub-Committee on Intergalactic Security and Recruitment. I am Councilmember Troya, and I will be coordinating today's proceedings. Please submit your initial set of exhibits to the V.E."

Telmx sucked in her breath and glanced at Goshing, now fiddling with her viewer. Telmx slipped the first disk into the slot. "I thank you, Councilmember Troya, learned representatives. I am honored to represent Triad Travel Team 1678-7." The hover-glows were slightly tropical and emitted a faint aroma of hylith and camroad. A bit comforting, but she was unused to depending so thoroughly upon sight, sound, and aromas. Without empath, how do people truly understand each other and know if they are truly understood?

"This first exhibit is for new delegates—my initial Level VI graduate project simulations of planet C42, which I reference by its indigenous name, 'Earth.'"

She paused, watching various members around the dome entering their V.E.-viewers. The younger Pomdos concentrated, while her elder reclined in apparent boredom.

After a few minutes, she continued. "Based on those initial simulations, my team performed close-in scanning of this planet, which has, since my initial graduate simulations, just abruptly ended a global war by wielding their new Atomic Age weapons." The elder Pomdos closed his eyes and started to doze. The younger looked blankly at Telmx. The rest of their faction was fidgeting or comatose.

I shouldn't have mentioned atomic power, she thought. Too soon. Now they won't hear the rest. She looked at Goshing, but could discern no sign. Goshing said to be clear, accurate, without being alarming. So hard to navigate between accurate and alarming.

"Um, we, my team— (what if she starts to stammer—and they haven't even begun the cross-examination?). As on most planets, its indigenous have always used primitive empath communication, primarily without realizing it. They do it haphazardly, and with almost no ability to focus. But (here it comes, she hoped accurate without alarming) our close-in scan simulations—see exhibit two—predict with extremely high probability that by the beginning of their twenty-first century, they will discover its power and succeed in harnessing empath energy for space travel.

"By the middle of that century, they will be operating slave-labor mining camps on asteroids, moons, and other planetary bodies in their own solar system. They will conscript indigenous species and 'disappeared' prisoners from their own planet. And exhibit three: by their twenty-second century (a mere half century from now in our time reckoning), they will have enslaved indigenous sentients on Garethob, the nearest inhabited planet outside their solar system." She didn't dare turn to face the tiny delegate from Garethob. Goshing had warned her not to push the point too hard, but they both had agreed that mentioning that particular scan prediction was crucial.

Maybe that's enough, she thought. Surely the Sub-Committee would allocate additional empath energy reserves to this project without having to present the rest of her team's most alarming scan predictions about Earth's eventual mind-alteration arsenal.

A small amber-winged Equine rose slightly from her perch. "Young Telmx," she said, "what in this report would compel this body to authorize more empath energy reserves for your project? You present nothing but primitive stages of development on a remote speck of the universe. There are many other planetary scout teams whose visits and scans reveal far more disturbing predictions, on newly developed sentient civilizations, yet we wait patiently for these planets to develop on their own without concern that they are a threat to the rest of the civilized universe. Witness the multitude of species that developed ethics and empath technology in sync with each other, without interference from the Council. They now grace our deliberations in this chamber."

"Enslavement and exploitation, colonization and profiteering are not unheard of amongst infantile species," said the Oranga who sat behind Goshing. "This new species will mature over time and forgo such practices. It may be simply a matter of time, young Telmx, with all due respect."

Most of the Pomdos Alliance was fully asleep. The old Pomdos himself was verging on oblivion. Since she had already lost them, probably she could reveal a bit more, to sway the others. "This planet's empath technology will develop at an alarming rate. At least two of their influential scientists will soon be experimenting with primitive empath mind-alteration, bordering on a retro-sweep technology, and as you know, in the hands of an infantile species...." She avoided looking at the elder Pomdos as she ventured into this alarming territory. "By their twenty-second century they will be altering their own history, and, having conquered, enslaved and colonized other systems in their own galaxy, their retro-sweep arsenal will then be aimed at the rest of the civilized universe. In other words, this Sub-Committee meeting might never be recorded in our history."

She didn't mean to say it. It just slipped out.

What would become of little J if Telmx couldn't return to watch over her, to tell her again and again that even though she was so, so talented at mind-bending, she wasn't stupid and evil because she couldn't always protect her mother or make her parents love each other again? Goshing's warning in the café echoed: "Don't let your love for J distract you from cogently and patiently making your case."

Goshing was staring at her. Too strong, too soon, she radiated in her eyes, the slant of her mouth. Telmx thought, "I'm botching it. I'm too new at this."

"I am only making a pre..."

"Young Telmx," interrupted another Equine member, pounding her hoofs on her mat, "surely you are not proposing that we retro-sweep this obscure planet in the off chance that they would come zooming into our realm and bring back primitive behaviors by retro-sweeping our entire civilized universe!"

"No, no, I don't mean a retro-sweep at all. I mean, I believe I have presented the worst-case probability too strenuously. I mean—"

"Even if this outcome were remotely possible, this body would never approve drastic action such as a planetary retro-sweep, and even in the most extreme circumstances, the General Council would only consider directly adjusting the rogue planet's history a millennium or two. We haven't even launched a recruitment strategy. Why wouldn't we simply opt for indigenous monitoring and mindshifting? Train one talented indigenous recruit, who can warn us if and when their research truly becomes a hazard requiring more drastic measures."

Yes! This is exactly what she had been seeking! Approve recruitment of a single monitor/ Magnitude I mindshifter! "I do propose a recruitment strategy."

The elder Pomdos was suddenly completely awake. "Her presentation of 'worst case' is deliberate and calculated. She is fear-mongering us, Imari style!" He bowed in mock ceremony. "With all due respect to your genius, courage and commitment, and to the very revered elder council member, your learned sponsor T'chembe zel-Goshing," he continued too grandly, "you, like your entire overzealous paranoid Imari species, mesmerize these honorable delegates with preposterous assumptions. Self-centered manipulations went out of existence so long ago. It is only the Imari who insist on keeping such phrases in our vocabulary. No! That's an impossible scenario! Enslavement and exploitation? Such phenomenon will never be part of our lives because sentient species can't possibly find their way into our realm until they have ethically developed way past such stupidity! Malevolence from a distant sentient species cannot and will not arrive at the threshold of our civilized universe. Not remotely credible. You have no proof except for paranoid Imari empath-scan predictions. This Sub-Committee refuses to be persuaded by self-aggrandizing paranoia, Imari or otherwise."

The councilmembers stirred and murmured among themselves.

"I ask that the Sub-Committee allow the scout to finish her petition," said Troya.

"I ask that she present facts, not paranoid predictions!" bellowed the elder Pomdos.

More murmurs.

Telmx looked at Goshing, whose eyes beamed compromise. Well, she thought, she certainly had enough data about their current behaviors without going into any more probabilities. Perhaps their electric chair, persecution according to skin color or cultural heritage.

"In Exhibit 16 we have documented their current..."

The elder Pomdos interrupted in slow measured tones. "Learned Councilmembers, she frightens us to secure more precious empath booster energy for her paranoid scouting missions. Over the last millennia we have approved thousands of scouting triads gallivanting merrily around the universe, happily draining our precious reserves for personal travel pleasures. Enough is enough. No more traveler missions! We will not be manipulated again!"

Telmx could smell acid terror racing through her cells, stiffening each strand of cilia.

"You say self-serving maneuverings do not exist in our realm, yet you accuse Traveler Telmx and the Imari of the very same!" A baritone voice rose above the cacophony of intergalactic tongues. Telmx could not discern where the voice came from.

Troya shouted for order.

Goshing stood up to her full regal height. The roar in the chamber suddenly faded. "I agree that young Telmx has presented the case a bit too strongly, but we must not be blinded by or overthink her youthful exuberance. Her close-in scan simulations document serious infantile malevolence reminiscent of eras long past in our known universe. The histories are full of examples, even though our learned Pomdos Councilmembers refuse to study them. Occasionally we run across such planets—many of which are represented here today, that endured long eras of devastation before they evolved enough to take their rightful places in the Council. First they had to outgrow infantile behaviors such as enslavement and exploitation, now not even part of their active vocabulary. But in these chambers we require such words in our vocabulary—if only to exercise foresight. It has always been our sacred mission to ensure a planet's development is orderly and safe, for the survival of universal tranquility. The situation here is no different, although presented a bit too strongly by a talented and exuberant fledgling. I propose that we grant her traveler team permission to continue observing the planet and to recruit one, just one, indigenous. If in ten Earth years, more recruits are required, we will reopen the issue and decide what to do."

An Equine stood up to speak. "With all due respect, recruitment is extremely dangerous, especially by such a young Imari as your protégé. What if her recruit reveals too much?"

"We are clearly aware of the dangers," said Goshing. "Telmx's triad team includes an empath master traveler, the Elder Gir Eja-Gnutha."

"If we agree," said the Equine, "she will train the recruit in Monitoring, no more than that. If the recruit possesses more advanced empath powers, it could have a paradoxical effect: the earthling monitor could inadvertently do something that would actually accelerate their development into the Age of Empath even more rapidly than Telmx's predictions."

"I don't believe other actions will be necessary," said Telmx, surprised that she wasn't stammering. She was lying. Goshing knew she was lying. Well, it was just the beginning.

"And Telmx's scouting team must retro-sweep the recruit if she exceeds her mandate," said the Equine.

"I don't believe that will ever be necessary, either," said Telmx. The hover-glow seared her neck.

"Yes, yes," said Goshing, "Monitoring. The recruit will merely watch over her planet and report what she sees. In extremely extenuating circumstances the recruit might implement a single micro-bit mindshift, but only with the prior approval of the Council and close supervision by this triad team."

The murmuring grew louder. Goshing raised her head ever higher, swept her gaze across the entire dome, and raised her voice above the din. "The recruit, after many years of training, will cause no major shifts of perception, just minor ones, normal among students and other forward-thinking sentients, such as challenging unethical, narrow-minded professors in front of her class, and, and…" She stared sternly at Telmx, raising her voice even louder. "The earthling will be retro-swept by Telmx's triad travel team without waiting for Consular appeals if she even slightly oversteps her mandate."

Telmx only saw J: miserable, cowering under her blankets. She desperately hugged the beloved little child in her mind. She would make absolutely sure J complied with the Council's mandates.

"If there are no further questions of the Traveler…," said Troya.

The dome fell silent.

"Empath Traveler Scout Telmx Galencia Eja-K'arika, you are excused. Your V.E.-disks are entered and indexed for Sub-Committee study and further deliberation. If we have further questions before we vote, we will send for you. Please remain available in the reception area. The Sub-Committee on Intergalactic Security and Recruitment thanks you for your dedicated service and petition."

The chamber fell completely silent. She felt like she was falling into a black hole. Telmx searched for a supportive nod from Goshing, now completely absorbed in her V.E.-viewer. Then Asmurbari was standing above her to escort her out.

✳ ✳ ✳

Goshing was among the first to appear at the far entrance of the reception area. She walked in rapid strides toward Telmx. "Okay, my girl, your petition was granted, with some amendments. This time. Uh uh! Don't start apologizing or, whatever else you feel compelled to do. Your so called 'overstatements' carried the day. Without them no compromise is worth a jot. The Sub-Committee will present their recommendation for this indigenous Monitor to the General Council at secondary sunrise tomorrow. Micro-bit mindshifting is summarily excluded. No mindshifting!" And there's more.

"No mindshifting? But she already..."

"Shh!" hissed Goshing.

Goshing pulled Telmx into a hardy hug. "Not to worry, child. Just wait until we are alone."

Delegates streamed past their embrace. Some stopped to join. Others hovered about, waiting their turn.

The elder Pomdos and his allies padded laboriously into the reception area just as the crowd was dissipating. When he wasn't stooped over, he was almost as tall as Goshing. "At this time," he said, nodding to the two Imaris, "you and your allies hold sway over our deliberations. And precious raw empath energy reserves continue to be squandered on paranoid false alarms. Our life is replete with goodness and love. We do not welcome the hard jagged rips you make in our tranquility. However, those of us who believe in the purity and innate goodness of all living creatures are growing in numbers. We will eventually scuttle all travel missions and devote our energies to enhancing universal tranquility and culture. The 'greater good' will ultimately prevail. Paranoia will not reign in our universe forever. We will also rid the schools of the *Books of Kro'an'ot* once and for all. They corrupt our youth, and cause the very crisis we are now facing."

"The vote was extremely close." Goshing said after the old Pomdos and his entourage were gone.

"They vote without even fully listening!"

"I know, beloved. Nevertheless, we won another important victory. The Sub-Committee approved two more earthling recruits. So much for your 'overstatement.' Each of your team members will have a trainee, but they are not to meet each other until it is absolutely necessary—when and if it is necessary. Now how's that for a mandate!"

"How did you manage that?"

"I just let tradition take its course. Even the Pomdos couldn't override conventional wisdom. The Sub-Committee is very traditional. There must be a triad team, because no one works without comrades. A triad team means checks and balances."

"This is fantastic! I can't wait to tell Winstx and Gir!"

"Later, my dearest. Now it's time for some vintage bot and some exquisite taste treats! And I know just the spot." In spite of her jovial mood, Goshing was clearly more worried than Telmx had ever discerned.

✹ ✹ ✹

They walked along the northwest canal in silence. "Don't ask me anything yet, my dearest," empathed Goshing. "Don't even beam worry. I'm serious. Clear your head! Now! Before we cross the footbridge. Raise your shield to maximum. We will talk about food and cafés out loud."

Although Goshing's manner frightened her, she obeyed, and Goshing led her across a wooden footbridge into an area of the city she had never visited. It was just after secondary sunset, and the hover-glows cast soft blue ripples along the cobblestones. There were few people on the narrow, winding street, mostly sapien, and almost all the kiosks were empty of their vendors, although their wares remained on display. Laughter and music defined the ambiance of each café. Goshing, always a lover of good food and music, extolled their cuisines and decor with forced eagerness.

"Hush, Telmx, don't think it." In her mind, Goshing's warning came to her as if filtered through many layers of thick tapestry. "Follow me in," Goshing commanded through the layers, while out loud she continued to praise the attributes of each café they were passing. "Don't think. Just do. Come, I'm over here."

Telmx allowed Goshing to lead her through the winding streets like a blind person, while her inner mind followed her through empath tapestries of their melded thoughts. "That's it." Goshing's empath voice was gentle, familiar. "Excellent. You did it. Here we are. Now we can talk freely. But I should warn you, this level of shielded empath is utterly exhausting, even for a Level VI. You'll feel pretty dizzy when you come out."

"I had no idea."

"We have a problem." Goshing got right to the point. "The Pomdos faction forced a compromise. The Sub-Committee declined recruit training in even single micro-bit mindshifting. You and your team are only authorized to train these earthling children for Monitoring. And if they overstep their mandate they will be retro-swept without Consular appeals, and your triad team will be the one required to execute the retro-sweep."

"But...."

"I know. I know you already inadvertently initiated J's micro-bit mind-shifting capability. But not really. She was already doing it, in her own undisciplined manner. Let's not go through this again. Obviously the Sub-Committee does not know."

"But what if they find out? I should never have entered the child's mind so completely. I really couldn't help it. It just kind of happened. I am so in love with her determination to protect others with her mind. She is so, so precious...."

"Just listen to me. We're almost at the café. Given your V.E.-exhibits, even with your compelling predictions, the Sub-Committee still feels there are enough indigenous on that tiny planet who are evolving within safety limits, without the need for a recruit's intrusive empath whisperings. No, just listen. By our traditional standards, your comrades should not have allowed you to enter that child's mind so completely. But it's done. It's not a tragedy. No, I said it's not a tragedy. Your comrades' instincts to let you bypass tradition were right, as were yours. It just means that now..."

"I should retro-sweep J's memory of me, abandon her to a lifetime of pain, and find another recruit." Telmx' eyes were filling.

"Stop! Get rid of those tears. You do not have to retro-sweep anybody. Nobody! You have to do absolutely nothing. Yes, you were motivated by compassion, and didn't take enough precautions, but I cherish your behaviors nonetheless. We have to trust them. You're moving an iota out of traditions. Changing the rest of us a bit. Let's just decide to trust it. Restrict little J and the two others to Monitoring, just as mandated. But since J is already capable of empath entering and changing someone's mind in an undisciplined manner, train her in advanced mindshifting as well. Teach her Imari Discipline and the Judgment. Continue to provide her with the knowledge she requires for total Mission commitment, but her current official Mission is merely monitoring.

"I believe your predictions. That planet is becoming extremely perilous to all of us. Its exploited do not rise up quickly enough. There are only isolated patches of evolution and revolution. But if we don't have to interfere right now, why should we? If Earth's empath experimentation gets out of hand, our earthling monitors will alert us. And if we require J and her eventual two comrades to alter someone's thought processes a jot, we will direct them to micro-bit mindshift selected earthlings without waiting for this learned Sub-Committee to approve. They'll already be trained and ready."

"Without approval?" Telmx was astounded. She never imagined that Goshing would ever bypass the Intergalactic Council.

"The vote was much too close. If we rely on their approval again, we are likely to lose the whole Mission, perhaps all missions. They talk more and more about the 'greater good.' Well, my dear Telmx, there is a 'Greater Good' beyond their 'greater good,' and when we need to exercise our powerful prerogative as Imari, we need to do so. We have to trust your scan predictions and no one except us in the Order of Empath Traveler Scouts will ever be the wiser. You have, without meaning to, already infused your young recruit with the capacity for micro-bit mindshifting. We cannot take it back. You will mentor her, as approved. But, since you have done what you did, we will have to operate outside the exact mandate and purview of the Council."

"But that puts all of us, it puts you in great jeopardy."

"It puts me nowhere. It puts you and your triad team more on your own: you, Old Gir and Winstx. I cannot supervise you on this one except as we do now, infrequently and in deeply shielded mode. We cannot openly violate the mandates. I think we're stuck with that. And you? You're stuck with a rogue little planet and an impressionable little empath prodigy."

"How can she know what she knows and not try, subtly or not so subtly, to empath-influence another's mind? She already tries to mindshift her parents. My beloved Goshing, she's only a little girl, five earthling years. She will want things, wish for things, and maybe, just maybe, try to get what she wants through a tiny bending of someone's brain waves. One thing leads to another. She'll make mistakes and then....We're consigning her to an impossible struggle."

"No more of a struggle than some enlightened others of her species already endure without our recruitment."

Telmx was shaken by a level of responsibility she had not foreseen in her scans. "I have to teach a brand new empath not to mindshift, even by innocent mistake. And, if she does, we will have to retro-sweep her. I just hate this so much! She's only a tiny innocent child. And what about the others? Three earthling recruits on their own?"

"Well, here we are!" Goshing said out loud, yanking Telmx out of the empath tapestries. Telmx reeled from the energy drain. "Follow me!" Goshing boomed, and led her wobbly student down an even narrower alleyway into a boisterous avian bar. "They have the best grub and bot in Locur Centrex! Just you wait! Hey, Larrimar! Would you allow us to savor your best vintage bot? We have some serious celebrating to do."

CHAPTER TWO

J

Billy started talking to J when she was two, a few months before V-J Day. When she first met him, Aunt Sara said he was just an imaginary friend and that was okay. Other aunts had different opinions about him. But J's mother didn't care because she was a natural mother, which meant that she knew things naturally. "You don't need to read books about how to raise children." She argued with Aunt Sara all the time about this. (Aunt Sara read Spock and quoted him a lot.) Her mother boasted: "I raise my children by natural maternal instinct. That's all you need, not that intellectual stuff." Her mother was older than Aunt Sara, so she had to know better anyway. In fact, her mother didn't care one way or the other whether J spent a lot of time with Billy. Good thing too, because Billy and J spent a lot of time together, traveling to places she couldn't remember when she got back, except that she knew more than when she had left, in a scary inner way that she couldn't say out loud.

When she was older, six or so, Billy said they were "both unstuck in time." But by then she knew better. She was unstuck and he wasn't.

Listen. I became unstuck in time after Telmx first visited me on the rooftop when I was five. Things I saw and did in my V.E.-future-travel-dreams were not true memories, but rather convictions of occurrences in the future. Once a future-memory got there, I knew about it in a very visceral sense, like a dream that's still there when you wake up, except it never goes away, like a truth. It didn't occur to me to be amazed I could predict things. I thought everyone could. They just called them déjà vu's. —J

No, she shouted at Billy, she wasn't planning to spend the rest of her life on his Tralfamador! And now, without knowing how she knew, she was talking in terms of ten dimensions, not just four. By the time she was six, he was accusing her of letting Telmx brainwash her with a lot of horseshit. They had long arguments about that. He could only travel within his own time. And she had already visited her Great Aunt Bessie when she nursed Lenin's toothache on his way back to St. Petersburg in 1917. And she could travel ahead and read books that weren't even published yet, except that she didn't quite know what she was doing. Also, she proudly boasted to Billy that she and Telmx had a very important and secret mission to do that would last way after the year 2000, and that he wouldn't be a part of it. Billy didn't believe her. "You're crazy!" he screamed.

Soon after that argument, in the middle of first grade, she decided Billy was in fact an imaginary friend, made up from a book called *Slaughterhouse Five*. Not like Telmx. She was real. At least she hoped so, although she worried that Telmx also was just another imaginary friend.

At six, even though I was just learning to read **Dick and Jane** *in school, in my mind I was able to read difficult grown-up books, ones that weren't even published yet like* **Slaughterhouse Five***, which came out when I was 27. So I discovered that Billy was just a character in a book. I didn't stop talking to him, but now it was just for fun. So Aunt Sara was right about my imaginary friend. Of course I never told her, or anyone except Billy about Telmx, and I figured it was okay to tell Billy about her because he was just in my imagination. –J*

V-J Day was a living V.E.-history-nightmare.

Because I was unstuck in time, the past and the present and the future had no boundaries. After Telmx's first visit when I was five, the events of the past, like V-J Day when I was almost three, took on blended meaning when I dreamt or thought about them later on. So this is my blended memory: —J

First she was asleep in a dark room but it was light outside. And her mother was telling her to get up because the war was over. What war? Oh, THAT war. Billy's war. There was paper flying and swirling from the sky all over the street and she saw a soldier in a jeep. Yeah, Billy's war was over. She pretended she was scared of a blue piece of paper that had floated into her stroller. She thought, I'm pretending to be scared of this falling piece of paper, when I'm really shrieking with horror as that Little Boy bomb drops from the sky to suddenly end Billy's war.

When she was two-and-a-half she saw this jeep and the blue piece of paper, and she knew this was a daytime, real-life, not a dream nightmare. Her legs felt like sand and she would have screamed without screaming—if this had been one of those other V.E.-nightmares. But it was real, like when her father's drunken rage roared into her mind at night, so she steadied her eyes, saw the blue piece of paper and the soldier in his jeep and pretended to herself that she was pretending to scream, even though she really was screaming.

The tiny child screamed into the blizzard of confetti, the tolling of bells and the roar of crowds pouring into the streets, milling and streaming past the diminutive Jewish couple wheeling a straw stroller, the mother standing stoically, mesmerized, the father kneeling in front of the stroller, pointing a clown face at a tiny screaming two-year-old to make her laugh.

"That's just a piece of paper. It's nothing to be scared of."

She wailed louder. She thought how stupid her parents were for believing she would really be frightened by a piece of paper, and what a bad girl she was because she was lying, and how scared she really was because people really made atomic bombs, and people actually dropped them on people, on little kids like her.

Every time Billy used to harp on Dresden, I would scream at him, "Billy! Don't you know? Dresden was a dress rehearsal!" —J

Everyone was actually having a good time on V-J Day. My father said bombs and plane crashes only happen in Africa. I thought my father was stupid or a liar.

When I was five, I had proof positive he was a liar, so, in addition to some other V.E.-dream trips I had already taken, or will take, to Dresden with Billy when we first met, and alone to Hiroshima right after V-J Day, I had a strong sense at two-and-a-half that plane crashes and bombs were not destined only for Africa, especially since a bomber had crashed into the Empire State Building right in my own city just a month before V-J Day. —J

Later Aunt Sara wondered where J had learned about the atomic bomb and accused her parents of frightening her. "There are things you just don't tell a child until they're old enough to understand," she said. "We didn't tell her anything about them," her mother said. "She has a vivid imagination."

I was scrunched up behind a very big man in this huge plane. He had named his plane after his mother, Enola Gay. He could just do that. Name a plane after his mother. There were lots of big tall men in the plane. They were on a mission. Everyone on the plane doing an important job for this mission. One man was doing things to a huge bomb. I knew it was a bomb. I don't know how I knew. I knew it was very big and heavy and very bad.

They all were very excited when he said he was finished. He had put some parts together so the bomb could work. I knew for sure that I had to change their minds. They had to turn this plane around. I had to do something about this bomb. I was so scared.

I was all folded into this tiny space behind the driver of the plane. I found his mind. It wasn't hard. I just did it. He was very happy. But it was his excitement that made it so hard to change his mind. He was thinking about candy bars and how he and his uncle (I think it was his uncle, some man very important to him) would drop candy bars from a little plane when he was a little boy—much older than me, but still a little boy. Everyone on the ground beneath them was running around grabbing these candy bars. He was eating one too. He was thinking how happy and grateful everyone was that he was dropping these candy bars for them to have for free. He was a little boy hero.

Now he was a hero all over again. The candy bars were his little "babies," and now he had a "Little Boy," a little boy dropping a "Little Boy" like candy and he was about to be a great American hero. I remember thinking, how can a little boy do such terrible things to people, to little boys and girls like me? I started to wonder if I should just go away. But I couldn't. This little boy was not going to throw candy bars out of the plane. He was going to drop a "Little Boy" that wasn't a little boy out of the plane and burn up thousands and thousands of little boys and girls. He was going to do that no matter what. I just knew it.

Someone on the plane said they were flying over "Hero Jee-ma," something like that, and all of a sudden I saw soldiers screaming and dying, thousands and thousands in the minds of the men in the plane and in my mind. I vomited on myself. I was afraid they would smell it. I wanted to wake up. I had to wake up. But I couldn't. They all started talking and thinking about this Hero place. And I felt their minds getting static, jagged static, all of them. And it was like their noses were all pointed in front of them to the place that would make them feel a million times better because they were about to get sweet revenge.

I tried, I really tried to stop them with midshifting, first with the man who loved to drop candy bars, and then with a man with a mustache named Tom. His mind was a little bit easier to push at. I thought so. Uncle Jim has a mustache just like his. I thought, he's easier because he's just like my Uncle Jim. He'll listen to me.

In Tom's mind was a huge cross. He was looking for a cross, like the cross the Catholic kids wear around their neck. A kind of "T." That's all he saw in his mind—and I couldn't figure it out. I thought, if he's thinking about a cross, he's thinking about changing his mind. How could he be all that bad? Especially since the window he was looking out of looked just like a church window, except without all the beautiful blue and red and yellow panes, just a beautiful blue with a few wispy clouds.

I knew I had to keep pushing at his mind no matter what. I had to make him stop. It was all up to him. It was all up to me. I vomited again. Huge heaves. So loud. Surely they smelled it, heard it. Vomiting made it harder to push his mind. I tried so hard.

And then we both saw the "T" right beneath. He said so. I tried to make him not say so, but he said so. And the driver told everyone to put on goggles. I had Tom exactly in my mind. For a second he really did change his mind, I thought. He changed a little, I thought. He's changing his mind. But he just changed the way the plane was going. Just slightly. To aim better!

I pushed and pushed at his mind. I tried to take the "T" out of his mind's eye—but it just kept coming closer and closer. He just held it there in his eyes. I yelled at him. Out loud and in his head. I yelled as loud as I could. I pushed him and pulled at him. It didn't matter if they found me out. I had to do it. But he just kept going.

White light blind, and falling. Flapping my arms to keep from falling into the white. In the white I saw a little girl running toward me. She was screaming. I couldn't understand—in my head she was screaming. I had to save her in the white light. I tried to grab her, to hold her but she just became nothing right in my hands. I was grabbing in the air and screaming. But she was nothing. There was nothing all around me. A terrible, terrible silence. Then a terrible terrible wind. And black paper flying everywhere.

The paper fell in my baby carriage. I was still screaming. My Daddy said, "It's just a piece of paper." And someone said, "The war is over!" I was screaming with the little girl screaming in my head. Even now I see her, I grab her, and then she is nothing. Over and over again. You know what? I just figured out I wasn't pretending to be scared. I was! –J

She saw, she felt, she smelled, the melting of flesh, the running, the scream-ing, the moans, the fires, the dust silhouettes of people against a wall. She just saw them! Now they're gone! The groaning women at the hospital doors. And the child no larger than she, simply running toward her, her clothing burning, and her screams. Oh that screaming. A million children scream-ing, all from one tiny mouth. She tried to grab her and bring her into her baby carriage, to save just that one little child, just that one child, and she couldn't. She didn't know how to pull anyone out of her dream. "I can't do it," J screamed to the screaming child. "I'm not strong enough. I'll come back for you. I promise!"

I never did come back for her. Instead I became an anti-war activist. My first demonstration was when we all refused to "take cover!" in high school. Everyone stood in line in the lunchroom and didn't budge. I think we sang "We Shall Overcome." All over the city, high school students were refusing to take cover, because it wasn't going to do any good, and it simply scared everyone, and it was propaganda about the so-called "Red threat" and we were demanding that the government "make peace not war." It wasn't even the 60s yet: a dress rehearsal for Berkeley, Jackson State and Kent State. For me, of course, these early little demon-strations had special personal meaning. —J

Starting right after V-J Day J would cry uncontrollably for no reason. She just cried and wouldn't tell anybody why. Sometimes she would wake up at night, sit upright and moan. One time, Jacki, the baby sitter, found her like this: in a trance, eyes open, moaning in steady whispered beats. When Jacki sat down next to her and held her and then put her in her lap and held her again, J didn't seem to know she was there. Then Jacki attempted to wake her from her nightmare. J wouldn't wake. Jacki stayed in the room until J stopped moaning and closed her eyes.

J heard Jacki tell her mother about it. She said, "Oh really?" and sent Jacki home.

J's father was really mad. He was afraid Jacki would tell her family and the neighbors that his kid was crazy. "We can't fire her," he said. "All the neigh-bors will talk." Her mother wondered if her sister was right, that J "needed professional help." Her mother didn't say anything to him. Too complicated, and he'd take it all wrong. He'd start carrying on about her family, so ho-ity-toity and critical of everything he did. It was embarrassing every time J cried for no reason. And Aunt Sara and the others, but especially Aunt Sara said, "She's a worrywart. Has the weight of the world." Her mother thought, "Sure she has the weight of the world on her shoulders, with such a crazy drunkard for a father." Why had she ever married him? Well, it was the best she could do and she so wanted a family. A normal everyday Thanksgiving-Day-type family. Now she had her perfect family and she'd be damned if this little devil child was going to smash perfection. "J was just faking to get attention," she said, and walked out of the kitchen.

Now then: V-J Day was her awakening, her first actual real-time awareness of awareness. Off and on since then she tried to make a big deal out of her awakening at the awakening of the atomic age. She'd say, "My earliest memory is V-J Day," and then be philosophical about it. Billy and Telmx were already fighting over their rights to her mind, and whether there were ten dimensions or four, but she didn't know that until much later. Didn't even sense that. Oh, she knew about Billy. They were constant buddies by then. That is, she also knew that Billy was firmly in her life at her awakening, not just about to be met (she didn't remember when or how they met). Even Telmx was hovering around before she actually brought J to the rooftop almost three years after V-J Day.

Telmx said to me many years later that one of the reasons she had sought me out was that I awakened to conscious remembered life on the very day Earth experienced the conscious horrifying knowledge of its own ability to eliminate all consciousness. The atomic age was born as my awareness of self was born, and V-J Day was the reliving of the horror.

I said to Telmx during that same conversation (I think I was in my thirties and visiting her on Galern II) that I had been convinced that few people truly understood the meaning of the phrase "ignorance is bliss." I asked her if five wasn't much too young to be initiating a student, and Telmx wept and said she had been a new mentor and there had been very little time to sort things out accurately. I accepted quietly, knowing that the infliction on my young mind was no comparison to what I saw and would see.

But throughout my childhood, I bitterly resented having all the knowledge and none of the power to do anything about anything. Instead, I stammered in public, especially in school. And was afraid to ask or comment about what I learned there for fear of giving away my knowledge, my nightmares, my pain, and my excitement about the future. I both shunned and craved the attention of any teacher who seemed to care.

Occasionally I would try to write poems about it all. Perhaps poetry would communicate with some obscurity and clarity what I was feeling, and it would be fanciful enough to not give away what I could not yet divulge. But nothing I wrote expressed the depth of my experiences.

It helped to know that I was a part of the change. And that I would live to see the change, because Telmx had chosen me to do so. It did not make me a messiah or a world leader or a revolutionary, just one of the many who participated in changing what needed to change, however long it took. —J

CHAPTER THREE

J

"You're a dream and not a dream," J said out loud, her eyes shut real tight. "I think I have been dreaming about you for a whole year. I thought you'd never come back for real!" Her own voice startled her, because things had been so silent, except for the nighttime stopping and starting of the bridge traffic.

"Hush, child, just think your thoughts. I promise I will hear them loud enough. We don't want to awaken anyone."

"How'd you do that?" Her lady was talking to her in her head, not out loud like everyone does, but in the silences in-between her thoughts, like they were almost the same as her thoughts, but they were coming from the lady. "I just did it too, didn't I?"

"You sure did. You're very quick."

"Are you here for real?"

"I'm not a dream, and I've some very important things to tell you—so you need to listen very hard, okay?" J felt a slight shiver in her lady's voice, and for an instant she shivered ice cold with fear. "My goodness, you felt my uneasy, didn't you? Quite extraordinary. Please don't be scared. You're only feeling my feeling about how very important it is that you understand what I tell you."

A sudden warm tingling on J's cheek covered her from head to toe like a deliciously warm bath, except there was no water. She allowed her lady to take her hand, and lead her to the window.

This time they did not climb up to the rooftop. Telmx led her to a corner of the fire escape. From under her travel hood she retrieved her mat and deftly unrolled it with her free hand, gently guiding the child onto it and into an Imari squat. Facing her, she eased herself into the same position.

Like the year before, her lady shimmered in the moonlight, this time kneeling on a soft rug of many muted hues. She was almost completely covered in a silky turquoise cloth, and her dark deep-set eyes peered down at J from a very dark brown face J could hardly see for all the cloth. Telmx lifted the outer layer of cloth and wrapped it around the child's shoulders, so that they were cocooned together.

"J, My name is Telmx."

"I was scared you were only a dream. You didn't come back in real life for a whole year. Only in my imagination."

"Well, you see, I'm not just a dream. You must listen to me now. There isn't much time. First of all, you can't say anything to anybody about me. You have to promise me that."

J sucked in her breath, squeezed her eyes and covered her face. It was her mother making her promise not to tell about the "skeletons in the closet." She struggled to disappear her lady, to wake up in her bed, cozy and safe and alone.

Telmx's arms swiftly folded around her, pulling her even closer. "Oh no, my dearest J. Not like that. Not like that at all. I am so sorry. Ours is not a shameful secret. It's a beautiful, wondrous secret, J. I promise you. Oh my love, I truly promise you."

How could she tell this terrified child about the consequences of revealing her visits? Too much. But she had to. Even if it felt like too much. Wait, she would make it easy. Subtle. In the back of J's mind. A tiny assumption. Not a strident warning. "I always move a bit too quickly!" she thought. "My impatience will destroy this little girl." All the time, caressing the child's terrified synapses, smoothing out the edges.

When J was fully relaxed in her arms, she obliquely conveyed the Council's retro-sweep mandate into one of J's deeper chambers.

"Well, you know that I'm not make-believe," she said, working on a version of the warning that she thought J could take in a bit easier, "But others might not understand, and say you were making it up."

"Like what Aunt Sara says about Billy."

"Yes, exactly like that."

"And my Daddy, well, you know, he'd give me a good red spanking for fibbing, if I said I didn't imagine you, that you were really real. So I promise. Swear to God and hope to die."

They fell silent, even in their thoughts.

"But where do you live? Why didn't you come back right away? Why can't you just stay here and be with me? Why can't you be my real Mommy?" The questions tumbled out of J before she knew they were tumbling. And then she was ashamed for wanting another Mommy.

"Oh my dear, unhappy child. I do love you very much, but I live very, very far away, up there beyond Orion the Hunter, and way beyond the horse's eye, on a beautiful warm planet with two suns called Galern II. You'll visit it some day. I know you'll love it." For a tiny moment, J thought she could see a beautiful forest of green against a red purple sky. "Yes, something like that," Telmx whispered into her head. "You're so extraordinarily quick, J. When I first met you I had no idea…."

"Wow!" J tried to get the picture in her head back, but couldn't. Then she tried to imagine a horse in the sky, and found herself staring at blurry patches of red and black just inside her eyes. Just a tiny moment, and they were gone.

"I don't see any horses. You live in an eye? I'm scared of eyes."

"No, my darling, it's just a picture in the sky. You'll see. It's very beautiful up there in the sky. You'll see."

J's head was beginning to hurt like right before one of those horrible nightmares.

"Show me one of your nightmares, J."

"You know about them? You really do? Can you make them go away? Please make them go away."

Telmx enveloped J in her arms, and held her tight.

"Show me," she whispered into her head. "I'll come with you. Don't be afraid. Look, I'll hold your hand."

"You can really just come with me to my nightmares?" And then she was there in one of her most horrible nightly nightmares: J stood shivering and naked on a cold foggy place with no trees. A pale ghostly lady with no smile, wrapped in too many dark blankets for one person, was standing over her, turning her around and around. The ground was swinging back and forth like the great body of water she had just crossed for endless, vomitty days and nights. She wished the no-smile lady would take off a blanket and wrap her in it, because that's what elders did for children. She opened her mouth to tell the pale lady about all the evil men who had snatched her from her family in the African village of Western Moanja. Certainly this lady would make the men take her back home. But her words got stuck in the thick fog. And the no-smile woman just turned her around and around, forced her to open her mouth so she could look at her teeth, and pinched her burgeoning muscles above her elbow. Then she actually smiled at the same pale men. Someone pushed her right into the thick white fog. In the next instant she was screaming and flailing in Telmx's arms.

"Hush, my dearest. They're gone now. I'm right here."

"Can you make the nightmares stop? Please make them stop."

I'm afraid I can't do that, J. I'm really, really sorry. I didn't know you would, I mean, I didn't mean for you to be able to have those kinds of dreams. When you're older I'll explain them to you. For now, try not to be too scared.

And I'll try to make them less like nightmares. You're not actually in them. They're not really happening to you."

"But they're true aren't they? I know they're true!"

"They're what we call history or natural V.E.-dreams, J, and I'm afraid I can't make them not happen. You were dreaming of the Diaspora and the Middle Passage, the selling of African children into slavery here in your country. It's kind of, part of...listen, I'll try and make them less scary. But you'll have to be brave. Enough for now, my dearest. We'll have plenty of time to figure all this out—but just not during this visit. I have to go now. I love you...."

"Please stay a little longer." J and Telmx shivered as if they were in the same body.

"Oh, you so quickly touch my uneasy! You are so truly extraordinary, my dearest. I'll visit you again as soon as I can."

Telmx squeezed J one more time and stood up, and J still felt her close by in her head even though she was so tall she couldn't see her eyes through the darkness anymore. "Come J, I will guide you back into your bed."

❋ ❋ ❋

The Little Ben alarm clock was clanging and J's mother was shouting from the doorway of her bedroom to get out of bed already or she'd be late to school. J lay in bed under the coziness of her covers, inside the hugging for just a few more moments. She was still only six years old, but she felt seven feet tall, as if she could just put on her dungarees and sneakers and no one would ever hurt her or her Mommy again, not even Daddy. At the same time, she was really scared, as if one of her nightmares could come true and she would never wake up from it.

❋ ❋ ❋

Miss Keating, J's first grade teacher, was young and tall and had the kind of deep voice that was smart and strong. She paid attention to all the children, even knew each one by name. J loved her, almost as much as her special lady from beyond the horse's eye. And her special lady was real. Wow! She really *was* real! After the previous night, she knew for sure that she was real.

When J thought about her teacher, she got that same special feeling up and down her back that she reserved for Telmx. Surely, like Telmx, Miss Keating heard everything she thought inside her head. Maybe Miss Keating and Telmx were friends. Maybe she was really from the sky also, and it was a secret. Surely, since Miss Keating was from Galern II, J and Miss Keating would have a secret to share with each other, and J wouldn't have to wait and wait for Telmx to come back, wondering if she ever would. But she had to be very careful, because she had made a sacred promise not to tell anybody about Telmx. Well, she'd be very clever about it and simply test Miss Keating out.

Miss Keating was sitting at her desk in the front of the room looking particularly beautiful with her long deep brown hair. J had been planning the moment all morning, the time just before lunch, when everyone has to sit quietly at their seats, fold their hands and wait for the lunch break. She could just walk up and ask Miss Keating the question that would settle it once and for all: was she also from Galern II? Her teacher would certainly be happy to discover that a child in her very own classroom knew all about her home planet. It would be their special secret. And Miss Keating would understand everything she felt, maybe even tell her parents that she wanted to adopt J, take her into her home, hug her all the time, and make her nightmares go away.

No, she had to be more sneaky. First she would try talking to her without talking. If Miss Keating talked to her in her head, she wouldn't even have to come up to her desk, and no one would even guess they were talking. It was the safest way, since she was supposed to keep Telmx a secret. She'd ask her a simple question in her head, without giving away that she knew Telmx, and if she answered, it wouldn't be breaking her promise, because after all it would mean that Miss Keating already knew all about Telmx. It was very clever, J thought, and Miss Keating and Telmx would praise her for her cleverness.

She closed her eyes real tight, pointed her head directly at Miss Keating's head, and concentrated with all her might. "Where were you born?" she thought real loud. That was a safe enough question. Everyone asks that kind of question when they are simply talking to each other. Silence. The rustling of paper, the shuffling of a shoe from one of the desks behind her. She asked again. Nothing.

She opened her eyes. Miss Keating was staring at her. She WAS staring at her. She DID hear! But then she turned back to her papers on her desk. Perhaps Miss Keating heard something but didn't know it was from J. Before she knew what she was doing, J was at the side of her teacher's desk. "I need to ask you a very important question," she said out loud but softly. Miss Keating looked up from her papers.

"Have you, I mean, do you know about the horse in the sky?"

"Do you mean a constellation, dear?"

J didn't know what a cons-ta-eight-tun was. "I mean a horse with an eye way up past the moon, past the hunter, and, well, then there are…." She hesitated. Something told her to just not say anymore, except: "You know, don't you?"

Miss Keating looked at her blankly. "I'm afraid I don't know very much about astronomy, J. Where did you learn about this?"

Uh-oh, thought J. She's pretending not to know, or she really really doesn't know what I'm talking about.

"J why don't you ask your mother to help you look up constellations in the library and find the hunter and the horse you heard about. Then you can tell the whole class about it. A special astronomy project."

"But you must know about the eye. Don't you know? For real? You can tell me, because I know about it already." She held back her tears and felt the beginning of that kind of throbbing headache. She was so very sure. Miss Keating was so very nice, just like Telmx. Only special people like Telmx could be so nice.

"J, I would love to understand what you are trying to ask me, but I really can't and we have to get ready for lunch now, so please return to your seat. I would love to see what your research comes up with. Certainly you can get your parents to help you. Besides," she whispered, "after lunch I'm going to give out parts for a little play on Christopher Columbus, and I have selected you for a really special role. You'll see."

The room wobbled a little bit and somehow J made it back to her seat. She decided she really hated Miss Keating for being so stupid.

When the class came back after lunch, the room was decorated with little sailing ships, pictures of Christopher Columbus and other "famous explorers," and happy Indians offering trinkets to them in their outstretched arms. Miss Keating called her lesson a "Unit on America." She said, "I know you were always taught that Christopher Columbus discovered America, but men in Viking ships had come here first. You all should feel real smart because you know something more than just 'Christopher Columbus discovered America.'" They sang "Columbus Sailed the Ocean Blue in 1492," and she gave out parts for a little skit to be performed in the auditorium at the next assembly.

J's throbbing headache was getting worse. Her eyes burned and she felt dizzy. She went to Miss Keating, even though she hated her now, and said she felt sick. Miss Keating said she looked pale, that she should go to the bathroom, and if she still felt sick, she would send her to the nurse and they could call her mother to come pick her up. "No that's alright," said J. She went to the bathroom with her wooden pass and stood in front of the mirror looking at "pale." Maybe she needed glasses like Cousin Carol. Maybe she was really sick. She just hoped she wouldn't throw up in the classroom in front of everybody. That would be worse than a nightmare!

She came back to the classroom, determined not to be sick. Miss Keating was giving everyone parts to the play. J was an Indian because she had dark straight hair and bangs. Miss Keating took her by the shoulders and placed her in front of the room. She had to stand on the "rocky beach" and say "How" and offer Columbus and his sailors some beads in their outstretched arms. "Now we'll do a rehearsal," said Miss Keating. J's head continued to throb. Columbus came across the front of the classroom with his sailors, and J screamed, "RUN! Run for your lives!" Kids started to giggle.

Miss Keating yelled at the kids to stop. And she yelled at J to stop shrieking. "You just don't understand," cried J, suddenly feeling much older than six. Her words tumbling out of her as if someone else were actually screaming. "He raped and killed my sister! He makes my people real sick, robs my village, makes my people slaves and sells us in Hispania. We are just like the Negroes. And lots of little children are dying in his huge canoes. I know; I saw them. They're mean and stupid. Don't you understand? Why don't you understand? It's not fair! You're not supposed to lie. You're one big fat liar! I hate you! Everyone's lying. People shouldn't lie! You're all a bunch of dirty liars!" She raced past everyone into the echoing hallway.

"What on Earth are you talking about?" said Mrs. Dunkin, the vice-principal. J was in her office waiting for her Mommy to pick her up so she could be punished for "making such a ruckus that the entire school was going upside down, and didn't she know any better, and was she crazy or something?"

"I don't know."

"What do you mean you don't know? People just don't go running down hallways screaming 'Run for your lives!' What in God's name do you mean by screaming 'Run for your lives?' Don't you know about screaming 'fire' in a crowded theater? What's the matter with you young lady?" J hated this big fat old lady with her squeaky voice and blue hair. She hated her more than anyone in the whole wide world. "I don't know."

"Do you have to run for your life at home? Is that what's going on? I am here to help. You can tell me."

In spite of her throbbing head, J was suddenly on high alert. Nobody will ever ever find out about her secret about her Daddy and Mommy.

"I was just dreaming." That part was true. Today her nightmare came right into the classroom. Oh, she thought, what am I going to do now? She needed Telmx to come right back and fix things.

"Sleeping in front of the class while rehearsing a play? You expect me to believe that, young lady?" She paused. "Do you see and hear things that aren't really there?"

J decided to just shut up.

CHAPTER FOUR

Telmx

Telmx slipped out onto the fire escape and hovered slowly back up to the rooftop. The child was profoundly upset. And what's more she was experiencing V.E.-time-traveling-dreams. Horrible, terribly accurate ones, too. What was going wrong? Perhaps old Gir would have some answers when he came back to pick her up. She leaned over the barrier at the edge of the roof and gazed at the sprawling city. She struggled to push her uneasy aside in order to think. Clearly this child was special. The degree of empath energy far exceeded her original calculations. It was as if her contact a little more than eleven Earth months earlier had triggered a huge spurt of empath development—so much so that even Telmx could not reverse it or slow it down without retro-sweeping her. Something has to be done, she thought. The child is suffering. It was only a matter of time before she reveals her undisciplined empath and exposes the Mission.

Could the child's first contact with Imari just one earthling year previous have itself triggered rapid empath development on this planet? Telmx had been extremely careful to factor this out in her original scan predictions. She and Goshing had gone over and over the scans, factoring in possible problems from contact with the Imari.

Telmx was overwhelmed by fears. What if the child's rapid empath growth wasn't particularly unusual? What if any child they recruited was destined to become the agent of that dreaded rapid Empath Age development? Perhaps it was a mistake to recruit from this particular geopolitical area, where empath development was most dangerous. But they had to. They needed to recruit an earthling monitor from the very center of the hazard zone where the danger was greatest. If her scans were accurate, within seventeen Earth years, this recruited earthling monitor would be indispensable. There was no choice but to have the child fully trained and ready for action. At what cost? To torture an already tortured child?

She winced. Her cilia ached. She closed her eyes, reached under her travel hood and stroked her undulating strands.

* * *

Telmx broke the froth and passed the goblet to Gir, squatting opposite her on his mat. They were silent, even in their empath, the only sound the hum of the booster maintaining their ship in high orbit around Earth. Gir nodded and smiled, and drank the bot brew in rhythmic gulps. He was somewhat shorter than Telmx, and his ebony chiseled features were beginning to take on the blue hue of advancing years.

"Ah, my girl," he empathed gently, "you must not indulge that uneasy of yours. What's done is done, she's resilient, she'll do just fine. Just a few hard bumps now and again."

"She's going to give herself away. She's not going to be able to help it."

"No one on that planet's going to believe her, not for one iota of a second."

"It'll drive her crazy."

"You'll be there to help her. Besides, 'crazy' is not so bad."

Telmx was grateful for Gir's reassurance. It meant something coming from him, but, she thought, he is also making light of a huge problem, just to make her feel less uneasy. Besides there was something else she could not quite grasp.

"What is it, dear Tel? What is this something else you can't quite grasp? Let's look for it together. I think I hear what you hear, but it is not causing me alarm. What is it Tel? Bring me there."

Telmx felt him probing her uneasy, gentle and respectful of her barriers, yet anxious to feel what she was feeling. "I'm actually afraid to probe the child too closely, Gir, for fear of shattering her—or provoking even more runaway empath powers, so I don't quite know. I mean she enters runaway V.E.-dream-histories. And she's dreaming them with her entire being. Not that she gets hurt, but I'm distressed by her unbearable dread. First of all, she's stuck in the one about the enslavement of the dark people from one of the other large continents. We wanted her to understand viscerally enslavement and exploitation, but she is living and reliving the nightmare as if she herself were captured. And there's something else." She sensed Gir's shudder as he merged with her uneasy. It frightened and soothed.

"Amazing!" Gir empathed. "She possesses spurts of empath energy more intense than a Level VI. Could it be that there is more raw empath energy on this planet than we calculated?"

"You see it too. Do you think our presence here is actually encouraging the very powers we mean to discourage in this species? Gir, have we made a terrible blunder here?"

Gir was silent. The blue in his face deepened to a glowing violet, highlighting the gentle creases around his eyes and cheekbones. Telmx lifted the goblet of bot to her lips and melded with its sequential pleasures. Whenever Old Gir entered his inner chambers, she felt intensely privileged. Other than Goshing, there was no one whose wisdom she respected more.

"I don't think so," he empathed quietly. "It's all the more reason to recruit the other two allies for her. It was only a matter of time before earthlings would have unleashed empath energy anyway. At least we should have some powerful ones on our side, don't you think? And we'll monitor them all with the utmost of care. Just as we train them to monitor and ultimately mindshift their own species." He took her face in his hands. "I am confident, my dear Tel. Listen to Old Gir. The child is capable of entering history empath V.E.s without a viewer, without even wearing V.E.-goggles, and comes out rattled but intact. Cause for concern but not alarm. She goes into a peculiarly earthling type of V.E., complete with more empath energy than a Level VI can muster with a low-range empath booster. Fine, we'll grant that too. Alright, we didn't know what we were releasing when we started recruitment. But here we are, just another puzzle in the universe to figure out over a good vat of vintage bot."

Telmx knew the argument. They'd been over and over it since they had first entered Earth's orbit and run their updated scans. She liked the idea of J having some friends, but in order to assure that each recruit was safely committed to the Mission, and not likely to give each other away during their early development, they couldn't know about each other for at least a decade or so, and in the meantime, her dearest J would have to go through those nightmares and the devastating isolation of being so different. There must be something she could do for her in the meantime. She couldn't be there every minute. Old Gir was very wise and, yes, they had to train the other two earthling monitors, but what would the Council say if it knew how rapidly empath takes over? Not even Goshing knew.

"If Goshing knew about the runaway empath, she might not even approve of our lining up the other two, in spite of the mandate to have a triad monitoring team," she empathed. They had been through this part too, but she never made major strategy decisions without consulting with her mentor.

"'Bout time you depended on your team," Gir empathed gently. "Goshing's been around for a while, you know. She expects spontaneous unexpected team decisions. This earthling species is turning out to be quite precocious. One tiny entry has triggered runaway empath expansion in that little student of yours. The raw stuff has been there all along, in all of them. That's why they're developing into the Age of Empath before they're ready. Because of the raw stuff, not because you popped some thoughts into a child's head. Not unusual. We can deal with it. But time is of the essence. If we don't recruit now, if we wait for you to consult with Goshing and if we do just what we're mandated to do, and put every little thing before the Council, the recruits won't be trained in time, or worse, they won't be recruited at all."

"But we are trained to be wary of such arrogance. We swore an oath. We..."

"Pish posh, so we're a bit out of sync with the Council. Yeah, not what you bargained for when you applied to the Order of Empath Travel Scouts. But Goshing knew what you were about. Wise lady, that mentor of yours."

Telmx knew all this without knowing it. Of course. "It's not arrogance, my love," Goshing would say when Telmx would have a stray thought that broke all the rules. "It's invention! Like an errant cask of bot that turns out to be even more exiting and intoxicating than we ever imagined. And then we have it forever onward. Go for it my love."

"Yup," empathed Gir. "You just better get used to that nugget of Imari wisdom, my dear Tel. We have special obligation and special responsibility. We must monitor, mindshift and work outside the purview of the Council. It's always been so. You just fell into the responsibility a bit sooner than you, or we, expected, 'cause like your little recruit, you're also a bit precocious. Ah well, we'll learn from you and you'll learn from her, and she'll learn from you and you'll learn from the rest of us. As what a fabulous roundabout, don't you think? So there it is. Now I've told you all. You're in it up to your cilia."

"Well, I don't like it." At least she had old Gir to consult with.

"Uh, uh, my dear Tel. You don't have me or anybody for forever and ever! I'm not a fledgling cadet anymore, ya know. Even though I still got that sparkle and spunk. These bones are gonna give out one of these decades."

She knew that also, but didn't want to think about it. But there it was. She was thinking about it.

"Don't fret so much, dear Tel. Everything'll be just fine. Special circumstances call for special treatment. Here my girl. Drink up. Then Old Gir has whipped up something special just for you. Just you wait here." He unfolded his body and rose from his mat in one grand motion. "I'll be right back!"

Telmx watched him disappear with his characteristic grace into the galley. Special circumstances, special treatment. True enough the warm bot was soothing, but she couldn't just forget J's terrified eyes and the quiver in her voice. She would have to find a way to make J's V.E.-history-dreams less realistic, less tied to actual earthling history, or she would indeed expose the entire Mission, and then she and the whole planet would be lost. Gir was too complaisant in his old age. Seen too much, been though everything. She hoped she never became so untroubled. It made him less caring of the little moments of loving someone when they felt distressed, she thought.

"Now, don't try and penetrate my shield. I have a little surprise," he empath-yelled from the galley. "I'm shielded so tight from your brilliant empath nodes, that even your precocious more-than-Level VI empath can't penetrate my masterful plot!"

He strutted back into the observatory and deftly slid two trays onto the mat before her. "For you on your Name Day! Ha! You forgot, didn't you? Well old Gir doesn't forget one little thing." The tray closest to Telmx was filled to its edges with sizzling pink emeh roots smothered in amber sauce and surrounded by thick strands of k'motbe. "And," he empathed, pulling a colorful Imari cloth off the other one with a proud and triumphant flourish, "one succulent order of No'an bread, baked in traditional Imari style to old Gir perfection!"

"How did you...?"

"Ah, Madam Arrogance," He folded himself on to his mat. "Your elders still have tricks up their sleeves that you young pups don't have one tiny empath clue about. And we do, my dearest, cherish those tiny moments of loving! Now then, if us old dogs can cook up such surprises on your Name Day, don't you think we can figure out how to keep one tiny earthling monitor from organizing her own retro-sweep or her planet's retro-sweep by some stupid intergalactic council three galaxies away? Now then, let's dig in while I tell you about this lad I've spotted and how we'll protect him from inadvertently giving himself away. To your Name Day!" he proclaimed aloud, gulped down a huge swig of bot, and passed the goblet to his comrade.

Yes, thought Telmx, she had forgotten her Name Day. It was truly a wonderful surprise. Her favorite treat. She leaned over and touched his cilia with hers. "My dearest Gir," she empathed. "You are forever a joy. My Name Day was the furthest thing from my mind. And I'm sorry if I...."

"Psh! And enough!"

But she could not just give it up. She continued to ponder it back in the deeply shielded chambers of her mind. Her uneasy wasn't just coming from the real and known dangers of making decisions without going through the tedious and delicate approval process of the Intergalactic Council. It had something to do with J herself, not only her current terror state. Something she was picking up from the child's uneasy foreknowledge. This child knew much more than she knew she knew. And now she was giving it back to Telmx, in a form Telmx couldn't quite fathom. In spite of her team's collective wisdom, she desperately needed to consult with Goshing, but it would be many months of travel before she would be able to visit her mentor's compound on Galern II.

Gir interrupted her reverie. "Listen, eventually J will have some buddies. It's going to get easier, you'll see. Let's see who Winnie recruits, and meanwhile, let me tell you about this young Johnny fellow I'm lining up. You're really going to like him…."

CHAPTER FIVE

J

J had learned she could find her Mommy's mind and talk to her without talking out loud (she may not hear her but she could talk to her anyway in her mind), even try to make her stop doing things J didn't like. Push her a little bit. After she had stopped her Daddy from doing those things to her Mommy, she stopped mindbending altogether. Telmx had warned her about using her powers like that, and so she just didn't anymore.

And also, what if her Mommy somehow caught on and maybe even caught her special power and could do things back to J, or simply listen to all her secrets. So for all of those reasons, she mostly looked and listened to her out-loud—but there were times she found herself listening inside her Mommy's head anyway. Not for long. Just a split second by mistake. Actually, by the time she was ten she realized that she knew from her out-loud Mommy all she needed to know. Her inside Mommy was actually pretty scary, and not what she really wanted to hear.

I don't know how this came to be—or when—but one day when I was ten I found myself staring at my Mother as if I were see-ing her for the first time. I had to grow myself up. My Mother was ill-equipped to deal with my simple needs. And then, some-how I sensed a greater gulf between me and my family. Alone. Really alone.—J

She wondered if every kid went through this. Was this feeling special to her because of her special powers? Telmx would help. Well, not alone, then. But only if Telmx were really real. Between visits, she never really knew.

J cried for no reason any grownup could figure out. She believed and didn't believe that Aunt Sara was right, that she "needed professional help." Nope. She had secrets to keep and she would keep them.

So not really crazy. Just funny in a way that was not crazy.

Like future and past V.E.-dreaming. Or knowing things she had no way of knowing. When she was ten, J was sitting in the living room listening to her Aunt Sara and her Mother talking about the Rosenbergs. "Ethel held her breath," Aunt Sara said. "She didn't die right away." J thought, "I knew that already." The night before she dreamed she was standing on a handball court and saw them lead her Mommy and Daddy to the gas chamber. And then her Mommy held her breath, and then a social worker was talking to her about where she and her sister would live now that their parents were dead. Before Aunt Sara talked about Ethel holding her breath.

My dreams were not always future V.E.-dream-histories, sometimes sort of mixed-up journeys. Worse, I couldn't just decide where to dream-travel to. They would just happen. –J

Certain phrases in fifth grade would set her off like: "our friendly neighbors to the south" or "the policeman is your friend" or "the land of the free." Off she would be in another place, another time—desperately trying to stop rugged American cavalry from slaughtering Mexican children. Or she was dancing the Toi Toi.

Soweto. That one. I wanted to shout it very loud: do you know what? DO YOU KNOW WHAT? Those kids taught their parents about changing the future, and when Mandela is freed... I watched him walk away from the prison gates forty years before he walked away from the prison gates. He had a new suit on, and he was thinner. His wife Winnie by his side. —J

* * *

"What did you say?" Here it goes again. She better shut up now. Mrs. Hanson was huge next to her tiny sitting self at her tiny wooden inkwell desk. "I asked you a question, and you won't find the answer on my face. You're not doing your work and I asked you why." She was back in fifth grade again. Ugly stupid Mrs. Hanson again. It was 1952. Mandela wasn't even in jail yet. Soweto hadn't happened yet. Winnie hadn't met Mandela yet. Biko wasn't even born yet. "What's the reading about this week? Tell me that, young lady!" The kids were staring at her again. "Soweto," she said. Everyone laughed.

Her face was hot.

I saw Hector Pieterson's body carried from the carnage in Sowe-
to. And then a weeping child in Birmingham at the funeral of her
best friend just killed by a bomb in the church bathroom. –J

She couldn't say anything because it might not have happened yet. She
tried to wipe away the dreams.

Better not say anything else.

"I don't know."

"Who's So-way-toe? Don't mock me, young lady."

Better keep quiet.

She looked around the class. The kids were staring. Well, maybe if she
just said something really really true to Mrs. Hanson, she would understand.
"Mrs. Hanson," she whispered, "You have to tell President Truman to stop
killing kids in Korea."

"What?"

"I mean, they're killing kids all the time. I mean…"

"J, why do you talk about killing all the time? We don't kill people. Our
country saves people. Makes the world safe for democracy."

"Maybe you're afraid to understand because they'll kill you too. They do
that to revolutionaries, you know."

"Child," Mrs. Hanson was suddenly nice. After all, she called her 'child.'
She's not mad at her after all. Maybe she'd understand if she just said things
the right way. "That's enough. Now open your Weekly Reader and answer the
questions at the end, like the rest of the class before I send you down to the
principal's office."

Maybe not nice.

"If you weren't afraid of losing your job or dying for your beliefs, wouldn't
you want all kids in the world to be free from hunger and fear?" Maybe that's
the way to say it. A question no one can call stupid.

"Are you starving?"

"No."

"Well then stop worrying about the rest of the world and…" J didn't hear
the rest because she closed her ears in her head, bent her head down, and
opened the reader so no one (especially Mrs. Hanson!) would see her wet
cheeks. It's just my eyes tearing. They tear a lot, she thought.

It never helped to know afterward that she had been dreaming because
somewhere she knew she was re-experiencing real stuff, with the horrible
clarity of a nightmare. She cried without meaning to cry: in class, on the

street, in bed, on a trip with her family. Tears just came out. Sometimes she couldn't remember what she was thinking just before the tears came. Just a vague feeling of an inner journey just completed. Other times she would relive with tremendous clarity an event that she knew had to be true. Torture.

She was lying next to Clarence as he lay dying in a street in her very own city, a policeman's bullet in his chest. "It's just a toy pistol, don't you see? Why did you have to shoot him? Look he's dying, don't you see? Call an ambulance. Hurry!" She heard herself screaming. Mrs. Hanson was standing over her again and writing a note. "Take her to the principal," she was saying to Ronald, a clean-cut little boy, the teacher's pet, "and give him this note." Giggles. J. closed her eyes. Giggles and silence. "Go ahead now."

J followed the boy downstairs to the principal's office. "Dr. Bradley's a principal," she thought. "And a doctor. He's smart. He'll understand and fix everything. Maybe he'll talk to the President." Maybe she won't have to keep secrets anymore. Maybe she could be a regular kid. Telmx would be very angry at her for saying too much. Once she finds out, everything would stop. The "retro-sweep." No more Telmx. Well, better that way. No more secrets; no more nightmares. Besides, maybe Telmx wasn't real. I'm ten years old. It's about time I gave up imaginary friends. Maybe she really does need some "professional help" like Aunt Sara says. She would tell him everything. She had to tell somebody. Finally.

Dr. Bradley wanted to know who Clarence was. J told him how he had been killed by a policeman "because he was black and had a toy gun and he was only ten, and the police didn't call an ambulance, and let him die, and I tried to save him, but I couldn't because I was only watching and wasn't really there."

He wanted to know if she liked "Negroes," whether Clarence was her friend, and what she did with him, and why she thought policemen would do such terrible things to children like let them die, even Negroes. And whether she saw things that weren't there—and if she heard "voices." Her dreams were real and only dreams. Clarence was real, but he wasn't born yet.

"Umm hmm. What else do you think about?"

She told him about the African Diaspora.

"The what?"

"The Diaspora."

"Is that some sort of disease, or did you make up that word?"

"It's, it's…"

"And what else?"

She told him about screaming Vietnamese children, their skin burning raw from fire in the sky, about Iraqi Bedouin children dying in hospitals from depleted uranium dust and how the Americans wouldn't allow them to have medicine. "It's true, and it hurts a lot. You're a doctor. You can make them stop. You can make my mind stop. I want my mind to stop. Please, Dr. Bradley."

"Are your parents reds? Communists? Uh, do they talk about Russia?"

"No, I am...will be... was. Katie is a socialist, not my parents. They don't understand."

"Who's Katie?"

"I don't know, but I met her in college when I was eighteen. But I don't really know, because it's sort of a dream."

"How old are you, J?"

"Ten."

Silence. Then: "I'm going to call your parents in for a little meeting." No! Her father would kill her. She had to push on Dr. Bradley's mind. She just had to. It didn't matter anymore. She entered. ("Are they in the PTA? I have to check. Must rid the PTA of all these subversives. Anyway, this kid's crazy as a bedbug. I bet all commie kids are nuts. How could they not be? She needs to see a shrink, get some shock therapy or something. Probably shouldn't have her in my school.")

Then, as if someone else were screaming: "You're stupid and biased and backward. You think you're an expert on children but you don't know fucking squat about human relations or troubled children or curiosity or history, or struggle, or dialectic materialism! How dare you! You're a fucking asshole!"

"What did you say?"

Not quite knowing where her words had come from, not quite remembering what she had just said, or why, she whispered, "I said 'I'm only ten. Can I go back to my classroom now?'"

"Absolutely not! I'm calling your mother. You're suspended."

Her mother told her about the special meeting with the principal. "I told them you just have a vivid imagination. Just stop all this daydreaming or we'll have to send you to a special place upstate for crazy kids. Do you know what they do to children in places like that? Rape. Torture." J knew about shock therapy because she had stumbled on it more than once in her head. Kids just like her, strapped down, screaming and vibrating. The burning, screeching trolley car stink. Maybe a future dream? Then her mother told her usual story about the orphanage in New Orleans, the "Home." How the counselor would sneak in at night and rape all the little girls. No way, upstate! She'd run away with Telmx first. Telmx will stop all these nightmares. If she ever comes again. If she's real.

Telmx came to visit about once a year. Sometimes I waited almost two years for her to appear. By now I fully understood the danger of retro-sweep and I really dreaded her next visit. I was sure she would do it this time. Maybe I was also hoping she would, just to relieve me forever of the burden of so many secrets and particularly, of course, of the awesome Mission I only vaguely understood. Telmx did get angry for that slip with Mrs. Hanson and Dr. Bradley, but she didn't retro-sweep me. She only said, "Don't do it again." And she promised to come more often.—J

CHAPTER SIX

J

When she was in 9th grade J had to chose a semester project—a term research paper with illustrations and a fancy cover to present in front of the class. Well, perhaps this project was an opportunity to surreptitiously share her V.E.-nightmares. She had bottled up most of it, occasionally letting something slip—only to be told by her aunts, or some other knowledgeable adult, that her stories were fabrications and that she had a vivid imagination. Aunt Sara accused her mother of taking her to see too many newsreels when she was small.

Well, that was also true, but the V.E.-states were much more than that. Only Telmx understood her desperate nighttime (and occasional daytime) terrors, and had admitted that she couldn't free J from them without also compromising the empath energy skills she was developing. "You are experiencing a kind of virtual time travel," she had explained to J when she was much younger. "It is an advanced skill that takes training and discipline to manage, and you have the raw talent. There is no way I can teach you everything you need to turn it on and off or to decide where and when you will travel. I am so, so sorry. I am afraid you'll have to live with it. And perhaps learn from it, as well. When you are older, together we will devise a way for you to manage it."

Indeed, when J saw *Triumph of the Will* in her early twenties, she had already "seen" it over and over again as a young child, in her mind, understanding the meaning without any outside explanation. She could find no rational reason why she knew what she knew. Perhaps her mother had taken her to see it as a little girl (like Aunt Sara said), but more likely, she had visited the film in her dreaded V.E.-dream-states. Or both.

Her haunting and nightmarish V.E.-dreams had transported her to so many children in harrowing adversities by now—in the past, present and future—that she felt she had already done more than enough research for this project. Perhaps sharing them in a kind of journal would finally free her, and she wouldn't have to forever relive the scenes.

She felt she knew these children, watched them struggle, suffer and die, but of course had been unable to save them, when she visited them in her recurring V.E.-nightmares. Their bravery in the face of suffering made her want to be brave as well. Perhaps compiling an anthology of their stories would help her be brave.

However, after many hours of searching for the "remembered" ordeals in encyclopedias and history she found very little information about the children she knew so much about. Yes, she found *Anne Frank: the Diary of a Young Girl*. That was great. She used some passages. But many of the stories and images in her head had yet to be published, either because the events hadn't happened yet, or hadn't yet been chronicled.

So she decided to draw word pictures from the images in her V.E.-dreams, and to go back over the past and future newspapers, books (especially A People's History of the United States), poems, and movies she had visited in her dreams and find stories and images that would somehow illustrate what she thought might be true.

She really loved the children she included in her project. Even if they didn't all come from the library or from the encyclopedia. And who cares anyway? She needed to do it. At last she had the opportunity to put what she knew together. It would be fun and freeing to make such a project.

She was driven. The dates of these documents didn't concern her. It was the fact of the occurrence that mattered. Sometimes she found newspaper clippings and pictures, which verified the many images she drew from her memory of V.E.-travel-dreams. Other times, she simply had to make up references, changing only the future dates to the present or past, because she just couldn't find anything that verified her memory. To keep within Mr. McNamara's assignment, she listed real and fake dates and references as best as she could, believing he wouldn't care enough to check.

Sometimes she would redraw an image from her memory (mostly in crayon, but for some she used a children's watercolor set) and then vomit in dry heaves. Often she vomited so loud she was sure her mother would wake up She never did. Her mother said something about not working so hard on homework because good grades didn't matter, and she was "using up" her eyes.

She copied verbatim the stories and poems from her V.E.-dreams, and then rewrote them so she wouldn't appear gory or crazy or an idiot or different from the children in her class. In the end she put almost everything back in because it was braver and it didn't matter what anyone else thought.

She called her project *Save the Children: A Brief Record of their Sufferings and Bravery.*

It opened with her earliest V.E.-dream-history-nightmare memory:

Hiroshima, 1945:

> A Japanese schoolgirl…saw a B-29 fly by, then a flash. She put her hands up and "my hands went right through my face." She saw "a man without feet walking on his ankles: She passed out. "By the time I woke up, black rain was falling…. I thought I was blind, but I got my eyes open and I saw a beautiful blue sky and the dead city. Nobody is standing up. Nobody is walking around. … I wanted to go home to my mother." [Zinn Pamphlet, p. 1]

The weekend before it was due she spiked a fever, but she didn't dare tell her mother. Nothing must interfere! She still had to finish the cover. It was almost 1:30 in the morning when J, sprawled on her bed, decided to use her version of the Schneider poster as the cover of her anthology. Done, except for fashioning the whole project together into a book. All the kids in her class competed for who made the most beautifully illustrated, beautifully bound projects. She just had to keep up—at least make her book look like the others—with lots of colorful pictures, and a table of contents (a table of contents made it even better!), and no spelling mistakes. She especially wanted this one to look incredible, in itself a work of art. Mr. McNamara said the project had to be a true labor of love. J took "labor of love" to mean just that.

Liz wriggled fitfully across the room. And J gently pushed her sister into deeper sleep, a benign, allowable way to enter someone else's mind. No bending, just gentle pushing into a place the seven-year-old needed to be anyway. Telmx didn't mind that kind of intrusion. At least that's how J rationalized it. There was little Liz, older than J was when J and Telmx first met, and still she could not share the experience with her. "Someday, my baby girl," she whispered to them both. She loved her bright hazel-eyed little sister to pieces, always asking the right questions, always trying to figure out J's mysterious ways.

Well, here was a mysterious project she couldn't share at all with Liz. It would simply terrify her. No way. Wait a minute, she thought, why wouldn't it also send her fourteen-year-old classmates into deep despair? No, this isn't right. It's not finished yet. The anthology has to be about struggle and change, not just about suffering. There was much more to be done. She looked at the picture of the Soweto kids again. There it is, she thought. She had to bring it to the next step. Ohmygosh! Okay, she absolutely had to keep awake, not vomit anymore, somehow will away her throbbing feverish headache in order to type yet again from her V.E. memories. Now Liz would really have to stay asleep. She brought the child deeper in, and then forced herself back into her project.

She closed with The "International":

> Arise, you prisoners of starvation!
> Arise, you wretched of the Earth!
> For justice thunders condemnation:
> A better world's in birth!
> No more tradition's chains shall bind us,
> Arise you slaves, no more in thrall!
> The Earth shall rise on new foundations:
> We have been naught, we shall be all!

Except she changed one line: "Arise, you children of starvation!" No one would notice or care, she thought. But it sure meant a whole lot to her.

By four a.m. Monday morning, she finished binding the pages together with brass butterfly clips, and collapsed into the scraps of discarded paper on top of the blankets.

And was late to school the next morning.

❋ ❋ ❋

Mr. McNamara gave her a C over A-plus. C for research and A-plus for effort and creativity. He asked her if she wanted to become a writer—but warned her not to lie about research (he had looked some things up!) and he wanted to know who Audre Lorde was because he couldn't find her OR the poetry book J claimed to have used. "Where's that book? Who actually wrote that poem? Did you write it? Tell me, is this your own work?" (She giggled to herself. This was plagiarism in reverse.) Finally, he wouldn't let her read excerpts to the class, because "children shouldn't hear such things especially when they aren't even true."

After her conference with Mr. McNamara, she walked home so dizzy she got lost. She had no idea what time it was or even if she was on the right street. She got home after dark. Her mother had just gotten home to an empty house (no dinner, no kids) and she was furious. J hid her project in her underwear drawer—and said she was sick and not hungry. And didn't care what her father would say about it all when he got home. Then she slammed her door with a grand flourish and waited for her father to get home. The big crime was that she had been rude to his wife and had disobeyed her. She genuinely wished she had remembered to pick up Liz from the babysitter. She was her responsibility. Nevertheless, this time he wouldn't get his hands on her. She was too old for that. But that wouldn't stop him from trying. Well, she would be brave.

CHAPTER SEVEN

Beyond the Horse's Eye

J thought this night would never come. She had started her private "count-down" on Christmas Eve, seven months, three days, four and three-quarter hours to four-thirty a.m., July 5th, 1957. She started packing her knapsack on Christmas Eve, and packed and re-packed in secret almost every night, snatching moments when Liz wouldn't come bounding into their room to ask too many questions.

"You don't need to take anything at all," Telmx had insisted for the mil-lionth time, several nights earlier. Vague smoky July 4th festivities still hung in the air. They were huddled in the shadow of the oak tree in J's tiny back-yard suburban garden. "My home is tropical, and I have all the stuff you need right there for you. You'll see."

"It's just a knapsack. I can't go anywhere without certain really really im-portant things. I bet you don't have a Fuller brush, or Levi's or, you know, Tampax or anything like that on your planet. I'd have a cow if I didn't have Tampax and you know, if things started to happen on the trip. They say it happens sooner when you travel, so...."

"I don't know who's more nervous about this," empathed Telmx, pushing the bangs out of J's eyes. J discerned new sensations, mingled with the fa-miliar tingling. She yearned for Telmx to press her firm body into her own. Wanted to caress her hands, her fingertips. She caught her breath, embar-rassed that Telmx had heard her. It was rough enough when she found herself having such thoughts about her best earthling friend Barb. Fortunately Barb couldn't hear her mind.

"It's all right, my love," empathed Telmx. "We can have those feelings for each other. It's natural. Exquisite." As usual, Telmx had heard. But as usual, it didn't feel intrusive. Just a sharing. She put J's hand in hers. J tentatively pushed down her uneasiness about the future and allowed these new antici-pations. "You'll feel easier on my homeworld. You'll see."

✳ ✳ ✳

That was several days earlier. Now the launch was four hours away—that's all, just four hours. J's mother was snoozing in front of the 11 o'clock news and J studied her worried face. If she only knew what was really going on! She listened for any even vague concern about J's leaving in a matter of hours—that she'd be away for almost the rest of the summer. J had told her an elaborate lie, that she was going away with Barb's family for a six-week camping trip in the backwoods of Yellowstone, and that Barb's dad would pick her up at 4:30 in the morning so they "could get an early start." "I think I recruited you because your mother is so tuned out," Telmx had quipped in the garden. Sure enough, J read nothing in her mother's mind except some vague worries that Barb's family would think her house was too shabby, and vowing to replace the old storm door in the spring. Her mother just didn't care one little bit what J did. Her mom never checked anything with anybody. She wouldn't ever talk to a stranger on the phone. And, of course, her mom would never get up that early to say goodbye.

J left her mom to her storm door monologue and tiptoed upstairs. There they were again. Warm anticipations. Now in her thighs, now in her lips. She couldn't wait. But also, her mouth was dry with frenetic worry. What if she got stuck on Telmx's planet and couldn't get home again? What if she's a victim of an alien kidnapping? A kind of seduction, a rape? What if she gets her period? Runs out of money? What if she's a total nutcase and wakes up in the crazy kids ward at Hillside Hospital?

She automatically shielded against her dad's frothy desperate static that invariably assaulted her through her parents' bedroom door. She wasn't terrified of him anymore, actually found some compassion for him floating around in a corner of her mind. Maybe they would have a heart-to-heart when she came back—if she came back. Her poor, crazy parents. How carefully they avoid each other. She bet they were never excited about anything. never felt such awesome anticipations. Her dad's dreams were boring, repetitive, desperately paranoid.

She quietly pushed open her bedroom door. Liz was sprawled fitfully on top of her sheets—now a wispy, spunky eight-year-old. J wished she could tell her all her forbidden secrets. Liz was a light sleeper, which made it tricky when Telmx made her occasional appearances. While she never awakened (with J's help), she'd be unusually silky and cuddly the next morning, lazily recalling strange and wonderful dreams. "I'll be back real soon," she empathed to the sleeping child, who couldn't hear her. "And one day you'll come too. I promise."

J did one last review of her knapsack, hoisted it on her shoulder, and climbed on top of her bedspread. In spite of Telmx's advice, she was determined to travel in her trusty Levi's, tee shirt, and sneaks. She just felt more prepared that way. She tucked her knapsack under her arm and hugged it tight. In spite of worries, excitement, delicious and forbidden anticipations, she forced herself to close her eyes. She needed to get to sleep, deep natural sleep—or when Telmx arrived to pick her up, she wouldn't be able to take her. Something about transport protocol.

✳ ✳ ✳

Beyond her eyelids that she would not, could not open, lighting sizzled. J was gasping, dying, 'Give me some air! I need air!"

"Come on J, hold on there, love." Words slowly filtered in, formed little pools of understanding under torrents of static.

"Choking! Can't breathe! Falling!" she managed, empathed or out loud or both. Screaming. Someone else's or hers? "I'm dying! Oh, I'm dying!"

White lights, tunnels and more tunnels of white lights with deep crimson edges. Falling. Voices all around. Terror within her terror—hers and others. "We're losing her!"

She heard, smelled the frantic loud and clear. It singed her skin, and every cell was tugged in a different direction. They're losing her, she thought. Who are they losing? Me! They're losing me! Who's losing me? I'm lost. Gone. Is this death?

Nowhere. No, choking. Past choking. Past feeling. Okay, this is what "nothing" feels like. But her mind was still working. Painfully working. Couldn't they turn off her mind now?

She didn't want to watch her own funeral and burial from here. No one would cry. Her mother would pretend to be stoic to make sure no one ever knows she wasn't crying. Telmx! Her lady! What happened to her lady? She never came for her. Will she cry when she finds her dead? Yeah, she'll cry.

Now back in bed, she squirmed stiffly inside her Levi's. Ah, she thought. Only a dream. On the day she's supposed to travel to Telmx's home planet, she's thrashing around like a lunatic on her own bed, strangled mysteriously in the very Levi's and tee shirt that were supposed to protect her. "If this is a nightmare," she thought, "I better wake myself up. Now!"

She held her breath and forced her eyes open, and found herself propped up on a chaise lounge. The colors of her blanket were intense, as if her glasses until now had been dirty. There were Aztec patterns, but even more vibrant, blues, and reds and yellows and greens and browns. Even the weave, the pattern of the stitches were incredibly clear! Then, slowly, she raised her head, and found Telmx and the universe.

Later when she tried to write about this moment, she needed three-dimensional paper, no, a V.E. authoring tool, so that others would understand everything simultaneously. No one piece of the experience could be fully fathomed without the whole.

"So you're awake," whispered Telmx. "I'm so relieved. It was, how do you say it? 'hairy' for a while."

"I thought I died. I got real freaked What are we doing? Are we at your house—your world? What's happening? Now I feel nothing but an amazing calm. I was so freaked out. And these colors are far-out."

Telmx's hand on her head. Familiar lumps in her throat, her lower back, her spine. And those new anticipations, the forbidden ones, weren't so forbidding anymore. Just thrilling, open, alive. One could be brave with this. She could be brave when she didn't feel so alone. She could be brave when she felt loved.

Still dizzy, she reached for Telmx's hand and looked up. She was in a round room, completely enclosed in glass. She and Telmx were in the middle, and the room was very bright, like brighter than daylight. They were in a gigantic kaleidoscope: she, Telmx and the multicolored cover transfixed together a thousand times over in unending mirrors.

"I've been here before."

"In your V.E. prescient memory. But until now, not actual. How do you feel?"

"Oh wow."

"Are you still dizzy?"

"A little. Don't take your hand away even for an instant. I thought, I thought I was choking to death."

"We had trouble figuring out the titration, in order to equalize your g. I got so frightened for you. I thought, well, I thought we had really made a mistake taking you this way. I was crying. You were crying. No, you were screaming. Howling. Screaming. I thought we'd never get it right. We did though. We figured out the right mix, finally. Gir assured me he had the titration right the first time. He..." Telmx took J's face in her hands. "But here you are. You're fine. I thought, well, I don't want to tell you what I thought. I thought we had your time track wrong. Well, we had it right. And I know from what we know, that you're fine for a very, very long time to come, so..." She paused to take a breath. "I'm talking too damn much. I talk too damn much when I'm excited and scared." Telmx cried and laughed. Then they hugged for a long time, and J knew that her prescient knowledge of a consummating sweetness with her beloved lady was real, and would soon take place. Not yet, but soon. A grand, long exquisite prelude.

Years of isolation and yearning dropped like so many layers of clunky medieval armor. J cried with gasping heaves and forced out, "I thought this day would never happen for real. You can't possibly know—"

J thought she fell back to sleep. The next time she opened her eyes, Telmx was lying next to her and their arms were entwined. Telmx was saying that there was something she had to show her before it was too late.

When Telmx reached over and touched a small rectangular display on the lounge, the lights and mirrors disappeared. The dome dissolved into a glowing mass of stars, like at the Hayden Planetarium, but J knew with awed certainty this was actual, not a projection. More stars materialized than she had ever seen, even on the darkest nights in summer camp.

"Do you see? That's your solar system." To one side a glowing globe no bigger than a dime was surrounded by millions of tiny dots of light, all rapidly shrinking. "That bright dot just below your sun is Jupiter. And just to its right is Neptune. Earth is so tiny—you can't tell which speck is Earth because it's too tiny. Actually by this time it might not even be visible."

J felt free and terribly, deeply lost, like when she was four years old in the large and crowded Woolworth's, the time she turned around and mother suddenly disappeared in the confusion of people.

J needed an anchor. "Where's the horse's eye?"

"In a while, my dearest."

J fell in and out of a slumber for most of the journey. At some point, Telmx was empath whispering in her ear, "Wake up my love. Here it is: the horse's eye. You don't want to miss this." J didn't know if she was awake or dreaming. It didn't matter, she thought. She forced her eyes open. There it was—like in the photographs she wasn't to see in Sky and Telescope for two more decades. For the first time, she saw the actual combination of colors that had been the awesome emblem of her experiences since her first dream-like episodes of the future. The horsehead surged, a dark mammoth sea horse rearing out of the water. It hovered in a raging sunset of reds and oranges and purples, the entire tableau set among dazzling lamps of various intensities and sizes.

Until then, she had always looked toward Pegasus to understand where Telmx's homeworld existed, but this, indeed, was not Pegasus. The collage was her recurring dream image, familiar, yet unfamiliar, an enormous, dark billowing cloud, distinctly in the shape of a horse's head, its regal profile gazing into the cosmos.

"That's where we are going," said Telmx. "Except, as we get closer, you'll see it's really not in the shape of an earthling Equine—it's actually dense stellar dust illuminated by radiation from Gyuf-ka, a bright star that your astronomers call Sigma Orionis. That's in Orion, the Hunter, one of your earthling constellations. It's just how it looks this far away. We'll be circling far around it. Can't go through that stuff. We'll end up directly behind that eye, four booster jumps straight on beyond it. My planet is actually at the spiral tip of a galaxy your astronomers don't know about yet. You'll see."

J was fading again. "No one'll ever ever believe me," she whispered. "Not in a million, million billion years." She slipped back into a deep slumber.

* * *

Except for some brief moments, Telmx kept J in high titration for the entire journey. Because J was becoming exponentially more susceptible to the ship's empath travel boosts as they approached her solar system, Telmx was even more reluctant to awaken her. She and Gir had anticipated some minor empath enhancements (such as intensified reactions to sounds and color), but these leaps were off the scale. She was able to fathom the ship's bearings and speed, even as she slept, and unconsciously make tiny adjustments even before Gir could calibrate them himself. At one point he had to thicken the console shields so that he could retain command of the ship. It wasn't malicious. She just automatically went there. Most alarming, the child's shielding was weakening. Almost non-existent. Telmx refused to leave her side, personally monitoring the g-titrations and J's energy flows, her hands constantly hovering the old-fashioned way over her body, enclosed in J's own self-proclaimed "protective" shielding: Levi's, tee shirt and sneaks.

Now they were in their final orbit, minutes away from docking. Galern II's splendid volcanic side loomed ahead: eternal swirls of green and yellow storms and occasional flashes of blue-white lighting. Icy ridges popped through the whirling colors, and for a second, a huge hole—the eye of the largest swirl, revealed the long curving row of mountains—the great Barrier Vromels that separated habitable from inhabitable, where only the tiny copthas and a few other hardy species thrived off the rich mineral spills from the volcanic peaks. Telmx wanted J to see it all. She could hardly contain her excitement. Just one more brief awakening, she thought.

"All right, my love, we're almost here. Come on, J. It's time."

"Are you sure you want to wake her just yet?" Old Gir empathed from the helm. "This is going to be quite a shock, you know. Got to take her in very, very slowly."

Telmx knew instantly he was right. Impulsive and impatient again.

"We're about to land. Why don't you bring her around right after the final retro-boost? Then I can devote my energies to the two of you, just in case. I know, I know, you want her to see Galern II from orbit. Give it time, my love. She'll see such things soon enough."

She loved Gir, but sometimes he was a bit too conservative, too careful. And usually right. "We're here?" whispered J, so softly Telmx thought it was empathed. Simultaneously, Telmx discerned the titration level slipping, raising, slipping again. J faded in and out of consciousness. She could not have a crisis now—not with Gir's energies diverted to the retro-boost. "I'm right here, my dearest J. You'll be awake soon enough." She rallied her energies and massaged J's temples with her palms, while deftly pressing her fingers on her cheekbones. She caressed her eyelids with her mind. Without having to adjust manually the flow on the chaise lounge, she simultaneously managed to equalize the titration. She knew exactly what to do without knowing. Perhaps she could equalize her just enough for her to get a glimpse. But she also knew better than to disregard Gir's wisdom.

"I want to see what you see," empathed J. J's faint empath whisper entered Telmx's mind, penetrating her surface shielding, as if it were not there at all. Telmx felt the child struggling to open her eyes.

"Not just yet."

"But you want me to see what you see."

"Please, my love. You're reading my impatience. We must wait until Gir can help you emerge. It's tricky, dangerous. Ignore my impatience. Just for a few minutes longer. We're about to land." The child's empath penetration and reception were phenomenal. Her shielding was gone, completely gone, and they hadn't even landed.

She would have to teach her Level VI shielding as soon as possible. If anyone from the Council were to discern her true powers…. Perhaps this was a mistake. They would have to jump immediately to her cottage, and bypass the inner city. Just for a while, until she learned the ways. Telmx shielded deeper, in order to hide her panic from J. "Wait until Gir hears the latest," she thought.

✳ ✳ ✳

"We'll have to keep her sedated," empathed Gir. Telmx followed his probe of J's mind, as he worked through each inner chamber, methodically, gently. He was a bit smaller than Telmx, but in these moments of deep concentration, he seemed to rise beyond himself, dwarfing the now dimly lit rotunda of the observatory deck. Telmx adored Gir in these moments. His chiseled and craggy face became smooth and glowed with a deep mahogany hue. His cilia wafted in unison, occasionally hesitating, then subtly shifting their inclination and cadence. He was squatting on his mat at the head of the chaise lounge, now lowered to the floor. At his instruction, Telmx squatted at the other end, and delicately held J's feet, now finally relieved of cumbersome socks and sneaks.

Telmx followed him through each of the child's inner chambers, sharing his astonishment as the child's rapid empath expansion manifested, layer by layer.

Gir's empath voice reached through Telmx's deepest chambers, to her most shielded portion, to that place only she and Goshing shared. Telmx followed him in, fearful and knowing what he was about to say. "I'm sorry to tread on Goshing's territory, but I know she would understand." Telmx braced herself. "She was perfectly able to pass for a new off-world scout recruit when we left Earth," she empathed. "She had even mastered the art of slight shield. No one would have guessed she had developed beyond our mandate."

"Well, she's way out of whack now. Lost her shielding altogether, and so open that when she awakes she'll be empath flooded and flooding—and any self respecting level VI around here will suddenly notice her wandering aim-lessly around their inner chambers. This is phenomenal. It's most astonish-ing that we never anticipated her capacity for such rapid empath develop-ment," he empathed.

"Or perhaps we didn't study her well enough."

"At a later time, we can re-analyze. But for now, we were only mandated for a Level I recruit—and one that isn't even allowed to tweak even slightly another's intentions. So we are faced with a staggering problem." Gir never used the word "staggering" idly. "I agree that you must take her to your cottage immediately, and we must envelop her in our own protective shields when we disembark from the ship—but we must do this without appear-ing that anything unusual is going on. And once you have taught her to shield again, she must master a technique that prevents anyone from dis-cerning that she can perform a Level VI shielding. At all costs, the Council mustn't discover her true powers. Even the local Imari must not discern them. Questions raised throughout our own community would travel to others in no time."

"Oh, Gir, what have I done? How come I didn't know? Didn't anticipate? I should've known even after that first encounter—how swiftly she went be-yond our intent, the Council's intent. Those nightmares, her prescience. I should have terminated the project then and there. Should've retro-swept. I could've protected her from her pain anyway, could've checked in on her as I recruited someone else—you know, been there for her without her really knowing it. I'm totally responsible…."

"Stop it right now!" Gir was suddenly harsh, jarring. Telmx reeled. "There's a wisdom at work we can't fathom," he continued. "Don't second-guess it.

We must work with it. You know that. We've always known it. Believe me, Goshing and I would've terminated this project long ago if we'd doubted. Now, think with me, and pitch all this self-centered indulgence overboard. It doesn't become you one tiny bit."

His words reminded her of Goshing's when Telmx was still a fledgling Imari scout recruit. She wondered why she should so suddenly be thrown back into a state she'd left behind several decades previously. "Old patterns don't ever entirely disappear. They just get minuscule and ineffectual," empath mumbled Gir. Then emphatically: "Now, my love, let's figure out a plan of action."

"We're being asked to disembark," empathed Winstx from the helm. "They need to shove the ship into docking orbit. We're taking too long. They're not suspicious or anything. They just need to do their job."

✷ ✷ ✷

J squatted within layers of thick multicolored tapestries. They wafted and undulated, stroking her skin on all sides. She raised her hand. No hand, the feeling of raising her hand. She moved her non-hand to her face. No face she thought. The feeling of face. She thought she should be frightened, but instead, without trying, she explored the weave, the soft dips and crests of the fabric, with her non-hands. A familiar aroma greeted her caress from the fabric. Telmx's. Clearly Telmx's.

Telmx stroked her face. Her lady emerged squatting beside her. In sensation. Real and non-real. "Welcome to my inner chamber," Telmx empathed. J knew her empath voice without hearing it. It informed without intonation.

"Is this your home? Are we there?" She empathed. Easily, immediately, without pre-thought.

"No, we're physically at the spaceport, still in the ship, in the observatory. We are actually in my mind's inner chamber, our minds' inner chambers."

"A secret empath place."

"Exactly. Now I need your help. You need to think with me."

"You need *my* help? Here? On *your* planet?"

"Yes, my dearest. Now listen carefully."

J listened to the dilemma that she already knew, as if she had dreamt it earlier on the voyage and was simply recalling the details.

"We'll alternate," J empathed.

"Alternate?"

"Yeah. Okay. I can't shield at all until you retrain me. You guys can't appear to be maximum-shielding me. So: you, Gir and Winstx should rapidly rotate and overlap your common shields over my unshielded empath, alternating with my raw and vulnerable state, just so it shows up a little bit, so people think that I am very, very space-sick, that I haven't regained my sea-legs or something like that."

"Brilliant! It will appear to others, even the most sophisticated among the Imari, that you are overwhelmed and disoriented by all the stimuli on our planet...."

"And that the three of you are taking care of me, wanting me to see and hear and feel all the new stuff, but overprotective at the same time, and throwing random shielding my way because I can't protect myself from being bombarded by curious Imari empaths and all the marvelous stuff I'm taking in around me." J marveled at how they were thinking together, figuring it out together.

"Like there's a whole lot of love going around," Telmx empathed, "among the four of us. And no one will appear to be deep shielding, just a bunch of over-zealous, over-protective Imari's."

"Excited to show off their homeworld to an exuberant and curious off-worlder who has no idea that all this fantastic stuff is too much for her to take in all at once," exclaimed J. Telmx had known Gir was absolutely right when he had suggested she consult with J, which she initiated quite reluctantly. She still wanted J to remain her dependent little Level I Earth-child.

"I can't wait," squealed J. "Let's do it!"

The three Imaris emerged with their semi-conscious sleepwalker into the terminal from the decontamination chambers. Telmx and Gir flanked J on either side, a hand on each of her shoulders. Winstx walked just ahead, hover-guiding J's knapsack and other light luggage. The terminal was abuzz with intergalactic travelers coming and going, minding their own business, and too intent on getting their baggage loaded and their travel documents scanned to bother with anyone else. J teetered every so often, occasionally opening her eyes, and then rapidly shutting them.

In her brief forays into consciousness, J didn't have to pretend she was overwhelmed. A cacophony of out-loud and empath voices bombarded from all sides, in a myriad of different languages, cadences and frequencies. Voices ranged from deep guttural growls, way below her normal human hearing thresholds, to high frequency whistles and song-like utterances much higher than her range. To her amazement, she could decipher their intended meanings. But so many bombarded at once, she couldn't keep up. She caught phrases here and there. The aromas, perhaps the pheromones, of each species, spoke even louder than their words, communicating overwhelming waves of emotions, from intense passions to minor preoccupations about travel details.

The slightly red-yellow hue in the terminal seared her eyes, and although she was desperate to take it all in, looking was painful. She had to settle for aromas and sounds, and what she could sort of discern with her mind's eye. In the brief moments that she dared to open her eyes, the terminal appeared more crowded than Times Square at rush hour, but no one was rushing. There was a silky calm in their movements, a slow motion quality, and not everyone was moving on the ground. It was as if she had landed in the middle of an elaborate open field filled with every animal species in the world. They were not like earthling animals, but rather variants of what was familiar to her: creatures like large flying raptors, chattering chimps, hovering elephants. Most of the travelers were Imari: tall, wafting, human-like people in travel hoods, people like Telmx, Gir, and Winstx, of various hues of black and brown.

Telmx said something about getting their documents validated. That was the last J remembered of the terminal. At some point Telmx said they were transferring from the terminal to her home, gliding through some canyons that separated the more densely settled areas from the sparsely populated rural communities. J wanted to see the canyons, but even the daylight glare stung her eyes, and when she tried looking, everything spun around. The air was silky, and a bit warm, almost too warm, with an occasional cooling breeze. The air, the aromas, everything pulsated in luscious musical cadences.

When they reached Telmx's cottage, Gir and Winstx were no longer with them. As they emerged from the hovercraft, Telmx coaxed her to open her eye, just for a moment, to see her cottage, the land, the canyons. Though J was desperate to take in everything with all her senses, she sobbed in frustration. "I can't. I'm spinning. I need to be inside, right now. I'm sorry. I need to sleep."

Although she knew she was capable of sensing what was around her, she managed to shut it out, and couldn't wait to lie down and sleep once again. She felt Telmx guiding her inside. Maybe when she awoke….

Then Telmx put an "apple" in her hand. "It'll make you feel better," she empathed. J turned it around in her hands. It was bigger than an apple, and she sensed from its aroma that it was fairly tart. She bit into it: it was more like a pomegranate, or an apple with seeds like a pomegranate, each seed exploding in her mouth, tiny capsules of sweet and tart, pulsating in her mouth in delicious rhythms. Then the pulsating was more than she could bear. "Oh shit! I'm going to barf!"

This time when she awakened, J found herself lying face-up on a soft rug, and covered by a light fabric that seemed to hover just millimeters from her Levi's and tee shirt. It seemed to cool all of her except her face, which was warm, almost too warm. Telmx was sitting next to her and smiled when she opened her eyes. The room was dim. Cloth wall hangings, like the comforter on the ship, surrounded her. Many colorful fronds and bulbous plants in large red-clay sculptured vases filled the space. Some hanging, some on richly textured floor mats.

Telmx said, "I made a mistake. I'm sorry. I wanted you to see and hear and taste everything at once. Even as we traveled from the terminal to my home. Please forgive me. I won't do that again."

J forgave her, for whatever it was she thought she had done. And immediately slipped back to sleep.

When she opened her eyes again, Telmx wasn't there. But the room and the rug were the same. She sat up, feeling better than she had for the entire journey from her bedroom on Earth to Telmx's cottage on Galern II. Now she was hungry, and desperately needed to pee. Okay, she thought, I'm actually here. She felt chilled and frantic. But more important, she had to find a bathroom. Maybe she was getting her period. "Oh my god," she thought, "where's my knapsack? And where's Telmx?"

The room had no windows, no furniture. No lamps, no door! But a soft glow illuminated multicolored plants and trees. There were other rugs scattered about. She pushed covers off and realized to her horror that she was stark naked! Her Levi's and tee shirt were gone. She felt as if she were back at home, with her dad's dizzy stink suffocating her brain. A nightmare? Where was she? Where was her lady? She was just there a minute ago.

She opened and closed her eyes, trying to rearrange the scene. Nothing. And she still desperately had to pee.

Still terrified and shaky, she risked standing upright, trying not to think of her nakedness. If she could at least pee, she thought, she could figure things out. A few paces away she sensed a door of sorts—an opening in the wall partially obscured by large blue and purple leaves and a variety of ferns. She aimed herself toward it. It opened into a kind of cordoned off room, about the size of a closet, with a hole in the floor emitting a pulsating spearmint aroma from water or a water-like substance flowing below.

There was no way to lock the "door," but at this point she didn't care. She squatted and peed forever, desperately hoping it was a bathroom. When she was finished, she didn't seem to require paper—the aromatic air from the hole in the ground seemed to take care of all that, and, what's more, she didn't have her period. That would've been the freakiest of freak-outs, her period without knowing where her knapsack was!

There was a stirring in the main room. "Come, my love. You're safe. You're not in a nightmare. Your dad's a billion light years away. Look, there's a comfortable Imari wishaptha, much more suitable to the climate, waiting for you at the foot of your mat. I'll show you how to wrap it." Even though Telmx was her lady, she still felt out of control and desperate for her trusty Levi's. And there was no towel to cover herself.

"Alright, my love, come on in. I won't look. I promise."

J tentatively pushed open the curtain and found Telmx bent over an elaborate urn she hadn't noticed before, examining a large ornate vent on the top. Her gangly large frame was loosely wrapped in a kind of multicolored cloth.

J felt naked and vulnerable in the presence of her beloved Telmx. She was torn. Disoriented. Dizzy and nauseous. Flustered by her reaction, but unable to control her prolonged and mounting terror, she made her way swiftly and silently to her mat, jerked the blanket off, and scrambled to hide her nakedness. Standing safely from the vantage point of her mat, J stared in dismay at her beloved lady, now in profile. Her lady was not exactly human, actually an alien, a real alien!

In all her visits with J, Telmx had never quite allowed herself to be fully visible. J knew she was ebony. Real ebony, like glowing onyx. But now her travel hood no longer covered her head. Beneath closely cropped brown/red hair, two pairs of ears, the higher larger than the lower, were all adorned with a multitude of various sized, intensely resplendent earrings. She was very still, except for something very wispy over her eyes: long, soft filament eyebrows wafted over the vent.

Without turning around, Telmx empathed, "I'm tasting the aroma. You can stare for a while. I'm preparing the, uh, samovar—we call it a frimulator. The tea is strong and stimulating. I know: four ears, cilia eyebrows, not stuff you expected. Please don't be too put off. I'm acting like I don't care what you think. But I do. Are you put off? You're put off. I can tell. Unfortunately I can tell."

J inched backward awkwardly in her blanket, almost tripping in her desperation to keep the alien at a distance.

"Oh my love, you're so scared. Well, what did you expect? I'm not completely human. I'm sentient, but I'm not from Earth, but I'm still Telmx. Oh, J, please don't be scared. We'll figure it all out, all right?"

"I'd really like my Levi's, tee shirt and sneaks. Where'd you put them? Did you bring my stuff like you promised? I mean, my knapsack is here, right? It was right next to me in my bed like we talked about, I mean, I really really need it. And my Levi's. Now.

"It's all right, my love. My goodness you're shivering all over. Of course. Wait right here. See? I have everything you packed. Right here." She reached behind a large cluster of huge purple and blue leaves and produced J's knapsack. "And I packed your earth clothes inside. See?"

J let Telmx hover the knapsack toward her and waited until she returned to the frimulator-thing. Her lady was strange, not exactly creepy—but so different from what she was used to. She read Telmx's dismay at her own distress and didn't know what to do about it. She wanted to ask her not to look at her while she dressed, but she also didn't want to insult her—strange mix of the familiar empath closeness and an equally strong aversion.

"You don't want me to look at you while you dress. I'm not looking at you. It's really alright. I'm not going to do anything to you. Oh, please forgive me for frightening you. I really didn't mean to. I just thought you would be so much more comfortable in this climate." J fumbled with the straps and finally got the knapsack open. She knew she had packed exactly the wrong clothes, but she'd feel more in control in her Levi's and tee shirt. She fumbled with the buttons to her fly, and ended up having to start over again. "Where's my sneaks?" she empathed.

"We don't wear shoes in the house," Telmx empathed. "I'm sorry. You do understand, don't you?" She was still bending over her brew, with her weird thing-a-ma-gigs waving in front of her face.

"I'm still the same Telmx I always was," she continued empathing without looking up. "Oh dear, I'm doing everything wrong, aren't I? I should have covered up better and let you see a little bit of me at a time. I was so anxious for you to take in everything. Gir warned me not to do things so quickly. I wanted to show you how we auto-effuse. I thought you would think it was, as you say, so 'cool.'"

J's Levi's and tee shirt felt completely hot and wrong. She remained on the other side of the chamber with her knapsack by her side, tears soaking her cheeks, unsure what to do next. She wished Telmx would just stop talking long enough so she could just listen to her own thoughts. Maybe she was asleep in a long incredibly realistic nightmare. Maybe her lady wasn't really an alien with four ears. Maybe she could will herself awake, find herself in her own bed, waiting for her real lady to come to take her to her home planet on the other side of the horse's eye, just like they had planned.

"I'll keep quiet now, my dearest. And look, I'm covering my head so you can recognize me again. I'm so, so sorry. You're not dreaming. It's not a nightmare. You're really here on Galern II, my homeworld, like I promised. Here, look. I really am Telmx. I really am. Now, I promise to keep quiet."

She raised her head from the frimulator and J took yet another step back. She watched warily as Telmx glided over to a large basket tucked away under the same purple and blue fronds. Telmx's words were soothing and familiar, but J kept her hands thrust in her pockets, afraid to let herself relax lest she be vulnerable to some unknown threat that must be lurking on the other side of the next moment. Telmx squatted at the basket, pulled out the familiar deep brown travel hood, and quickly pulled it over her head. "There, now."

Telmx longed to fold the child in her arms and sooth her jagged edges, but she wouldn't even dare reach in to those chambers they had shared so recently to soothe her empathically. She and Gir had decided it was best to offer no unusual intrusion, and to use only the most surface of empath communication. For the time being they had managed to seal off J's deeper powers by erecting a strong Level VI shield around her inner chambers. Here at the cottage, no one would notice, no one would come. There was an unwritten agreement: when an Imari retreated to his or her own cottage, the retreat was honored. In the safety of the cottage there was time and space for the child to warm up slowly to the experience with Telmx's help. She went back to the frimulator and filled two cups of tea with a ladle hanging to one side of the device.

She placed them on the mat next to the frimulator and squatted. "It's really good tea," she empathed gently. "It's something like your chamomile, but more minty, and it also contains a hint of licorice. It's not anything like your cherry coke, but I think you'll like it."

Now there was silence. J was grateful. She stood awkwardly on the other side of her own mat, and tentatively looked at the figure now squatting peacefully by the frimulator, sipping her tea. Perhaps it was all right. Her lady looked like her lady again. Her aromas, her aspect. Her inner peace. Telmx seemed to have folded into herself, deeply shielded, she surmised, giving J the time she needed. J began to experience inner peace as well.

Up until that moment, J hadn't noticed that the air was anything but silent. The fronds and leaves inside the cottage and in the surrounding area sent soft comfort through her temples. She closed her eyes and discovered that she could easily peruse the neighborhood outside—not visually, but in essence. Tiny and not so tiny creatures scampering and flying about just outside, sending their own melodic strains, in counterpoint and sometimes punctuated by what seemed like faraway rhythms, drumming perhaps, marimbas, shakers, and very, very distant strains of a harp-like instrument. Perhaps from a neighboring cottage. It seemed that they were in a kind of valley—and the sounds bounced lazily, repeating, fading, rising, fading again. Aromas, mostly similar to lilac, mingled with the more distinct mint and licorice. She was transfixed. More like what she had anticipated. More like what Telmx had promised.

Perhaps some tea, after all, she thought. She opened her eyes. Telmx had not moved, her eyes also closed, her mind firmly shielded. Telmx did not stir when J approached her mat and reached for her tea. The tea was still warm, smooth, with a distinct sequence of tastes. Everything was more intense here, she thought. Even her feelings. She examined Telmx's face. Familiar now: angular, high cheekbones, broad slightly quivering nostrils, and full, slightly parted lips—without the extra ears and long cilia, now all hidden by her travel hood, she indeed looked human again, J thought, regal and gentle, the lady she adored.

J hoped, knew, Telmx had not been put off by her freak-out. Just a freak-out. Of course Telmx wouldn't judge her. It was not her way, not the Imari Way. She regretted her outbursts now, for making Telmx work so hard to cool her down. She yearned to touch her face, to squat opposite her and meet her forehead with her own until they almost touched, like Telmx had taught her. Yes, she would allow Telmx to take her through this experience. In spite of the stiffness of her Levi's, she managed to squat opposite her beloved lady, and silently asked her to forgive her frenetic uneasy.

❋ ❋ ❋

The suns were down now and J was on her third cup. She was intensely uncomfortable in her dungarees, even after Telmx had reconfigured the room. Mostly J stayed quiet. Telmx talked and talked sometimes in empath, sometimes out loud, and expected nothing in return, for which J was grateful, but it was also the first time their empath communication bothered J. J wished Telmx was not able to read her thoughts—it would allow her space to continue figuring things out on her own. It was a bit too much intrusion, even though on Earth she had cherished it, looked forward to it like a game—a secret game—like the two of them belonged to a special secret club. But here, the impact of empath was too loud, too jarring.

"You need to learn how to shield again—even from me. I'll show you how. But first, some dinner," empathed Telmx. "It'll make you feel better. You must be hungry. I mean, I know you're hungry—and you really would be more comfortable in an Imari wishaptha."

J's Levi's did feel increasingly uncomfortable—they clung to her skin and seemed to tighten as the evening wore on—but not quite yet, she thought. But she sure was getting hungry.

Telmx rose and began fussing at the frimulator. She reached into some other place behind a set of large purple fan-like flowers, and produced a large wooden tray containing several bowls and small clusters of colorful items, each emitting a distinctive aroma, some familiar, all extraordinarily inviting. J marveled that she could discern which aroma came from which, even from the far side of the room. "I prepared my favorites for you." Telmx continued.

"One day you'll introduce me to your favorites. I left out some of the spices that are completely new to your system, but, well, it's like your Thai, uh, Siamese cuisine, I know you like peanuts, but not exactly Siamese, perhaps also a bit like Korean, the spicy sesame aspect, with a hint of East African."

J realized she was no longer nauseous.

"It's the tea," Telmx empathed. She set the tray down between them. The tray looked like a large lotus leaf. Each bowl contained a different color sauce, some more pungent than others, grouped in a pleasing array in the middle. Arranged around them were large green leaves, each one tenderly filled with a different delicacy cut into small bite-size pieces. Smaller neatly stacked leaves adorned the outer perimeter of the tray. "These over here are three varieties of mushrooms. Those are amber roots, something like your daikon radishes, and these, these are my favorites: fowqua berries marinated in bot and frimulated in a mixture of guxto sap. You eat them last, like a dessert." Telmx went on and on, but J couldn't take in the details. She felt like touching anything on the tray would be destroying a masterpiece.

"It's all right. I'll show you how to prepare all this," empathed Telmx. "Oh no, almost forgot the bot," she exclaimed out loud, and went to fetch a large delicately carved goblet.

"It's my great great grandmother's. The carvings all have meaning. I'll tell you about them sometime." She held the goblet out to J.

"What is it?"

"It's a kind of beer, but just a tinge of alcohol."

"How do you know I won't get sick again?"

"It'll do just the opposite. You'll feel better and better."

J thought it might be a drug. She hesitated.

"Not a drug, in the sense that you mean," empathed Telmx. "Here, it's ceremonial. You don't have to drink more than a sip, if you don't want to. Take the goblet and we'll break the froth."

"Break the froth?"

"It's an Imari ritual for friendship and camaraderie." J lifted the goblet to her lips. The taste was initially sweet, lingering, and then burst into a sequence of tastes, perhaps ten in all, each slightly stronger than the previous one. It warmed and cooled her pallet simultaneously, and within seconds she experienced an overwhelming sense of well-being.

"One could get addicted to this stuff," she empathed, handing the goblet to Telmx.

"A healthy addiction, if you want to call it an addiction. Now we have broken the froth. Come, try the goptha root first. You wrap it in the limbus leaf, like so, and then, now watch carefully, the sequence of dipping sauces is important. First this one." She handed the leaf to J. J hesitated. The aromas were tantalizing, but even so….

"Savor it slowly. I prepared them so you could enjoy them without surprising your system, but your body's not exactly used to all this."

"No forks, not even chopsticks, no nothing." J thought, bringing the morsel to her lips.

"We also sometimes use a kind of bread to pick up food, like your Ethiopians."

After a few tastes, J knew that she would never be able to eat normal Earth food again. She wondered how she could reproduce the tastes when she returned. Telmx promised her that it was possible, that she would help her figure it out.

"Now, then," Telmx empathed. "You feel quite a bit better. I am so pleased."

"I just wasn't, like I didn't expect you to be, you know..."

"Non-human."

"Right."

"Except for some minor differences, actually, we're quite the same."

"Not really."

"Well, that's just because your planet is fairly young, as things go, I mean technologically. I don't mean that some day you'll all have four ears and cilia. Actually, your species does have six ears, it just that four of them are combined inside your outer ear—they haven't come into their own, so to speak."

They continued talking way into the night. After secondary sunset, they laid out a mat on the patio and Telmx pointed out constellations and nebulae. The general direction of Earth's galaxy was just above the treetops to the left of her home, but it could not be seen, not even with a powerful telescope. By tertiary moonrise, they were huddled close on a single mat, silently imbibing each other's company, just as they would on Earth, except the blue/white moonshines on Galern II cast subtle overlapping shadows. J finally succumbed to exhaustion and couldn't possibly stay up for primary sunrise. They went inside, and J allowed Telmx to wrap her in the wishaptha, the Imari Way.

CHAPTER EIGHT

Galern II

Still fearing vertigo when she ventured outside the cottage, J kept her eyes closed on the patio. Telmx was picking up provisions from a small depot on the other side of the canyon. The air was unusually still: no sounds of Imari anywhere, not even from the neighboring homes she could feel, but could not see. Not even from the hovercraft drones that earlier echoed in the valley. Pungent eucalyptus and something called chud—a very sweet fruit that was quite intoxicating—even the fragrances felt like a contact high. She was basically a city kid, even though she now lived in the suburbs. Perhaps this is what the Tropics feels like on her own planet, or California. Barb had visited California and raved about the eucalyptus.

The birds and the insects were very velvety. She listened intently, on purpose intently but surprisingly without effort. Maybe other people on Earth feel and hear and smell and yearn for more all the time. These enhanced sensations were new to her, but perhaps all her friends, perhaps most earthlings knew about them already.

A crunching and padding. She opened her eyes, risking dizziness. The tiny animal at the end of her mat pawed at the goztca fruit seed from her lunch. It mostly resembled a large squirrel, but it also had layers of colorful shingles, like the pictures of iguana she had seen in school. Perhaps this was the famous regipe. "Okay, eat the seed," she said. "Hey, here's a whole fruit." But the creature scampered away when she raised her hand.

Would she see and hear and feel things differently when she returned home? Here even the small patterns in the grainy wood felt completely awesome.

And double sun shadows, just as with the moons.

Dizzy and safe together. At first, safe frightened her. Safe actually made her more uneasy than constant, ineffective preparations for unseen but inevitable doom. Telmx had explained why safe felt unsafe, something to do with being comfortable with the familiar, but she didn't get it. "You will," Telmx had said, and wouldn't elaborate.

She wished Telmx would hurry up and come back. She concentrated on the far edge of the canyon, listening intently for the distant sound of her hovercraft, the familiar sensation of her lady returning, as she had done for so many years on Earth, knowing for sure, if only in a dream, that her lady was close by, perhaps orbiting her planet, and about to appear. She always knew, and she was always right. Here things were different. After feeling so invaded by Telmx's empath the first day, Telmx's shielding was now allowing only surface communication empath between them.

"Your powers have evolved so rapidly," she had explained, "that I decided to shield my deeper self, my deeper empath chambers, to protect you from being overwhelmed. Not forever. You'll grow your own shields, and your own empath controls. And then we can move in and out of each other's inner empath chambers in the Imari Way. With consent and respect. Mutual understanding. But we must take it slow for now. There's time." J had no idea what time was like on this planet. Or how old she was now, having traveled millions of light years in no more than one human week. "An elaborate but completely simple trick of time travel," Telmx had said, and she promised to show her this amazing elegance of science with V.E. pictures "one of these days soon," but warned that J should not expect to understand it yet. Another "soon, but not yet."

She felt antsy, motivated to walk around, just a bit, perhaps explore, in spite of vertigo. She decided to pry her eyes open again and hold her head upright for more than a few moments at a time. Just for the double shadows. Or to see another regipe. Or the mammoth palm trees, much larger, Telmx had explained, than any on Earth and bearing such rich fruit that it was prudent to avoid standing right under one, in order not to be bonked. After J learned the technique of hovering, she would be able to select the ripest, and hover it gently to the ground herself. "Soon, but not yet."

She opened her eyes, expecting to be accosted by searing brightness. Instead, the sky was a deep gray-purple, with hardly any glare. Perhaps the setting of the suns, she thought. In fact, the suns were now behind her. She could feel their warmth on her back. Double shadows were long and thin.

Telmx was actually gone a very long time. She had left soon after secondary sunrise. What if something terrible had had happened to her? Telmx had indicated there were certain political rumblings, certain sentient species to be wary of, that even some disgruntled Imari had turned against their own species.

Suddenly frenzied thumping and scurrying shattered the forest rhythms. Then profound silence, as if someone had abruptly switched off the sound.

The air turned briny. Pungent odors assaulted her nostrils. In the distance, beyond the canyon, a soft but persistent roar. Her hair swished with the trees.

Two giapias scampered past her into the brush. Telmx had also warned her about killer storms: to get inside and stay inside, that she would be tempted to catch a glimpse of the storm, enjoy the magnificent colors of its lightning, but that it could blind even the most sophisticated Level VI Imari. On this perfect planet, flaws: political factions, and storms that were completely normal and completely lethal.

J grabbed her lunch tray. She was spinning now, completely in sync with the giapias' terrified pheromones. The roar intensified, as if a huge swarm of hovercrafts were about to appear over the crest of the canyon. She could not look around toward the roar for fear of fainting. She simply was determined to reach the door at the end of the patio. But she couldn't scamper like the little creatures. Fearful of stumbling, she walked slowly and deliberately toward the cottage door, guided by the aroma of the cottage, more than by her blurring eyes.

A sudden gust threw her over, and the tray whipped out of her hand as if a fire hose had been aimed right at it. Her knees hit the flagstones. Sharp pain. Lightning in her head from the pain. And now lightning from the canyon. She was sure of it without seeing it. Her knees gave way to the pain, and she sunk to her belly, inching toward the door like a soldier under fire, moving on instinct, eyes shut tight. A staggering clap of thunder shook the ground beneath her. Rocks smacked at her back and head with deliberate precision. Suddenly icy pellets under her hands and a vicious hissing. Pungent steam roasting her face, tearing her skin.

Somehow J reached the gelatinous door shield, willed it open, as Telmx had taught her. A sudden gust of wind propelled her inside, sending dust flying and objects crashing. The door coalesced behind her. She lay curled up on her side, just inside the shield. No more droning from the canyon. A steady thumping. Very, very quiet except for that thumping. The room glowed softly in a red rose hue, seemingly oblivious to the chaos, except for the auburn dust that had swirled in before the door coalesced. Broken fronds hugged the corners in clumps. She tried to move, and realized that the sticky slippery wetness beneath her was not from rain. It hadn't rained: she was bleeding. She empath and out-loud called for Telmx, using every piece of energy she could muster. Raw stinging and spasms alternated with concerns about Telmx. A half-hour provision run had taken a whole day. Perhaps the storm. What if she had crashed? How long should she wait before she tried to summon a neighbor? She didn't even know which neighbor to trust, and she wasn't supposed to be in contact with anyone yet. "Soon, but not yet...."

✳ ✳ ✳

Telmx found J unconscious on the floor, crumpled and tangled in her wishaptha, surrounded by the chaos blown in by the storm. She had been grounded by the storm warnings, and hoped against hope that J had not wandered outside. She had even tried in vain to empath reach her from the other side of the canyon, but the boosters were down. She had no time for self-reproach, for leaving J alone only one day after their arrival. She retrieved her crumpled mat, gently hovered her onto it, and peeled off the bloody wishaptha. J's body was riddled with huge purple welts, and bleeding from jagged gashes. For now, she would not try to arouse her. She had to close the wounds. She quickly entered J's cranium, and rearranged her cells to obliterate concussion.

Telmx had a stash of salve that closed her wounds and cured all the welts and bruises within an hour. J would be alright—some scarring, but those would fade within the next two hours. Then she again examined every inch of her body, looking for burn marks, scratches, any indication of potentially permanent damage, because the radiation from the storm could be lethal over time. Her own encounter with the hail, when she was six, had left a bruise that had never quite healed. It continued to be a faint worry. Sometimes she would wake up in the night and empath-probe her scar to see if something had changed. It never did, and now doctors were convinced it was not part of the scarring, but simply a birthmark or a benign scraping that for some reason left a little trail. Nevertheless, she recently had started treating it with a potion she had found in an unofficial self-help shop along the back alleys of Curmot. With daily applications, the scar had actually begun to disappear. That was a couple of years ago, and it was in fact almost completely gone. Like a chronic headache she had no idea was pounding at her until it began to go away.

There should not be speck remaining on J, especially since J would soon be back on Earth, not able to obtain proper treatment.

As for leaving her vulnerable to the storm: How could she have even thought of doing that? But they needed supplies, and J couldn't go with her. Not just yet.

These concerns filled her even as she applied a new coat of the potion to J's traumatized spots. Certain parts of her body, specifically her hands, were especially sensitive. Whenever Telmx worked on them, J would fall into a deeper and more peaceful sleep, and almost as quickly surface to a shallower slumber when Telmx moved to another area.

Telmx had mastered Earth people's body fluid energies early in her visits. To mentor and protect J, she needed to know precise issues of physiology and then apply her advanced medical knowledge without being tempted or tempting others to jump huge gaps in medical knowledge. Many earthlings were already well aware of body energies and fluids, and other more empath issues that formed the basis of cures among the Imaris as well as other sentients of the known planets. If she found J an earthling cranial-sacral expert, even though that knowledge on Earth was primitive, the situation could be monitored.

Telmx lingered on her hands so she could work her eyes up and down the rest of her body. Her sonar scanning had detected no inner traumas. Still it didn't hurt to check again. She worked her way around every muscle, every curve in every organ, in and out of arteries and around soft meniscus tissue in her joints, (lingering briefly on the light murmur in the third ventricle—there would be time to address that later), moving carefully, for even this amount of invasion had its effects on the cells and psyche, like deep massage.

J felt unusually light, as if each cell in her body were being individually caressed and wrapped in cool smooth silk. She would not abandon such a sublime dream. She felt desperately like touching herself, like she often did at home, after Liz was asleep, imagining making love to Barb, or a favorite teacher, or even to Telmx herself. It would be the most intense conclusion to the silky gentle breeze that caressed her.

Telmx slowly became aware of J's arousal. Flushing, she imagined what it would be like to make love to her at last, to teach her the Imari Way. For the Imari, fifteen was about the right age to ascend into womanhood. But this was too soon for an earthling. Loving her the Imari Way would be misperceived by earthlings, perhaps even by J herself, as an alien abduction, perhaps even as a rape of a minor. But she had been younger than J at her own Ascension. Perhaps it was alright, even appropriate. After all, without the Imari rite of passage, how could she complete all the stages of her recruitment? Did she really think she could bring J to her full empath potential without it? She wasn't surprised by J's reaction. In fact, she and J had both anticipated her own Ascension even as far back as that first roof moment. The rite would enhance her healing. Yes, she was ready.

Telmx couldn't possibly recreate the wondrous experience Goshing and the other elder women had created for her. She struggled against her own urges. Perhaps she should gather the elders from the compound, and properly prepare J for the inevitable, the full Imari Way. No, Goshing and the elders would chastise Telmx for her habitual flawed impatience and lack of foresight. And they'd be right. If a few aromas and sensations had thrown J into such states, what would a genuine full Ascension rite do to her? She had to be cautious, prepare a more Earth-like ritual. But so soon?

J imagined her special lady gently pulling away her sheets and blowing cool and reassuring puffs of air between her legs. She imagined Telmx stroking her forehead and her nipples and her abdomen as if her lady had six hands separately and expertly schooled in massage and shiatsu. She imagined her lady could penetrate her gently, with quiet words of comfort, pressing into the small of her back. Eight hands now, each one addressing a different desire, each with its own rhythm, gently stroking and entering, pushing with quiet deliberate strength against her own throbbing internal membranes.

She was afraid to move, lest she break the spell, conflicted between allowing everything to release inwardly, then extend outward and inward and up, and the intense desire to keep the sensations going exactly as they were, for a long as she could. After all, it was her fantasy.

Telmx had no choice. J's staggering empath growth, unharnessed and raw, forced new strategies. Ascension was natural and beautiful. No one would object. It did not have to be perceived as a gateway to deeper empath training. Just a natural rite of passage between mentor and student. Not to perform it would be, in fact, unnatural.

Besides, J's Ascension was also essential to the Mission. Without Ascension, albeit altered to fit the physical and emotional limitations of the earthling, no advanced learning could be attained. Now Telmx and J must face the complications of cross-cultural taboos. The issue was quite complex, and Telmx had to prepare herself and J for all that the rite of Ascension implied.

But not just yet. In a few days, she promised herself. They had to get through this crisis first. Also, she had to stop chastising herself up for leaving J vulnerable to the storm.

Telmx's hand was stroking J's cheek, and J found her mind in her mind. No, Telmx was right there, and this was not simply a fantasy. "You would like to make love with me," J heard herself empath. She was beyond herself, open, so open. Abandoned to sensation, her loins, vulva, and velvety places, far inside. Swelling, and pulsating urgent and calm. "I accept your gift," she managed to empath. "Now. Not in a few days. Please. Now. Alright? Now. Before I change my mind. I promise you. I know your struggle and I accept full responsibility. I promise you. Please. I know what this means, more than you're willing to tell me."

J reached up and caressed her beloved lady's face. "I don't care if the setting isn't exactly right," she empathed, "or whether I am fully cured from the storm. Please. Please lower your travel hood, so you can finally and fully fathom me. I am ready for your Imari ritual. I really really am."

Telmx drew back her hood and unwrapped her wishaptha, and laid it gently next to J's. J welcomed her firm and tender hands willing her legs apart. She sensed the heat of Telmx's face and the gentle swish of her long silky cilia on her thighs. J's back and buttocks, urgent and calm and firmly supported by an unseen force, hovered slightly off her mat. At the moment Telmx's lips pressed gently on her lips between her legs, she reeled in expectant ecstasy. Telmx cupped her hands around her breasts, so that J's erect nipples were slightly crushed by their grip. And Telmx's tongue gently graced soft spots J didn't know existed.

She yearned desperately for Telmx to enter her, and she did, with her tongue, her heart and her mind, round fullness, growing, swelling, heaving, releasing, heaving and releasing again and again. Sequential layers of urge and release.

❋ ❋ ❋

"Here you go, J. You should break the froth."

J accepted the goblet, nodding her head slightly, as if she had been performing the ritual all her life.

"It's a special vintage bot, reserved for these occasions. Sip it slowly. It has a powerful after-punch."

J took a sip and handed the goblet to Telmx. "Now your Ascension is complete," empathed Telmx. "Your learning will be all the deeper for it, and swifter." They sipped in silence. "You're fifteen Earth years. In our culture, you were more than ready for the Ascension, and," she smiled, "you noticed yourself that you were more than ready. But on Earth, what we did would be unacceptable, probably considered criminal."

"I know." J could never imagine sharing the experience with anyone at home, not even with Barb.

"This is not a value judgment, or a matter of saying which culture is better, more evolved," empathed Telmx. "It's just different. On some other worlds within our Council, the Imari Ways are tolerated but not encouraged. It's a problem because there are some very talented raw empath youth out there who never have the opportunity to develop through the levels."

"But they enjoy their lives, don't they? They are fulfilled?"

"No question, and for sure without the variety of cultures and tradition, the universe would be a very dull place, don't you think? But you have to know, every being in the universe is capable of achieving what we achieve."

"I wonder if there are any others on Earth that can achieve, without your Imari training."

"Oh yes," smiled Telmx. "Some earthling cultures, even your most sophisticated anthropologists don't know about, and some of your animal species, your dolphins, some species of bovines, including your elephants are natural empaths, even more than the humans."

J didn't care one bit about learning anything. The urge to lie with Telmx again bordered on painful. Such insatiable yearning.

"Yes, and of course more loving. Of course more loving." She pulled J close to her so that their breasts merged. "Tonight we celebrate your Ascension."

CHAPTER NINE

J

J lay still with her eyes closed, her incredible dream lingering at the edge of real. She didn't want it to end. A downer to wake up in Queens after such a long and exquisite night of making love. How would she be able to confess to Telmx the details of her passionate dream? Well, she thought, I truly am a kooky, horny adolescent with a hell of an imagination. And look at this! Dad's stuff didn't stop me, not one tiny bit! If I change a few things, like making my dream lover an earthling guy, I can even share this one with Barb. She'd get a kick out of it. She'd say, "See? I always said you weren't scarred forever!" Amazing. But only a dream.

"J? Would you like to get up now?" Telmx's empath voice softly entered her head, the Imari's strong arms surrounding her pulsating body. "Not a dream. You're a million light years from Queens."

J pulled away, sat up and opened her eyes. "Holy shit! Too much!" The blanket fell away from her naked body, reverberating from the dream that wasn't a dream. She reached to pull the blanket around herself, but instead let it drop, the aroma of lovemaking mingling with the frimulator brew. The soft hoverglows cast shadows on the lavish ferns, and now-familiar tapestries.

"Take it slow, J. I have suffused a light bot-chi for us, and baked my special yil biscuits. You were sleeping so soundly, I didn't want to wake you, but it's getting really late and there's so much to do, so much I want to show you and we only have a few more days before you have to go back to Queens, for real."

"I can't imagine this ending. I want to stay here with you forever," J said. "I know, not possible, and I have this Mission. I can do it; I think I can do it, knowing you are with me on this. But I can't imagine being without you again. This is going to be really, really hard."

"For me too. But you'll visit many more times. And I'll come to you as often as I can." Telmx rose from the mat. "But let's not jump ahead. Not just yet. I have planned out the next few days. A lively group of Imari students from Galern II University are dying to meet you. So the day before we leave for Earth we're all going to the Cultural Center of Obtti, Galern II's second largest city. I made reservations for a really exciting concert.

"It's a great way to introduce you to how we live here, and you'll get to meet some of my closest buddies. You'll also get to mingle with various sentient species in the civilized universe, without having to interact any more than you feel comfortable. We'll take it very slow. I'll know as soon as you are getting overwhelmed. It can come as a huge shock. Most sentients are variants of your earthling animals. Others look nothing like any creature you've ever seen. I'm always surprised. I wish I could spend more time knowing and learning from all these species. Even just the ones who come to Galern II. Perhaps when I retire.

"The Mnz_Obt orchestra will be performing works by composers known throughout the civilized universe: Mozart, Saint-Saëns, W.C. Handy, Uro, and Ywins.

"Mozart? How Mozart? Did he travel here too?"

"No, no. I brought their music back when I first visited you. Earth is considered backward in almost all aspects except the arts. Its composers and performers have inspired many of the universe's most famous composers, unbeknownst to those who inspired. Using V.E.-future and past travel scans, I brought music here from Earth's ancients to those who haven't yet started to compose. So your planet is in the vanguard."

"Wow! My planet's music has done all that? You mean your discovery of us has already influenced the rest of the universe? That's far-out."

"Yes, it's pretty incredible. Earth's music has won over the younger generation of intergalactic composers. You'll see. VuNhat tan, a Vietnamese composer who will create music after they throw out the Americans, and your East African Chapi xylophone music particularly influenced Uro. And Ywins integrates an indigenous ritual chant from your continent. I can't wait for you to hear their works. Uro is from the university here. She's a brilliant young Imari composer. Ywins is an ursine young man, from our neighboring satellite galaxy. Plus there's a universally renowned clarinetist from Kv'jumng VII. Now, I know you're still not used to all these different species. It's going to feel a bit weird seeing her play Mozart's Clarinet Concerto. She looks somewhat like your earthling ring-tailed possum." She flushed with excitement. "I thought that would be a special treat for you since you play that exquisite earthling instrument, and that particular concerto."

I couldn't believe I was going to hear my all-time favorite on Telmx's planet, performed by a possum-like sentient from yet another galaxy, backed by an intergalactic orchestra made up of a multitude of species. —J

"In the meantime, after our bot-chi, I want to take you to see some sights."

In the next two days, they alternated making love, savoring Telmx's home cooking, and going on short hover-trips to spectacular vistas and unusual geological formations. They glided past dazzling fiords, rock formations and glacial skyscrapers. They clambered over lava beds and trekked along dizzying canyon rims. "Here's where Goshing, my mentor, taught me the first principles of controlled empath," Telmx said as they climbed behind the roaring cascade of an immense waterfall.

Telmx maneuvered her hovercraft so quickly from site to site that J glimpsed only aerial views of streets, plazas, factories and expansive tracts of vegetation farms. She had meticulously planned every last detail of their itinerary, timed so they never ran into any people, not even at the public viewing areas.

"I'm dying to meet all these species you told me about. When do we do that? And your Imari friends. And Mozart's Clarinet Concerto."

"I know, my beloved. I've been putting off having you interact with others. It's on purpose. I'm slowly modulating your shielding to camouflage your empath skills without anyone picking up that I'm camouflaging. It's extremely important that no one, not even my best buddies here on Galern II, know your full empath ability. As far as everybody is concerned, you're a Level I Empath Monitor, with no capability to hover, mind-bend, enter V.E.s, or V.E.-dream-travel, none of the unauthorized skills I inadvertently endowed you with as a child. It's difficult, and I'm being extra cautious. Your empath capacities are very elusive, and they are synergistically enhanced the longer we're together. I devised a shielding algorithm, which by tomorrow afternoon when we go to the concert should be in full working order."

✻ ✻ ✻

The Mnz_Obt Plaza parking zone was crowded with hovercrafts of all sizes and shapes, each one, like Telmx's, colorfully emblazoned with a whimsical identification logo. Most were on the ground. Others were tethered to floating buoys several meters above. A three-dimensional vehicular display. "I'd like to get you on the ground, but, hmm, not possible today." After circling around for a few more moments, Telmx moored her hovercraft above some crafts similar to hers. "I'm initiating the shielding algorithm. Remember, I'm hiding most of your empath skills. Although you certainly can still empath communicate."

J felt as if a bit of cotton gauze had been pushed into each ear, a slight dulling of empath listening, a relief from the vibrant sensations barraging her as they approached the Plaza.

"Don't try to hover down to the ground," Telmx said before she opened the hatch. "I'll take you."

It was not the first time Telmx had caused J to float gently. Even though she could hover on her own, it was still a thrill when Telmx guided her. At home, in the privacy of her own room, when her family was not around, she'd hover up to the ceiling (not her desperate imagined flight as a little girl, but for real) and push off from one wall to the other, just for the fun of it. But now they were in public, and like on Earth, to exhibit her various tricks was dangerous and unthinkable.

"Most will discern that you are a newly discovered species. It's not as if people don't know about Earth, ever since the debates about it came up in the Intergalactic Council after my first report. But, you know, most people are rushing to their events or involved in their own festivities, so it's not likely that many will notice."

Telmx gently placed J on the ground amidst other disembarking people, who rapidly rumbled, hovered, and glided past them toward the Cultural Plaza. J was used to the Imari, who were quite humanoid. It was difficult not to stare at all the different species animatedly conversing together in an empathed and out-loud universal language that she miraculously understood: raccoon-like people in excited exchanges with Ursines, small bear-like sentients, and a multitude of other species, many looking as if a child had taken the head of one animal and pasted it on the body of another. It reminded J of drifting through a sea of multicolored coral reefs and exotic life forms when Barb's family took her snorkeling in St. Croix. Except there were no underwater labels on Galern II for all these species.

"Don't be afraid to close your eyes if it's too overwhelming. I got you."

"No way am I closing my eyes! I don't want to miss even a nanosecond of this! Shit, I wish I had remembered to take my camera! Holy cow! And I even understand what they're saying. Why's that?"

"The same way we understand each other. It's a technology the Equine Oglassis traders developed several hundred centuries ago. I'll tell you about them sometime."

Telmx led J into the plaza, which seemed to span forever in all directions. They strolled past the large provision kiosks that circled the periphery. Interspaced within, as far as J's eyes could see, were hundreds of smaller ones, each one decorated in vibrant layers of colors and filigree featuring their offerings in hanging baskets, frimulator urns, and floating trays. Dispersed throughout were trees, ferns and a variety of flowering plants and shrubs, along with a variety of sculpted fountains.

When I was in my forties, I visited Italy for the first time, and when the déjà vu came, I knew where it had come from. Then I wondered, did Telmx's civilized universe come first or did Michelangelo, the architect? Did Michelangelo empath travel? What did he really know? —J

"The kiosks offer samplings from the Old Town stores," Telmx explained. "People with specialty crafts, services, cuisines, set up these little shops for their own pleasure and the needs of others. They offer for barter handcrafted items, antiques, traded objects from other planets and galaxies, specialized healing potions, whatever your whim. Retirees often set up a small shop offering their favorite expertise, and keep contact with others by trading what they do best. Some set up field kiosks like these in various town squares, with samplings to take, and codes to put into a hovercraft to transport a person or group of people to their shop. You'll see! We'll get to some of them before you go back home."

Many Imari and non-Imari sentients were walking, flying, hovering, in small groups to various theatres, amphitheatres, indoor concert halls, and museums arrayed around a mammoth central fountain. Others were eating and drinking at the myriad of small kiosks that displayed varieties of bot and other beverages, sweets, snacks and actual meals. An orangutan-like group stood by a blue and white kiosk, sipping from small porcelain cups and discussing the play they had just attended. A tiny couple, a raccoon-like woman and her lover, a woman who appeared to be an amalgam of red fox and J didn't know what else, squatted next to a small-multicolored fountain silently enjoying the display. Several brown bear-like families rumbled past them, apparently late for a sporting event on the other side of the plaza.

Telmx squeezed her hand in reassurance and led her quickly past a small group of Imari adolescent girls who had stopped to stare. "Later," Telmx kindly empathed to the curious bunch. "We'll be late to our concert. I promise, if you stick around, you can meet this interesting earthling when we come back out to the plaza." The teens raised their necks in formal acquiescence and deference to the Imari Scout.

"It's not only that you're so pale; I'm glad you insisted on wearing your tie-died tee-shirt. I should have told you to bring a few extra of those marvelous tops to give as gifts," empathed Telmx. "We're meeting Tarow, Milla, Cario and Karine near the G'iosti Amphitheatre. Tarow and Milla are ecology students. Karine is studying intergalactic diplomacy, and Cario, well, he doesn't know what he wants to do yet. He may still prepare to qualify for the Order of Empath Travel Scouts."

"What do they know about me, about us?" What would Telmx's friends think of her, a short, pale, awkward adolescent earthling, newly ascended, and almost completely ignorant of their ways? Plus she was still obviously tingling with the ecstasy of the last several days.

"Not to worry, J. They're wonderful people. They don't judge. They know everything I wish them to know."

"Hey Tel! Over here!" J heard a loud empath call emanating from a small kiosk just ahead.

"Ah, there they are."

Several Imaris, dressed in the typical wishapthas, but without the travel hoods J was accustomed to, were standing in a cluster alongside a kiosk filled with baskets of biscuits and dispensers of various flavors of bot-fruit cocktails. J read their excited anticipation. Like Telmx, they were tall and exquisite, their long and silvery cilia adorning calm and enthusiastic faces of various shades of brown and black. Her apprehensions fell away.

"Greetings, everybody! This is J. J, this is the gang."

"Hi," said J out loud, not knowing who to practice her newly learned formal greeting with first.

"Hi J, I'm Milla." He took her hands in his, and, in soft measured tones, said out loud, "I am honored to meet you. Welcome to Galern II." J tipped her head slightly, as Telmx had taught her, and he arched gently toward her until their foreheads touched. "I am honored to be here," J said. "I'm Tarow," said a much taller woman, touching J's forehead in like fashion. "And I am Karine." A winnowy adolescent grabbed J's hand before J could return Tarow's greeting and held it tightly, her face radiating with eagerness. "I've been waiting forever to meet you, J," she said. "If up to me, we'd skip the concert and just talk the whole night! But, oh well. So listen, how about going off-riser with me at the concert?" J had no idea what she was talking about. "Don't worry, I'll show you how to do it. You'll see! And oh! Congratulations on your Ascension. We must celebrate after the concert."

J flushed. There's nothing they don't know, except what Telmx doesn't want anyone to know. That's what Telmx said. They can read her thoughts, just like Telmx. And J couldn't manipulate her own shielding, because Telmx was secretly doing it for her. So Telmx felt it was okay for them to know about such intimate things.

"Don't be abashed," whispered Karine. "I ascended just twenty sunrises ago. I know. It's pitching you backward. Me too, don't you sense it in me? Sure you do!"

"You just ascended too? I mean, yeah, I'm dizzy and excited, and scared. I didn't know anyone could feel this way, especially after what I went though as a kid." J was surprised that she could just spill what she was feeling to this overenthusiastic stranger.

"Well it really threw me, too, and I didn't grow up on a primitive planet. It's alright if I call Earth primitive? I mean, you think so too. You must be really disoriented, right? Yeah, I can tell you're still catching your breath from it all. Don't worry. I'll take care of you. We all will."

J heard Telmx's voice touch her inner chamber, quietly and discreetly. "It's alright J. I've told her to slow down. She has a lot to learn about pacing things!"

"Alright, J!" yelled Karine, thrusting J's hand into Telmx's. "I know when to hang back. I have a problem with moving in too fast. Sorry!"

"It's okay, Karine," said J. "You remind me of my best friend Barb."

Cario, who would have been Telmx's height if he didn't stoop so much, stood quietly by, waiting for the opportunity to hand J and Telmx mugs of hot mocha bot-chi. "We've already had ours," he said. "They were running out, and I know how much you love this brew, Tel." After handing them the mugs, he also touched his head to J's in formal greeting.

"You are lucky to have Telmx as your mentor, young J. I wish you well in your difficult years ahead on Earth. Your task is daunting, and anything I can do, now or in the future, to make it easier for you, well, just let me know. I am thinking of training to be a Travel Scout, you know. Perhaps I too will one day visit your planet. I hear earthlings create magnificent art, and of course, to hear its music in the original. I can't imagine how fabulous that would be!"

As they started walking toward the amphitheatre, Karine grabbed J's hand again and pulled her ahead, anxious to explain everything and anything to her. Telmx and her friends followed behind. "Don't worry Tel, I won't overwhelm her again! Alright, I see you are already overwhelmed. I'll just tell you a few little things, alright? Just a few things you really need to know."

J, spinning from her onslaught, was nevertheless drawn in by Karine's exuberance. She struggled to keep up with her long strides.

"Uh, Karine, could you slow down a little? I want to see everything."

"Oh, right! Sorry again. Sure. But I've so many questions. Not now. I know. Just let me be your official tour guide. Alright? I already know what you want to know. Like you're wondering what those blue hoverglows are doing. Right? Well, because we get these occasional deadly hail storms (like the one you were in the other day), there are underground shelters within most of these fern clusters. They're interconnected, and you can safely reach the periphery where emergency hovercrafts are parked completely underground. They're also stocked with emergency provisions and first aid kits.

See? You need to know that in case we all get separated. Now you know! Not everything on our planet is perfect."

✻ ✻ ✻

There were lines at the ornate arched entrances to the G'iosti Amphitheatre, a large round outdoor structure. When they got to the front of their line, J took her turn walking though a scanning device, which she assumed was a matter of security. Who were they protecting against? It didn't fit the mood of the place. "No not security, J," empathed Milla. "The scanner calibrates how the music waves are to be distributed that night based on the topography and physiology of the audience. Because each of us goes through the scanner to identify personal resonance, each can enjoy a unique experience of the musical vibrations. The scanner gave each of us a temporary internal tag so we can wander anywhere we want and the settings will find us."

"Wander?" J was used to sitting in one seat during a concert, or standing in the back when she couldn't afford a ticket. Here no one was paying for tickets, and there were no seats. Telmx, Cario, Tarow and Milla spread out their mats on a riser several meters above the sunken central stage, where an orchestra, made up of over a hundred musicians from different planets, was warming up.

"Come on, J," Karine urged. "Let's go off-riser. It's a lot more fun!"

Karine pushed J around small clusters of sentient species to a spot right above the wind section, anxious to show her the different kinds of pipes, pipettes, and reeds tubes. "For the music from Earth, they'll play replicas of your earthling instruments. But the compositions of Ywins and Uro require entirely different configurations, and the musicians won't just stay in the pit. You'll see, they'll be scattered and wandering through the audience, with empath to keep them communicating to each other and, unlike on Earth, they don't need a conductor. It's also fantastic to wander around during the concert and move with the music. Will you do that with me? That's being 'off-riser.'"

The risers were filling up, and the standing and hovering space near the orchestra pit was getting crowded, but not intrusively so. Way above the series of risers, other species were hovering under the triple moonshine and unfamiliar patterns of stars. J absorbed the vibrancy of everyone's anticipation.

Soon she and Karine were dancing to Uro's familiar and unfamiliar musical sensations that coursed through her body, resonating to the vibrations. Colby, a composer she had listened to in one of her future V.E.-travel-dreams, had hinted at these internal vibrations, but this orchestra had taken it to its ultimate. And everyone, including the musicians, was expressing personal sensations in dance! Amazing. She would have to push for new ways to listen to music when she returned home. Not just for the mosh pits not yet in vogue, but for the "serious" music as well.

The air in the amphitheater, made artificially "hot," not in temperature, but in sound, literally quivered with the music that surrounded her. Occasionally an instrumentalist, or several of them, would play and dance next to her and Karine. Or someone taking a solo would suddenly appear in the central pit alone and the single instrumentalist would take off in improvised and structured harmonics.

The instruments themselves, and the electronic vibrations they emitted, were precisely calibrated to cause gentle resonations with bone and viscera. It reminded her of the first time church pipe organs surrounded her, and the times she played duets with her clarinet teacher. Oh how her bones soared with the internal bliss of being one with the music, but it was only with certain harmonies, when she and her teacher played together.

Now she basked in the harmonies of the Clarinet Concerto. Mozart would have been in ecstasy, she thought as she and Karine gyrated with a group of adolescent Ursines. Not that he ever would have imagined such a variety of species playing traditional, western earthling instruments. But, the interpretation and the sensual dances were probably exactly what he had in mind when he composed it.

Many decades later, I rediscovered the "downtown" composers in New York I had met in my V.E.-travels, and found out I didn't have to visit off-world to hear the burgeoning precursors of what was to become the next masterpieces of the universe. –J

After the concert, the group, still internally vibrating with the music, ambled through another quadrant of the plaza. People were coming out of various buildings and coliseums of recreation, some from the small sports complexes and others from the myriad of small and midsized theaters and concert halls. Others were moving in and out of small restaurants, or stopping at kiosks to pick up various foods and beverages to take home or to bring to small mats around the various clusters of gardens and fountains. Groups of people were pushing mats together at outdoor cafés. Telmx and Milla were now spreading their own mats at a cafe that Karine was particularly fond of. Karine and Tarow then went to the cafe kiosk to gather refreshments.

Cario squatted to talk to a group of fellow students from the university at a neighboring mat.

J was ecstatic, proud to have been born on the planet that inspired such rapture in form and feeling. She also felt bewildered and in awe of how easily she found herself loving the other sounds and sensations the Imari and the other species called music, which by no stretch of the imagination would be considered musical on Earth. Telmx was clearly beside herself experiencing J's joy. The music had transported J beyond her and Telmx's wildest expectations. Each day on this planet had been something new and special, but this was way ahead of anything J had encountered so far. "Telmx's discovery of Earth's music has enhanced the repertoire of the civilized universe by quantum leaps," empathed Milla.

Now squatting over bot and snacks, everyone was anxious to tell J everything about another kind of music, the vibrating tones of the cosmos. "You see," said Karine, "we don't hear cosmos music in the air because it's constantly all around us. We automatically tune it out, just like we ignore cosmos dust, so we can hear each other, so we can concentrate on the modulations and vibrations that we need in order to live and communicate comfortably. Many centuries ago, Tark'let and Urth from the F'jarut System proved mathematically that the cosmos was constantly serenading. Then the actual harmonies were finally detected by musicians from a planet in yet another galaxy, where the atmospheric and thermal conditions allowed for such experimentation."

"Actually," added Tarow, "some of the elders begin to hear the music of the cosmos naturally, as their capacity to filter it out diminishes. My great-great grandmother, for example, has very mixed reactions to the phenomenon. On the one hand, she can finally hear its harmonies, but on the other, she has a harder time hearing all of us!"

Although lightheaded, J did not want people to stop talking. She just couldn't hear all of it. Telmx was so happy, happier than J had ever experienced her. That was most important. When they moved on to topics that were completely out of her reach, she let their voices go, simply savoring the completeness of the evening.

When they drank to her Ascension, J accepted the bot goblet and allowed the multiple tastes to linger. But the words Telmx and her friends were trading slipped again into the background din of the plaza. Some wandering minstrels came across the cobblestones and a crowd gathered as they settled next to a nearby fountain. Pipes, violins, a tambour played. This was as perfect as a fifteen-year-old could imagine perfection to be. People were clapping and calling for more. The musicians started again. How could Telmx and the others continue talking with all of this splendor around them?

She could feel the heat of an argument brewing. Telmx was saying something about arrogance. J felt herself becoming heated by the force of their discussion, without hearing the words, but the word "arrogant" stuck. Barb had called her arrogant and stubborn just a few weeks before her trip. They had been at an organizers' meeting for all the high school groups participating in the action against air raid drills. All the groups had agreed to organize their schools to refuse to "take cover" during the next drill and to sing "We Shall Overcome" instead. It was exhilarating and right. Barb was bubbling with excitement after the meeting. J ventured to suggest that they take the opportunity to do more, to educate the organizers to the ideas of Marxism, to show how all the issues fit together. Barb disagreed: It would diffuse the point, obscure the real cause.

J had persisted. "Perhaps we could build a movement. People might come together in a way that would unify many of the various causes that are beginning to build." Barb started screaming at her in the middle of Broadway and 46th Street and left her standing alone with her own flood of ideas, in the hubbub of tourist traffic.

Yes, she was indeed arrogant and stubborn, but not in the sense that Barb would ever understand. J had wanted her friend to read Kelly-Broone's discussion of Materialism and the Ten Dimensions, but she hadn't been published yet, not for another 90 years. Holy cow! How did one deal with the burden of knowing so much yet knowing so little about how to deal with knowing so much?

In the midst of Barb's accusation, she remembered how Jerry had wanted her to read Marshall McLuhan. He had given her a copy at the last Ethical Culture youth group meeting. Okay, she'd read McLuhan. It made sense to read him, Marx, Lenin. Them and Marcy (but he hadn't published yet either) and Kelly-Broone. To hell with Barb!

At one moment she was in the Plaza that she remembered dimly from earlier V.E.-dream- time traveling. The next, she was actually in the real-time Plaza, within the event that bookmarked the V.E. trancelike experiences of before. And the reality of it was beyond her wildest expectations. If only she could stay. But Telmx said they both had work to do. It was good to taste the future, but now J had to join in making it. J hated this burden. In spite of her reassurances to Telmx, she felt unfit for it. Did those other earthling empath monitors she hadn't met yet feel the same way?

Someone passed her the bot goblet again. The minstrels had long since left the Plaza. The sound of the nearby fountain filled her head. What are Telmx and the others talking about? Telmx said later that it was fine for her not to listen, because she had so much more to learn before she could understand what they were discussing anyway.

That night J and Telmx cuddled in each other's arms and talked until tertiary moonset. J asked her about arrogance and timing, and Telmx told her about the human capacity to integrate new ideas and the necessity for personal and political upheaval. Telmx was explaining the relationship between scientific truth and inevitability and between individual and universal reality when J, not understanding a word, fell asleep.

CHAPTER TEN

The Mission

Telmx made a special breakfast the next morning. The time had come to tell enough about the Mission to get J started. She was uneasy. Overwhelming this young earthling with too much responsibility before she was ready would throw away so many years of preparing for this moment. J had to be willing to accept the weight of what she was about to put on her. Just be calm. Don't frighten her. She peeled another sovbot for the fragrant soup she wanted J to experience.

"It has to do with gold and aluminum," Telmx empathed, seemingly out of nowhere.

"What?"

"The Mission."

Telmx squatted opposite J on the mat, caressed the bot goblet in both hands and took several long thoughtful swallows before passing it to her. Here we go, she thought. "You see, the powerful people on your planet, particularly in your country, are extremely greedy. They're constantly scheming for ways to get richer. That means cheap labor and lots of profit. Without going into detail about it, J, in the next year, your government will establish a group called the National Aeronautics and Space Administration or NASA. Along with various corporations, it will be intensely 'curious' about space, but mostly motivated by the drive to attain domination over the universe. The new frontier. You know about the new frontier. Like finding Inca gold to steal and people to enslave to get rich off their labor. The universe, well, even just your solar system, is rich in precious metals, like gold, nickel and aluminum. Your moon is extremely rich in nickel and aluminum, and they'll be mining there even before they admit to the rest of their world that they've even landed.

"Prisoners from your own planet, mostly people of color from your American inner cities, will be enslaved as miners on your own moon. Your asteroid belt has a trillion times more gold than South Africa and the Congo combined. And then there's the moons of Jupiter and Saturn. Some happen to have sentient inhabitants whom they'll enslave for mining. It's the history of your world. And you happen to live in the middle of the current 'power of arrogance.' That's our term for a planet's major imperialist empire. The corporations that actually run your country and much of the world are frantically investing in research to harness empath technology so that they can quickly travel back and forth from the outer planets and asteroids and ultimately beyond. So much for one large step for, how is he going to say it? 'For mankind.' No, one 'large step' for a certain tiny definition of mankind."

"Wait, wait, justa minute. First of all, you sound like Katie. Ohmygod, I haven't even met Katie for real yet. But you know what I mean, like a Communist. All this time, I mean almost my whole life, you've been visiting me, caressing me, sending me on these V.E.-history- dreams, and it all has to do with stopping corporations from gold mining the stars in the future? You're training me to stop all this? Me? Just me?

"If your worlds, if the Imaris, know so much, if you have all, all this, this empath power, and everything, why can't you guys take care of it? What do I have to do with it? And anyway why do you even care? Look at all you have here. We're so insignificant, we don't even appear on your official maps. What does it matter?"

"We can poke around in certain people's minds, and we can do certain tricks with time travel, but by our own time-honored regulations, governed by a multi-species body, the Intergalactic Counsil, we must not make significant changes on another planet. We can only run simulations, you know, possible future simulations, and then make educated predictions, and then, well, then, if..."

J was getting more and more agitated. Too much at once. Yet Telmx was absolutely positive that J was an excellent candidate. But only a candidate. Her student. She had to remember that, no matter how much she loved her. Telmx's arrogance had blind-sided her own judgment before. And then she had to remember the Council factions. And the mandate that the recruit be only a Level I Monitor, not even a Level I mindshifter. And here was J with exponential empath and mindshifting powers and unfathomed potential. Plus her team had two more monitors, and Gir's and Winstx's earthlink monitor recruits had also empath-developed well beyond the original mandate. The whole project had become so ridiculously complicated and dangerous.

J broke the empath silence. "If what?" She startled both of them by screaming out loud.

Telmx hesitated, and then said out loud: "Well, if, I mean, let's say that they, your species, the arrogant power-hungry part of your species, let's say they harnessed empath travel in the wrong way, I mean, for the wrong reasons, a lot, a whole lot, could go wrong. For all of us. Put simply. We need you to monitor and report their scientific progression to the Age of Empath. That's all. Not stop them or anything. Just watch…."

"You mean spy, don't you? You know what people get for spying? You know what happened to the Rosenbergs? Besides, I'm too young. I mean how can you expect me to keep all this stuff in my head? It's too far-out technical. Too much dangling of this idea and that idea. It's just not fair, just because you happen to think I'm smart."

J's furious static was exploding in Telmx's temples. It was hard to think.

"J, my love, you're not too young. And you're extremely smart, so smart that…."

"I'm still only a kid! Besides, you absolutely tricked me. That's the far-fuck-ing-out bad news about all this. You tricked me." J was weeping uncontrolla-bly. Her empathed words rode on her tears. "I thought, I mean I really thought I was here, that you were in my life, because you loved me. I mean that's what I thought. So it's not that you love me! You brought me here for your own selfish political purposes. Oh my God! I amazingly can't believe this!"

"No, J, that's not what I'm saying. I love you. I chose you because I love you." She reached for her across the mat. But J recoiled, and Telmx drew back, tears blurring her eyes.

"Take me home. I want to go home now!" J was standing now. "Not to-morrow, not in an hour. Now, goddamn it! Take me home! What a god-aw-ful nightmare. I can't believe this. You better wake me up real soon, okay? Like now!"

She looked down at her precious lady. "Why did you do this to me? I really, really believed you were saving my life, the mother I never ever had. Then you do these, these amazing things to me. We, we have the most amazing— Like I can't imagine in a million years ever feeling like that after all those years, after what my, you know, my father did to my mother and, and to me—I don't know if anyone I know can even imagine such, such incredible, you know, utterly way-out bliss in a million years. I mean how can I ever have a normal life if I ever wake up from this, I mean how can I sleep with anyone else except you? No one, I mean, no one can…. Everything is so confusing, so far-out awful, so upside down."

I stood there and wept uncontrollably. I was alone, marooned on Telmx's world, unaffiliated, and too stupid to understand even one iota of it, and too goddamn smart for my own planet, which was all Telmx's fault in the first place. I just wanted to lie down and die. We stayed like that for a very long time. Me standing in the shadows of the windblown plant clusters and she squatting

on her mat so she wouldn't tower over me, her head bowed and,
I know now, in such incredible pain. I am most upset now about
the incredible pain I inflicted on my beloved Telmx that morning.
   She gave me plenty of time to cry. Then, quietly, in the way we
later reserved for our most intimate moments, she empathed
softly: —J

   "J, my dearest love, I know you're scared. Who wouldn't be? But I really wanted to show you my life, all my friends, our life, my planet, the universe of known planets, so now when I talk about the Mission's purpose, you'd know what you're protecting and what your planet can become. Besides, I couldn't wait for you to visit me here because I love you so very much."

   She waited a beat.

   "Please, come back to me. I love you. Let me hold you. I love you more than you can possibly imagine. Come."

   Telmx wanted to send more soothing empath sensations to J's inner chambers, but after the first rebuff, she refrained. Can't be intrusive. Let her calm down on her own. With words and feelings. Just that. No intrusion. "I'm truly sorry, J. I do love you, so very, very much. I'll be patient. It's not your fault. I get impatient."

   "It's okay, I think. I mean, I don't know what I mean. I'm so alone. A fifteen-year-old, self-conscious, stammering five-foot-zero earthling barely out of tenth grade. I am so, so not strong enough, old enough, smart enough to do all this. It's so, so awesome. How am I supposed to spy on a bunch of lunatic scientists, 'monitor' as you call it, all their top-secret sophisticated research in labs I don't even have a clue about? Oh, I can't stand this!"

   "First of all, you're not alone—"

   "No, I have you. You visit once every two or three years."

   "No, there are others."

   "Others? Other what? Other monitors like me? You gotta be kidding!"

   Silence.

   "On Earth? Other earthlings? Other Monitor Recruits? Where? Who? I gotta find them, talk to them. Ohmygod!"

   "Not yet, my love, not yet. There will be time enough to meet them."

   "Soon but not yet! Always soon but not yet! Ohmygod, Telmx! People like Barb? Or, or—"

   "No, not Barb. Don't try to guess. When you're all ready, everyone will know everyone. It is too dangerous at this point for you to communicate with each other. In the meantime, I am causing you to forget I told you, for your safety, and theirs."

"Always wait and see—Oh jeez, Telmx, wait and see, wait and see! I just don't know how to do this alone, I mean, what if—"

"I'm asking something of you that's very, very difficult. Get closer and closer to your earthling friends, your political comrades. You're not going to change the course of history all by yourself. You need to become acutely aware of justice and injustice. You know what you know, and can see what they don't yet see because they haven't traveled there yet. Some of them can see the possible futures, because of their brilliance, their political analysis. Embrace them, join in, but don't ever bring them where you are tempted to bring them."

"If I tried to tell others about time travel dreams and your homeworld, I'd be locked up in a loony bin."

"Well, at best those in the outer fringes of sanity would be the only ones to believe you. Plus—" And this was the hard part, although she more than once had warned J about consequences.

"Plus, as you know, I would be forced to sever all communication between us, and it would be as if we had never met. Not a trace."

I hated when she talked like that. It felt unloving. Although I knew she was not being callous. Rather, what she said was absolutely mandatory by Council fiat, and she profoundly hated her participation and compliance, because, I knew, she loved me so deeply.

The double bind for me was astounding. To eliminate Telmx from my experience would in fact also risk changing my world's future. That knowledge trapped me. She had chosen me to participate in the forward flow of the world, even in its backward flows, and to revel quietly in its future. I don't really know if it was my love for Telmx or this love for the future of things that kept me going. I would like to think that at fifteen I was able to love people who were yet to be born, but I guess it doesn't matter. I grew to feel that way, and kind of knew that I would.

I have to admit: the intellectual and scientific stuff went way over my head. Most of it, but over the years I got it. During that first visit, I was mostly in love. That's what counted. I was also mostly afraid I'd lose her if I didn't understand her. That's what I think made me so frantically terrified and furious. –J

"It's been hard on me to think that there's actually, actually and really something profoundly different between me and the rest of the human race, but now you say not entirely different."

"You can always cancel the whole arrangement. It would be as if it never happened."

"No, it's too exciting now. Besides, how could I stop loving you, even if you did cancel everything? No, it would be too much loving to give up. I'd be feeling really awful all the time; I'd know it, without even ever knowing why."

"You'd not be as unhappy as you think. You'd seek out therapy, and find what you needed, if you worked hard at it. It's just a different road to the same place."

"Well, I have this, and the Mission is urgent. It's awesome and utterly terrifying. I'm sorry I freaked out. Let's not debate it anymore."

"It'll not be the last time you think about foregoing the Mission. That's alright. It's quite a daunting and uncomfortable task. Come, please. Break the froth with me. Please."

J squatted across Telmx on the mat and accepted the goblet. Then they bent their heads toward each other and touched, cilia to cilia-to-be.

"I don't want to admit it, but it actually makes me glow inside when I think about it," J empathed. "Sort of like slowly falling in love with the whole thing. Like I'm so in love with you and your homeworld, and everything. All the colors. The Horsehead Nebula, getting so close to it. I couldn't ever think of ever erasing those colors, or tastes, or bot. I know; I know that's not exactly the purpose of it all."

"Yes it is, actually."

"Okay, in the sense that I understand the Mission, and what would be lost to the universe if the Mission failed, or if people like me didn't take it on. So in that sense...."

"Not to mention what I'd lose. You see, I'd still remember you, that wouldn't go away. For you it would be as if our relationship had never existed, although you are convinced you would forever feel the loss. But for me, for my triad travel team, it would be an unbearably painful loss. You can't imagine. Your decision to break from the Mission would never erase my memories or alter my reality. Only yours."

"Just one more question," J. said. "Why did you choose such a self-hating kid, of all the people in the world to choose?"

"I fell in love with you," she said. "Actually, if you really want to know the truth, it started out not so personal."

"Oh?"

"Well." Whenever Telmx felt squirmy, her ebony face got even darker and began to shine. Like now. "We needed mission monitors from your country. You were born in the country where the monitoring had to be organized. Also, the Imari, and most of the sentients in the universe, are dark, and we thought when we selected you we were giving a pale minority species a chance to be involved in the monitoring Mission. I was excited. No one in my home planet had ever met a colorless creature like you. I mean, you're not completely colorless, but, you know, just not dark. Not even tan.

I actually thought I was tan, swarthy tan: a very short, tan Sephardic New York Jewish, not-exactly-but-wished-she-were-until-she-knew-better, Princess. —J

"Then, of course, in spite of your odd colorless complexion, I fell in love with you, J, so you kind of made up my mind for me."

We talked for a long time that day and well into the night. And made the most exquisite love until both suns came up. Off and on during those hours I wondered what Telmx found attractive, and just as quickly decided not to wonder. Telmx was too selective to be doubted.

To me love had been an abstraction no one really believed in. Someone touching you because they want to and because they take pleasure in it was unspeakable and unimaginable. Yet Telmx was doing just that. Occasionally over the next several years, when we visited each other, I would think, Oh, is it only because Telmx finds me intriguing and exotic because I'm from another planet? That's all. I would say that to myself, especially when something would happen on Earth between me and my parents or me and my friends, and I would sink into a deep self-hating place. Somehow I always came back to a feeling of amazement, that Telmx could actually take pleasure in touching me, talking to me, laughing with me, even being curious about what I was thinking, although she was so far, far advanced. She still wanted to know what I thought. And reveled in it. Also, she became very, very—how can I say this?—human. She had faults, complications. For example, many moments of arrogance that she hated in herself. Also, I wanted her to understand my world, my developing philosophy, my plans for how I was going to use what she was trying to teach me.

All through my adolescence, I said to myself: this is what love is all about. But that made no sense either because my friends said all the time that they loved their boyfriends or girlfriends, and even my miserable parents said they loved each other, but their love couldn't possibly duplicate my round and full and colorful and extremely private passion. Then I would convince myself it was all stupid adolescent stuff and wouldn't tell my deepest feelings to anyone, not even to Telmx (although she of course had to know!): That I saw colors that never existed before, and stumbled upon places on my body I never knew. It was also like an addiction. I couldn't wait for the next time and wondered how in the hell people could stand waiting for the next time. Especially if they didn't know when the next time would be. It was an agony I had never imagined was possible. Always the opposite, never like this.

I also thought, especially in those darkest moments after my first trip, that I was simply and stupidly under the spell of her tropical homeworld. A brief summer romance. When she finds out I'm not what she thinks I am, whoa! People on high pedestals fall hard, you know. —J

CHAPTER ELEVEN

J

J almost left her knapsack behind the next evening, when they were preparing to leave Galern II. Oh, the thought of putting on dungarees and sneakers again, like putting on an alien costume. No room to breathe. Well, she could wear her new travel hood until they reached the Europa outpost. But she couldn't take it with her to Earth.

She sat in the same chaise lounge, in the same observation chamber, and waited for takeoff. This time she was awake for it. Telmx insisted she could handle it now. She sure hoped so, because she wanted to see everything, even though she really didn't want to leave. "You'll be here again," Telmx promised. "Many, many times. And next time we'll tour several of the older and quainter cities in the system." Next time? She bet there wouldn't be a next time. She'd wake up and be all changed and yearning for a next time, and there just wouldn't be one.

Back to "normal." Normal? Everything was so un-normal on her home planet. "I can't stand it! Isn't there a way to just stay here from now on?" She hoped and hoped for a huge glitch. No way to take off. Sorry. Have to stay here on Galern II for a while, perhaps forever. We ran out of booster power. Something!

Plus the Mission ahead of her on Earth was daunting. Impossible. No way not to do it, no way to. Not that she understood all the ins and outs. Not to mention the politics within the Intergalactic Council. This was overwhelming, and terrifying, like almost falling. Like standing at the edge of a huge cliff, the Grand Canyon, and imagining plummeting all the way to the thud at the bottom. This was not just a five-story fire escape with her legs dangling! The whole actual falling she would experience again as the zooming, accelerating ($vf = g^{*}t$). Oh, it was impossible to grasp!

Once, when she was six, she had a terribly real falling dream. She had plummeted to the ground, where she lay really still, a round rubbery chunk, dead on the alleyway cement five stories down. Didn't even bounce. Just there. Dead and knowing it.

"Oh, my dearest child," Telmx had said when she visited that dream. It was her second visit. J loved when she called her "my dearest child." It made her all warm and safe down to her toes. She didn't feel alone and defenseless for many days afterward, replaying it again and again to keep warm and safe. It helped her fall asleep. Finally she was not listening for keys in the door, not monitoring shadows.

"You'll see," Telmx had promised, "how different your life will be in just a few years. Besides, I love you, my dearest. It makes me very unhappy when you feel you have to watch over your Mommy, so don't think like that anymore, okay?" She told J that she couldn't stop the nightmares, that she couldn't even stop her Daddy from beating up Mommy, and when she couldn't stop him with her special mind-protecting, it didn't make her evil. Not in the least. With Telmx's help, J began to sense a much better future. She had to learn how to wait.

Well, she guessed she did learn. Now she was actually seeing. Now Telmx wasn't only her beloved lady, but her actual lover. She still couldn't quite believe it. They were now, Telmx had said after J's "Ascension," forever intermingled. A kind of emotional/sensual melding, and something more that J couldn't quite define. Something new happens in the melding that redefines and heals, and stays forever. "Like a commitment, like going steady," J had suggested.

"No, not at all like that," Telmx had empathed. "We awaken an inner chamber presence that runs much deeper. You'll see it when you see it." So there was always more to see.

* * *

They had just completed the first leap out of the Galern system and were now laying over at the Oldebridge rest stop, a small, extremely dense planetoid twelve megadiaps out. The planetoid's orbit in close synchronization with an Imari outpost planet in the Orgh system makes it a convenient booster station for intergalactic travel ships.

"You may not need these, but better to be precautious." Telmx squatted down next to J's chaise lounge and pulled her close to her, brushed her bangs out of the way and reached around to adjust the straps on her sun goggles. She had been extremely preoccupied troubleshooting various small glitches in the first hop from Galern II, and they were taking complete advantage of this precious moment. "I don't know how soon I'll be able to wander with you, but you go ahead. I'll catch up."

In long space flights, ships have to make occasional landings on a high-gravity rest stop to renew components, connect with empath boosters, etc. Also, for the health of the crew and passengers, everyone has to disembark and be on solid ground for a specified period of time.

Like most rest stops, Oldebridge was filled with kiosks, restaurants, motels, kiddy parks for kids, exercise gyms, V.E.-holo-maps, V.E.-tours of popular tourist sites, and hover-rides across the undeveloped areas of the planetoid. Not your average Howard Johnson rest stop on the thruway. Most rest stops are on small planets and moons. Some (like this one) are near warp-wraps, to prepare for the strain of folded space-time continuity travel.

Mostly the kiosks display arts from the various worlds. Sentients universally love collecting tapestries, especially ones that depict different cultures, atmospheres, planets, events, color combinations, fabrics, collages. There are also bins of electronic mail-order zines displaying various kits for elaborate gardens (with precise directions for how to build a mini-terraform in an indoor living space, or on a small swatch of land), and custom-made furniture for all varieties of sentients for hundreds of different terrains. Usually several shops are devoted to hundreds of brain-teasing V.E.-games that challenge even the more advanced empath levels.

Of course, I've now visited and revisited perhaps hundreds of rest stops, and there are small shops and restaurants where I'm considered a "regular," but this first visit remains very special. It's where I met K'dasti. —J

J lingered in one of the tourist shops, browsing through baskets of artifacts. As she picked up one or another tapestry, she briefly sank into their exquisite and intricate stitching, sensing that they conveyed embedded V.E.-stories which she didn't know how to access.

She was particularly drawn to a wooden sculpture she found buried in a tapestry basket. She knew she couldn't take it with her because of the strict customs regulations, but she was so drawn to the filigree of soft carvings in the handle that she just had to pick it up. It was carved out of a single block of very hard mahogany-like wood, but in her hand it reshaped itself to fit her grip, and adjusted its grip on her hand, so she hardly had to hold it. It was an uncanny sensation, as if it were alive, and at first she recoiled, but it seemed to seek out and send soothing vibrating sensations to her sore wrist, still a bit strained from the storm on Galern II. It was something like Telmx's massages, and she couldn't put the object down. Suddenly an intriguing presence was at her side before she could anticipate him.

"Don't worry, it won't hurt you. The wood is aged with empath, from use by so many Imari farmers. You're holding centuries upon centuries of farmers' hands in your hand."

His empath voice was crackly deep, a bit hoarse, with a slight high-pitched twinge, like a pubescent boy's, yet confident, swaggering, ever so slightly, in sensitive motions of strength and attentiveness. He entered her first tier inner chamber with unabashed enthusiasm, but with consideration, as if to ask, "Is it comfortable for you that I approach you this way? I was drawn to your fascination."

"No, of course it's fine." Her empath was blurting, self-conscious. She savored his Imari energy and was instantly aroused. She raised her fledgling shield just a tiny bit, as best she could. It was hard to modulate. She was new at it, and at that moment, not thinking clearly. How could she feel such immediate sensual attraction to someone else with Telmx's loving coursing through her blood!

"These are special to my homeworld. That's a frinbar. It's very, very old," K'dasti continued, clearly and kindly ignoring her confusion. "It's used to pull the fibers off the g'tim flower for clothing. I should say, *was* used. You hardly see them in use anymore because it's a hand tool. Not very efficient these days. But isn't it exquisite? I felt you admiring it." K'dasti was just simply the most breathtaking male Imari she had seen: tall, gangly, muscular, as dark as Telmx, with closely cropped hair framing his long wavy strands of cilia.

"It seems to be moving in my hand, just slightly, or is that my imagination?" she managed.

"They do that. It has absorbed the subtle hand motions of centuries and centuries of Imari farmers at work. Isn't the sensation fantastic?"

"Farmers used them?"

"Yeah, their empath lives in the wood. It's the most amazing thing. But they replaced the tools for modern hover machines. There are still places, especially on the Galern worlds, where farmers still use these, insisting on being close to the soil, but hover-empath technology has really made all these old tools practically obsolete."

"Why would something so precious be found on an outpost rest stop like this?"

"Oh, they're precious because they're no longer used. I mean precious to me, and others who preserve the old ways, but they were originally manufactured by the hundreds of thousands when they were used for agriculture. So they're common for souvenirs and some people buy them for healing sore hands and wrists. You chose it wisely. Would you like that one?"

"I would love it, but I'm told the customs agents will freak out."

"Freak out?"

"You know, go ballistic, be upset. Maybe arrest me? I don't know. I just know I can't take anything back to my 'primitive' home."

"Oh, I see. You're from an underdeveloped, pre-revolutionary place. Well, maybe we can figure that one out. There are ways, you know. Where are you from? You're so pale, and have no cilia, yet you empath like a native Imari, and shield like one too, I might add."

He could certainly push past her fragile shielding, J thought, but he is so Imari respectful of her privacy. In an inner chamber, she worried that Telmx would be furious about her talking to this boy, probably no older than herself. And he also seemed quite willing to break rules. She had to be careful what she shared. There were things she could say, but much that she couldn't. The politics had been difficult to master, and she didn't really understand all the intricacies, but the guidelines were clear. She could be honest up to a point. But not allow anyone to know how profoundly her contact with Telmx had pushed her capacities beyond the Council mandate.

"I'm a Monitoring Recruit from a system you call R-345 in the G'uw galaxy. I'm here on holiday with my mentor Telmx."

"Oh I know exactly who you are! How exciting. You're the Level I recruit from that little planet you call 'Earth.' Telmx's Mission is well known, even in the high schools. We use the topic as exercises in debate. I'm so honored!" His quick excitement embarrassed and frightened her, and she lowered her head, shielding even more emphatically for fear he would take in more than he was allowed.

"Plus I have already shielded, just in case your shielding doesn't hold. I knew Telmx was among us today, but I never imagined you'd be with her… but of course, you must be at the age of Ascension, I mean of course you are at the age of Ascension, so of course you would be visiting with her."

"You know her?"

"No, not personally. Just by reputation. She's one of the most prominent young Scouts in the Council, a student within the Order of Empath Travel Scouts. I believe she's one of Elder Goshing's protégés. I'd thought about applying to join the scouting order, but, well, I want to do so many other things."

"Like she's prestigious?"

"Well, yeah, but no, not the way you seem to think. I don't hold her in some kind of awe, unapproachable, that kind of thing, like with ancient rulers, and stuff like that, but she's very respected and there's much to learn from her. You're very lucky. Please, come break some froth with me. I was just about to have a snack."

She hesitated, weighing what to do. Telmx had warned her about spies, even Imari ones. She couldn't let anyone beyond her outer shielding, for no one must know her true capacities. No different from hanging out with her closest friends, though. Plus she had to get used to levels of shielding, part of the responsibilities of the Mission, but one of the responsibilities she hated the most, because it made her feel lonely in another's company. Telmx had said she lived with that also: the plight of responsibility. Well, if Telmx could, so could she!

"And I promise I won't pry. I have no need or desire to…. Oh, and I didn't need to break through your shielding to know your uneasy. I can read it in your eyes."

They spent the rest of the day together.

Indeed, K'dasti's eyes were piercing, as if he could read her not so much with his empath, but with a vision that seemed to V.E.-capture every word she thought or said out loud. His empath caressed and probed, always wanting more, just a little more than what she had just allowed, but he didn't probe intrusively, waiting for her thoughts to form fully before he read them. Knowing she was being very careful, he fully respected her hesitations.

His thoughts, however, were rarely fully formed. He had so much to say that his words tumbled out of his mind in rapid bursts. Then he would apologize because he had said things too quickly, without making sure she had already absorbed what he had just said so she could then understand the new thoughts he was bursting to share. He called himself a vague and rambling undisciplined philosopher, but he was hardly that. His formulations, though scattered, were incredibly deep and troubled. He was clearly on a quest, and didn't know quite how to orient himself to the universe around him, most of which, he said, had moved much too far into technology, harnessing empath for unnatural phenomenon, and not leaving it be, like the old farmers did.

She didn't know what to do with his energy.

"I'm so excited to meet someone from a pre-revolutionary era! What's it like to be worried about everyday survival, to know multitudes of people are dying because a few others have almost all of the wealth of the planet?" He asked a lot of questions, with respect and enthusiasm. Basic questions. She answered the best she could, and felt embarrassed and apologetic for her planet. He sensed it and told her not to feel that way. It was only "youth wants to know" kind of thing. He asked her about teenagers, sexuality, parents, teachers and mentors, rebellion in adolescence. He would think for a while, shaking his head, as if he were chewing something delicious. Then he would look at her in delight and ask another question.

He talked about a movement on his home planet to be purists, ones who have nothing to do with mechanical things. To rely only on one's own empath, senses, hands, resources, each other. There were groups of people who lived in self-sufficient utopias, and refused to space travel or to participate in anything other than what was available naturally on their planet. He had been involved for a while. But he wanted to taste more. "There's too much of the universe to understand, savor, feel. It would be too delimiting of one's being to ignore it all. After all, when an animal makes a habitat, it uses its natural technology. We recognize and respect that. Well, all creatures have technologies, some of which are much more sophisticated than others. Or at least different."

J loved how K'dasti's eyes opened wide as he talked. He obviously adored thinking. "I've come to the conclusion that science and technology are as fabulous as a hibernation hut or a nest or a web spun by an insect or a tree stick the h'out uses to gather fleshy protein from a g'plit. Just different." He emphasized how he also loved living off the land and was looking forward to spending more time on his compound's farm.

After hours of talking at a bot bar, they took a walk along the protected tourist path, up to the ridge just beyond the pavement, before it dropped off into areas that were only accessible through guided hover-tours. Like them, many travelers were required to skip the tours because they had to be on solid ground for a predetermined period of time, depending upon how long they had already traveled and how far they planned to go before the next rest stop. So they squatted on the ridge and talked some more. She was beside herself with sensual excitement. She had thought that she was only excited by females (never ever a male! No way!), and that Telmx was the only one forever, and here was a stranger, a guy.

"Actually, I'm recently a guy. My given name is K'dastx. Does that disturb you?"

"No, I mean I don't know. What do you mean by 'recently a guy'?"

"Just two years ago I was female. I suspect this is quite weird for you, coming from Earth. I don't know if people do that sort of thing there. I'm told that pre-revolutionary worlds are strange like that. But here it's pretty common. I wasn't happy as a female, so I got myself changed. This is sort of a new me. I love being this new me. I can't tell you exactly why or how, but it's made a huge difference in my life."

"So you're really a female?" She was actually relieved, even though it was, she thought, the maleness in "him" that was exhilarating.

"No, I'm all male, through and through male. Just that I somehow retained some female energy as well. I worked on that. Not everyone does. I like keeping the old with the new."

Well, she didn't exactly follow, but she didn't exactly care. K'dasti was voraciously intelligent and attractive, and so amazingly friendly. And he had absolutely no inhibitions. He was scheduled to depart that evening, so they promised to see each other in the future. She didn't know how, but he did. He said he would find her the next time she was on Telmx's home planet, and he would arrange to travel there as well. And not to worry, it was fine, really fine, "Not like your planet! Believe me, here we all can love and love and love. Perhaps, also, in the next ten years or so, when you get more used to traveling, we can take a trip together."

Her life, as vibrant as it now had become, increased yet again in intensity and hue. She so much wanted him to grab her and hold her tight. Of course he knew it. And she knew he knew. Finally, after hours and hours of talking, he did just that. They kissed for a very long time, just kissed, just held each other and kissed, and they both came, deliciously and unashamed.

She longed for him the moment they parted. Telmx had insisted that she would never be her only love, and that anything and everything was possible. J didn't believe her for one second. She still didn't. Plus, she had just met him. She hardly knew him. It was just a fleeting passion. She was sure Telmx would be so angry and jealous. And worried. Had her shielding held? What if he was really a spy? How could she know for sure? He sought *her* out. Maybe he pretended not to know who she was, even though he could probably read that much information right off the bat. She was so new to this kind of intrigue, so how could she possibly be a good judge of people?

Most upsetting: How could she explain to Telmx (much less to herself) that loving K'dasti and Telmx was like loving "Just 'Round Midnight" one minute and the "Trout Quintet" the next, each time thinking the music she was listening to at the time was the only music worth listening to. Plus, how could she love someone so quickly? Something was very wrong. Shit, accepting this Mission was already much too complicated, like a stupid mystery or spy novel (reading those novels provoked the kind of thinking she most disliked). Nor did she feel up to the challenge.

✳ ✳ ✳

Telmx sought out her favorite chi kiosk and carried her creamy double shot chi-bot brew to a quiet shaded corner of the plaza. She squatted gratefully and scanned the plaza for J. There she was squatting at a bot bar with an adolescent trans and seemingly thoroughly smitten by the boy's vibrant enthusiasm. "Ah, what a difference a few weeks makes," she mused. J has taken on the Imari Ways without even trying, indeed without even exactly knowing that she did so.

She savored another sip and found herself becoming giddy with excitement about how quickly her student had assimilated. How will she deal with her earthling ways after this? She'll just have to figure it out. There are certainly cultures and groups within J's own culture that don't demand the ownership of loving friendships. But she'll need some help through the confusion. With Goshing it was different. They shared even in the Ascension rites, the Imari Way. Multiple organisms, multiple partners, multiple pleasures. Oh, if life could always be that simple. Perhaps she would make a detour to Goshing's compound after she deposited J on her homeworld. Surprise her? Not quite possible. Besides various Council issues were developing, really disturbing ones that would potentially and dangerously affect the earthling Mission, and Goshing and her living group might require her to stay away right now.

Telmx reached silently and unobtrusively into the boy's shielding and discovered no malice. And J was already exercising good judgment. "I'm just like an intrusive mother," she thought. "No, it's alright to be concerned." She battled that one for a moment, and let it go, turning around to face the other direction and modulating her shielding to afford maximum privacy for them. People from that trans boy's homeworld, now there's a group that refuses to get involved in any political tangles. Well, that's another reason why we need to keep vigilant, so groups like that can continue without losing their bliss.

The Imari closed her weary eyes, and allowed the chi fragrances to bring her into her own blissful chamber, free from onerous Pomdos maneuverings and out-maneuverings, and the complicated calculations and transport adjustments that had dominated for the last several days.

J's face was hot with confused embarrassment when she "confessed" to Telmx about K'dasti (no way not to). But Telmx topped her excitement by vowing to arrange for them to get together as soon as it was logistically possible. J knew Telmx and her people didn't "own" their lovers, yet such genuine enthusiasm for another friend's happiness! Wow. Telmx's statements were not just theoretical notions.

CHAPTER TWELVE

J

One of the first realizations I had when I got back to Queens was I could stand up under the sky and be really close to, no, actually be in the universe. Not just be in a room, under the covers, in my novice empathing, but in fact, I could physically, PHYSI-CALLY be next to Telmx and K'dasti by standing upright outside under the stars!

Look at all the people standing, walking upright under the stars going about their business. Do they realize that their bodies, the tops of their heads, are pointing directly up (or down?) to incredible people whose heads are pointing at them. Where Telmx, Karine, Tarow and K'dasti stand: I'm touching the space they all touch; no solid walls exist between us. I wasn't thinking about ten dimensions and complex things, just being with them because there's nothing, absolutely nothing in-between.

At fifty-five, I still think about this, even after all the trips to other worlds, after all the complicated maneuverings, the politics and the struggles: every creature going about their business touches the same space. Sharing our space especially helps in the lonely times. Even when I can't be with my friends on my home-world. Scotty, or Katie or Barb or Shenea are standing or walking, going about their business in our very same space.

Also: I was throbbing. All over. Especially my crotch, my clitoris, my insides. Deafening vitality. I'd always imagined losing my virginity as an awkward, perhaps even somewhat violent, experience. My father's red spankings and everything else he did were terribly real, and they caused me to imagine unspeakable scenarios, like being gang-raped in an empty lot by a bunch of Hells-Angels-type guys who took turns. But I would fight them at first, then I imagined being forced to give in, enthralled and horrified by it all. Fifteen-year-old masturbatory fabulous and safely secret. But violent. Oh, how I didn't know that sex and love weren't violent until Telmx! Actually, when I thought about it a lot, I thought my parents' relationship had already ruined, spoiled, damaged me, so I couldn't ever have a healthy relationship. No one would ever want to touch me. They would know, just by feeling me cringe. I didn't think I could do it, or even want it. It would always have to be horrible. The Imari Ascension rite is a sacred thing. It gave me true loving. What happened with my parents wasn't love.

It seemed weird to me that I would so easily and suddenly enjoy her caresses. I don't know why I never asked her, never even probed empathically.

I replayed my moments with Telmx, experienced the sweet sizzling, tasted it and felt the sweetness infusing me whole. Then K'dasti's lips, his strong yet tender arms around my waist. Beyond belief. Two people, each one comfortable with the other's existence and I managing to be comfortable with (and excited by) their comfort. I would lie down in the cool grass in my back yard and replay any one of these moments any time I wanted. I ached for these so sublime and different feelings. Her face, her smile, her energy, his hands, her voice, his energy. Now! This very moment! Not anticipated empath dreams, but true memories!

Not enough. Throbbing followed me everywhere. The separation was torture. I had to believe that Telmx was right. Oh boy. Was she right. By tasting her loving, I was ready for more. How else to explain K'dasti? So easy, for them, and then, miraculously, for me too. I had no choice but to believe her: even earthling lovers could feel this wonderment! I'd love again and again. And there'd be room for more and more. "There's always room for more, once you start loving," she insisted, pulling me closer so that our breasts mingled into one melting ecstasy. "It's addictive, you know." Could that be? Making love with earthlings addictive? Maybe, but uh-uh, not yet. At first I didn't dare look around. Actually it didn't even occur to me to look around. My body was exploding from the inside out as it was. Not a scintilla of energy left for another explosion.

Nevertheless, I started eleventh grade, started to look around and saw everything and everybody for the first time. People were rounder, their skin moist and ready. They had distinctive aromas, intoxicating and virulent. All these adolescents, tightly wound, awkward, and ready for anything. Each boy was a bit of K'dasti. I averted my eyes so they wouldn't know what I was thinking, involuntarily shielded from the empath they didn't know they could harness. Each girl was a bit of K'dasti and Telmx, especially the women teachers. Especially my new Trig teacher.

I also thought about becoming an actual boy. I wondered how many girls were really wanting to be guys and afraid to even think it. And vice-versa. I wouldn't dare search their minds for such secrets. I did remain disciplined about that. Although it was incredibly difficult.

Everyone was screaming and hugging, the only way Performing Arts kids could do on the first day back: dramatically effusive, some really really meaning it and feeling it, others trying to act that way to fit in. When Barb saw me she couldn't stop screaming. "What happened to you? You got laid, didn't you! Oh wow! Where? When?"

"Why? What's so different?" Of course I knew, but I wanted to know what she saw without looking into her mind.

"Well, all I can say is that you are walking firm and light all at the same time. Whatever happened to you this summer looks utterly far-out."

I couldn't exactly tell her about it, at least not in detail, so I made some things up. And got them all wrong, so Barb didn't believe I was telling all. But she didn't seem to think the less of me for being coy. "Okay, okay, just a summer romance, so who's it gonna be now? Gotta get you laid again 'cuz it looks so terrific on you, girl!"

"Not right away, Barb." I needed a few more weeks or months or years (I didn't know) of being wrapped in these sensations.

As Barb and I sat in HoJo's on 47ʰ and Broadway chugging down fries and milkshakes after school on that first day, I tried to talk to her about all of us sharing the same space in the universe. It came out kooky and sophomoric. She said it was bullshit to think about things like that, and a distraction from what we really had to be doing, getting laid and supporting the Civil Rights Movement. She said I was still a mystical dreamer and that I had better look around at the real world that needed a lot of loving and fixing.

I knew the world needed a lot of fixing. That part was just plain true. And, yeah, we all also needed a lot of loving, and I found uncanny truths in songs like "Jude" and "Give Peace a Chance." Then I started talking about Martin Luther King and Malcolm X, how they died trying to fix things and that we should be inspired. I heard my words coming before I could stop them. Barb was looking at me with disbelief. "What in the hell are you talking about J? You sure as hell shouldn't be talking like that. What ever are you thinking? Someone'll think you're plotting to kill the greatest civil rights leaders of our times. And who the hell is Malcolm X? You better be careful. If I told anyone what you just said they'd lock you up and throw away the key."

My face burned and my tongue was suddenly thicker than my whole mouth. It was my first, but not my only, out-loud slip into a future V.E.

I covered myself: "Justa 'maybe,' you know, Barb, like maybe some civil rights leaders will be so inspiring that they'll die for it, especially after they start merging their visions. But you know, that shouldn't stop us from getting things done by, by any means necessary."

"Well there's a great phrase, J. I like that one. 'By any means necessary.' Wow, sometimes you just rock me right off my feet!"

Like always, Barb was just crazy about her crazy friend. I loved that. And every once in a while, when I tried to convince myself Telmx and K'dasti weren't the only loves of my life forever, I would dip into Barb's mind (I almost never did that, because it would make our friendship so awkward and uneven) to see if she had some feelings for me besides being just a friend. I found them deeply there, but so deep it would probably push our friendship over the edge if I tried to do anything about it. I left it alone.

Except for Trig, I was so spacey (literally!) I couldn't keep up with high school. In the afternoons, during orchestra rehearsals, there were long stretches when the tympani were silent (I studied clarinet but played tympani in the high school orchestra). I stared out the widow across the street to the sweatshop that I hadn't noticed the previous year. Time and time again, Mr. Goldstein, the orchestra conductor, would cut into my reverie. Even if there was no part for tympani, I had to pay attention.

I was mostly confused, dizzy and forgot what world I was on, or what year I was in. I stopped at newsstands to check the date. Then I didn't know if I had just traveled to that year or I was really there. I'd talk to someone in the street, or I'd call Barb to make sure I wasn't just in one of those V.E.-dreams.

At night I played and replayed moments with Telmx and vowed that the very next day I would find a woman, perhaps an older woman to love (Maybe my Trig teacher. She was so, so beautiful, and she liked me a lot, but...). The next day came and I didn't know how to find this perfect woman. Well, what about one of those soft, firm adolescent boys? What about one of them? In spite of what I had learned from the Imari, such thoughts felt like betrayal. I wasn't ready. Certainly I could empath travel forward and learn who it would be and then work backward or *forward or both, trying to find my way into a new relationship. But I couldn't travel where I willed to travel. I was still a novice. V.E.-history travel states were still not in my power to call up. They just happened when they happened.*

But there were other things to contend with: the curse of knowing and seeing. The curse of impatience. The curse of having a heart. The curse of being empathic. I cursed my curses and envied stony people. I cried much too easily and longed to cultivate a way to sit tight.

And most sobering, most jarring: As I squeezed into the F train back to school a few days after returning from Telmx's homeworld, I remembered how utterly insignificant Earth was in the universe. "Have to keep it that way," Telmx had said. Because the Earth, in spite of its insignificance, could develop to the Age of Empath before it was ethically ready, it could also destroy other worlds. I was beginning to understand the Mission.

Every once in a while I'd also get wildly furious at Telmx. She had no right to give me all the information and not let me shout stuff from the rooftops. I was trapped. Still, I knew that shouting my revelations from rooftops had its time and place. There'd be time enough for that when people were ready to hear things. Now the harder work: how to motivate people by involving them in struggle. Especially the workers, who earned their right to control the means of production. Marx had said this, but I didn't really understand it until sophomore year at CCNY when I met Katie's friends (she called them "comrades"). Then I learned about struggle and class-consciousness. It wasn't enough to experience the wonderful life on Telmx's home planet and (by then) some of the other cultures in the "civilized" universe, as Telmx called it.

"You'll learn about your planet's struggle in your own time," Telmx said. "I don't want you comparing our history with yours. Each planet has it different, although the basic principles are the same. Exploitation is exploitation. Paranoia is paranoia." I was still struggling over the paranoia part. It would be another few years before she gave me the first volume of The **Books of Kro'an'ot** *to study, which explained the function of paranoia in a primitive society, and, I think, prepared me for my eventual confrontation with Matt.*

A throbbing headache started brewing as I reached 47th street. I pushed out of the train and raced up the stairs. What year was I in now? Shit! Once again late for homeroom. Fuck-a-duck! —J

PART II:

1967

CHAPTER THIRTEEN

Matt

Matt felt as starched as his new corporate suit. He didn't know what to expect at Bell Labs, but it was a huge corporation, and he had to look the part. Wildly different from his undercover field trips to SDS for the Company. He parked his new red Trans-AM in the visitors' area and checked his chin in the rear-view mirror. Why was he so damned jittery all of a sudden? The nick he got shaving monopolized the entire mirror, rivaling the zit that had suddenly exploded the night before. That plus a good case of crotch rot. Jeez.

Already at 7:03 a.m. three smart navy uniforms and identical briefcases were strutting across the walkway from a separate parking area. He pulled his new briefcase with his gold leaf monogram and coded snap locks out of the car and waited for the uniformed officers to pass. Then he strutted after them. Better than making a goddamned fool of himself by going to the wrong entrance. He patted his suit pocket for his clearance and letter of intro. Okay, just be cool.

At the end of visitors' parking, the lot widened and stretched around a two-story, many-angled building that extended beyond the horizon. Just at the nearest angle of the building, the uniforms turned onto an inconspicuous side path marked several yards further on with a minuscule sign reading: "AUTHORIZED PERSONNEL ONLY BEYOND THIS POINT." No security guard, but he was well aware of the cameras mounted on adjacent trees and lampposts. Not caring to create any hullabaloo suspicions, and worried that he already had, he turned and followed the main footpath around the building. At Bell Labs they practiced professional security. Now men and women, but mostly men, and mostly civvies, were converging in dribs and drabs from all directions onto the walkway ahead and disappearing into a yet unseen fissure in the building. He quickened his pace and followed them through a cluster of revolving doors.

By the time Admiral Dawes came to pick him up at reception he had been photographed, fingerprinted, x-rayed, searched, urine-tested and grilled. Even his Company ID didn't save him from abuse. Probably made things worse. Matt was pissed and humiliated, but he also understood. Fully. Well, at least they sent an admiral to greet him, even if the troll inside all the stars and stripes was as ugly as hell.

"You have a very impressive resume, Matt. May I call you Matt?" Dawes had a gravelly, almost inhuman voice that sounded as if it were filtered through an old telephone receiver. Later Matt realized the weather-beaten Rumpelstiltskin was talking through a tiny microphone from a creepy opening in his throat.

"Yes, sir."

"Quentin's the name. Admiral Quentin Tyler Dawes. People call me QT. I like that." His chuckle was a raspy cough.

Matt chuckled back. The admiral was anything but cute. Maybe they mothball the short ugly ones in back-office research. He'll just call him Admiral Dawes, or "sir" to his ugly face. "I'm very excited about this research, sir," he offered.

"Mmmhmm. Let's wait until we get past these goddamn electronic ears, son, okay?"

Well, that was a stupid ass fool's mistake. Made a fucking lousy first impression. "Yes, sir." Just shut the hell up and follow his lead.

They turned left at the end of a long corridor buzzing with people milling about with their AT&T coffee mugs. Now out of sight, they stopped at a broom closet. QT slid his ID card over a tiny scanner beam. "By tomorrow morning, your ID will open all the doors." After descending two flights of stairs, several ramps, and more stairs, they entered another set of corridors and passed through several more ID scanners. Matt figured this was the underground approach to the area where those navy stiffs had marched, but he was completely turned around, even though he prided himself on keeping track of such things.

"This is how I get my daily workout," QT rasped through coughing and wheezing. "If I'd known my life would be clambering around the caverns of New Jersey, I would've stopped smoking decades ago. My doc thinks I'm doing the Canadian Fitness program. Ha!"

At the end of a long corridor on what seemed to Matt like at least five stories below ground, they turned yet another corner and approached a glassed-in reception area, flanked by six burly sailors pointing Uzis directly at them. "Welcome to Shangri-La," QT grumbled, as a seventh sailor emerged out of nowhere, saluted both of them and "begging your pardon, sir" commanded Matt to raise his hands in the air. "This welcoming committee only happens once," he went on. "Then for some asinine reason, everybody trusts everybody." While the sailor patted down Matt yet again and made him open his briefcase, Matt decided the whole navy security team was recruited from closet or not-so-closet faggots. He imagined his knee flying swiftly and smartly into the sailor's groin.

Then the ensign from behind the glass buzzed them in and snapped to attention. "Okay, okay, son," graveled QT. "Ensign, this is Dr. Matthew J. Hobbs. He has Level One-A security and will be a regular customer. Etch his mug and ID number into that photographic brain of yours so these goons don't go after his ass anymore. Besides," he said to Matt, "what you bring into this area from now on is more secure than anyone out there in reception has clearance to see. Even if it's in code. And of course, you bring nothing out, absolutely nothing." Matt was beginning to like Rumpelstiltskin more and more. O'Brian never gave two shits about his status in life. Not to mention his integrity. Yeah, Dr. Matthew J. Hobbs, Level One-A: that did sound downright aristocratic.

✳ ✳ ✳

Matt entered the small library clutching his top-secret project manuals and found a chair opposite the door. He planned to be intensely engrossed when Admiral Dawes came back with the principal physicist of the project. "Without Yazzie, we might as well pack up, go home, and kiss the whole project goodbye," Admiral Dawes had rasped during the morning orientation. "He'll take you through the hands-on." Yes! The lead physicist. He couldn't wait. He was anxious as hell to get into the photon chamber lab itself, and so far he had spent the whole godforsaken morning in meeting after meeting with Dawes and several non-technical officers going over protocols and security procedures. At least they had finally given him the manuals! The admiral went to track down Dr. Yazzie, and they would meet in the library. Sometimes, Dawes had warned, Yazzie was hard to locate. Good. Maybe he had time to take a piss and study the first chapter or two. Be prepared. Be impressive.

At first Matt hardly noticed the squat leathery old sailor dozing with his head in his hands in an easy chair across the room, except to calculate where he himself should not sit. He opened the first three-ringed binder and took a Sharpie from his collection of pens racked on display in his shirt pocket. He wanted to ask all the right questions. But the wheezing and coughing coupled with a vaguely familiar odor emanating from across the room took his attention. The sailor was colored, perhaps mulatto, with deck overalls, a single stripe on the sleeve of his blue denim shirt, and a red sweat bandanna wrapped tightly around his forehead. He was clearly an orderly or some deckhand sneaking some z's when he ought to be scrubbing urinals. Well, the admiral and Dr. Yazzie will toss him out. This was top-secret stuff. He had no business sneaking into the tech library.

As Matt stared, the sailor began rubbing his forehead in his sleep, in small circular movements. No, he was not actually rubbing his head, but rather, his hands were hovering several millimeters away from it in a manner that perked Matt's curiosity and contempt.

Having completed perhaps twenty circular motions, the brown man sighed serenely, moved his cupped hands just beyond his temples, and started the circular motions once again. In so doing, he opened his eyes, smiled faintly at Matt, and closed them without missing a beat in his carefully orchestrated motions. Matt shoved his attention back into his manual, but was again distracted by the old sailor's movements and indecipherable murmurs. While his right hand continued to float above his temple, his other hand was deftly unwinding his bandanna. Having wiped his brow with the unraveled headband, he smoothly folded it with the gnarled weathered fingers of his left hand into a neat rectangle, which he slipped, with one continuous motion into his breast pocket. Then he took out a watch on a chain from some inner pocket in his overalls, snapped it open, studied it intently, murmured or rather intoned something under his breath, closed its lid, returned it to its home, and shifting his weight on the chair, brought both hands behind his head, leaned comfortably against them, and returned Matt's transfixed gaze. Matt was dismayed and comforted by his intense, penetrating brown eyes conveying something intrusive and yet serene, like in the previous smooth unselfconscious ritual, and even in his faint odor which he now recognized as a mixture of corn and freshly cut grass. He realized with annoyance he was drawn to a stranger whose existence he would never have deigned to acknowledge, except perhaps to proffer a tip for some service well done. The sailor's eyes reminded him of Uncle Donny's, whose profound deep-set gaze always made him feel uncloaked and secure when he was a boy.

"How's your day been so far?" the sailor glided into Matt's reverie.

So taken aback by his gentle, simple baritone voice, Matt couldn't answer, and instead fumbled with his pen, as if to resume reading, lest he be caught in casual conversation with a colored deck hand. Colossal breach of security just for starters. The sailor continued as if Matt had not even considered aborting conversation.

"Don't read that manual right off," he said, in the simple melodious tone Uncle Donny used to guide Matt to the Andromeda galaxy without fancy star charts. "First off," Uncle Donny would insist, "don't look direct. Use your peripheral vision. Let your eyes relax. Don't concentrate so goddamned hard."

"It'll turn your head and get you started on the wrong trail," the deckhand continued. "It's really about unity in the universe, this project of ours. It's actually quite simple. Think of the universe as a unity, one entire thing, you know, then it's not such a mystery that one thing here moves another thing there," he went on, and without waiting for comment, pushed himself upright, murmuring, "These blasted headaches slow me down something fierce these days," and then walked slowly and smoothly to the coffee urn in the little alcove next to the door.

"We just see it better when the things are close. Like my fingers, you know, move this cup. That's easy to see. Anyhow, so twin photon particles are pretty close, so they move together even if they're far apart. Unity of the Universe. That's what it's all about."

Matt squirmed. Ignorant deck hand talking about something he knows absolutely nothing about as if he knows everything about it. He wondered if the admiral and the other officers knew just how much this guy blabs to his cronies about things he shouldn't blab about. (Right in the middle of the hottest top-secret project in the world. Should he report this outrage to the Company?)

"You take milk and sugar?"

Matt nodded. In spite of his better judgment, he was pulled back in by his kind, gentle manner.

"Still, don't worry if you don't get it right off. I'll aim you right, as long as you don't go and read those fancy theories and technical procedures first. If I live that long," he added under his breath. If *I* don't get it right off? Who in the hell does he think he is? "Here try this on for size." He handed Matt a large Earthen coffee mug, and groaning slightly, sunk back into his chair. "Goddamn headaches."

"Ah, I see you found each other." Admiral Dawes was standing in the doorway. Matt stood up, flustered and confused. "I'll join you two briefly and then leave you in his capable hands. Now don't you go keeping this lad up all night. It's his first day, and he has already taken in a lot. And you need some rest too. How's that migraine of yours, Yazzie? Seen the medic yet?"

Yazzie smiled. "Ain't nothing your medicine men can do that I can't do better myself, sir. Yes, we've already begun."

Matt sat down to hide his wobbling coffee cup. "You know," said the admiral, "there's lots of magic in this universe until scientists come along and find practical explanations. We have no explanation for what we got here, not yet, and we're not even close. So it's gonna have to be magic for a while. And Yazzie here has that magic touch, along with his own theories. I have a feeling he's right on the money. Maybe you'll translate his theory into formulas the rest of us can understand. He makes a hell of a good cup of coffee too." Then Admiral Dawes was gone.

Wait'll the boys at NASA hear this. Jesus, what a big, fucking mess.

"You believe in magic? How do you want me to call you, Matt, Dr. Hobbs? Tell me what's most comfortable for you. You can call me Yazzie. Everyone does, you know, at least when they're not talking behind my back. Then I'm 'that redskin,' 'Merlin' or 'Half-breed Harry,' oh golly, I don't know what-all."

So the lead physicist is a redskin. Might have known. It never occurred to Matt that an Indian could get a Ph.D., much less a plain old college degree. Whew, things are changing fast these days of "equal opportunity." What next? Well, now he had to say something about magic. "I used to think me and the cows were in cahoots using mental telepathy," Matt said. Indians would like that sort of thing, he thought. "When I was a kid, you know. Way back, and I thought me and the moons of Jupiter could, you know, talk and stuff." Now why in the hell did he have to tell him that?

"You a farm lad? Me too. Where'd you grow up?"

This was getting too goddamn personal. "Iowa. This coffee is top notch. Uh what about the particle chamber, uh, Dr. Yazzie? I'd like see what you're doing"

"Iowa? Well, I'm from Arizona, I mean originally from way north of there, you know. But that's before I was born. So you talked with animals and stars, did you? Well now, don't go bragging about that to some of the other guys around here, you know." Bragging? Who's bragging? This was really getting out of hand. He had never admitted that ESP stuff to anyone, not even his wife.

"Hmm I knew there was something about you, Matthew. Can I call you that? Don't call me doctor, by the way. I just about finished tenth grade."

"But...." Matt started.

"Ah, what an upside-down world we live in," continued Yazzie as if the words on his tongue could not linger to listen once they got there, "when what's good about us is bad, and what's bad is good." Then, as if it were his natural right to know, he went on: "How does it come to be that a lad that talked with cows and stars ends up a particle physicist from Harvard?"

"I wanted to be an astronomer, and they gave me a slide rule. Then it just kind of happened."

"So that's how you ended up in NASA. Do you have a family? A wife? Children?"

Matt never talked about his terrified childhood, his drunken father; and never ever would he divulge that he and his milk cow would commiserate with each other. Not even to his wife, especially not to his wife who was impressed he knew the multiplication table and could manipulate a slide rule. But to his great dismay, he already yearned to spill all his secret beans to this nosy old half-breed. Awful. He held his tongue. "My wife and boy are in Baltimore," he said lightly.

"Do not take loved ones for granted, Matthew. Nothing in life replaces the intimacy of loved ones." He poured them both more coffee and pulled his chair closer to Matt's as if in agreement that he tell his story, even if Matt would not reveal his own. "When I rejected the home of my father and grandfather and the land of my ancestors, I lost so much. I was young then. What did I know? I wanted to experience the world, the whole world, not simply the bears and the rivers of Arizona. I wanted to experience history in the making, not spend my life learning and repeating the tired stories of our ancestors. I wanted to be the story, you know, make new stories as sacred as the ancestral ones.

"Now I regret it. The white man drove us from our home, you know, way before I was born. Marched us to Fort Sumner, in New Mexico, the Long Walk. Have you heard of that? Of course you haven't. Many of my family perished on that 300-mile 'walk.' My people, we are the Dineh, the Navajo, finally won the right to come back to our sacred hills. Did you ever hear of Kit Carson? I'm sure you've heard of him, a hero in your history books. Well, he's the greatest enemy of our people.

"As a teenager I thought, well, if they conquered us, well, it was meant to be. That's what I thought. Let me join the community of the conquerors and go forward. Especially since there were enemies from across the ocean aiming to conquer our land. So I joined the call for volunteers in the Second World War, not as a Wind Whisperer, maybe you've heard of them? Probably not. Still classified. I joined as a 'sea listener.'

"My father was devastated. I even scoffed at his devastation. Scoffed! Can you imagine? I said to myself, he will learn from me that there is more to the world than the Earth and the trees and the animals. Ah, the arrogance of youth!"

Why was Yazzie telling him this stuff? This, his first day on the most important, most secret, most expensive project in the history of the world. So much for his report journal. "Discussed the arrogance of youth with an Indian." Maybe O'Brian tricked him. Knew it was a goddamn freak show all along. He drifted in and out of the melodious baritone. "...and so it comes right around," he caught. "Ah, I see you're quite exhausted. Let's continue tomorrow, when you're fresh, and I'll make my little photon twins perform spooky motion for you."

"For sure," Matt said. Tomorrow he would check it all out.

"I'll walk out with you. There's a shortcut out, you know. I need to do my evening prayers, before I get back to work. Are you a religious man, Matthew? Of course you are. You're wearing a cross. Great man, that Jesus."

When they emerged into the twilight, Yazzie led them to a collection of trees and shrubbery just behind the parking lot. "If you sit facing this way, and you don't tilt your head too far to the left, you can actually trick yourself into thinking you're in the solitude of a forest, if you block out honking cars, turnpike din, and jets from Newark airport." Matt left the Indian in a ridiculous pose, talking gibberish to ghosts in the small clump of trees behind the parking lot. What is it with these people? Nothing in graduate school had prepared him for this. Usually he'd study all night to prove he wasn't no stupid-ass farm boy from Oshkosh. Usually he'd memorize a bunch of formulas, make up one or two of his own, just to fit in. Now he just wanted to sleep.

✳ ✳ ✳

During Matthew's third week on the project, the Pentagon imposed revised security guidelines and a new deadline. By the fourth week, which was closing in on the Thanksgiving holidays, the core personnel had been cut by a third, work hours had been stretched for the dozen who were left, and holiday leave was rescinded. There were rumors that someone had leaked essential code to the Russians, and no one was above suspicion. Matt was insulted and incensed by the intrusive investigations and surprise searches. His wife called in a panic. Their neighbor saw a strange man stalking her and their son and she wanted him to come home immediately to confront this serial killer, rapist, kidnapper who right that very minute was watching the house in a car from across the street. Besides why couldn't he come home for Thanksgiving?

He could understand it if the Company was going after Yazzie. After all, he wasn't a true American. The redskin took the new restriction in stride. "These little twins won't sing and dance for anyone else like they sing and dance for me, so let those little bucks enjoy their fool's hunt."

Then it was rumored that the pimply faced ensign who manned the glassed-in security post, had died of an overdose in a brothel. Suddenly this uptight, small-town favorite son was linked to a local scandal. The next day several prostitutes were charged with giving him a lethal injection of tainted heroin, and the mutilated body of their pimp turned up in the Delaware Water Gap, apparently the victim of a gangland assassination.

Within the next two weeks, more tragedies occurred: five of the transferred physicists were listed among the 127 fatalities in a plane crash. They were on their way to an international quantum mechanics conference in

Stockholm. Two others committed suicide, and one was incarcerated in a prestigious Baltimore sanitarium, where he sustained shock therapy and a frontal lobotomy. As the days passed, Admiral Dawes became more gravelly and short-tempered. The rings under his puffy eyes grew exponentially.

No one among the surviving members of the team would talk openly about their apprehensions, except to banter that expulsion from the photon project caused "spooky action at a distance." They started calling themselves the dirty dozen.

Yazzie was denied permission to perform his parking lot prayers, and finally going outside at all was considered a security risk. The navy brought in cots, and set up a number of bedrooms in the emptied offices. Christmas was celebrated underground complete with a synthetic tree and a secret Santa grab-bag. And Matt's wife and son celebrated the holidays at her mother's house back in Des Moines.

Several times, as the deadline to complete the first phase of the research to demonstrate to the boys in Washington approached, false security breach alarms were sounded, and MPs clutching Uzis with both hands ran frantically from one end of the lab to the other, breaking Yazzie's furrowed concentration and ever more frequent library retreats to meditate away his migraines. One of the MPs accused Yazzie of tripping the alarms with "Injin Voodoo" and demanded that he cease and desist his bizarre library rituals. Team meetings often dissolved into panic sessions and cross accusations.

The three sub-units, the particle physicists, the technicians, and the MPs, were united by a single objective: master and harness the twin photon phenomenon before the Russians, transfer the model to space travel, and conquer the solar system for the free world. It was even rumored the Reds had contrived the ultimate weapon: photon time-travel chambers. They would travel back to the twenties, save Lenin's life, and conquer the free world. Before long, there would be slave labor gulags in Milwaukee. It could be in the works already.

The sleeping arrangements established when round-the-clock schedules were instituted found Matt and Yazzie sharing the office-now-bedroom next to the library, based on mutual need for ready access to that facility: Yazzie for his easy chair to nurse his migraines and Matt for his assignment, developing theoretical formulas to harness the twin photon technology for space travel. Because Yazzie was specifically assigned to train Matt on every aspect of his work, they ended up inseparable, at the chamber console and in the library, where in spite of his medicinal meditations, Yazzie was always ready for speculative discussions about space travel fueled and guided by twin photons.

"Look here. You see, when I access my favorite little photon right here, it resonates with its twin way on the other side of our galaxy. Indeed, last year I discovered a photon had found its partner in Andromeda. Imagine that. And do you know what happened? The twin in Andromeda had another twin already singing and dancing with several other twins, way beyond Andromeda. Can you imagine? Now I have sent aloft close to two thousand particle twins, and I can sing and dance with each one at will. When Einstein contemplated these spooky actions, he had no idea!"

"Soon we will be able to send out quadruplets, and septuplets. Yes, now that's a real secret, even more secret than anything else you have learned. Not for another couple of years though. Oh, Matthew, the possibilities are infinite!"

Three days after Christmas, Yazzie fell into a feverish delirium, after a particularly strenuous non-stop 24-hour stint at the console. A physician was flown up from Bethesda, and became the thirteenth member of the team, restricted to the premises and, of course, recruited to handle all ailments now besetting the exhausted group. As Yazzie deteriorated, Matt avoided the seaman's cot, catching catnaps in the library lest he enter their room while Yazzie was awake. Matt could not explain it to himself, but the grimmer the doctor's report, the harder it was to approach the room. When he did go in, to retrieve his shaving equipment or a change of underwear, the man's incoherent babble resembled their endless conversations of the weeks before. Now they were strung together into an incomprehensible rhythmic incantation. When the odor emanating from him became rotting corn and manure, Matt avoided the room even more and made every effort to forget he existed.

While trapped in this project Matt began to fathom, not with his Harvard training, but with the part of him that believed that he and the cows really did talk to each other, that his rational and logical calculations were not producing the fulfillment he had always assumed they would, but instead, that his dreams and fantasies were far more exciting, especially when he allowed his mind to wander into illogical realms that belonged in fairy tales, or at best, "soft" science fiction.

By the end of April, with no one to speculate with, he had formulated another more terrifying conclusion. That none of his formulas were worth reciting to his colleagues, that they amounted to a hill of rotten beans, that in fact, he had no scientifically accurate proposal to offer in answer to the Russian space threat (let alone time travel), that all he could offer his colleagues was a mystical, unfounded, almost unheard of conclusion, that if Yazzie died, the project would die with him. They would laugh Matt off the project, and that prospect terrified him more than he was willing to admit.

He tried working at the photon console, duplicating the procedures the old seaman had taught him. "What do you think of all this, Matthew?" Yazzie had said during the hours and hours of training. "Do you want to try it? It's quite simple, really. Some of the other techies think I'm crazy for spending so much time on one photon trial. But you know what? They don't get through to their twins anywhere nearly as many times as I do. Do you know why? They don't talk to them quietly when they send them on their way. They don't promise them safe journey. They don't even name them properly. How can a little baby have a number for its name? It feels loved when I name it. How can twins sing and dance with each other when they don't know the name of their brother or sister?"

Now without Yazzie's help and encouragement. Matt would set the controls, calibrate the vertices, the temperature, the spectrograph, and then like Yazzie, he would begin, secretly, of course, the traditional Navajo naming ceremony for his designated photon twins, which of course demanded more time and concentration. He'd have to close his eyes without letting on what he was actually doing, and pick a name like "flying eagles" (his names were always much less creative than the ones Yazzie thought up), or "panther partners." He began to achieve "hit" rates even higher than those of his colleagues but certainly nowhere near Yazzie's success story. Simply following the manual without adding the Yazzie rigmarole, produced no hits at all. He'd walk away from a session spinning and exhausted, his head pounding as if the devil himself were hammering relentlessly at the bottom of his skull where it joined his neck. When he took a break and folded his large frame as best he could into the easy chair in the library, as far as he could get from the mounds of paper he had produced for his space travel report, he ignored the pain in his head and thought about irrelevant things.

The closer the deadline, and the more Admiral Dawes pressured him for a preliminary draft, the further he drifted from his formulas and graphs. The night before his presentation was due, he finished collating his fifteen copies, and labored over his summary and conclusion chapter, surrounded by wads of rejected sheets. His conclusion chapter was mottled with scratch-outs, arrows, inserts, sketches and doodles. Reams of notes and rewrites, most of which was destined for the shredder, crowded all around him, on every available surface, and in labeled piles on the floor. Admiral Dawes flitted in and out of the library, sometimes annoyed that he had not yet seen a preliminary draft, and other times ecstatic that something substantial was finally being assembled into binders. He would bustle in with slices of hot crusty pizza or a new supply of donuts and a freshly brewed pot of coffee from his own private stash, fussing over Matt's comfort like a nervous father-to-be, anxious to do everything to make his pregnant wife comfortable yet timid and careful lest he do something to upset her.

Although Matt tried to convince himself that Dawes would be the most accepting of all the team members of his unscientific conclusions and proposals, he was very worried. The proof of his argument was that at least 80 percent of the so-called "hits" recorded by the other techies and physicists seemed spurious, suspiciously fudged. Only Yazzie's hits were right on the money 97 percent of the time. It clearly had something to do with the seaman's spirituality. Dare he admit it? His maverick methods of talking, listening to and coddling his photon twins, each bequeathed with an invigorating name, caused a kind of energy surge. Matt had finally found a way to graph it, a kind of spike of energy that Yazzie named a "real blue" because it seemed to produce a faint blue glow in the air between Yazzie and his console. Indeed it was only when Matt himself managed to achieve that "real blue," after exhausting concentration, that he registered a hit.

Maybe Dawes would get it, but certainly no one else in the team would, especially since his argument hinged heavily on how much fudging was going on among the other technicians. Each time Dawes entered the library with more goodies, or a worried inquiry, he would say to himself, "This time, just say it: like 'by the way' or 'we got a slight problem here, sir,'" and each time he would think, "Well, just keep working on the proof and conclusions so they're airtight. Just try harder to square it all away. He'll be back soon enough."

Such was Matt's state after Dawes' last delivery of tollhouse cookies when he discerned a weak and familiar wheezing behind him. Turning he found Yazzie sitting in the easy chair, wrapped snuggly from head to foot in his blanket, beseeching Matt to come closer in his weak, wobbly voice that still retained a trace of its baritone resonance. When Matt leaned over to better hear the old seaman and saw his emaciated leathery face regaining a tiny trace of its previous serenity, he felt his own chest begin to heave with hope and expectancy. Maybe this old man might not die after all! This thought made him gulp for air. He searched for excuses to escape the library and not reveal how much he cared for the old redskin, but he remained kneeling next to his head, pretending detachment.

"You're up and about," he said lightly.

"In a manner of speaking. One windowless room, another windowless room, what's the difference? Ah, Matthew, it's how one transcends windowless. On the submarine with no windows, I rediscovered our Mother Earth under the great rivers, and I found a new realm of animals. Matthew, have you ever met a whale? I mean really close? Have you even sung with her, rejoiced in her birthing? Have you ever merged the energy of your eyes with the eye of an octopus? I mean really floated on the energy flowing between your eyes and hers? And you know what else? Out of that experience, I gave myself a new name: Singing with Whales, better than Coyote Blindly Hunting, don't you think?" He chuckled softly using one sustained breath which gave way to such desperate wheezing and squeaking, Matt stood up to fetch the doctor.

"No, no Matthew," managed the seaman. "Just give me a sec. One blasted sec." Then he managed to talk for a very long time, in a forced but resonant voice that ebbed and flowed as he lost and regained his energy. Occasionally he paused from wheezing but he went on as if he were desperate to make sure all was conveyed to his next of kin before it was too late. Matt, transfixed, held on to every word.

"I don't know how to explain it, but my sonar work in that windowless submarine carried me back to my roots. I merged with the music of the Earth, sang its songs. Here in the lab, I found a new music. Did you know that the universe sings? Oh, its songs are strong, and full like the roar of the waterfall, whispered and proud, like the leaves in the breeze. It blends the songs of the sea with those of the bear and the antelope, and the voices of my ancestors are there too. I need the photon chamber to bring me to our universe. It was meant to be. Isn't it strange? I needed the sonar on the sub to bring me to the sea, and the photon chamber to bring me to the unity which is the universe. My ancestors would understand. I had lost touch. Not having the drums of my ancestors, I caressed the instruments of the white man and brought myself back to the powers I had lost when I rejected the home of my father and grandfather and joined the navy. I am so grateful.

"In the sub you really had to listen, and that's goddamn hard you know, when they got all these walls of metal between you and all the sea critters you're trying to listen to. Gotta listen to those critters, so you know the difference between a German sub and a humpback whale. I got pretty damn good at that after a while. You see, if you find the oneness with the whale, it feels, it sounds very different from a German U-boat. Me and my earphones. Just listening and listening to the sounds of the sea, and the captain would come to me. To me! And say, 'What do we got now, Yazzie?' You know, I was never ever wrong. Me and those earphones and my oneness with the universe stuff. Pretty damn neat, eh? So whatever works, the navy'll take it. This is one hell of a good job, this job here. I get almost one hundred percent hit rate, almost one hundred percent.

"You know, back in that sub, I wouldn't admit my ultimate achievement to my captain, for fear he would find cause to send me topside for madness, but finally I had to reveal the secret of my sharp ears. The humpback whales were my ears. They offered, I accepted. I only had to sing to them and they would do the rest. If I aimed my song true to them, the humpbacks' songs sent me the location of every German sub in a three-hundred-mile radius. The only use I had for that sonar panel in that sub without portholes was to assist me in aiming my song true to my new friends.

"And so, when no other sonar engineer could pinpoint those enemy subs but me, I had to come clean, or they would have shot me for having information I had no business knowing, like I was a German double agent or something. I had to explain it, so I recommended that sonar engineers be animal lovers and professional musicians. Artists, you know, real artists, or people like yourself who know how to talk to the cows and the planets. Believe me, when the Pentagon wants something badly enough, they will even listen to a kooky old redskin like me, if that's what it takes."

That night, Matt and Yazzie told Dawes the truth. And within weeks MPII (Manhattan Project II) was launched.

CHAPTER FOURTEEN

Johnny

Johnny pushed his trumpet to a high C-sharp and let it lay there until Raygoth and Lenx pulled into unison. Then he took a deep breath and reached for the F-sharp—right on the nose, yeah. The club went wild. He held his note, reverberating and vibrating in every cell of his being, in every cell of every listener, and his fellow players. The club on this planetoid rest stop was packed from floor to ceiling with sentient species from the local star systems and several groups of long-distance travelers from planets and systems he had never heard of.

He glanced at Raygoth and Lenx, poised at their instruments, took another long breath, and brought the fusion tones of empath energy jazz into its fiery climax, and closed the set. The crowd roared, and clacked and stomped and slapped their tails. "Thank you, Thank you," Johnny empathed and shouted. "Yeah. Thank you. Let's hear it for Lenx on Imari cymber horn, Raygoth on Pomdos reeds, Rico on Empath Booster Console." He was desperately out of breath, but he could at least get out the credits. "And yours truly on earthling trumpet. Yeah!"

The crowd was demanding another encore, but jeez, everyone was spent, totally spent. Already drawing on the last vestiges of tonight's energy, Lenx peeled and unwrapped his cymber horn from his long Imari torso and shoulders, delicately lifting each layer of pipe and setting them carefully on his mat. And Raygoth was already in her usual Pomdos semi-trance. "Thank you," Johnny shouted out loud and empathed through the relentless ovation, with the last ounce of energy he could muster. "Come back tomorrow night. I'm sorry. We're quite done in now."

It was a great set. One of the best since he and his friends had formed the band several months earlier and had started touring the Galern System and the nearby intergalactic travelers rest stops. Now people traveled to rest stops just to hear the combo. Word traveled, it seemed exponentially since they had started their tour. Pomdos and Imari making music together, a first—along with an all-new species and an all-new sound. Not to be missed. There had even been complaints that people were booking flights between systems just to visit the rest stops where the band was headlined, crowding out others who truly used the rest stops for long-distance intergalactic traveling.

If the guys back home on Earth could hear him now. See this scene; experience this fusion jazz. "No, man," he would say, "it's not what you think. Not like what you think of as 'fusion.' This is way out; I mean way, way out, man. It's 'fusion' with empath energy. Yeah. Like a blend of ecstatic mind/body sensations you couldn't even dream up in your wildest sexual fantasies." He could see Jim's eyes opening wide. "Give us a taste of it, will you Johnny? Just one hit," he would say. One day Johnny would be able to bring them all in on this, not yet, but in his lifetime. That's what Old Gir had said. In his very own lifetime, he'd be able to share fusion empath jazz with anybody he pleased. Just be patient. In the meantime: "Go out there with your new sound and show the galaxies that Imari and Pomdos can make wonderful music together," Gir had said. "We'll call you when the Mission requires your return to Earth. Don't you worry."

The crowd was beginning to disperse. Clusters of sentients, moving, flying, hovering slowly toward the exits: some sapient like; others resembling Earth's brown bears, except bigger; and equine-like adolescents, clattering and braying with unfettered enthusiasm.

Then there were Johnny's favorite, a cluster of three water tanks in one corner of the club, with perhaps a half dozen dolphin-like people, clicking and nodding to each other and now empathing loudly to him to join them for a quick swim before they hover-transported their tanks back to their ship. If only he could. He was loath to give up this opportunity, especially since one of the group, Merla Colum, was a galaxy-renowned lyricist. "Not tonight, I'm sorry," he empathed. "Is tomorrow afternoon alright? As you know, we're all really, really spent." Yeah, they already know, yeah, tomorrow would be fine. And one by one, the tanks lifted gently into the air and glided out with the rest.

Then there were the Pomdos, more panda-like, sluggish but brilliantly enmeshed with every note of the set, their eyes fixated on Raygoth, watching every move she made, monitoring her eye and empath contact with this little earthling twerp and with the hated Imari. One Pomdos female had been to every single concert since they had started the tour. Everyone in the band thought she was a dedicated groupie, testimony to how successful their fusion combo was in bridging the gap and soothing over animosities.

As in previous concerts, he would suddenly feel this vague tug from out in the audience that endeavored to un-fuse the harmonies, and he would have to struggle to keep the blend going. This time, he had vowed to locate the source. He had his suspicions, of course, but until now, he hadn't had the energy to compartmentalize his mind so one chamber could focus on keeping the harmonies blended in spite of the interference, and another chamber could root out the source. Raygoth had insisted his suspicions had been groundless. Pomdos don't do spying, she assured him. "They're not paranoid enough. And certainly they wouldn't spy on their own kind, even if I do hang with two Imaris and an earthling recruit." But Johnny knew about this stuff. He had experience. When he was five, white Chicago cops smashed through his apartment door and gunned down his parents right before his eyes in a trumped up drug raid. Finally, after a million foster homes, his real Uncle Wally took him in. Then the same racist thugs went and killed his new real Dad, right under the El. That's when Gir pulled him the from their clutches. Since then, every time he visited Earth, he suddenly had to watch his back again. Now in the midst of intergalactic peace and harmony, here it was again. Always the target. Although his efforts to figure out this so-called "groupie" during the gig thoroughly exhausted him, he decided not to break the mood by discussing his proof tonight. Raygoth would get furious, and he wanted to continue the long spate of good feelings they were all experiencing with each other. There'd be plenty of time on the jump to the next gig. And he'd look for that same creepy Pomdos, for sure, when got there.

By the time Johnny had packed his trumpet, Raygoth was out of her Pomdos trance and crunching a bamboo stalk. Lenx was almost finished wrapping his delicate set of Imari reeds in their hermetically sealed cloth pouches. "Your room or mine?" he empathed to Johnny.

"Not yet. You're all recovered, but I still need a little time after a set like this." He also wanted Raygoth and the two Imari musicians to spend more time together outside of rehearsals and gigs. Especially since he had to broach this new discovery about the sabotaging Pomdos in the audience. "Always the diplomat, sweetness," Lenx empathed. "But let's not use up our whole evening on diplomacy, especially after a set like that." He enveloped Johnny in his strong, gentle arms and nibbled at his ear: "That was really swell playing. You have the sexiest sound in the universe."

"Not so bad yourself."

Johnny was no slouch. Six-foot-two and built like a football player, with a solid pair of lungs that filled his broad muscular chest. When he visited Earth over the years, he would turn the jazz scene upside-down. Dizzy proclaimed that he played the meanest and most melodic horn in Chicago's North Ward and on Bourbon Street. Then he would mysteriously disappear, leaving the music world and the ladies who wanted him for their own completely in the lurch. Well, Lenx had him for his very own, and he wasn't about to disappear on him. No way! Even if he did have to visit Earth every once and a while, just to keep his Mission perspective alive, and reconnect with his jazz buddies there. In spite of having to endure separate bathrooms and drinking fountains. But his next visit to Earth wasn't scheduled for another three Earth years. Maybe by then he could bring Lenx with him. It would be more tolerable with him there. Maybe things had changed since last time. They would take Easy Street by storm. He brought his lips to his. Yeah!

"Hey you guys." Rico's empath filtered gently. "You coming or what?"

When the foursome finally emerged from the club into the open air, the huge cobblestoned plaza was still teeming with people, clustered at kiosks, squatting or sitting at various spots among the central fountain or gathered in the small splotches of colorful gardens, gently suffused with soft hover-glows.

Johnny still felt like an oddity among the multitude of species ambling and hovering and squatting in the plaza. Even though most of the Imari were as dark as he, and in features not noticeably different, they carried themselves with a strong sense of peace, a beatitude he still wasn't used to, and he was sure, no, he knew, everyone, every species, read his tension, his preoccupations, his assumptions that he would be forever treated with disdain, or worse with disingenuous civility or solicitous over-friendliness, like on his homeworld among the pale people. Not to mention, it had taken him months to trust leaving his trumpet, indeed all their band equipment behind at an unknown club with no security system or at an open amphitheater, unlocked, and unguarded.

He sucked in the fresh, rich air and found his energies returning, Lenx's strong Imari arm was wrapped around his shoulder and Raygoth and Rico were ambling ahead of them sorting out the clusters and kiosks, determined to find those honeyed root cakes the rest stop was famous for and that new bot/cranberry juice cocktail everyone was raving about. Their exuberance and their renewed, always renewed, spurts of energy were contagious. "C'mon, you guys," Raygoth empathed to the dawdling lovers. "We found a great spot." Lenx squeezed Johnny's shoulders. "I don't know how you did it, but I'm actually beginning to love that crazy Pomdos, even when we're not jamming. But don't you go and tell her."

"You underestimate their empath powers."

"I know how to keep them off my private channel. Now, you better keep my secret too, you hear me? Now where did those two run off to?"

When Lenx and Johnny found Rico and Raygoth, they were already setting up the tumblers and dipping sauces. "They ran out of bot/cranberry for the evening," Raygoth said, pouring out a deep red mixture into the goblet, "so I took barcoberry instead. It's almost the same."

"At least not every little thing in the universe is permanently perfect," said Johnny, accepting Raygoth's offer to break the froth.

"To fusion empath jazz!" Raygoth empathed.

"To Imari and Pomdos friendship," chimed in Rico.

"I'm beginning to really love you guys even though you're Imari and," Raygoth giggled, nodding at Johnny, "you're a paranoid Scout recruit."

"Well, you're in deep trouble now," Johnny teased. "Better make sure that Pomdos spy doesn't see you breaking the froth with these Imari rascals. Now you surely noticed her this time, didn't you? Didn't you at least feel her, sense her interference? Surely you picked up her dissonant pull?" Johnny broached the subject in spite of himself. It's too difficult to keep things from empath buddies. They would ultimately pick it up anyway. "It's real bad, Raygoth. She knows how much all four of us dig each other too. And she's not happy about it at all. I'm sure of that. She was just to your right in the second tier of mats."

"Cut it out, Johnny," empathed Raygoth. "She's just a really devoted fan, that's all. You do suffer from deep Imari-inspired paranoia."

Laughter. Johnny closed his eyes and rolled the sequential tastes of bot around his tongue. He didn't want to engage. He shielded his discomfort and listened vaguely to the empathed and out-loud banter of his comrades. Something about their next gig. Rico was always sending ahead to the next group of bookings, making detailed arrangements, checking atmospheric conditions, travel times, audience development.

No, something else was demanding his attention in his right temple. A familiar and yet slightly unfamiliar wavering line coalescing into a sharp bright yellow dot in the very front of his mind's eye. Couldn't be his mentor. Gir was scouting off-galaxy somewhere, and not due back for several months—no another equally powerful Imari, a Level VI at least, fully shielded yet probing, so deftly he couldn't even raise a weak shield in defense, especially after such a concert.

"Don't fight it, Johnny, please," the dot empathed. "Oh shit," he thought. "It's too soon. Not for another three years." He opened his eyes. Two Imari stood very still several centimeters from their mats. The tall lean Imari, of regal continence and high sculptured cheekbones, wore the travel hood of the Imari Scouts and a long flowing wishaptha with the traditional overlapping Galern patterns of reds, blues and yellows. The other Imari was a shorter, less imposing woman similarly adorned. "May we join you?" the taller one said out loud. Lenx stiffened and pulled his arm tighter around Johnny's shoulder. They were not bringing good news.

"Of course, in unfettered spirit," said Rico, automatically switching to the ancient greeting reserved for traditional bot sharing with revered elders. He refreshed the goblet as the two Imari newcomers squatted between him and Raygoth and opposite Johnny and Lenx. The smaller Imari bowed her hooded head in silent thanks, accepted the goblet and took a small ceremonial sip. She passed it to the taller one, who also took a ceremonial sip and passed it along.

"My name is Telmx, and this is Winstx," the taller Imari started out loud. Johnny read her disquietude, but could not decipher its content. "Please do not fret, Johnny. Your mentor, Gir, is fine. I do not come with bad news of that sort."

"But you come with bad news," Johnny said. "I have to leave my friends, don't I?" Burnt briny rage and loss filled his nostrils, like when the stupid white social worker told him she had found a "nice" place for him to live, and that he couldn't even say goodbye to his murdered parents that were surely alive, if only he could go hug them and make them sit up and hug him back.

"I'm sorry," Telmx empathed to the other members of the band, but especially to Lenx, who now held Johnny in a stronger grip, tears trickling down his cheeks. "We're truly sorry to take Johnny from you so suddenly. We didn't plan for things to happen on Earth this quickly. Our faulty foresight in this matter is in itself quite troubling." To Johnny: "We need you right away, the Mission needs you right away. An emergency. We are taking you to meet Gir, who's speeding back to Galern II to be there by the time we arrive. Then you and he will set course for Europa, in the Earth's solar system." She paused with obvious pain. "We must, I'm afraid, leave immediately, without a moment's delay."

"What could be such an emergency that it can't wait until we're at least finished with this booking?" Raygoth was also crying, large globules matting her black and white fur. "You waited this long. Why not another few days, another few hours?" Johnny read Raygoth's pain coalescing into rage. "You Imari empath scouts are all alike." Her voice rose several octaves and echoed across the plaza. "Your words are law. Everyone's gotta jump when you dredge up your 'emergencies'!"

"Raygoth, please. Let me figure this out with Telmx. Perhaps there's a way...."

"Always raising alarms." Raygoth was shouting. "Always suspicious of new species. Nobody, nowhere ever plots against anything, yet you forge on making all your insane paranoid predictions, depleting our energies, our pleasures. You even got Johnny here hallucinating spies everywhere he goes. Pomdos spies no less. Imagine! The most un-paranoid species in the universe. I won't let you break up our group. Not this time!"

"Please, Raygoth," Johnny empathed. The plaza was suddenly quieter, people trying to look as if nothing was happening, but terribly cognizant of the familiar conflict between Pomdos and Imari, the very disease his little band was starting to heal. Pomdos and Imari in fusion empath jazz, music and camaraderie? Unheard of in the galaxies!

"Cut it, Johnny!" pleaded the Pomdos. "Why do you Imari Scouts always have to ruin our good times?" Her voice was fading, her eyes slowly closing, the inevitable Pomdos response to disturbing news.

Johnny looked at Lenx. His lover was extremely quiet, shielded up tight, his lips set straight in a line. Lenx was well disciplined. He knew what had to be. It didn't make things easier.

Johnny felt a sudden emptiness, the familiar emptiness of the foster child losing his sense of self-worth to a so-called higher order of things that made no sense. "I must have my trumpet," he said softly to Telmx, like he had said to each and every social worker who, for the umpteenth time was pushing his belongings into a bunch of shopping bags, he and his shopping bags destined for yet another unknown family that always smelled so different from his home it would make him puke and pee in his pants for weeks and weeks. At least he knew the homeworld he would be traveling to this time round, sort of. "I really need to get my trumpet," he said again, just like his seven-year-old self. Telmx and Winstx were just like those social service pimps. They would never understand, never believe that a black orphan would cry for his mom and dad, and have a passionate talent or a possession in the world worth cherishing. In that foul-smelling world Johnny couldn't control, his trumpet was his only refuge, the only thing he could truly trust and control.

"We have your trumpet and your traveling sac. We must hurry," empathed Telmx. Her urgency and compassion enveloped his temples and made him feel safe in his pain. "The next empath boosting surge is in less than an hour. We need to be there in time to catch it."

"I gotta get away from here now before I lose it!" Lenx suddenly stood up, wheeled around, and walked briskly off through the plaza.

"Wait Lenx!" yelled Johnny, still his seven-year-old self. "Don't just fuckin' split! We'll figure it all out. Maybe you could come with me! Wait!"

He leaped after him, charging around the clusters of people and kiosks. He caught up with him at the edge of the plaza, leaning against one of the huge teraforming pillars that encircled the center of the planetoid. He was wheezing and coughing. "Don't make it harder," Lenx managed. "Just leave. I knew it would have to end. Take your precious trumpet and the blasted Mission and leave."

"I didn't think it would be this soon. No one thought, I mean, certainly Gir didn't have a clue. I bet it's a big mistake, a big miscalculation. It'll all be straightened out when I meet Gir. I'll talk to him about letting you join us. You'll see. I'll be right back here to get you. And if I can't bring you with me, just keep going with the band. For everyone's sake. Please. I'll meet you at the next gig, the very next gig. You'll all be playing along, and all of a sudden you'll hear this horn solo, in f sharp, you'll see, in f sharp minor and there I'll be taking it down, trading fours, just like it never stopped, I'll be back in no time. You'll see. I promise." He could vaguely read Telmx's pain resonating with Lenx's across the plaza. He knew that Winstx, Rico and Raygoth in her semi-trance were resonating with him too.

"He'll be back within a year, we think," empathed Telmx across the plaza. "I don't think he can take you with him. I'm truly sorry. It's of great concern to our Imari team that we did not anticipate the emergency. I'm not able to say when he'll be back for sure."

"Or *if* he'll come back at all! Spare me nothing. He's not coming back at all, is he?"

"Unless we have lost more ground than we think, our scans assure us he will be back, my dear. We just don't know exactly when. Come, Johnny. I know this is very hard on both of you, but we must hurry." Telmx empathed.

Gir misled him. No, no, they miscalculated. It was too soon. Not predicted. He needed more time! They made it an emergency. He must be strong now. It's not as if he didn't know he would be called away from his bliss at some point. That was his commitment to the Mission. His advanced technical training. But look at what his band was doing! It was becoming an incredible force, building trust between the Pomdos and the Imari. Like Dizzy on Earth, he was a musical ambassador. He pulled Lenx to him, empath-whispering assurances. But there were no assurances. The Mission was dangerous. There were no guarantees he would return, or if he did, that he would return very soon. They kissed long and slow. And wept. He had to accept his commitment to the Mission. He couldn't back out.

The clusters of species were almost silent now, as Johnny and the two Imari traveler scouts made their way back past the fountain and gardens to the other side of the plaza. He felt self-conscious, like a local hero leaving for the front in some crucial global war. Nah, he was no hero. He was angry and grieving. Well, it was a war, of sorts, yeah, well better than going to Nam. At least the war he was about to fight was for a cause worth fighting for. He would still get to teach fusion empath jazz to the guys in Chicago, some day. That was Gir's promise, if the Mission is carried out right, if he keeps his focus. If only Lenx could go with him, if only he could have his arms around him, if only what? If only he wasn't an earthling, the very species who posed a huge threat to the amazing serenity he was enjoying!

Okay, okay, it's only a goddamn detour on a large, fabulous tour. "I know I can't bring Lenx with me" he empathed to Gir, wherever he was. "I'll even forgive you for that too. I can handle it."

"I know you can," empathed Telmx, as they boarded a hovercraft at the edge of the Plaza. Winstx closed her eyes and sent a narrow blue beam from her cilia to the shimmering console, and the craft lifted silently, veered to the right, and carried the trio toward the intergalactic port far on the other side of the planetoid rest stop.

CHAPTER FIFTEEN

J

J snuggled into a corner at Figaro's and tried to concentrate on *Ulysses*. Everyone was reading it. You couldn't be caught in a village café without poring over it, or mixing a passage from it into everyday conversation, like you had read it from cover to cover, studied it, analyzed it several times over. So finally she had given in, might as well know what this *Ulysses* is all about. But she couldn't get past the first page.

The hazy mixture of pot and caffeine in the air didn't help at all, especially to her overly sensitized brain. Extremely dangerous for an empath. Contact high in two seconds. She fought it. She was used to fighting it.

What if everyone was just pretending to understand the book!

"Here we are, J!" Katie slid in next to her. J read her giddy pride even before she introduced Joe, the only topic of conversation for the last three days.

"Hi guys."

"Joe, this is J, my bestest friend ever." Joe squeezed in next to Katie. He was just as she had visualized, just as Katie had described him "An Adonis, you'll see, like a true Greek statue, and wow, does he live up to it!" Adonis was a ruddy tan, with full boyish, almost girlish lips, and long golden hair, combed down over his forehead, Harvard style. Even sitting down, he towered above the women, but he cast his head forward in a measured contemplative fashion that, in fact, shortened his stature. He held out his hand and cast her a quick nod.

"So you're J. Katie has talked so much about you, we hardly need introduction."

J read fiery political energy and knowledge. But she didn't have to delve inside to discern his sizing-her-up gaze, and the ever so slight disdain, his dismissive feelings about capable women. What contradictions. She wondered if Katie had figured this out yet. If she had, she hadn't let on. She would search her friend's mind later. Just a tiny bit. "Hi," she said, trying not to react to his hand squeezing hers just a bit too forcefully. At least she chooses them smart and ravishing, but always with the same fatal flaw. "It's the temper of the times," Katie would say. "We just gotta teach guys about that part of the

struggle also. It's a process, J. Don't be so hard on them. They're half the population. Besides, shacking up with men who are just a wee bit macho is a real
turn-on." When would she ever learn?

Joe glanced at *Ulysses* and slightly curled his mouth. "Did you know we're
at war?" He wastes no time, J thought. Which one? Desert Storm, Korea,
Vietnam, Sarajevo, Somalia? Panama? Chile? Indonesia? Iraq?

"Joe's roommate's gonna burn his draft card at the demo this afternoon.
Wanna come?"

J was drawn to Katie's energy, how it intensified exponentially when she
was with her comrades at the demos, and to the powerful understanding
between the determined young people in the street. Familiar. A precursor.
But the demos also hurt her head big time: all the conflicting issues, agendas,
and knowing what the cops were going to do before the marchers knew. Of
all the situations, demos were almost impossible. She had to fight with herself
all the time so she wouldn't give herself away. Look at what happened at the
last demo: Katie chanting right next to a real gorgeous girl with all the right
slogans, beads and peace buttons. That ravishing peacenik was undercover,
and she had risked exposing her true nature, her empath self, by pointing the
agent out to Katie. No wonder a headache was already brewing.

"Sure."

"J can smell agents a mile away, Joe. You'll see. It's like she's got a sixth
sense or something, you know, ESP."

＊ ＊ ＊

J raced past a herd of restless brown horses and a phalanx of shiny blue
helmets and night sticks toward the Recruitment Center, on its own island of
concrete in the middle of Times Square. The familiar "Hey, Hey LBJ" echoed
above the din of rush-hour traffic. Something special was going to happen.
J knew it like she always knew things. She wanted to run in the other direction, but Katie would be furious.

"Something's very, very wrong here," she yelled above the din to Katie.

"Don't worry, babe. This is the best! Look at all the pigs we brought out.
C'mon!"

She gripped her *Ulysses* tighter, wishing she had forgotten it in the cafe.

Joe and Katie were rushing just ahead of her now, their heads pitched forward, excited by the excitement.

The Recruitment Center itself was completely ringed by wooden barricades and wooden-at-attention cops. The static in the air was deafening to
her empath ear: waves of putrid pounding from her temples to her jaw. J
hadn't felt so frenetic and debilitated since she was a child. Something was
very, very wrong here.

Then they were in the middle of the chants and someone shoved a placard into her free hand. Too much disorganization, she thought. Who's in charge? She fought the static to sort out a leader. "Who's in charge? Who called the demo?" She turned around to Katie, but she was gone. Why all that static in her head? Worse. Beyond impossible. Perhaps she should shield up. No, she had to stay completely in tune, come what may.

The crowd pressed closer, and somehow she found herself at the front-line, face to face with a badge without a nameplate. She struggled to protect herself from his paranoid, vicious thoughts, powerful stabs from the past, but his terror and contempt, and his raging case against his fiancé were inexplicably stronger than her capacity to focus.

The whiney thin voice of a bullhorn wafted into the mix. "You are hereby advised to disperse."

Someone yelled, "No! We're staying! We're not moving! Hell, no! We won't go!" People all around her were sitting. As she crouched at the boots of her helmeted guard, she felt his mind stiffen, and his knuckles harden around his billy club. "Sit down!" she joined the chant. "Hell No! We won't go! Sit down!" For a moment she saw Katie in her mind, arguing furiously with Jimmy. But the static was too strong. Her temples were pounding. If she stayed right there, next to this goon's boots, she would be his first arrest ever, and if he panicked.... Maybe she could empath some sense into his skull. No, stop being an asshole. No empath mind-bending.

Then a voice amplified louder than the others. Someone specific was yelling into her head. Not in her ears, in her head. But not like a hallucination. More like right before Telmx would visit and she could hear her coming, a few hours away—maybe at the edge of the solar system on her way in. She would hear her singing or teasing her: "I told you I wouldn't be long. See? It's only a few more of your Earth hours. J, I know you can hear me. Please, my dearest, please let me in. Please answer me." But J would not answer, would wait, as if Telmx's voice were just a hallucination, as if everything up to that moment had been a wonderful psychotic fantasy that she just didn't want to reality test. She would wait and wait.

Telmx would become frantic: "J! I am not just in your imagination!. Stop fighting it!" J would then open her mind and struggle to perform all the long-range empath techniques Telmx had taught her, not believing they would really work. If she strained too hard, they didn't work. She had to overcome frantic: trust deep breathing and calm repose. Then empath would take over. Then they'd have a real conversation, and they knew they'd be in some kind of sublimity together in just a few hours.

J, squatting by these Gestapo boots in the street, perceived that particular almost echo sensation of empath, a strong and husky empath, not like Telmx's, but similar, the way a phone voice is similar to another phone voice but you know it's a different person. A clear empath voice was insisting, "No! Don't sit down! Get everyone up. Hurry! Not the right time to get busted! There are provocateurs here! Don't listen to them!"

Yeah, it's not the time to get busted, she thought. Too soon: for me, for the movement. But Katie would be furious if she finked out now. "Seize the momentum. There's never a perfect time," Katie always insisted. But no! There was Katie yelling into her megaphone, urging people to stand up and march, as if she had heard the empath voice too! But no one was listening! The din was overpowering. No one was listening! Gestapo boots shifted weight and clutched his Billy club even harder. This was about to get really, really messy.

"Absolutely not the right time to deal with legal shit," the empath voice coalesced into her right temple, loud, emphatic. "There's not enough support! Let's not tie up the movement with legal shit! Not yet!" Some force had joined Katie's warning, amplifying it and simultaneously empath-pushing the whole crowd, the entire demo. Actually empath-pushing! Without thinking about how Telmx had absolutely forbidden her to, J joined in the empath-push.

"Get up!" J yelled and empathed simultaneously, her sudden out-loud voice amplifying her empath. "Everyone up! Let's just march!" It was as if she were her own microphone and PA system. The Gestapo boots moved this way and that, both tense and relieved. People around her were already standing. Others were shouting to get up. Someone shouted, "To the UN!" The crowd abruptly propelled her through a sudden opening in the barricades.

As the crowd surged forward, J empathed to the empath voice, "Who are you, where are you?" In her mind's eye she saw Katie and her comrades urging the crowd forward into a march to the UN. Jimmy was negotiating with an officer whose bronze metals declared him clearly in charge of his brigades. J persisted in her head, "Hey, who are you? Where are you?"

Now the static in her head vied with the calmly urging empath voice wafting in and out of her temples along with the shouting: "Hey, Hey, LBJ!"

"I knew it! All these years, thinking I was the only one," a voice said out loud, and then suddenly a woman, not much taller than herself was in step beside her in the street. "All these years, and then they said, 'Go find her. She's somewhere in New York City.' And here you are, just like they said. Wow! There *is* someone like me, another earthling empath monitor!"

Was the figure real? A hologram? The boyish bounce, the breathlessness from running, a slight brogue. Irish? Or Scottish?

"Who are you?" J empathed. She was suddenly frightened. Perhaps this was a trick. An intergalactic traveler Imari-Gone-Bad (the newest threat to the Council). Maybe a shape-shifter. She started to shield.

"It's not a trick. It's for real," came straight into J's mind, cleanly cutting through her shielding, and the deafening static. "Holy Moley! There's finally two of us! I can't believe it! There're actually two of us! My name is Scotty."

J already knew her name. Always had. She had roamed a secret part of her brain so often, never lingering, and strangely fearful of what she would discover. And now Scotty, a real person, had entered or erupted from that place, beckoning her to join her in real time, arms outstretched like an old friend. As they stopped in the street and faced each other, J empathed, "I know you." Those deep piercing blue eyes, tousled auburn hair, the slightly freckled high cheekbones were all too familiar. Even with the chanting crowd sweeping around them, J let go of her uneasy and moved into Scotty's warm exuberance.

Scotty empathed through the static, "I just knew I would run into something life-changing today. It had to be! I've been searching for you without knowing you since I got to New York. I woke up this morning and just knew I had to join this demo!"

"You're a human, aren't you?" J empathed back. Of course she was. An earthling empath monitor, an extraordinary empath monitor. Right here in New York City, empath mind-bending without even a nanosecond of hesitation. How could she have assumed she was the only empath recruit on the planet? Why didn't Telmx tell her there was another? Perhaps she had in that remote secret corner of her mind. Of course, Telmx had told her. "But you.... Oh wow, of course. You've been to Galern II. Who do you know?"

Suddenly a bolt of static surged into her neck and scalded her shoulders, abruptly crashing their connection.

"Shit!" shouted Scotty out loud. "You felt that too, didn't you? Something's very wrong here. I smelled it when I approached the barricades. It's not safe here. We're too vulnerable. Can you shield?" The two women stood perfectly still, eyes meeting eyes, while the stream of demonstrators roared by.

"That's the strongest jolt I've ever felt. I got a whopper headache," J said out loud. She was dizzy and nauseous.

"Me too. Let's shield up high and cool it on empath, just in case." Scotty also spoke out loud. "Something really, really shitty's going down."

"What do you mean?" J felt the other's strength and wisdom penetrating her, like a power she had only felt with Telmx. She also smelled their mutual dread.

"I don't know what I mean. Something's really spooky, and I think it has to do with us empaths. Listen, it's making us sick. C'mon, pull your shield way up to max!" Scotty urged. "You do know how, don't you? Yeah, I know you do."

J groped for energy to raise her empath shield. The jolt had sapped her strength beyond belief. The street wobbled.

She felt Scotty enter her temples. "Let me pull your shielding up to max, just to be on the safe side." Scotty's soothing presence inside J's head abruptly receded into a faint echo. J suddenly felt confused and alone. "Wait," said Scotty. "Don't get nuts about it. I'm going to explain. Just let me modulate your shielding for another second."

As Scotty closed her eyes, J involuntarily closed hers too. It was as if someone turned down the volume in her head, way down, leaving vast eerie silence after years of humming, like when the refrigerator suddenly stops and you suddenly realize it's been droning all that time.

"There! I raised both our shields to max," Scotty's out-loud yell above the din pulled J's eyes open and J realized that without the enhancement of empath she had to read her lips to catch her words, even though she was shouting. "Where'd you learn that?" she could hardly push out her words. Though the static fell away, and the street steadied, her headache increased exponentially.

"I'll show you how later. I just wanted to say what I think without being overheard by another empath entity, just in case," Scotty grabbed her arm. "I bet two earthling empath monitors have never been in such close proximity before. We must create a very vulnerable field when we empath to each other. We gotta go," she yelled. "It's bad news for us around here."

J knew she was right, even though Scotty's words made no logical sense. Her migraine was stronger than ever, jagged blue and yellow flashes behind her eye. She let Scotty pull her out of the street, steering them toward the library lions, where she hailed a cab.

"163rd and Amsterdam," Scotty directed the cabdriver. "We'll go to your place. Is that okay? I'm staying at the Y until I can find some digs."

"I know, I mean, sure." If only Scotty would grab her arm again and never let go! Or she could grab hers, like protector and protected.

The cab lurched forward. She leaned back, closed her eyes, and pressed her fingers against her temples, desperate to quell the vicious throbbing pain and lightning assaulting the top of her head, temples and ears, and shooting down her shoulders to her fingertips. The din of chants gave way to the din of relentless traffic.

"I betcha our headaches cease and desist in a couple of more blocks," yelled Scotty over frenzied, disgruntled horns. "Golly, this city is loud. Don't need no stupid empath scanners to give a girl a big fat migraine."

"Empath scanners?" Headaches at demos were about being at demos and struggling not to give herself away. Katie often leaned on her so-called ESP, like when she fingered that provocateur. Warning her friends without revealing her empath powers. Who wouldn't get headaches?

"Kind of empath divining rods, searching for empath energy."

"To harness our powers?"

"To nab us." Scotty's empath voice entered J's right temple. Empath again. "See? We don't need the shielding anymore. Headache's almost gone. I told you they were concentrating on the demo."

"They? Who? What's happening? How do you know?"

"I don't know. I am only just figuring it out. I mean, we know that there are scanners, but I'll tell you all that later." She turned to face J and giggled mischievously. "I bet you have bot, don't you."

"And dipping sauces," J cut herself off with a laugh. Of course, Scotty already knew about that!

Empath communication with an earthling! No barriers. How her friends carried on about her so-called "ESP." J had to shut them out from so much. Even Katie, for the sake of the Mission. To be so close to people and yet so distant. Although profoundly lonely, J always felt a little safe and special in her empath differences. Now Scotty just pops up out of nowhere, maybe only for a little while. Her too-precious specialness suddenly wasn't so special in the presence of this possible true, no-barriers friend.

"Don't worry, I'm not going anywhere," Scotty empathed. "It's been super hard on me too. I really appreciated the empath cultures in the last three years. The closest friends I ever had were my roommates at the Jioram Intergalactic University. I can't wait to tell you about it. So, you know, coming back to Earth, with all our secrets, especially to this loud, primitive city is like landing on yet another planet. Besides, I'm a small town kid, you know."

J flushed with excitement. When they arrived at her apartment, she'd fix her living room up for Scotty just like she always did for Telmx, whose next visit was long overdue. Scotty would really love an authentic Imari meal. Sharing bot with an earthling! How incredible! She couldn't wait.

"You have authentic Imari goblets, and the actual tapestries! I can't believe it! How did you get them past regulations?" Scotty could survey her apartment from twenty blocks away! A true empath! A true earthling empath!

"Long story. I have to hang them up for you. They're all hidden, you know. I just set it all up when I'm completely alone. Or when Telmx, my mentor, comes in for a visit."

"Holy shit! I shoulda known. Telmx is your mentor. Of course! Mine is Winstx. Do you know her? Of course you know her. And Gir too! We'll talk.

I gotta find out everything! So much to talk about. Oh golly, Vintage bot, like on Galern II. We'll talk forever! I couldn't take anything with me when I returned. You thought restrictions were heavy. You should see them now! Not even a tiny hubnut. I'll tell you about it. Wow! Can you auto-effuse? I can, you know. I learned at the university. I can show you."

Tears saturated Scotty's flushed cheeks, and J realized she was weeping as well. Mostly J felt relief, after almost two decades of intricate and ludicrous double-think with earthlings, not to mention her nightmares. She wished Scotty would touch her arm again. Of course, she could take a chance and....

Scotty grabbed her arm. "No secrets," she commanded. "No need for coy." J flushed again. Scotty was intense, the way her head bobbed up and down, punctuating every empathed and out-loud statement, how she tossed her short auburn hair this way and that with her hand, how her mouth formed a kind of pursed ooh when she took a breath between sentences. She loved that Scotty hovered at the tip of her emotions, holding nothing back, not uptight and controlled like J, more like Telmx after several droughts of bot. As with Telmx, her shield was stronger, and she couldn't read Scotty the way Scotty was reading her. Okay to have unbalanced shielding with an Imari, but so peculiar to be empath weaker than another earthling.

The cab turned onto J's block.

"I'll try not to be so intrusive, J. I'm so used to purely empath folks now. But isn't this incredible? We have so much to talk about." Now they were crying and laughing. By the time they reached J's house, their headaches were completely gone.

✳ ✳ ✳

"I don't want you to do a thing," J said to Scotty, as they stepped into her living room from the dark tenement hallway. Thinly woven, somewhat faded lavender burlap covered the windows. They cast a soft hazy sunset glow on the several large pots of tall ferns, two rubber tree plants, and several Honduran desert mountain trees that filled most of the room. A multitude of throw pillows covered with madras cloth were casually grouped in one corner next to an intricate Navaho rug, strewn with a small portable typewriter surrounded by spiral notebooks, crumpled papers, oversized college texts and library books with small index cards sticking out of the pages. The rest of the floor was covered with books, magazines, pamphlets, flyers announcing rallies and sit-ins, and piles of New York Times and radical movement newspapers from various political tendencies. Across one wall, gray rough cinderblocks supported a set of planks that rose halfway to the ceiling, also brimming with paperbacks and piles of notebooks. On another plank sat stereo components and several milk crates filled with albums.

"This is really cool," said Scotty. "But first things first," and she raced into the bathroom.

"I just gotta clean up a bit," called J. She wanted her new friend to experience the full Imari effect, like the tranquility of Telmx's cottage on Galern II, even if it were makeshift, the way she did when there was no chance of Katie popping over without notice. "It'll take just ten minutes or so." Her quivering hands betrayed her anxiety, but then again, Scotty could read it anyway.

She pulled her "research" rug, typewriter and all, further into the corner of the room and piled everything she could from the rest of the floor onto the rug. Then she tugged several cartons out from the closet in the bedroom and shoved them into the now emptied center patch of living room. One by one she drew out the richly colored Imari mats and tapestries. When Scotty came back into the room, she was carefully covering her "research" rug with a large finely woven Imari cloth.

"What a fabulous collection! empathed Scotty, placing the reminder of the mats on the floor exactly where J wanted them to be. "I really wish I could have taken some of these with me." Together they completely covered the walls with tapestries. J wanted to surprise her, but completing the transformation with Scotty was even better. She dragged two folding screens from the kitchen, placed them in front of the bookcase and stereo, and draped her two largest Imari cloths delicately over the panels. Scotty rummaged though the cartons, and produced three small translucent balls. "I can't believe you have all this! Authentic hover-glows! Wait, I'll get them going." She placed them exactly in spots that J would have chosen, bent over each one as she went, and deftly auto-effused them to life. Together J and Scotty adjusted the glows to match the mood they wanted to create. They were like a couple of kids in a candy store. Transforming J's living room had never been this much fun.

The third carton concealed a hermetically sealed traveler's chest. They pulled out several bottles of J's vintage bot, and three pouches of powder for dipping sauces. "Holy shit, girl, you even have the proper church key!" She held the tool up to the light of the hover-glow, and ran her thumb over the delicately engraved ancient Imari script on the azure metal lip below the carved wooden knob. "Oh wow! This is an antique! I've never seen anything like it. I can't even decipher the letters. What's it say?"

"I found it in the old town on Galern II. It belonged to a practicing empath elder, who wouldn't let me leave her kiosk without accepting her gift. She said it brings good luck to those who struggle. Roughly translated, it means 'no inner or outer wall is forever.'" Scotty hooked the shimmering device onto the top of the bot flask and deftly popped the waxy orange seal. J caught the mahogany froth in a large porcelain goblet and offered it to Scotty. If only her hands would stop shaking.

"One sip of this stuff will stay your trembling hands," empathed Scotty, beckoning her to break the froth.

J savored the familiar sequential bursts of tastes and the reverberating af-ter-tastes and handed the goblet to her new friend. "We'll have to do with some desperately unworthy substitutes for crisps and pickled roots: I'm afraid it's onion matzo and daikon," J empathed. "But first I need to heat the dipping sauces." They should have waited to open the bot, by all traditional standards, but Scotty was right, she could feel the bot simultaneously enter-ing the anxiety zone of her mind and wending its way to her fingers.

Scotty accepted the goblet from J and took a healthy swallow. "Wait one second, J. You're not going to heat that precious powder over the goddamn stove? Give it here. I'll suffuse the sauces. Where's that fabulous assemblage of Imari ceramics?"

Now they were squatting on J's favorite Imari mat. In the gentle blue-green radiance of the hover-glows, the large ferns cast soft shadows on the multi-colored tapestries and quilts. J handed her a shallow ceramic bowl intricately glazed with red, yellow and black shapes similar to those on the tapestries. Scotty placed the bowl on the mat in front of her and tapped a small amount from each powder pouch into its center. Then she closed her eyes and J fol-lowed the vague blue beam from Scotty's forehead to the bowl. The powder began to steam and swirl, and then rapidly jelled into the familiar magenta dipping sauce. For an instant, she was fifteen again, her first morning on Telmx's homeworld, waking up to the rich aromas of Echinacea and the pun-gent eprira ferns that reached out and caressed the intricate Imari tapestries.

"There!" empathed Scotty, "I can't imagine how it could possibly taste right using that stupid stove. How could you have managed? Just you wait, I'll show you everything!" She held out the swirling dish to J with a flourish of satisfaction.

"Where'd you learn that?"

"I got really sick on the way from Nikehma to a conference and I couldn't travel long inter-stellar distances for three years. And so," Scotty gulped bot gustily and continued. "I entered the Intergalactic University right there on Jioram. What a planet, what a grand experience, let me tell you. I'm on Earth two months and I'm still in culture shock, you know. Anyway, Kimstx, an Imari kid in the dorm, showed me how to develop some eyebrow strands as kind of substitute cilia. See?" She pushed her bangs aside and displayed several vibrating silky filaments. "I can show you how to develop these. It's actually quite easy."

Without realizing it, J leaned in toward Scotty until their heads were almost touching. J's desire burned onto her thighs. Not since Telmx's last visit two years ago had she felt such yearning. "You're a Level VI. You're a mentor, with cilia and everything, aren't you? But I thought an earthling monitor couldn't qualify yet."

"Not a licensed mentor. Sort of a secret maverick one. I matriculated in inter-species anthropology and psychology, and secretly learned all I could from Kimsx. I'm not someone to pass up opportunities." She paused. "You're not that enthralled with our Mission, are you?"

J flushed. Scotty had cut right to the heart of those years of misgivings. For the first time she could talk freely to someone other than Telmx about how she felt. She and Telmx would end up arguing. She loved being different, more powerful than anyone else, kind of a secret Supergirl. Telmx would become very quiet and serious. "You absolutely must stop using your empath powers to keep yourself apart from friends." Telmx would explain that J could be, without contradiction, both close friends with earthlings and an empath monitor, that the Mission was primary, that it didn't have anything to do with secret powers and prestige. And most important, J would lose Telmx and all memory of her if she revealed, even by mistake, her own empath energies and the Mission to anyone. Too much double-think! Too much responsibility! No time to be just a kid, a teen, a young adventurous adult. Didn't Scotty feel burdened and ambivalent?

"I used to," Scotty empathed. "In the last three years I developed much stronger respect for the Mission. It's very complex, but it's also very simple. And dealing with these goddamn migraines just now, really erased my very last shred of doubt about why we were recruited. The Mission *is* upon us. What we've been training for. Something, someone's scanning for us, and not just for Russian missiles and spies. I think they're scanning for us guys right here. That's why I had to come back. The Imari Scouts want us to figure it out and find a way to give them the information without being detected.

"Dodging NORAD on the way back to Earth was super difficult. I came in on an outpost mini-shuttle from Europa, and we were almost detected. Such a drag. They couldn't drop me in the states. We ended up off the coast of Nicaragua. I just jumped out about a mile from the Managua airport and ran, leaving all my luggage behind. They were gone before I could turn around and wave goodbye. At least we made it to Earth without being shot down. And getting back to the states, that was an adventure and a half. I'll tell you about it sometime. After today's close call, I now know it's only a matter of time before they replace NORAD with sophisticated empath scanners. Winnie and her crew suspected that. They couldn't take a chance themselves. The Imari can't come in again, until we do something about the scanners. No more visits right now. Too risky."

"Wait wait, you're going too fast for me. Too much to take in. No more visits?"

"Winnie, Gir and Telmx stayed on Europa to help upgrade the outpost, and to get me to you on Earth. Then they were going off to do some other Scouting somewhere, I don't know where, leaving a team on Europa and me to my own devices. They have too many assignments, I think. Plus they have to negotiate around the Council's restrictions. So much intrigue going on in the Council. You know, the nay-sayers and the threat from factions that want eliminate the Order of Empath Travel Scouts.

"The Council doesn't trust student scouts to do anything past monitoring on any given planet. No mind-bending! Not yet, anyway. Not until things start getting hot, and pose a threat to other planets. Well, earthling scientists are empath scanning, they *are* on the cusp of the Age of Empath before they are ethically ready, just as Telmx predicted. The Imari make good guesses, you know, but their time estimates are off. So things are getting very hot a few years before her predictions."

"Do you think there are more of us earthling monitors? And they just didn't tell us yet? Actually I think Telmx did tell me. It just didn't quite come to the front of my mind until now." J paused. "Actually, I know there are three of us ... do you think? I mean, we gotta find the third one!"

"Dunno. Probably. I think so. Maybe too dangerous. Until they let me come back, they didn't risk allowing earthling empath monitors in close proximity. Maybe it still is. Look what happened to us."

"No. They need us to find each other now, no matter what the risk. We need to find the third and start sending info to Europa."

"Well, we might have to make decisions on our own, third earthling monitor or not. It may be time to move past measly observations, especially if we can't figure out a way to tell the Europa outpost what's going on. It's within our Mission to make a decision like that, even if the Council didn't officially authorize us to intervene without Telmx's triad team telling us to do so. Besides, you're already a talented mind-bender, in spite of all the formal Council rules and regulations.

"We're supposed to empath-send a report to the outpost when we know more. But it's not possible right now, given the extent of scanning going on. It'll be detected for sure. The Europa team will try and send us a device to help. But because of the scanning they didn't even tell me any details, for fear my information would be detected. We'll have to let the device find us! If it can. If they can. Any clues from your monitoring about why they might be scanning for us empaths? You've been doing tons, haven't you?"

"Nothing about anyone developing empath scanning," empathed J. "Not even at Duke, where they're doing all that ESP work. I thought I was on top of it all."

"I'm sure Duke has something to do with it, but I actually think it might have something to do with dolphin and bat research as well."

"I never thought to look at animal research. What makes you think so?"

"They might be searching for creatures, human and otherwise, who possess the empath energy they need to fuel their experiments."

Of course, J thought. How could she be so shortsighted? They're rapidly working toward entering the Age of Empath, so why wouldn't they go after the most empathic animals? How could she be so utterly asinine?

"Hey, cool down, J," empathed Scotty. "You flip like me, jump right to 'jerk-of-the-year' award. Hey," taking J's hand, "I have a fabulous idea." J read it before Scotty could even pour it into empath words. "We'll be a team. You with your research and me with my jury-rigged Level VI stuff. Plus I can teach you everything I know. Let me tell you. I'm really glad we found each other. We need each other to figure these headaches out, find out if they are actually scanning for empath humans. That's what they're up to, I bet. If they find us, I can't imagine. No, I *can* imagine. You've been at it alone, right? Well, here I am, I mean, here we are. It was meant to be. I just know it. Nothing's a stupid coincidence with the Imari. I'm so far-out fucking psyched!"

J hadn't realized how alone she'd been. Scotty's warm hand was reassuring, and tingled with enthusiasm. It sent calm through her quicker, more emphatically than even vintage bot. And giddy, erotic yearning. "I think I'd like that," she offered.

"Hey, you don't have the corner on loneliness, you know," empathed Scotty. She pulled J's hand to her moist cheek. "Check it out, here we are. It's far-out, don't you think?"

As J wondered what it would be like to press their cheeks together, merge their tears, Scotty pulled J's head toward her own and pressed their cheeks together. J tasted their mingled salt and savored the fresh lemongrass aroma of her new friend. New and young. A joyful, tingling mixture of quiver and calm. She turned her head and found Scotty's lips. Simultaneously they wrapped around each other on the mat while the hover-glows, quivering and shimmering, receded silently into the ferns.

"What should we do, Scotty? What do you want? This is going really quick," she empathed. It felt peculiar to desire her so quickly and so fully, as if they shared years of memories and experiences.

"I think we can't avoid the inevitable, can't stand on stupid ceremony; that's what I think," empathed Scotty, and J knew so before she said it.

"Except for Telmx and a trans from R-345 in the G'uw galaxy, I'm quite inexperienced," empathed J. "I mean, I haven't slept with an earthling yet."

"I know. Me neither. Aside from Winstx, my only other lover was my Imari buddy at the university. Also, we don't have to do this, you know."

"I know."

"I'm a tiny bit scared," empathed Scotty.

"I know. Me too."

As the two women undressed each other slowly, tentatively, the hover-glows, nestled in the ferns, modulated into a faint shimmer. Two women in their mid-twenties, already seasoned intergalactic travelers, trembled like adolescent virgins.

CHAPTER SIXTEEN

Telmx

Telmx brushed past the early morning shoppers without a glance, making her way toward her favorite kiosk at the northernmost corner of the plaza, in Grjimbe City, on the planet of the same name. If they didn't have caramel chi today, she didn't know what she would do. She had to have it, the only elixir that would get her juices flowing this morning. She was so out of sorts, couldn't remember when she had been this off. Like a relentless itch. Perhaps an unresolved dream. Something she just had to solve. Warn Goshing about. Someone, or something was foul in her nostrils, in her inner chambers.

It was finally time for the three earthling monitors to find each other and form their cadre. Telmx's triad team had been pained by the earthlings' isolation from each other, but the risk involved in bringing the young monitors together had been too great. Now Earth was accelerating into the Age of Empath more rapidly than they had anticipated, and the recruits were mature enough to forge their own triad team. She hoped.

Because of their primitive cold war, earthling super powers were monitoring their airways with ever more sophisticated radar systems. Scotty and Johnny had to be sent in very discreetly to connect with J. Hopefully they had landed safely, maybe had even located each other by now. Johnny had been trained in empath booster communication technology, and after Gir had guided Johnny to Earth, the Europa team would decode Johnny's communiqués about the status of earthling research and whether further intervention would be required.

It was the first time in years that she, Gir and Winstx had not traveled as a triad team. Worse, Gir had warned her that he might not survive this particular mission.

Not now! Not when things were so confusing and chaotic. Wait! Stop! Too devastating to think about. Besides, there was another level of trouble, beyond urgent. Perhaps when she talked to Goshing, she would figure out what was bothering her so desperately.

After leaving the poor reluctant Johnny with Gir, she and Winstx had set out for Grjimbe, making an appointment with its empath relay station along the way. She hoped she would be able to get through to Goshing before the empath circuits got too crowded. She had to have priority on this one. She trusted her uneasy. Always had. Goshing was in deep seclusion now in her compound, recovering from her eighth transformation-molt. Telmx was gratified that she herself would never have to go through that. No one needed a transformation-molt anymore. Just the elders. If Goshing were still in stases, no one would be able to fetch her, nor would Telmx want anyone to fetch her.

There were several people, all Ursine, milling around the kiosk. She would have to shield. They would know she was shielding and wonder why, but she would make light conversation, and throw enough unshielded preoccupations their way to keep things comfortable.

These Ursines were mere cubs, brown and black, with soft pre-pubescent fur. She nodded politely, and they made way for the Imari empath in deference to her age and wisdom. This time she would take it. Ordinarily she would strike up a lively conversation with them about status and prestige. But not now. She'd take up that fight some other time. She gratefully pulled a double order into her goblet and looked for a shady area to squat. Although it wasn't home by any stretch, she liked Grjimbe City. It took care to cater to travelers, and made sure off-world cuisines were in good supply.

On this world with only one sun, it was a bit more difficult to gauge her day. So much to do, and not enough time to do it in. And people here took things real, real easy. No one rushed around. No one felt alarmed about anything. A very different rhythm from hers at the moment. She had to fall into their rhythm or she would call too much attention to herself. Single shadows were interesting and extremely rare. She should find some time to enjoy them. She could never take that kind of time when she visited J on Earth.

The nodes around her cilia ached and tugged, a vague prescience. Nothing she could do about it until she could enter the long-distance empath booster relay system on the far side of the plaza at her appointed time. Even with optimum boosting conditions, the time delay between transmissions was agonizing. Stop being so angry. Anger caused heavy unnatural breathing, and then transmissions were virtually impossible. The first chi sips started working their wonders, taking the edge off. Plus she would diligently perform the required rituals before she entered the relay booth. She finally relaxed into the rhythm of the plaza and looked around.

The plaza was beginning to fill with its Ursine denizens and a variety of off-world people. Multi-colored aromas and inner energies, a din of discussions with selves and others. Toward the center of the plaza, a small group of Ursine adolescents started singing local ditties and playing their pipes, strings and ancient cempa drums, intricate lilting harmonies and rhythms, which attracted a widening circle of intergalactic tourists. The rhythms were intoxicating, and within minutes, the crowd swayed in unison: a large family of hathas (like Earth's hippopotamuses but smaller) with their youngsters peering out of their pouches, various sizes and shapes of Sapiens, beating their tails and nodding their heads in unison, and a group of sleek spotted Felines, with tiny infants hanging off their sides and jaws. Telmx swayed with the music, and realized that it steadied her discomfort more effectively than the chi. What a wonderful culture, she thought. The Ursines were particularly unshielded, very trusting, fun-loving and so welcoming of strangers. It was no wonder their planet attracted the diversity of visitors. They even had large intergalactic retirement communities on some of their many forested islands in their warmer climates. Telmx so desired to visit there one time, just to see, just to interview some of the elders from around the universe, but like always, she had work to do. No time. Never any time.

She hovered her chi goblet in front of her and smoothed out her wishaptha, taking pleasure out of the soft textured touch of the cloth on her fingertips. She wondered what it was like not to have the pleasure of fingertips, and thought about all the other species she didn't know much or anything about, in addition to those yet undiscovered. Even in an Imari lifetime, there was not enough time to learn all things, to meet all species. Besides she had work to do, and although the uneasy had abated somewhat, she knew she did not have the luxury to people-listen. Just a few more moments before she had to keep her appointment with the relay station. Then her precious shore leave would end.

Her last assignment, which she and Winstx took on without Gir, hadn't been particularly hazardous after all, although the Council led them to believe that the newly discovered planet, further away from Earth, which was their primary Mission, was so hazardous that only talented young Imari scouts like themselves could tackle it. When they reached the outer fringes of the potentially rogue planet, not only weren't they even remotely detected, there wasn't even a scintilla of evidence that primitive empath existed, except perhaps in the neonates of the species and a smattering of wild animals. And unlike Earth, whatever dangers lurked in the future of that world were so remote as to pose no immediate danger to anyone else in the civilized (or even the uncivilized) universe.

But it was difficult to leave without warning them about the hazards to their own planet: overproduction, implosion from greed, catastrophic climate changes from haphazard and self-serving industries, and if their planet survived all that, cataclysmic warfare. She and Winstx held their tongues, however. A major breach of protocol to interfere, unless in the future some uneven development did threaten the rest of the civilized universe. Too early to train monitors. And probably not necessary.

According to her scans, history on this planet would do its natural unfolding, and uprisings from underneath would ultimately prevail. And finally it would join the confederation. It would take many centuries. Maybe not. Sometimes things on developing planets just crept excruciatingly slowly into place and other times they raced into a better future exponentially.

Finally, as much as it distressed Telmx and Winstx to leave them be, they were relieved they could return to Galern II for shore leave and spend some vacation and consultation time at the elder compound. They also wondered if the Council had sent them on a wild goose chase just to keep them occupied for a while. Or perhaps to challenge their discipline. Goshing had been very suspicious of their assignment off-galaxy this time. It was too easy, especially after all the objections about their wasting empath energies, etc. But Goshing and the scouts had decided they should not challenge these orders from the Council, as contradictory as they were. They were already considered mavericks and upstarts. No need to fuel those rumors.

On the way back to Galern II, Telmx and Winstx sensed something sinister, more than the crisis on Earth. Their forebodings made their bones ache. Instead of returning directly to Galern II, which would take too long, they revised their itinerary, registering it as R and R, in order to contact Goshing from the booster in nearby Grjimbe City, just in case. Besides, they needed to make minor repairs and give each of them a chance to gravity adjust, and Grjimbe City often served as a perfect rest stop for them. It was almost like returning home.

Winstx had elected to stay in orbit first, to watch over their ship and to do necessary repairs so they could move quickly to wherever Goshing felt they needed to be, whether or not the Council knew about their actual plans. But getting supervision from Goshing might be difficult. The timing was wrong, as if that timing were planned in advance against them as well. Goshing was due to be in her molting while they were away, and might not be available. A chance they would have to take. If she couldn't contact her, could they consult with one of the other members of the elder compound? Maybe they'd have to go directly to Europa and help move that Mission to the next stage, with or without Goshing's council. Maybe Gir himself was in trouble.

A gaggle of winged Oglassis were soaring and dipping, also attracted to the Ursine ensemble. She had seen them emerging from the decontamination chambers at the port earlier that morning, chattering in excited tones, ready for a long offshore leave after three months of nonstop travel. She was too preoccupied with obtaining her emergency appointment at the relay station to find out where they had been for so long, but they sure were raring to wander. Now, here they were again. Some were flitting from kiosk to kiosk, while curious Ursine schoolchildren looked on, giggling amongst themselves, and stomping their paws in excitement.

The Oglassis were an elegant Equine species, lively, curious, unpretentious, yet artistic in their attire, braiding their long manes with colorful strands of hemp and mica, and girding their loins and rumps with silken, billowing textures. Their large Pegasus-type wings were unadorned, shimmering blue-white in the sun, and emitting a deep droning tone as they glided along. She loved watching them, truly a rare sight for her, not to mention the children of Grjimbe. She wondered how they manufactured their fabrics, how they did anything without an opposable thumb. Rumor had it that they had strong hovering powers, and a very sophisticated mandible, and that their children learned at a very early age to cooperate in pairs around everything. Someday she would find out more about them.

"May I join you?"

A large Oglassis was slowly landing next to her, folding her wings behind her mane, as she hover-squatted opposite Telmx. "I saw you resting here, and thought to make your acquaintance. My name is Orja, from Oglassis-Prime. My partner Beja is hovering at the edge of the music, in respectful distance, just in case you in fact want and need to be alone. We just thought it was an opportunity to meet an Imari. We rarely have the pleasure."

"I am Telmx. Of course you and your partner can join me. I only have a few more moments, but I was just lamenting my lack of knowledge about your wonderful species. You speak flawless Imari." Telmx was aware that the Oglassis remained just at the edge of her empath zone, so respectful of her boundary, that she did not even attempt to empath communicate, instead speaking out loud in a delicate and lilting accent, a somewhat archaic dialect of Imari.

Orja nodded in the direction of her partner, who within seconds glided next to her holding a sack of grains and aromatic grass with her jaw, which she placed ceremoniously in the center of their circle. "I suspect this is not a delicacy for you, but you are welcome to try," said Beja. "We have not had access to these ingredients for almost half our tour this time."

Telmx read warmth and strength in their combined presence. As intoxicating as the music. She accepted their offering, and placed her chi goblet between them.

"This is Telmx," said Orja.

"From Galern II," added Telmx.

"Ah." Beja nodded and tilted her silken amber head to one side. Her mane rippled and sparkled in the morning light. Exquisite from a distance, its hues took on new qualities up close, the craftsmanship of the filaments interwoven throughout. "Please excuse our boldness…."

"She has but a few moments," said Orja. "Do you mind if we speak to you in a closed empath chamber?" She cast her head around the marketplace and lowered her voice. "We don't mean to intrude, but we actually sought you out. You see, we were rerouted to your coordinates because of certain information we had stumbled upon at a crafts fair. May we invite you to enter our empath chamber?"

Telmx noted the quiver in the Oglassis' voice, and nodded. She unshielded a narrow band, and easily found their shared chamber. Here the Equine aromas were stronger, lemongrass, with a hint of hickory smoke. Orja dipped her head into the chi goblet, took a long draught, and gently pushed it toward Beja with her nose. "Thank you for taking the time," she empathed. "It seems that your own urgency resonates with ours, but you do not yet know what we know."

"My team has been in foreboding for a few months now," empathed Telmx. "But there has been something more sinister assaulting our inner chambers in the last day or two, ill defined, but very urgent. What is it that you know? My appointment for a priority empath relay to Galern II is scheduled for 0800. If you have information…."

"Then indeed, we do not have much time. As you probably know, we are craftspeople and artifact traders. We frequent marketplaces and intergalactic crafts fares, which of course brings us into contact with a rich variety of cultures and non-political, homeworld bound sub-cultures and independent, isolated species groups. We have forged close relationships and partnerships in remote areas of the galaxies, especially among the worlds that retain their original heritage and do not strive for technological evolution. So we are privy to information, conveyed innocently enough, from individuals who have no idea what they are divulging in friendly, casual conversation. We have, over the eons, developed the ethic that we would never engage in intergalactic espionage, and if we learned something of consequence, we would auto-erase ourselves, to make our species, and trade, free from duplicity, politics, and alliances. We never enter another's empath zone without explicitly obtaining permission, and even then, we do so infrequently, lest we inadvertently learn or divulge information. We are trusted and revered, for which we are humbly grateful.

"But something we have learned about your Mission on that planet they call Earth has forced us to break from tradition. Three months ago, having determined your itinerary, we cancelled off-ship leaves, changed our own itinerary, and booked a crafts fare on this planet in order to meet with you. Please forgive our intrusion, and duplicity, but we are frightened, and we suspect you will agree that we had no choice but to violate our own code of ethics. As it is, we are now seen together in the marketplace, and it would be prudent for us to hold off further discussion until we can meet even more privately. In the meantime, I would propose that we execute a trade to put off those who may be watching us, endeavoring to listen in. How about your Imari goblet for an intricately woven tapestry, which possesses, within its stitches the technological schemata associated with what we have learned. Please forgive us for pushing so boldly and abruptly."

At that, she nodded to Baja, who reached under her wing with her head and produced cloth woven from dried grasses of many hues into a subtle, intricate pattern of tweed and filigree.

"Please pick it up," empathed Beja. "Absorb its texture and warp. Inhale its aromas. We humbly offer it in a somewhat unequal trade for your sacred Imari social goblet. We could not hope to match the goblet in tradition, vitality, the vintage of its materials and its centuries of maturity." She gently lowered her head and offered the fabric to Telmx.

The foreboding in the Imari's cilia nodes deepened as she reached for the mat. The tips of her fingers tingled, and before she grasped it, she knew it contained an extraordinary version of a V.E.

"Please don't attempt to enter it now," empathed Orja softly. "We beg of you to accept it, ensconce yourself in your inner chambers at your own convenience and safety to read its contents with appropriate V.E.-goggles. Also please accept our invitation to visit our quarters right after sunset for early supper. I am sure you will have many questions. There is no need to know its content before you keep your appointment with the empath booster. Indeed it would be safer if you did not read it until after your transmission to your homeworld. There is much danger in knowing what we know while you empath-communicate across the relay."

Reluctantly pulling up enough shielding to block her curiosity, Telmx grasped the fabric and touched it to her cheek as if to examine its quality. Then she nodded in agreement. Beja lowered her head, drank the last drops of chi, and, gripping the goblet delicately with her teeth, tucked it under her wing. Telmx noted a deep rubber-like pouch under her ribs, where the Oglassis swiftly inserted her new acquisition.

"Well," the Equine trader said out loud, "we must be on our way. We thank you for this trade. Use the tapestry in good health. We look forward to trading with the legendary Imari Scouts in the future." They rose to all fours in unison, nodded gently, unfurled their wings, and glided elegantly toward their comrades amongst the tourists assembled around the minstrels.

Telmx followed the Oglassis with her eyes, her mind racing with dread. She thought momentarily that she would postpone her relay so that she could immediately enter the fabric's story, but then thought better of that plan, for such a change in schedule would call attention to their meeting. Instead she carefully rolled it up and placed it in her travel pouch, rose slowly, and walked across the marketplace in the opposite direction of the minstrels, toward the relay station.

She would have to shield the scantiest trace of new apprehensions during her conference with Goshing, difficult because her mentor could read even the slightest quiver across the thousands of light years of space. Well, she certainly did not have to hide some of her foreboding. That was already present before her encounter with the Oglassis, and why else would she ask for a special priority relay to Galern II? She and Winstx desperately needed Goshing's input. Perhaps they would have to detour to their homeworld, before rejoining old Gir on Europa: an excuse to linger in her own compound, share bot with the elders, and talk privately with her beloved mentor. Perhaps, if Goshing were well enough, sufficiently recovered from her molting, they would make tender love, and then they could enter the tapestry V.E together, and make a plan. No matter what the V.E.-story uncovered, they would require, she was sure, Goshing's wisdom in order to proceed.

The marketplace was crowded now. Groups of retirees from the out islands ambled and floated past her, in muted animated excitement, and she was vaguely aware that some small clusters stopped to examine her as she glided by, and occasionally a wizened individual empath-greeted her briefly in clear formal Imari. She modulated her foreboding and exchanged pleasantries, all the time straining inside to filter out her reactions to the Oglassis meeting so that she could enter the relay station unencumbered.

The station was built several hundred meters above the marketplace plateau. She joined a handful of others on their way to their relay appointments, and paused to admire the huge marble and granite archway and the wide ornate steps beyond. She had to slow down her uneasy. There would be no way to mesh with the empath relay if she didn't calm down. In spite of her uneasy, she had to take the time to perform the slow, familiar ritual as she ascended to the top. Discipline. She certainly knew how to be disciplined.

When accessed by foot, the eleven groups of steps up to the peak constituted an architectural experience: each landing featured a small park, with clusters of flowerbeds, fountains, several kiosks, and various nooks and crannies created out of hedges and shrubbery for private meditation. Built by the Intergalactic Council, they were designed to preserve every scintilla of empath energy during the climb, which would be lost if one hover-approached, so most people chose to approach the station by foot. Telmx was quite used to the routine, and took advantage of the privacy available at each tier to compose her thoughts. However, even in the safety and comfort of the approach, she was vaguely aware of a sour presence lurking at the edges of her consciousness: the same foreboding, but a bit more defined. Still, she had to keep herself from rushing to the top. One step at a time.

At the ninth tier, where an adobe building was provided for body excretions, and a strong empath boosting potion, she squatted just outside the large pale blue arched entrance, and tried to take comfort in the handful of other climbers slowly entering and leaving. Most were sapient, who, like herself, were generally in need of contact with their homeworld groupings, or had to check in with their small children to assure them that their mom or dad was homeward bound, or would be back on a particular date. Someday she would allow herself the luxury of children, when her work was not so life-threatening, not that her grouping wouldn't take care of them if she were to perish. No, not fair to children. It's one thing to be a trader or artisan or construction worker assigned for small leaps here and there in the known universe, although occasionally one would die in an absurd accident or natural disaster. It's another to take on her kind of assignments, which by definition caused her to enter the unknown, and to take unheard of risks. Perhaps even Goshing and the elder compound were in trouble. With the Council? With some other crisis to be revealed within the Oglassis tapestry V.E.?

The booster potion made her hearts race, and she climbed the next two tiers quickly, without pausing to meditate. At the eleventh level, she turned to the left, leaving the others to file into the main building, and hastened down the dirt path to the small oval station jutting out from the mountain face. She hated having special privilege, but there were times like these when she was grateful. Nevertheless, privileges like these caused great rifts in the Council, especially among the Pomdos Alliance. Fortunately, she saw no members of their group among the climbers, nor had she sensed any Pomdos in the market place. Not that the Pomdos traveled that much, but there were usually one or two adventuresome individuals at the major intergalactic rest stops.

Telmx walked slowly up the path to an old unadorned wooden door, and absorbed the sweet harmonies emanating from the dome that ballooned up and out over the precipice. During the last few weeks of dread, compounded by the meeting with the Oglassis, she had forgotten how glorious a visit to a relay station was. Like most stations, it provided relay services but was dedicated to fathoming distant galactic harmonies, sorting out distinctive patterns in the effort to locate new species. She scanned and eliminated any stray shielding and uneasy she might have retained on the ascent, took several deep breaths and stepped up to the door to be security scanned. Within seconds, the door opened gently, and she entered the darkened vestibule, where a richer blend of harmonies surrounded and entered her, vibrating in her bones like they were delicate obgeth reeds. She made her way to the center of the vestibule, squatted on the circular mat, and closed her eyes in order to merge fully with the deep tones.

"Ah, Telmx, you have come."

Telmx recognized the gentle empath voice.

"Raymond," she empathed. "I had a feeling you'd been transferred here, but I wasn't sure. How delightful."

She reached out her hands and allowed her old schoolmate to raise her up. They folded into each other's arms, intertwining their cilia. "Oh Raymond, I am so excited it's you. How've you been? How's your grouping?"

"You're quite troubled, Tel," he empathed. "Please, come to my repose chamber before you enter the booster. I've been worried silly since you requested priority status, but I didn't want to alarm the others. Besides, you can't empath relay in the booster with so much static. Goodness, Tel, my dear Tel. You're weeping."

Telmx tried to feel safe in his arms, but realized that indeed, tears were forming in the corners of her eyes. "I thought for sure I had cleansed my uneasy. I'm losing my touch." She laughed.

"You've always been too hard on yourself. Come."

They walked though an Imari fabric on the left side of the vestibule and after a few steps, they passed through a similar fabric into a warm, tropical chamber. "Do you like it?" he empathed. "I just put in a new bunch of eprira ferns that a colleague brought back from Galern II, along with, of course, a few cases of vintage bot. We'll break out a liter after your relay. It's almost like home, don't you think? I mean, not quite, but well, you know...."

"I love it," she empathed. "I'm uneasy, but it feels to me that you are also in some sort of conflict or confusion. Almost like when we were cramming for the graduation exams. What's wrong?"

He laughed. "I struggle not to visit those difficult times. Of course, I'll never forget how you helped me, and how disappointed you were when I didn't quite make the cut. But I do well. Look at me. I am director of one of the most important empath relay stations in the Galaxies. So I don't get to travel like the Scouts. It's fine. I'm happy. But first things first. We'll lose your empath window if we don't cleanse your uneasy right away. Can you dump it on me? Should I shield the room so you can deposit it safely within my inner chamber?"

Telmx felt vaguely troubled by his forced contentment. He had never forgiven himself (nor the Imari elders at the Institute) for failing to make Scout Status, but she pushed her concerns for him aside. Later, over some bot. "You know I've never kept secrets from you, Raymond, but this time I hold the safety of others within me. I've actually never had to...."

"Don't waste time explaining." He pushed back a large eprira leaf, and lifted from the undergrowth a small mahogany box, chiseled into a repeating raised pattern of tiny squares. She looked at the T'cha box with dismay. She learned about it at the university, but never had to actually resort to the artificial means of cleansing her mind and nodes.

"Stop chiding yourself," he admonished softly. "Even Level VI Imari can fall into a deep uneasy. And by the way, dear girl, you're not the first. That's why you learn repository procs. You won't be able to engage successfully with the empath booster relay unless you are truly at repose. So, touch the repository and release your uneasy to it as soon as I shield myself so that I cannot fathom anything emanating from you to it."

It felt as if she were on automatic, performing a ritual against her better judgment. But he was right. And she needed desperately to consult with Goshing. She reluctantly accepted the box and clutched it in her palms. She winced as his shield shut her from him, and then she slowly touched her cilia to the raised pattern.

The uneasy poured out of her nodes like so many demons.

"It's almost like what I imagine an auto-erase feels like," she empathed afterward. "Except I'm still aware that I was heavier with its load a moment ago, and that the ritual requires I take it all back after I finish the relay. Strange how light I feel." She actually felt a bit giddy. "I'll be ready for that bot when we're done." She took his hands. "Let's get this thing over with. Funny, I still know why I need to talk to Goshing, but I don't feel the least bit frantic. Hey, one could get addicted to this box, you know."

"Well, I've had to perform the T'cha proc many times for my work here. It's a well-used repository, believe me. But taking the uneasy back is not all that comfortable, so you'll see, it's not a procedure I look forward to guiding people through, but I have to. It is one of the most important aspects of my responsibilities."

They walked together into the main dome, where several other Imari were squatting at elaborate consoles. The music was no more.

"Ah, the emergency relay client," empathed one of the technicians. "My name is Geth," She bowed in traditional Imari greeting to Telmx, and pointed to a hook next to her console. "You can hang your travel pouch here and follow me to the booster chamber. We shut down the harmonics to recalibrate for your relay, but if we don't hurry we'll loose the strip of opportunity." The Imari was a mere adolescent, probably, Telmx thought, a Level II technical on her internship. So young to be isolated off world from her grouping, but better to be out-posted on this planet, than enduring some others. She thought of Gir and the surveillance team on cold, barren Europa.

She followed Geth up the winding steps to the cylindrical booster chamber that hung a bit below the top at the far end of the dome. Raymond stayed below, now squatting at a console and fiddling with adjustments. At the top,

Geth slid open the alloy door and Telmx lowered her head to enter the small space. "This is the newest model," empathed Geth. "You don't touch your cilia to a conduit anymore, just face toward the portal, which Raymond will open from below, and point your cilia straight out. He'll do the rest. I'll be right outside here if you need me. May you connect in good harmony." She uttered the last in traditional ancient dialect, bowed her head slightly, and slid the door shut.

Telmx raised her chin to meet the cool rush of air as the portal opened. She closed her eyes and opened her empath energies to maximum. She imagined she was again behind the waterfall in the shallow cave where Goshing brought her for empath training as a child, and pushed her cilia further forward as if to communicate with a fine misty spray. The relay would take several minutes to reach Goshing's compound, and then several minutes more for Telmx to receive the initial return greeting. If Goshing were out of molting transformation, she would answer herself. Otherwise, Telmx would endure silence until Raymond determined that connection was not possible. Then she would ask to connect to one of the other elders in the compound. She coalesced her energies into a single dot of light and waited for the boost from the console below. She heard it coming before it entered through the soles of her feet. Its blue surge warmth traveled swiftly through her spine, her primary and secondary hearts, and her throat. It reached the top of her head, arched slightly downward into her cilia and sped out into the open air. Exhilarating, with no perceptible energy drain. She relaxed into the transmission, as wave after wave of blue surge coursed through her body and rushed through her cilia.

"Oh my dearest Tel, I had a feeling you would empath relay today." Goshing's mind met her mind with impeccable clarity. Telmx let out a long breath of relief.

"We have required supervision, to speak with you, to hear your voice, but we were concerned you were still in molting. I trust it went well." She said this last, already registering with horror, that Goshing had not yet entered the molting.

"Yes, I have not yet molted."

"But if you don't molt soon...."

"Hush, my dearest and listen. There is little time. Conserve your energies. Do not use the relays again. Study the *Legend of Kro'an'ot*. No, my love, do not ask anything else. Trust your uneasy. Do what you need to do. We may not see each other again, even though our travel scans have indicated otherwise. So if we don't, I love you always and forever, no matter what the revising future brings." Then she was gone.

It was as if Goshing were dead. Telmx was aware of that thought, but felt nothing. She touched her cilia nodes because they were pulsating, but felt no concern about the searing heat emanating from them. She pressed the exit button on the console and her chair swiveled to match the opening of the sliding door. Geth's hand extended to hers and she squeezed out onto the top step, straightening to full height, only to realize she was unable to negotiate down the rest of the winding structure without losing her balance.

"You are weakened now. Let me help you down," said Geth out loud. "We have some chi down below. It will offer some renewal."

Telmx was dizzy, and she could neither shield nor empath. She also knew she had to leave the relay station right away, although she felt no inner urgency. Drinking the tea would be a diversion, a delay, but not drinking it would slow down energy renewal. The descent was slow. She would fall if she let go of Geth's hand, but at the same time, it was much too slow, and she could do nothing about it. All so intellectual, she thought. Facts without feelings. Bothersome stuff without being bothered.

Raymond placed the chi in her hands as soon as she reached level ground.

"A very strange sensation, isn't it, being weakened and without the capacity for uneasy?" he said.

"I can't exactly say it's a sensation. It's more like the knowledge of a problem which needs to be solved." The station now seemed immersed in a greenish tint, and the technicians seemed like children's movable dolls in a V.E.-story. "I must leave right away," she said, slowly, without sensation or urgency, although she was aware of its importance.

"In good time," he said. "Drink up, first. Then we will return to my chamber for the T'cha take-back, and to break open some bot."

"Lead me now," she insisted, handing the chi to Geth. "Please, Raymond. It's urgent, although I don't feel it, although I can't adequately convey it."

"If you insist," he said, and led her out of the observatory. Things were missing from the puzzle she needed to solve, but she couldn't figure out what they were. The puzzle itself had no substance, a horrible sense of unfinished business. Like without that piece of the equation, nothing would make sense ever again. Well, she'd figure it out after she reentered uneasy and renewed her strength. There's no way she'd get addicted to the T'cha. Even without taking back the uneasy, she was becoming overwhelmed with a distinct odor of foreboding. Without looking directly at him, Raymond's eyes looked larger, a bit desperate, a kind of gleaming. His smile seemed disingenuous, almost sinister. Exactly like her recurring nightmares as a very young child. She would awaken with this alien's eyes and smile still hovering and glowing just inside her eyelids, and she'd go scurrying through the musk darkness of the inner courtyard to her parents' chamber. Now she struggled to shield from Raymond. It was unfair to burden him with her paranoid distortions.

"You and your mentor are remarkable women," Raymond said. "You've performed the T'cha, but having communicated with Goshing, parts of you are now shielded in some unaccountable way, and you came out of your communication with a returned, if ever so slight, sense of uneasy, even though you have not performed the T'cha take-back process. Strange and intriguing."

His probing bothered her, but she cast her thoughts aside. There was no reason to be cautious around her old childhood chum. But it was curious, she thought, that she was able to shield selectively without having taken back the uneasy. Perhaps Goshing had indeed sent her more than she knew.

"Help me, Raymond. I do need to return to the central district right away."

"First things first, my dear Telmx. You must take back the uneasy or you will hardly survive the decent. This condition is more debilitating than you think. And certainly you can stay for some bot. I was so looking forward...."

"Well then let's get to the T'cha box quickly," she said. She couldn't imagine squatting with him over a bot ceremony, not even a brief one. But she decided not to break that to him just yet. One piece of the equation at a time.

He guided her into his chamber and offered her a mat facing the eprira. She squatted gratefully and quickly, careful to avoid his eyes. She hoped he would not notice the affront. After the take-back, she thought, she would be able to shake her childhood nightmare and renew their warm camaraderie.

"The initial rush can be overwhelming," he said. "Don't worry if at first you feel like you went to minus-7g without a g-transfusion." She accepted the chiseled box in her palms and lowered her cilia.

"Not there!" A whisper. She almost didn't catch it. Gone.

"Go ahead." Raymond's out-loud voice mingling with his empathed. "What's the matter?"

Telmx lifted her head involuntarily. "I can't right now," she whispered, also involuntarily.

"You must," he said. "It's dangerous to avoid the take-back."

"It's dangerous to take it back right now. I'm sorry Raymond. There's something very wrong. I can't quite grasp it right now. I must leave here immediately without taking back the uneasy. As you see, I am uneasy without taking it back, so perhaps I don't even need the procedure. Perhaps it'll be more dangerous if I do allow everything back in right now. I must leave right away. Please, I'm sorry."

She was shielded and wary. Without the take-back. If she could run, she would run. If she could hover herself away, she would do it now. "I must go. Raymond, I need you to ... no, I don't need you to ... I can do this on my own. Just give me a minute. Just indulge me a minute." She rose to standing, her chest pounding and resisting, as if the gravity field had suddenly increased her weight tenfold. This chamber also now had that greenish tint.

Then Raymond was gripping her wrists. Tugging her down. "You mustn't go without the take-back. I can't let you do this to yourself."

"Please let me go."

"It's my responsibility to see you through the whole process. I cannot let you leave without the T'chi take-back. What's going on? Tell me. I can help. I know it's addictive. Some people really do want to stay in such a restive state without the take-back, but you said yourself—"

"Raymond! You must let me go now." She hesitated. "I don't want to hurt you."

"You can't hurt me." He was hardly alarmed. "Even with your reputation, you cannot, not in this state. Besides, you know that's a very forbidden and drastic solution to a simple issue here. You would certainly be brought up on criminal charges and banished from the Scouting Order. When you have completed the take-back, if you still want to take me down, I can't fathom why, we'll talk, but not in this condition."

"Raymond, don't try me. I promise you I can and will take you down. This is no trivial issue. Please, my buddy, I know you mean well, but please stand aside. Even in my weakness I have the strength. Believe me! Do not obstruct me!" The words were not hers. They came automatically, and within her shielding she knew and feared her bluff. He let go. "I don't know where this is coming from, Tel. It hurts me deeply. We are buddies, old friends." However, his look, gleaming with determination, was trying to pierce her shield with the heat of his eyes.

She averted her head, and walked slowly and regally past him. She kept walking, the blast of cool air in the reception area buoying her onward toward the wooden door. It yielded easily to her touch. He wasn't stopping her. He wasn't following. Maybe she was doing what he wanted her to do, leaving the relay station without the take-back? Maybe he was tricking her into *not* doing the proc? No, dangerous to perform the proc in his sphere of influence. Knowing without knowing. Her feet, clumsy, plodding, guided her back along the path in the red/green twilight, then painfully down each step, not hesitating until she reached the bottom.

CHAPTER SEVENTEEN

Matt

Matt's monitor was the only light in the room. The cursor bobbed along, leaving an endless trail of numbers and letters in sets of eight. He hit the print button, and waited for the clacking of the printer. He wasn't concentrating anymore. Maybe he should take a walk while the printer filled yet another carton of green and white computer paper. The hell with paper jams and error messages. If he lost some data, so be it. He sure as hell needed better equipment and a larger team. Here he is, hotshot Harvard physicist, O-A-One for NASA and the Navy, now Associate Director of Super Top-Secret MPII, monitoring the printer tractor feed like some asshole office boy.

Even if he *did* grow up shoveling chicken shit. Emma was always impressed with his status. Not that he could tell her anything about this assignment. She was nothing but poor white trash from Iowa. When they first started dating, some ten years earlier, he was on his way to Harvard. That impressed her alright, but she was more dazzled by his long sleek slide rule hanging conspicuously from his belt in its fine leather case. That was right there, for all the world to see. She made him demonstrate all its functions, even though she couldn't understand a thing. Well that was good. He slid the ruler back and forth with great flourishes and spouted all those impressive words, like exponentials and conversions. She beamed with pride when he mentioned decimal places. She knew that phrase from junior high school.

But would she be as turned on by his other tool? Would she ever let him in? Finally she did when he came home for winter break. Good thing, too, because sure as hell he would never have been able to keep up with those hotsy-totsy Radcliff girls. Now that they were married, he worried if his two little boys would end up as stupid as Emma, them being home with her all the time. He'd have to take them on some sort of expedition when he got back to Maryland, maybe to the next launch at Cape Canaveral. That'd be exciting and educational for them.

He refocused on the monitor. No error messages. Actually, it had been a pretty productive day. The army recruitment center was practically just around the corner, so his team could've just as easily hung out the office window to get the data. Good that they decided to wade right into the stinking red rabble because the dirty commies had taken off for the UN and would've been out of range. This time only one scanning kit pooped out, so five real data collectors did the job. Processing all the data sometimes took all night, especially since the NASA mainframe was so goddamn slow, chugging data back and forth over half a continent. And by that time, even if the data analysis yielded a strong signal, the trail was stone cold. So frustrating.

Charlie's voice had boomed over the phone earlier that evening. Even louder a hundred miles away than in person. "You're always demanding technology that's years and years away. This is 1967, fella, remember?"

"We need to be analyzing the signals as they come in, not waiting for the mainframe to spit the data back at us. We're absolutely nowhere, Charlie. C'mon, you're our braniac techie. Can't you devise a real-time computer for us? This grunting, grinding batch processor is a dinosaur. Do it, man! We're at the cusp of the cusp here."

"Go scream at IBM, not me," he bellowed. "Tell 'em you want a little tiny mini-computer that sits right in your hand and bites your fingers every time it gets a lousy true blue hit. Tell 'em I said so and they can give me the bucks to invent it. I got ideas, you know."

Same conversation for months. What a goon. How'd he ever get to be such a brain? Maybe Matt should just go out and get laid.

When he and his team first got to New York, they were sure they had located a whole nest of high-energy natural ESP freaks, right in the heart of Greenwich village. False alarm. Diffuse signals and very unfocused. Just weirdoes doing their "thing." Then they went for the psychics and fortune tellers, just in case. After several weeks of false leads, and some major technical setbacks, they located their first clear blue ESP surge during a performance of *The Merchant of Venice* in Central Park. Just for an instant. Could've been one of the actors having a really high moment, but it was a clear hit. But of course they couldn't track it because the data didn't come in from the NASA mainframe until 4 a.m. and it took until seven the next morning to plot it all. "A clear blue! Got a clear blue in Central Park!" He was so excited when he called Dawes, he forgot to act cool.

Dawes sent him two more technicians and a second ESP energy detection console. Now, almost thirteen months later, he had a team of seven and their Griffith New York City Large Print Street Map hanging ceremoniously on the far wall sported almost two hundred blue pushpins. If their target is only one person, he probably lives on the Upper West Side, works or studies in Midtown, hangs out in beatnik cafes, attends folk and rock concerts, takes in a bit of real culture, like Shakespeare, and goes to commie demonstrations. Goddamn needle in a haystack. They all look alike. Probably never bathes, has a long Jew beard, does pot and LSD, and shacks up all the time with those hippy-dippy chicks with beads, bell-bottoms, rimless glasses and tits (If Emma ever made her tits pop out like that in public, he'd kill her on the spot). And that Jew beard has no idea in hell he's got enough ESP energy to fuel a space ship to Jupiter and back. Just what MPII needed, better and bigger than the original Manhattan Project, that's for sure. Hell, once they perfect *this* ESP technology, nuclear bombs'll be a minor blip in history. He was sure as hell proud to be the chief of MPII.

If the truth be told, he'd much rather be back at the lab with Yazzie spelling him on the console, sharing the excruciating headaches. Amazing. Who woulda thought that he'd care whether a goddamned Indian lived or died? But he did, in a deep sort of way that embarrassed him. "You choose, Matt." Dawes had rasped. "You can slowly fry your brain like Yazzie here or you can use all your smarts to find others and save Yazzie in the process. We need you guys. Desperately. There's some interesting stuff beginning to come out of Stanford, but we have to find our own ESP talents, without going through regular channels. That's the directive from the hill. Let them play their games, and of course we'll keep on top of it, but this work here, this is the real thing. And absolutely no one, not even the boys in Stanford know what we're doing here. I'm afraid it's up to you, Matt."

Not even Matt's scanning team knew what was really going on.

The clacking stopped. End of the final data run. He turned back to the keyboard, and logged off. After several more streams of coded messages, time stamps, annoying "are you sure?"s and "thank you"s the monitor splashed into four groups of little letters shaped to spell N.A.S.A., and blinked to black, leaving the room in total darkness. Jerk off? Go get laid? Or pour over the data sheets?

He switched on the stark overhead, and flopped the stack of data sheets on the bed. He was probably the only stud in New York, yeah, the only stud in the whole goddamn universe who'd lay a sack of data sheets on a goddamn double bed on a goddamn Saturday night. Okay, just a few calculations, just to see.

Hunched on his folding chair, he scanned the sheets, line by line. Occasionally he paused and performed a quick in and out with his slide rule and graphed the results in his blue bound, NASA embossed, analysis pad. When he saw the surge coming at the end of the fifteenth sheet, he could smell it. His little pencil graph showed a little blip in the data, then a series of stronger and stronger blips, and then a real "blue." Holy Shit! A double real blue! He redid his calculations. Double spikes on his graph, like two real blues talking to each other. The spikes rose and fell in doubles for over ten minutes of data, then slowly diminished in intensity, fading in unison. Yeah, like they were walking away from the scanning console. Two targets just strolling away like it was a goddamned walk in the park. Shit! Why couldn't they just detect the surges right there and then? We would've had them in our hands already. Already promising the poor bastards more money than they could make in a lifetime to be part of the hottest most top-secret history-shattering research on the planet. Then fry their asshole brains to smithereens instead of his and Yazzie's, who were needed for more important stuff.

He had to get his hands on all the photos and footage from the UN march. All of it! Okay! He was sweating and his veins were throbbing. Even better than getting laid! Tomorrow first thing, he'd get Dawes to obtain access to the NYPD helicopter surveillance stuff. Oh yeah, and the raw news footage from NBC and CBS. Dawes could pull strings there too. So what if it's Sunday. Two Jew beards. TWO! Walking away from the crowd about five minutes into the march.

Two fabulous, off-the-meter blue surges. The biggest fish in the goddamned sea, meandering away, away from the crowd like life was just one big contact high. Why would they leave? Maybe they know something. With all that blue ESP surge power, maybe they're on to us. Jeez! Nah. The surges came from Howie's console. Maybe he actually *saw* something, remembered two beatniks splitting off. Can't call Howie at this hour. Why not? Got to. Four a.m., do you know where your goddamn team is?

CHAPTER EIGHTEEN

Johnny

Johnny lingered in the observation lounge long after the planetoid rest stop had dissolved into a vague speck. Twenty-four hours before, he and Lenx had been entwined on their mat. What an idiot! Falling in love knowing he would eventually have to leave. His plight in life. Love and lose, love and lose. He replayed Lenx's eyes before his own, their love and their misery. "I'll be back as soon as I can," he empathed into their misery. "I love you." He would send a message to him as soon as he could. Maybe Gir would let him send it from the ship's relay system. Even the most powerful Imari could not empath messages such distances without relay.

He loosened his titration belts and reached for the aloe stick in the pouch under the recliner. He was applying it generously to the titration pinpricks on his arms and chest when he felt Gir's powerful presence fill his right temple.

"May I?" empathed the Imari. The old man appeared by his side, towering above him in his red and black traveling suit. His hood dipped down over his wide, charcoal forehead, framing his deep-set black eyes that beamed compassion for his young lover. "I'm sorry to intrude, but we will be veering around the Griffin Luminosity soon, and we'll be double shielding from its dust storms. I thought you might want some lunch before we have to buckle in and titrate under again."

"The Griffin Luminosity. On Earth it's called the Horsehead Nebula, right?"

"The very same."

To Johnny the nebula was the final barrier between him and Lenx and the Galern system, his adopted nirvana. Couldn't even see the horse's eye from Earth without a powerful telescope. As soon as he reached home (where would home be this time? New York? San Francisco? Maybe Boston?), he would point his trumpet to Orion's belt and pierce through the eye of that horsehead. Long sonorous jazz tones racing through space to merge with his song. Lenx would hear his tune in f minor. Recognize it. They would start trading fours. What a romantic he had become, after drowning in a lifetime of cynicism.

"We need to start training you for reentry," Gir empathed. Johnny picked up distress in his mentor, a surge of concern for Johnny's welfare that frightened and comforted. Johnny loved the old Imari. His caresses were slow, tender, deliberate, just the way he was in every aspect of his life. To have two such lovers was more than he had ever imagined in his wildest childhood concoctions. Not to mention, that he was in love with two *men*. That was way beyond the beyond. "I'll never see Lenx again," he empathed. "It's just temporary," Gir assured him. "He's not gone from your life no matter what your despairing self claims. Come, we'll have a light lunch and then start your training." Alright, he could handle this. Lenx will have to handle it too.

Gir was short for his species, not as stunning as Lenx. But his quiet wisdom and kindness, and especially his strength, inspired and inflamed him. Long after other elders had retired to their villages for their twilight years, Gir kept on, dedicated to the Mission and to Telmx's triad team. He was seriously focused, but not without whimsy and humor. Johnny felt safe in his domain. The old man could strategize out of any obstacle, and there were plenty coming up according to Telmx and Winstx.

"Please be patient with us, my boy. It's not easy for any of us. Not this time," Gir went on. "Like Telmx said, 'we must keep our eyes ever forward.' No, I'm afraid we can't relay back to the Galern system. We need to preserve all our empath energies for this trip." Johnny knew that they had to leave Telmx and Winstx back on Galern II. Entry to Earth was, in fact, too risky this time, and there was much to take care of at the Council. Telmx would await Gir's report, if he returns. Those were her words: "if he returns." Jeez. That's what she had said. Then she wept. The lady everyone revered like a goddess openly wept real tears. He was dismayed, but not surprised. These Imari are so human. She had heard his thought, and right before they parted, they hugged and cried like little kids. As he followed Gir out of the rotunda, her parting words echoed in the dim corridors of the ship. The invincible Imari uttering such ominous words. Maybe Raygoth and his other Pomdos friends were right. These Imari were calamity-janes, chicken-littles. Jeez, why couldn't life be simple for a change?

Gir's ship was smaller and more comfortable than the large intergalactic cruisers he was now used to. Its motors hummed softly, muted by plush Imari carpets that fondled the walls, ceilings and floors. The hoverglows kept precise pace with them as they moved slowly through the corridors. When an occasional bump pitched Johnny and Gir up and about, they floated briefly with the hoverglows, touching this and that patch of color carpet on the ceiling and walls, before the adjusting gravity pull returned them to the floor.

Johnny enjoyed those little bumps better than being tethered to a recliner. It gave him a rush, like hitting high C. Took his breath away.

He closed his eyes and floated in vulnerability, completely safe.

Once his older brother visited from out of nowhere—one of the three precious times he saw his brother as a child. Sonny took him to the famous Bakers Amusement Park, where the rich white kids went. Wow. The roller coaster, the bumper cars, the house of mirrors, all the places he had heard about and could not imagine ever being able to go. His favorite was The Centrifugal House. It spun around; the floors gave way. Each time he screamed in utter terror, until Sonny caught him in his large powerful wrestler's arms and the two of them floated blissfully to the spinning walls that cradled them and carried them to another realm of terror and bliss.

Now at 24, Johnny was two years older than Sonny was when he had guided nine-year-old Johnny through that park. They went for sliders afterward. Then Sonny had driven him back to his foster home in Bronzeville. They had double-parked on the dark gloomy street in that shiny new Chevy Eldorado with red velvet seats, and Sonny told him he was going far away. He said, "Johnny-boy, you take care of yourself and that golden trumpet of yours, you hear? Become the best jazz artist that ever lived in the entire universe."

Johnny cried like a baby, and Sonny wrapped his huge arms around him and held him close. "Gotta do it, Johnny-boy. If I don't cut loose of this town now, nothing good'll happen. I'll find you. I'll write to you, after I make it real big. 'Cuz I got lots of smarts. I'm gonna make it real big somewhere, Johnny-boy. No Man on my tail gonna take it all away. I'll send for you. You'll see. No brother of mine gonna rot to hell in foster care. Right now, I just gotta dump this whole life and disappear like I never even was."

Johnny knew he would never hear from him again. Clutching his musty aroma, like cinnamon, just like cinnamon, he decided not to cry again. "I'll play a real mean horn, Sonny. You'll see. You'll hear my tunes on the radio and you'll be right proud. I'll dedicate every song to you right there on the radio." He stood in the street, clutching the crisp c-note Sonny had squeezed into his fist, and watched the Chevy dissolve into the haze. He slowly climbed the five flights to the alien stink of his newest foster home.

Gir steered Johnny to the lift where they floated up two decks to his tiny quarters. They squatted on Gir's weathered mat and broke the bot froth together. The old Imari and the young earthling bowed in silence until their foreheads gracefully touched each other.

"There's been a change in landing arrangements," Gir empathed gently, and Johnny again discerned Gir's foreboding. He forced himself to concentrate. He just wanted to fold the old Imari in his arms and make tender love to him rather than have a serious conversation.

"What kind of change?"

"We're going to land on Europa, you know, Jupiter's moon. That's where our outpost is. Our comrades there advise us that it's too dangerous to bring the ship, or even a small shielded landing craft all the way into your home-world's territory. Not only are the Americans monitoring the skies, they are actively searching for strong empath energy bursts. Something to do with their arms race. We're taking no chances."

"Who's doing the scanning? NATO? NASA?" Johnny was not surprised, and he knew that Gir wasn't either. Part of the predictions, the original scenarios as Telmx and her research team had presented to the Intergalactic Council years ago. The Age of Empath on Earth was beginning. The Mission was upon them. Just much sooner than anyone thought. "What could they be looking for? Are they afraid of enemy empath-powered bombs? Visitors from outer space?"

"We don't know yet. We need updated information from the two other earthling recruit monitors. But only you have the technological skill to help them secretly send the information to our Europa outpost. In any event, the United States is determined to shoot first, ask questions later. So of course, if we enter the old-fashioned way, without empath power, we'll be picked up by their radar and blown out of the sky. We're not about to use our powerful weapon systems on them. Or worse, our very presence will start a nuclear war, before they realize we aren't the Socialist Russians, their mortal enemies. If they do figure out we're not from their planet, they'll probably shoot us down anyway. In that case, we'll cause a panic, raise real alarms about 'men from Mars.' They can suspect and spin fantasies about us. They must not know about us. Not yet, so...."

Johnny braced himself. "So we have to find those other two earthling monitors I've never met. Well that part's okay, but how can we do it without being blown out of the sky? How will we get there? What kind of ship will we come in on? Where will we land?"

"You're going to go in alone, Johnny. I can't come with you this time."

"What in fucking hell are you talking about? It's too dangerous for *us* to go in but it's not too dangerous for *me* to go in? One fucking moment, Gir? What the fuck are you saying?"

"Hold on, hold on. Hear me out. No way are we going to put you in any danger. We got it all worked out."

"Worked out? I don't even know how to fly a hovercraft. Jeez. I don't know how to harness an empath guidance system. I'm not even a Level II empath.

Besides, I'd be a moving target, no matter how I enter. How in the hell am I going to enter? What's going on here? I don't like this, Gir. I just don't fucking like it."

This was way more than he bargained for. Besides, he didn't entirely believe things were that bad. Not THAT bad. The Imari always play things dramatic. Quiet, convincing, and dramatic. That's what Raygoth said. Here it was. She was right. No, she wasn't right. She was a Pomdos, a dissociated Pomdos, just like the Imari said. No, he trusted Old Gir and Telmx. Jeez. Maybe not.

Gir took a long time to formulate his words. "We have until Earth-time August to teach you how to convert your body into a living landing pod."

"You gotta be fucking kidding!" Never since the CPD hacked down his door when he was five, shot his parents in cold blood and thrust him into foster care had he felt such raw terror. "You're shitting me! C'mon, Gir, you're playing with me. Quit playing around!"

"Bear with me, Johnny. You're going to learn how to maneuver in controlled free-fall and burn though the Earth's atmosphere without getting burned."

Old Gir was shielding just how much he feared for Johnny's life. Johnny knew he was. "Oh, Jeez. Oh good Jesus in Heaven! What in God's name are you trying to tell me? What are the survival chances of this? I'm really really fucking sorry Gir. You're hiding some real bad news from me. I know it, no matter how well shielded you are. I can hear it in your voice, you know. I ain't no musician for nothing, you know! Wait, wait, I need time to think about this!"

"Johnny, my boy, I won't hide anything from you. It's difficult, extremely dangerous, and has a 70 percent chance of succeeding, give or take a few percentage points." He took Johnny's hand in his. "We've done this maneuver before on other planets. With the proper training and attitude, the chances for survival go up. In addition, you'll be completely covered in a heat-resistant shroud. We have several months to practice once we reach Europa. I'll be right there with you for the practice runs."

"What kind of practice runs? What, you just kind of roll me in a blanket and toss me into fuckin' free fall? If the heat don't get me, a goddamned missile sure will, as sure as hell."

"Johnny, our triad team wouldn't have authorized it if it weren't absolutely necessary. And Telmx, I, have no doubt that you'll land safely and unscathed. I know this is going to sound completely absurd, but you're going to be disguised as a meteorite, camouflaged within their August Perseid meteor showers."

Johnny wished to hell he hadn't drunk too much bot. What a stupid ass-hole scheme. He simply puts on a Halloween costume and lays himself out for target practice by the Man. A black guy comes tumbling out of the sky and says, "Hey, here I am. Here's a new guinea pig for your white man war games. Come and get me." A nightmare. A bad titration nightmare. He had heard about such things.

"This is not a nightmare, my boy. What'll happen if we fail the Mission is the nightmare. One more thing." He smiled. "Your trumpet is coming with you."

Johnny looked at him with disbelief.

Old Gir laughed. "You didn't think we'd leave your trumpet out of the equation, did you? Now let me show you what real free fall is all about. You'll see, it's actually fun. Just better do it before lunch!"

For the next two hours, and for the remaining weeks of their journey, Gir turned the young jazz maestro into a master free-fall acrobat.

CHAPTER NINETEEN

Johnny

The time had come. When Johnny entered the ejection chamber, he could already smell Jupiter's sulfuric stench even though the airlocks were sealed tight. It was a prescient odor, a death stink. His death. Okay, it had been fine, even fun to do the practice stuff. He was even proud of how he handled various maneuvers. But now, here on Europa, less than an hour away from the real thing: no more fun and games.

For the first time since the cops had gunned down his parents, he wished he believed in God. Someone, something to lean on, not the Imari, who played God, raised his hopes real high, and then abandoned him big time. At least in Nam he would've died with his buddies all around him. He wished God would come into his head right now and say, "It's okay, Johnny, these Imari, they're good people. Yeah, they get a bit paranoid sometimes, but they sure know what they're doing. You can trust 'em." He searched for the Gospel songs he had learned in his first foster home. They believed. He believed. He could believe again. He prayed.

No god ever visited him, his dreams, nothing. Why should this night be any different? Nah, all in his imagination, a crazy nightmare. In a minute he'd wake up and find himself curled in some alleyway in Bronzeville, homeless, hungry, gagging from sulfur sewer stench, rotten earthling shit, yeah genuine earthling shit, but alive, ah yeah, alive, and not burning to a crisp in free fall. Yeah, that's all he wanted, even if he ended up starving to death.

"Of course you're scared, my boy." Old Gir's empath voice penetrating through the airlock was particularly soft. Johnny didn't want soft. At just this moment, Gir was intruding. He had a right to be scared. Calling it scared didn't take scared away. "And furious, my boy," Old Gir said out loud as he entered the airlock. It shut with a hiss.

"Yeah, I'm scared and fucking pissed off as all motherfuckin' hell, I am."

"Whoa there, Johnny."

"Don't appease me. You come waltzing in here telling me what I already fuckin' know. Sure as hell damned right I'm pissed. How is it that of all the

billions of people in the universe I'm the only one qualifying for target practice for some trigger-happy honky, so you can go on living the good ol' Imari
life? Answer me that!"

Johnny paced up and down the ejection chamber like a caged tiger. Gir's
shield was way up. Sealed tight. Yeah, but Gir could penetrate his shield all
he wanted. Just not fair.

"You got your shield so high and thick these days, I can't tell what the hell
you got planned for me. You sneaking around my mind, trying to soothe it,
making it all sweet and passive so I take all this bullshit like a pussycat. Well,
I'm not taking it. Do your own dirty work. Go down there yourself, why don't
you? Just you go down there in oh-so-blissful free fall and take care of things
yourself, if you're so worried 'bout those mothafuckers down there. What
they gonna do to you out there anyway, all the way safe out there in another
galaxy, a million light years away? Why am I blown to bits to save your mothafuckin' asses? I gotta fight my own battles for my own people, you hear me?
If I'm gonna die, I'll die fighting my own battles for my own people. It's about
time we took up for ourselves. And you take up for yourselves!" He stopped.

He wouldn't look at the old man. Enough to bump against his shield, to
feel him poking around his right temple, like he was some piece of stupid ass
silly putty.

"Johnny, it's your fight too," Gir empathed quietly, a wisp of air brushing
against Johnny's temple.

"God, Gir! Get out of my face! Leave me the fuck alone! Don't you tell
me what my fight is. I gotta get there in one piece to do what I need to do.
Now, how in hell are you gonna assure me of that? You have no assurances
that my ass won't be fried out there in that stratosphere. Jeez, not even some
sewer rat gonna keep me company while I fry, and everybody's gonna see
me burning to hell and shout 'Wow! You see that? Look! A big mothafuckin'
shooting star!'"

"I'm simply trying to get a word in edgewise."

"I should've seen it coming. I just should've seen it like it was always staring me in the face. Of course. Plan A: Find some orphan foster kid and set
him up for target -practice. Just 'cuz this one's here in outer space, doesn't
make it not a lynching, you know. Oh boy, how'd I get in this mess in the
first place? And then you say, no way out now. You're in it now. You just can't
back out now. No, uh-uh, I gotta get back to Earth anyway I can, and then
jump out of this whole Mission mess. But to get there. Holy Jesus, I gotta get
shot into a thousand pieces just trying to fuckin' get there. Oh God. I wish
I'd never met you. Any of you." He hurt so badly, he thought he would puke.

Alone now. Betrayed by everyone, including Lenx. "Who gave you, I say, who gave you the motherfuckin' right to take a tiny scared wisp of a boy and push him into this? And then lull me with your loving, and with Lenx? Loving both of you like there had never been any love as loving anywhere in the universe? I'll tell you why. Just 'cuz I got no family. No one would fuckin' miss my ass. You could do with my ass just like you goddamned pleased? Who, I'm asking you Gir, who gave you the supreme authority?"

Johnny was desperate to get out of the chamber.

"I'm sure as hell not leaving today, you know. I'm just not ready to die this week, you know. I'll go find Lenx and sign us up for something else; I don't know what, but something else. Maybe he and I can go to Earth. Yeah, Lenx and me, safely, not using your stupid stealth stuff. We'll figure it out. I didn't get all this fuckin' technical training for no reason. Yeah. That's what I'll do." He turned toward the airlock, yanking the ripcord of his travel suit.

"I'm afraid we have no choice about when or how or why we leave, Johnny." Gir grabbed Johnny's shoulders and shoved him into a squat. Johnny sank to the ground in spite of himself. He had never realized how strong the old man was. He couldn't move. Rooted.

"I'm sorry Johnny," Gir's empath voice came through like an echo, and captured each thought he tried to think and drowned it with incessant reverberations. Johnny gave up struggling, and the echo resolved into a deep mellower version of Gir's out-loud voice. "You're in such a frenzy, I had to exert an imptha fix on you. I'll teach this little trick to you sometime. But right now you have to listen to me, and well, if this is the only way to get you to listen, I guess I just have to resort to some dirty old war gimmicks."

Johnny's thoughts seemed far away, like they were outside of himself, struggling to form sentences somewhere on the other side of the chamber, hovering helplessly, without form. Plus he couldn't move a muscle.

Gir squatted to face him, his head bent so his cilia gently feathered Johnny's forehead. "Look," he empathed, "you convert all that scared and furious energy into fuel for this trip. If you follow my instructions exactly, you won't die. No way. You'll be just fine. And you'll be back with Lenx before you know it. Have I ever failed you? Remember, I'm a smidgen better than you in V.E.-time-scans. I'm afraid I have some odds on knowing the outcome. Even though I can't exactly predict one-hundred percent." He hesitated. "Besides, I'm coming with you."

Scattered thoughts, rushing headlong into a spot between Johnny's eyebrows, coalesced. He pulled his head back. Jeez, the old man was suited up.

"What did you say?" he empathed in slow even beats.

"I'm coming with you."

Now he noticed the slight quiver in Gir's empath voice. Ever so slight, mostly shielded, but Johnny had a good ear. "Yeah," empathed Gir, "I'm a little scared too, that you won't listen to me unless I pull an imptha fix on you. But we're going to be just fine. I'm not coming all the way. Just until we cross Earth's stratosphere. Then you'll be on your own. And you'll do just fine. I just want to—"

"Wait, wait, just wait. You told me the other day, just the other day, that you hadn't done this sort of thing in a really long time because of some big deal medical thing. Oh how I wish to hell I had never met Lenx. Now what do I do? And you? I wish I'd never met both of you. I love you both so very very much. Oh Jeez. Oh Jeez." He was going to cry. That's the last thing he wanted to do right now. "Oh Jeez."

For the first time in weeks, Johnny realized how much he'd been feeling sorry for himself, how completely out of touch with his mentor he was. How could he do this to him when he loved him to pieces? He hadn't even seen this coming. Not even slightly.

"No, no I'm fine. I'm a little slow sometimes when I'm tired, but I'm really well rested, and I'm just fine. The truth is, you're so pissed off and scared, you're likely to lose a nanosecond of crucial energy just before the stratosphere, and I need to be there to enhance the burst at that crisscross moment we've been practicing. You're great at it, but if the burst isn't one-hundred per cent, you know, so...."

"See? You don't trust this cockamamie shit any more than I do. And, *and* you don't one hundred percent trust I can do it."

"Not at that one place. All the rest of the maneuvers. You're impeccable. Just in that one place. You're not about to abandon 'scared' and 'pissed' for the journey. I can't let you go it alone with such energy drains eroding your empath storage supply. Even if you turn them around right this second, they might return at that crucial moment. It's not your fault. In fact, you better save 'scared' and 'pissed' for other stuff you need to do, in their own time. Let's just say, you need a hand, my hand, through the hard part of *this* trip at *this* time."

"But your own safety!" Johnny was desperate. "I can't let you take that chance. I should've known you would never send me to my, I mean...." Even though he knew Old Gir could read his thoughts, he wanted a way to tell him out loud he was real sorry. Now he was to blame for risking his best friend's life. "You're doing this so I can trust you. Shit. I trust you, Gir. Look what you've taught me! I adore you, Gir. I'm going to do that crisscross without losing a beat, I promise, even at the crisscross. You can't come with me. If you die…. You gotta understand. Everyone one I ever loved went and died on me." Desperate also smelled like sulfur.

"I won't do anything stupid, my beloved."

"No, but you just don't know everything. You told me so. And I can hear some stuff you mean to hide. You know, you're not so sure you're coming back. I can hear it, you know."

"You've learned your lessons well. My shakier side was there all the time. You've simply learned to plumb it."

"You don't shield as well as you used to. I mean, I'm worried about you. I love you like a, like a, you know, like I loved my Uncle Wally, you know, and then, you know, you patiently waited until I became a man, and then, well, I love you so much, I don't want anything to happen to you, especially not on my account, and I couldn't stand it if I never saw you again. "

"I know."

They looked at each other. Johnny wanted to be strong. No tears. Even if his prescient dread turned out not to be accurate, he surely wouldn't see him again for a very long time. How could such bliss turn so bitter all at once? It always did, so why should this be any different? He grabbed the old man's hands and looked up into his magnificent face. They leaned toward each other, the tall, sleek Imari folding his torso to touch Johnny's lips with his. They were quivering. Jeez, the old Imari was crying, actually crying. "I'll miss you too," Gir empathed. "You're part of me, Johnny. Now, let's get this thing over with. The sooner you go, the sooner you can come back."

Johnny felt emboldened, ready for action. A surge. Like just before a gig, with the multitude of intergalactic species buzzing and chirping out there in infectious excitement. When he and his group walked onto the round and took up their instruments, the sudden universal hush was deafening. Johnny counted off the first beats in a whisper heard throughout the huge amphitheater.

Now there was a deep velvet hush in the ejection chamber. The young earthling and the old Imari stood up in silence. They exchanged glances and simultaneously slipped their travel hoods over their heads.

Johnny closed his eyes, and, fighting back a second rush of tears, reluctantly folded himself into his catapult capsule. His travel sac was comforting. His trumpet was safely ensconced, strapped between his knees and now tucked close to his chin. With his mind, Johnny pulled the heat sheathing tight over his rounded body and head and fused it with his travel sac. In his mind, he knew exactly when Gir had completed his own sheath fusion in the adjacent capsule. Then the covers of both capsules clanked into place. Sealed. No turning back.

Entering the high-empath energy state came relatively easy for Johnny. When he played his horn, he could hit high C and sustain it past his wind capacity because he just kept feeding in more energy from his empath reserve. When he was on tour with the band, they would trade off energy bursts, and the fusion and overlaps of energy at the point of synchrony made for unbelievable harmonies, not only for the players but for the overflow audiences that came in shiploads just to savor the experience. Empath energy boosting in free fall without playing trumpet was tricky—at first he even practiced free fall with his horn at his lips, holding that high C as long as he could, just for training. It felt oh so great. A real high. He and Gir even considered having him play his horn for the whole trip down. No, he and his trumpet were safer without extraneous and telltale reflections and vibrations. He'd have to keep it in his travel sac, and conjure one hell of a high C in his head for the crisscross.

"Ready, my Johnny?" Gir's familiar jasmine balm washed over Johnny's right temple.

"'Round Midnight, take one."

"Well, then, count it off, my Johnny."

"Uh one, uh two, uh one-two-three-four!"

Weeks of rigorous rehearsal flipped into real.

The two oval capsules leaped out of the ejection chamber into Europa's stratosphere, arched smartly into the hazy yellow sky toward Io, and sped twice around the smaller Jovian moon. Then, like slingshot balls, they tripled their original speed, catapulted away from Io, and raced sunward to their precarious rendezvous with the Swift-Tuttle comet debris. Their fiery tails burned somewhat blue-green, as they rushed side by side out of Jupiter's influence, and then glowed a whitish yellow as they streaked into the void beyond the giant orange planet like a pair of speeding headlights on a deserted road. By the third hour of their journey, they simultaneously wobbled and hesitated, and then with renewed bursts, streaked so quickly through the void toward the Perseids, that their headlights, now phantom afterglows, could not catch up with themselves.

CHAPTER TWENTY

Telmx

Intellectual inclinations mingled in Telmx's right temple with vague uneasy, like a huge set of unsolved equations, like the G'bet conundrum, the tortuous bane of every freshman, but far worse, for she was tackling this one alone, not with her raucous wide-eyed, conquer-the-universe dormitory grouping. And not with Goshing. Somehow a whole day had gone by. The sun was not quite down, but the plaza and adjoining streets were already ablaze and buzzing with joyful night activity.

Her mentor's words flooded back, and her uneasy ballooned into dread and misery. She had to put those thoughts aside. Now it was like in battle: solve the crisis of the moment, and go back to mourn later. Alright. Mourn later. Right now, Raymond's behavior and Goshing's warning demanded her full attention.

Nevertheless, her mind was working very slowly. Misery and necessity were in collision.

Carefully stepping over occasional old lava ridges, she plodded slowly and aimlessly through the narrow streets, away from the central district, until she reached some steps leading down to one of the ancient canals. She climbed down, one dizzying step at a time, and squatted at its edge. The sky, now a hazy purple green, was almost starless, paled by the primary and secondary moons, one overhead, and the other rising, large, red, gibbous. Flickering hover-glows lined the streets on both sides of the canal. Vague empath of Ursine children echoed from somewhere around the bend. Briny water lapped against the stone sides of the canal below. Chilled, and shivering, she pulled her wishaptha closer around her.

Separated from Goshing. Cut off. She supposed it was inevitable that Goshing would not be available to her. Perhaps never again. Is that possible? She clutched her knees and rocked back and forth. It never occurred to her that Goshing could die. Even if she couldn't get to her at a particular moment, she was always available. An everlasting assumption. She never even thought to scan for possible futures between her and her beloved, just to see when and how she might die.

So many others depended upon Telmx, looked to her strength. Yet she felt vulnerable, and had learned to always display her best demeanor, invariably thinking about what Goshing would do in a particular situation, always buoyed by the knowledge that Goshing would nod or smile later, or curl her left cheek crease a little tighter, empathing her demur, ever so gently. Then Telmx would teach her as well. Never one way. One time, just a few years ago, when Telmx had to make a rapid crucial decision, with no time to consult, she did the most obvious, without a trace of misgiving. "Why did you do that?" Goshing empathed just hours later.

"Because I thought of what you would do."

"My dearest Tel, I never would have thought to do that. It came from the depths of your brilliance!"

Telmx conjured up Goshing's smile, and her gusty laugh. Certainly they would be together again. Just not now. But Goshing had said maybe never. What did Goshing know? She couldn't imagine life without her. The thought of having Goshing mingled into her inner chambers because she had died was unbearable. Gir, suffering so from his old injury, had talked to her and Winstx about his Incorporation into Johnny. He would do it on Europa before sending Johnny back to Earth, just in case. Telmx, Winstx and Gir had hugged and cried and made their parting. Telmx had managed during this last trip to come to terms with Gir's probable passing on, maybe even before she and Winstx could reach him to say goodbye. But Goshing? No way to endure. Just can't happen.

Most sentients believed that Imari never suffered, and certainly never died. How wrong they were.

Distant thunder intruded her reverie. She realized she was maximally shielded, and that she had taken back almost all of her uneasy on her own, without Raymond's T'cha take-back. Still exhausted and chilled, she climbed clumsily back up the steps, crossed the narrow street, and passed through the archway of the first inner courtyard she could find. Curling herself under and around the nearest orthno shrub and simultaneously auto-weaving its broad leaves into a protective tent, she was asleep before her head touched the underbrush.

* * *

Karothanmootthe was hardly two years old when her parents, along with their grouping, decided it was time to migrate to the northern hemisphere to avoid the semiannual flooding of their compound. However, her Legend, like so many others, was intricately woven afterward by her Imari descendents and then by the inhabitants of the planets they visited. By the time her story reached the rest of the sentient universe several millennia later, it had been altered and embellished into mythic proportions. Through a series of convenient transliterations and contractions, the child's name first lost its original lilt, and then the compounded syllables, because certain sentient tongues couldn't pronounce them. So, as her tiny story became embellished into an epic, her name was abridged first to Kro'than'mott and then, finally, to Kro'an'ot.

So reads the introduction to the annotated textbook version, in the original ancient Imari tongue, embedded in imbuiki parchment and meticulously studied by linguistic scholars. Scout candidates must memorize the original epic in its entirety before they are even accepted into Level I classes, and must be prepared to discuss each annotation lucidly and exhaustively according to the particular cultural and symbolic meaning placed by each of the separate and intertwined sentient species known to the Intergalactic Council. Consequently, the novice empath student has to develop her or his inner libraries and master smooth and rapid access to whatever iteration, translation, episode and interpretation the pre-admission examining board might ask at empath individualized oral examinations at the time of candidacy application.

She slept deeply, unperturbed by the raging ionic storm that whipped and roared around her cocoon. She didn't even dream. So she thought. However, when she was finally awakened by the predawn chatter and bustling about of families in the cavern compound, she was reciting to herself one of the verses from the epic in its original Imari lilt. Not the actual words. Playing before her in her half-awake state were the musical inflections of the verses and the images of the child Kro'an'ot. Little pneumonic devices Goshing had taught her during the grueling couple of years of pre-admission preparation.

Her cilia scanned and shielded in rapid fire, as if at any moment she would have to summon her unwanted, deadly and dreaded take-out powers from deep within. Mostly her empath was flooded with nearby cubs complaining about having to get up so early in the morning, and the various basso-growling tones of parents and kinsfolk cajoling each other in dawn ritual. Behind all that the lilting verses, and behind all that, the nagging terror. She couldn't as yet recapture the actual verses of the Legend, only the lilting inflections, a kind of song that looped in and out of the front of her head.

She raised herself to crouching with a start, ready for action. So much in her brain. Somewhat deafening. Nagging. An entire day had gone by and she had to reconstruct it. What was yesterday? How had she managed to be here, hiding in the courtyard of a cavern compound, inside an auto-suffused cocoon? The very act of reconstructing upset her. It was not like her to be so deeply asleep that the previous day had to be retrieved. Also she was parched. Needed some chi. Of course, chi. Then she would have to make her way to the intergalactic relay station. Must speak to Goshing.

Then her yesterday rolled slowly into place. She reached for her travel pouch to retrieve the elaborate gift, the beautiful tapestry from the Oglassis, and realized she had not honored their supper invitation the previous evening. Nor could she find her travel pouch.

When it appeared in her inner mind's eye hanging on the hook in the relay station console chamber, her forebodings about Raymond gelled into awful clarity. Now Goshing's warning and farewell. Now vulnerability and futility she hadn't experienced since she was seven when she couldn't breathe Eepppee back to life no matter how hard she tried. Eepppee was a tiny regipe, one of her best playmates since birth, whom she had named. Her very first out-loud word. Not even the elder, powerful Goshing had been able to awaken inert little Eepppee. "It's not that death is final," explained the elder as she rocked the devastated child in her strong arms, "It's just that you will never again talk to that particular personality."

"But you will never ever leave me. You will never enter the eternal silence."

"I can't promise you that."

"But you *did* promise you would always and forever be with me."

"Not in the case of a regipe, my dear Tel. You cannot understand it all until Ascension. Please be patient with me."

"But you must! You *do* know how! Do it for Eepppee now. Bring her back to me! I can't wait until Ascension." She pleaded and wept to no avail, and finally flailed out of Goshing's arms, kicking and beating at her face and chest.

"It's not fair! It's not fair! You're a mean old crone! I hate you!" She had run hysterically from the elder compound to the comfort of her own mat and did not allow Goshing back into her mind for almost a year.

She melted the cocoon, first scanning the immediate area, so as not to frighten the Ursines who were up and about. Fortunately it was still early and no one had yet emerged into the courtyard.

In the next instant she was racing back toward the center of the city, back to the relay station, and then, as she approached the arched entrance, where a line was already forming, she thought better of her plan. There was much wisdom in the Oglassis tapestry. She needed it, but it was too dangerous to retrace her steps.

Something was very wrong, and now that her foreboding was back full force, she required a clear head, more data, and the assistance of Beja and Orja. And Winstx, in orbit above the planet, had no idea what was happening. She had to reach her. Without an empath call. And with that, she realized she had to raise her shields to maximum and find her way back to the intergalactic port in empath silence.

She hesitated only briefly to obtain a goblet of strong chi and a small local bot biscuit. Then she summoned a mini-hover-cab, which took forever to hover down to the summoning post. She set the craft for emergency velocity mode, and punched in the coordinates for a spot several meters from the intergalactic port.

The putrid odor of chaotic peril and terror punched through her shielding, weakening it slightly. She scanned briefly ahead and bumped immediately into reverberating empath static. She automatically shielded to maximum again.

The port district was dotted with low, sprawling warehouses and factories, interspersed in between and around large patches of hardened lava pools. About three kilometers above a huge open area hovered the enormous central rotating docking area, for shuttlecrafts from the intergalactic ships docked in fixed orbit around the planet. Fifty or so tubes rose in spokes in all directions from the center. They served as decompressions and decontamination, gravity adjusting channels, each one terminating in a hexagonal reception and boarding station. The hexagonal terminals were then linked by a transparent outer circle from which hundreds of hover lifts picked up and deposited passengers at the port below, which lay a half kilometer from the surface of the planet. On the ground, directly beneath the port, loomed the circular synthetic structure that housed the empath energy generators for the port. Every few meters around the circumference were archways that served as initial customs stations, where passengers boarded the lower hover lifts. From above the entire port resembled a huge rotating spoked wheel. From below, a mammoth buzzing hive with hundreds of little beings coming and going in tiny tear-like vehicles ascending and descending from between the terminals and the station gates below.

The port appeared normal. A shuttlecraft was silently descending from orbit into the central hub and the general din of species traffic in and around the various spokes and terminal. Nevertheless....

She guided the hover cab manually as close as she could, her head reeling in a deafening static field that had not been there the day before. There was no way to maneuver it closer without being detected. So many things were wrong. She didn't require empath to know that the air was tinged with the scent of recent trouble, perhaps as recent as a few hours ago. She would have to park the hover cab and approach by foot.

It was much too risky to scan for the Oglassis intergalactic vehicle also docked somewhere in orbit. She would have to read its coordinates on the consoles dispersed throughout the terminal, and then figure out a way to connect with them unobtrusively.

Telmx squatted briefly to get her bearings. She was near the warehouses and the softy whining generators in the low-roofed structures that reached seven levels under the lava-splattered ground. Then she made her way from building to building, clinging to the whitewashed warehouse walls, now risking short carefully calculated scanning bursts so that she could know what lay directly ahead.

As she rounded the corner of the last warehouse, a circle of huge archways loomed ahead of her. Travelers were already queuing up for their routine passport check before entering a hover lift to the port. From her position, everything suddenly seemed much too quiet. Not even a static field, just utter silence. Even a deadly empath silence. The eerie quiet overwhelmed the vague hum of activity at the archways.

She opened her empath scanner a bit more. A putrid burnt stench invaded her nostrils. Just ahead, along the side of the warehouse wall smoldered a huge pile of charred feathers and flesh, in silent testimony to what she already knew in vague prescience. Nausea overwhelmed her. She dared not approach closer. She dared not linger. Whatever force had been wielded against the winged Oglassis Equines was not very far away. No time to scream or cry. No time at all for figuring anything out. She had to put grief on hold, get to Winstx, and get far away from the planet, even though Winstx had not yet had the opportunity to gravity-adjust. Once inside the port, she would figure out how to get to her shuttlecraft, which would take her back to her ship.

They had been in much more dangerous circumstances many times before and they always figured things out, in obscure worlds and asteroids. Certainly no one ever expected even the slightest trouble in Grjimbe City, so much so, that security was extremely lax. Some biological and ecological scans, paper checks, regular customs routines, but no political security. Political chaos was assumed to be non-existent, as far as the Ursine species was concerned. A dangerous assumption during these times. The *Books of Kro'an'ot* were almost unheard of in Grjimbe City. Apathy. Sheer, blind apathy was, in fact, the growing problem that she and her team, that the Imari Scouts in general were confronting.

Who had murdered Beja and Orja? Why wasn't there a general alarm, medics and patrols swarming around their bodies? What had the Equines been so afraid of that they had to arrange a surreptitious meeting? Who did they assume was watching them? And how had she been so easily duped, as to leave her precious travel pouch with its precious tapestry V.E. in the hands of her erstwhile childhood friend Raymond. The balance of forces was changing in ways that seemed beyond her ability to sort. She hadn't until yesterday, even a hint that Raymond was not to be trusted.

She crept slowly around the last building, fighting back tears and feeling more alone than she had ever felt. She yearned to call to Winstx. Was she all right? Surely Winstx would have found a way to reach her if there were trouble. But maybe under the circumstances, she couldn't. Given her power of prescience, shouldn't she have had an inkling? Well, maybe she did. Maybe the source of her uneasy was in fact Raymond himself.

The stench from the charred corpses, not fifty yards away, still hung in her nostrils, and the multicolored feathers strewn all over the pavement seared her temples and inner chambers. Her eyes burned with the struggle not to cry, to keep her mind focused on solving her escape. Winstx should have sensed trouble by now. She must be worried, with no way to do anything without leaving the ship unattended. To be on the safe side, she would have to approach her own vessel with caution and in empath silence.

Clearly hiding and slinking along the edge of warehouse buildings was not going to get her anywhere. It enraged her that she couldn't keenly and absolutely focus. Raymond's poisons were not completely gone from her system. She could feel the residual granules coursing though her veins, refusing to give up their last traces of hold on her energies and concentration.

She hadn't experienced such frustration since her first days of training behind the surging waterfall as a very young child, where Goshing had demanded she count the trees on the other side of the blinding spray, and she knew she couldn't see beyond the length of her outstretched arm, straining and struggling to see what Goshing could see without a trace of effort.

"It's your rage," Goshing had empathed.

"It's not my fault! I can't help it. I'm too young. I don't know the secrets. Tell me the secrets!"

The huge curtain of water and mist of that waterfall seemed to grow thicker and more impenetrable. "They are only droplets of water, thousands of them, hundreds of thousands of them, but each one separate from the other, each droplet with more space around it than the density of the droplet itself. Focus on the space. Gather the spaces." She knew what she had to do, but the task was beyond her. How could she gather spaces that she couldn't see?

"And your despair."

"You're supposed to be my friend, my teacher! Not my heckler!" she had thought, knowing full well the old Imari could read every word she was thinking, and having no way to stop her from doing so, no matter how hard she had tried to shield just like the students who had already reached full Ascension, which was at least three long and impossible years away.

"And your impatience," she continued, folding the child's hand in hers.

And now it was twenty years later, her mind so much more disciplined than a child's before Ascension. Yet at this moment she couldn't muster 100 percent efficiency. It was not as if all her powers were gone, just a bit compromised, fuzzy around the edges. She needed to convince herself of that. She needed to trust. And forgo rage, impatience, despair. They were wasting her time and precious energy. That's it, she thought, she just needed to trust her senses as best she could, and be satisfied that the rest of her empath powers would catch up in due time.

So far, there were no sounds, except the wind that always whipped up when a cloud passed overhead. She knew that the spaceport, not more than a quarter kilometer away would be teaming with travelers and tourist guides, embarking or debarking, making itinerary arrangements, waiting for a delayed ship, straightening out a reservation gone astray, calling for hover-cabs or boarding the lava skimmers to bring them into center city. All the things travelers do at spaceports. If she concentrated really hard as she approached the port, perhaps she would be able to discern some Imari among them, or locate Imari-turned-bad lurking in the shadows. Well, she thought, Raymond appeared to be an Imari-turned-bad. This Imari, a former school buddy, had somehow bypassed all her sensors. Even with her mind at full empath power, he had befuddled her. Perhaps the Imaris-turned-bad had concocted some new strengths that were outside her parameters, a new weapon in the intergalactic community where weapons were outlawed except for those carried by the Imari Scouts for protection from species understandably terrified of extraterrestrials. Perhaps this is what Goshing was warning her about. The whole mess was mind-boggling. And meanwhile she had the daunting task of getting to Winstx, then perhaps to the other Oglassis, and then, who knows what.

She braved the open space between warehouses and walked casually to a nearby entrance. She would go though customs, board a hover-lift, enter the terminal, and mingle with the crowd of tourists and traders milling within. Then, using the crowd itself to protect her from attack, she would get to her own ship and Winstx.

Passing through customs was easy for a Travel Scout. Then, wrapping her travel hood more securely around her head and bending into herself, she merged with the crowd lined up at the hover-lift entrance.

The lift was jam packed with a sleepy group of Ursine commuters, munching on besinkberry honey muffins. The lift door opened into the huge domed port, an ornate indoor plaza, with self-service kiosks and multi-species environment areas. Ordinarily Telmx loved spaceports, their energies, their vibrant, expectant, adventuresome aromas and colors. But this time, something else, vague streaks of yellow orange energy particles grazed her temples.

She cautiously scanned, maintaining an even outer empath shield, searching for the source, and finally found a pair of young adult Imari. She panned past them, as if not to notice, registering their steady stench of purpose. Did Raymond have a whole squadron? They were shielded, scanning in small strategic bursts. So far they had missed detecting her, and now wouldn't except by sight, because she had again shielded to maximum.

She crouched behind a cluster of freight carriers and, at the most opportune moment, slipped into a multi-species commode and chose a defecation stall calibrated for the muribali species. Those young Imari pups were just inexperienced enough not to look for her in a muribali defecation stall. She squatted just inside the stall, grateful that the terminal was modern enough to leave only traces of scat for the comfort of the species, a vast improvement over the old-fashioned assumption that everything had to stink appropriately and loudly for each species, to give them the comfort of feeling as if they were back on their own homeworld.

If there were only two renegades, she could possible handle them. But what if there was an entire squadron? Why hadn't she even picked up a trace until now? Perhaps they had just landed. Not likely.

With extraordinary luck, or uncanny foresight, Telmx was in a defecation chamber of a species very different from herself. She needed to maximize their scat tracings and cover herself with them. The scat dispenser was in the ceiling, and without hesitation she located its receptacle and coalesced a ray of energy in its direction. Using an infusion power she hadn't needed to make use of in at least a decade, she sucked the scat pheromones into her nostrils, then slowly and methodically distributed the molecules into the cells of her sweat glands. She applied the extra splash or two directly to the outer cellular layers of her skin.

She worked slowly and methodically, all the while wishing she had the power to morph, to shape shift, a skill everyone was researching, but nobody except for the Kiolanthe, who kept their secrets well to themselves, had yet been able to accomplish.

Telmx was not sure of her strengths. She wasn't even sure if the damage Raymond had inflicted on her was permanent. She doubted that. No one could permanently dislodge the Imari powers, not even a rogue Imari. But Goshing's warning was ominous. What had happened to her and her comrades since she had left Galern II? Goshing's warning had come too late. The uneasy she and Winstx had been feeling. Had Goshing been trying desperately to reach them by any means possible, sending relays upon relays, without arousing suspicion? Perhaps Goshing had ultimately sent a message to her via the Oglassis. No, the Oglassis specifically told her that she should not communicate what she knew to Goshing. It would be too dangerous. She had to learn what they had learned from the tapestry itself. "Study the Legend." Was the Legend message in the tapestry V.E.? Perhaps, but there was no going back for it now.

How had Raymond been able to make her so muddy she would leave her travel pouch with its precious cargo hanging there for him to confiscate without a struggle? Were other Imari Scouting teams aware of the danger? How come no one had foreseen with future scanning, these horrific events that were now unfolding? Well first things first. No checking with the Oglassis. She and Winstx had to get off this planet, and out into an area of space that they knew no one could get to, and perhaps find their way to the outpost on Jupiter's moon, perhaps to Gir. Her beloved J would be just a small leap away, now with Johnny and Scotty. She hoped.

Or they could go to the home planet of the Oglassis, where they would definitely be protected. Perhaps not, if the rest of the Oglassis didn't know what had transpired. Well they could tell them. But the Oglassis were determined to stay out of politics all together. They didn't want trouble brought to their doorsteps. The deaths in Grjimbe City would further justify their policies. No, Oglassis-Prime would be the last place they could go.

Perhaps they should travel to the Kiolanthe themselves.

She reached with her mind into inner chambers and located her take-out mechanism, the one she had threatened to launch against Raymond. How bizarre. She had never needed it, never even thought about that power since training. Whatever made her summon deadly force? In training, they were only simulations, except for one real trial per student, to know how it felt to wield its deadly power. Back then she had taken out a small artificial target, whose cells were automatically distributed back into the simulator. It was drastic, forbidden except under utterly extraordinary circumstances. Should that power be required in battle, (one hadn't been required in Telmx's lifetime; only once in Goshing's), no one, nothing beyond the intended target could be harmed in any way. Worse, if there were unjustifiable reasons to wield it in the first place, the Council would have no mercy.

Telmx tightened her travel hood, pushed her body into a semi-squat position, simulating a creature that alternated between biped and quadruped. Closest she'd ever get to shape shifting. She waited behind the stall door until she sensed a group of Ursines near enough to the commode to blend with.

She was hoping for a group of taller species, but Ursines would have to do. She stooped as low as she could and stepped into the grouping.

She mingled in the crowd of Ursines, aware that they were looking around to see who or what was in their midst that could exude such a scat. She had no time to calculate what scats would be offensive to particular species. Several smiled faintly in her direction and moved slightly away, nodding and bowing, as if to say, we recognize you as a shorter Imari. We greet you with honor and respect, but we are also a bit offended by your scat. Telmx accepted the motions with as much grace as she could muster.

The renegades were nowhere to be seen. But she could sense them. They were lurking somewhere in the periphery, perhaps relying primarily on their olfactory and auditory perceptions to guide them, to avoid empath detection.

Then without realizing it, her feet were carrying her faster. Too fast. She was racing, in spite of herself. Fear carried her. That wasn't right. Fear always informed her; it never carried her without her will. She wrapped her mind around her autonomic nervous system and tugged it to compliance. A struggle. A tug of war within.

She summoned her inner chambers for more strength. Simultaneously, she realized that she was now alone, no longer surrounded by Ursines or any other species, alone in the huge crowded central dome of the spaceport, alone but not alone. Scores of sentients moved in all directions around her. But she was no longer camouflaged by any of them. Suddenly, in the corner of her mind's eye, she spotted the two Imari renegades, walking rapidly toward her. Not too rapidly, but slightly quicker than the rhythm in the port.

She ducked before she knew she was ducking, screamed before she knew she was screaming, as fire ripped into her left shoulder. She lurched forward toward the shuttle gates, vaguely aware of screaming all around, merging with her screams. The odor from her burning flesh seared her nostrils: new, wrenching, infuriating. Now the attackers were almost on top of her, wildly firing bursts of shattering shrieks as they approached. People were falling all around her. Screams, blood, and babies crying, all of it reverberating in her temples: grunts and brays, shrill whistles, and cries of disbelief, as various species sounded their alarms. Overwhelming carnage and terror around her. Blood gushed from her wounded shoulder, now hanging limp and useless. Though jagged yellow terror and pain assaulted her, she felt numb. She cascaded forward in uneven zigzags, leaving a slippery crimson trail behind her.

What happened next would replay and replay in Telmx's nightmares for the rest of her years. Before she knew what she was doing, she was hovering above her crimson trail, blindly tracing the yellow shrieks to their origins. In rapid, seamless motion, she summoned her formidable take-out, and launched it in the direction of the blaring. The silence that followed the sonic booms from her take-out was more silent than anything she had ever imagined or experienced. White silence. Frozen silence. Nothing moved. She found herself on the ground, clutching her shoulder, and unable to discern any life at all around her. She dared not open her eyes to confirm the horror she knew surrounded her. Her take-out had to have been poorly aimed, ill-conceived, reckless, all that it was not ever supposed to be, all that she had been trained never ever to do.

Telmx had wantonly and indiscriminately murdered. Taken out not just a couple of misguided young Imari, that would be horrendous enough, but an entire spaceport of people, perhaps an entire city. Certainly she didn't have that level of capacity. Certainly she never thought that she possessed that amount of take-out energy. Winstx! Goshing!

Unaccountably, someone was lifting her up. A cooling and soothing liquid was bathing her lips, and vague murmuring began to people the area around her. She struggled in vain to push her eyelids open and to pull her head up.

"Please lay still."

The voice was clearly Ursine, an elderly male Ursine. "I have staunched the bleeding as best as I can. I do not know how you did what you did, Madam Imari, but the pups who were shooting up the place have just disintegrated, completely disintegrated. Without you, scores more people would have been injured. Without you, people would have been killed. No, don't try to get up. I'm holding your shoulder in place. A med-team is on the way. Where is your ship, Madam?"

CHAPTER TWENTY-ONE

J

J awakened to find her and Scotty sculpted together, two nudes, inter-twined on the mat. She had fallen into a deep slumber on Scotty's chest, her face nuzzled gently on her breast, with Scotty's arm wrapped around her back and their legs woven to obscure ownership. Scotty was still enmeshed in her dream, their dream: ah, the dream had awakened J:

{She and Scotty were naked in a small hovercraft about to land on Europa, not an interplanetary vehicle, but a regional, low empath powered hovercraft, as if it were common practice to travel nude through the solar system in such an inadequate vessel. As they glided to a stop on this newly terraformed Jovian moon, they gathered boxes and boxes of equipment for some sort of guerrilla action.

But they had landed in full view of the very army they were supposed to surveil and ultimately overthrow. Why didn't Scotty know what she knew? Couldn't she see NASA's weapons aimed at the hatch? After all she and Scotty could read each other without effort. Why hadn't they landed in secret? They needed to take off again, get themselves dressed and armed, prepared like guerrillas, but Scotty refused to retreat, and instead was unlocking the hatch, oblivious, joyful.}

Now half-awake, J sensed that Scotty was still in their dream, eternally refusing to foresee the danger, eternally unlocking the hatch, oblivious and joyful. And no matter what J did, she couldn't reach her, even though their dream was in common, even though she was still pleading with her not to open the hatch, in both aloud and empath modes.

Perhaps it was only her own dream after all. Perhaps she was dreaming that Scotty was in her dream, that they were dreaming in common. Scotty stirred. She could, if she wanted, actually enter Scotty's dream, just to see, and then thought better of it. That's an unfair invasion of privacy, she thought. Besides, they hardly knew each other. She'd ask her later. Right now, she needed to shake away her dread.

Her heart was still racing, her empath energy exhausted from her struggle with Scotty's folly. Right now, she didn't want to move a muscle. Her new friend's tranquil cadence was soothing. What amazing luck to run into her. How blissful, in spite of their (their?) dream. Why Europa? Well, they'd figure it out later. A prescience? Scotty stirred.

"What's up, babe?" she empathed, a faint indecipherable empath echo slowly coalescing into words. "What about Europa?"

"I don't know; I, we, I mean, were you dreaming about Europa? You were, weren't you?"

"Just for a second. Wait, I don't know. Wow! Look at that. You were dreaming about Europa. I can't tell whose dream is whose. That's freaky! That's never happened to me before. What about you? Wow. Something about NASA. You were opening the hatch and I was trying to stop you."

J was stunned. "No, actually I was trying to stop *you.*"

They looked at each other. "You're kidding!" empathed Scotty.

"No, it's absolutely how I remember it. And boy, were you obstinate. I tried calling to you…."

"I know, I know. I just don't get it. Whoa, we got a lot to figure out, don't we? But, you know, we should really shield to max when we sleep. It's that scanning, you know. They could catch us unawares, zero in on our enhanced empath energies while we sleep, you know. We have to learn how to be together without detection. Those scans can easily pick up the empath energies emanating between us, especially when our guard is down. Far-out! Dream-merging. I wish we could do it again, just to figure it out, but I think we have to be real careful." She entered J's temples and raised their mutual shields to maximum.

Unlike yesterday, when Scotty's shielding offered relief from the migraine, the sudden empath silence was painful. Scotty's words were almost like a foreign language. Not having Scotty's inner thought to round out meaning, she had to fathom each word. Scotty's intense blue eyes radiated concern and determination. At least she could read her eyes.

"You're not used to this level of shielding," Scotty said. "Weird, isn't it? Like entering a sound-proof booth. Takes getting used to." She placed her hands on J's temples. "It'll take some practice," she said softy and slowly. "I'll show you."

✻ ✻ ✻

J had a few more weeks before classes started again, and Scotty hadn't yet found a job, so they had the rest of the summer completely free. Scotty taught J how to modulate shielding levels, and J brought her up to date on the latest ESP research at Duke University and NASA. They risked low-level empath mode, monitored for headaches, and slept fully shielded without merging their dreams, even though they were intensely curious about the phenomenon. They made love and traded stories, occasionally venturing out for long walks by the Hudson River, along the drive, along the rocks, or to pick up within the shrubbery and weeds ingredients for various intergalactic cuisines Scotty had mastered during her years off planet.

J took out her journal, songs, poems and sketches she had mined from the past and future, starting when she was in junior high school. Her teacher told her she had a brilliant imagination, and should be a writer. She never took her up on that because she knew, or thought she knew, her images weren't simply made-up.

During her visit to Galern II, she understood more. And felt even more burdened by the powers she brought back with her. "Here we are at the beginning of the Vietnam War, and we knew all along it was going to happen," J said. "I have a friend from first grade who's going to die in this war. And I knew it in first grade. Freaky, right? I like him a lot, but I can't do a thing about it. Do you have anyone like that?"

"My brother." They were silent for a long time. "I tried to dissuade him, but I also knew I couldn't really dissuade him. Its all so crazy how this works. So he's in Fort Bragg now. They're going to ship him out in less than ten days. He's going to die with what they call "friendly fire," you know, when they fire on their own. Funny, sometimes I don't feel bad about it. He is such a redneck and he's such a fuckin' bastard. But he's still my brother, you know." Scotty's eyes filled.

"I have a cousin who's too crazy to be drafted. He just turned 18 and he's already 4F. The only good thing about being crazy. He's strung out on acid somewhere, Haight-Ashbury, or Berkeley, Sausalito. Something like that. His parents didn't notice he was gone for a whole month and a half, and I wasn't about to tell them. They're like that, you know. When my Aunt Norma finally figured it out, she made a big drama out of it, but by then he had turned eighteen and he was legally allowed to run away, do anything he pleased. 'Oh he'll come back when he's ready,' she said, and that she always knew he would end up in some no good way. My uncle cross-examined me, like a goddamned detective. Calls me every couple of days. But I'll never tell him. Rusty called me on his eighteenth birthday to tell me he was 4F. I don't know how the hell the selective service found him, with no forwarding address. I guess they have their ways."

After a few days, Scotty and J gathered some camping gear and took a bus up to Woodstock, where beaded beatnick undeveloped ESP would drown out and protect them from being discovered while they again risked dream merging and practiced shielding techniques.

They lay down together under the stars in the meadow up by Meads Mountain Road and in the wee hours of the morning looked right through the Horsehead Nebula with their naked eyes. Fathoming it with all the empath vision they could mutually muster, they called to their Imari mentors. Squirreled in mounds of Imari blankets, they folded into each other's arms in the brisk mountain air and found new combinations of empath and lovemaking. And began pondering strategies.

CHAPTER TWENTY-TWO

Matt

On Tuesday morning, Charlie arrived unannounced with a surprise: a prototype portable, battery operated, real-time, surge scanner. "Don't ask!" he said, beaming proudly through his Baltimore Oriole's baseball cap. "Just take me out for a couple of pints and we'll call it square."

"Not without showing me how the thing works, you old dog. How'd you do this? Who gave the okay?" Matt was ecstatic.

"Like I said, don't ask. And I ain't promising you anything. Especially you. If you use it yourself, it's like getting boomerang feedback bigtime at a rock concert. You don't want to try. Let the guys do it, far away from you, or the only blue surge they're going to get is you. I mean it. I tried it on Yazzie and he threw me out of the lab, almost headfirst, it hit him so hard. So Dr. Matthew, you just can't use it yourself. I'll train the guys and dry run for you, without actually turning it on, and then you owe me two pints, at least, because this was a bigdeal coup. The world's gonna thank me bigtime for this one. But right now, you and Admiral QT Dawes are all I got."

✳ ✳ ✳

The next day Yazzie collapsed. NASA slipped him to a secret ICU at Bellevue Medical. Everyone thought he was dying, and Matt shuttled between his MPII scanning work and fighting with the staff to allow him to see the old man. He couldn't go and die now just when things were on the cusp of fantastic discovery.

Meanwhile, the guys on the MPII team registered full blue surges, high peaks, mostly on the Upper West Side and Washington Heights. Then, just when they thought they had a fixed location, somewhere in the West 160s, silence. Nothing. Just vague tiny peaks here and there around the rest of the city. Blasted. His next report to HQ was due within weeks, and the entire project was going up for renewal. Fuck it all! He should fudge some data just to keep Dawes hooked on New York until he captured a real honest-to-god blue surge in person.

Right here under his very nose, just like he thought it would be, and now zippo. Maybe those high blue surges at the demonstration were tourists? Well, what would they be doing on goddamned Washington Heights? Touring on the cheap? Do tourists go to commie demonstrations? Maybe they were outside agitators, hiding out at International House. Maybe Russian agents. Agitate. Disappear. Yes, Russian agents. Brownie points for nailing them. Maybe he should go back to the Company.

Maybe the surges were in town for a few days, or on their way back to college. Ah, where would anti-war types go to college, besides CCNY? Berkeley? Yeah, New York Jewish hippies love Berkeley.

Gotta get going. Gotta do some scanning grunt-work himself, even if it gave him migraines. Even if Charlie disapproved. Even if it's Sunday. The crew's day off. Not that they had a union. God forbid! But bureaucratic bullshit, civil service, military regulations. Whatever it was. Sunday was a day off unless it was an emergency. Well, it was an emergency! Yeah, but not by their crazy standards. Only an emergency to him.

Somewhere in Brooklyn the guys had been getting tiny hits, just tiny ones, but bigger than the general noise, especially by the ocean near Coney Island. So fish have some ESP? Probably. Well it's Coney Island. Why not check it out? Lots of commie hippies are Jews, and Jews sure as hell are crawling all over the place out there. Sunday, and it's fuckin' hot. Coney Island ain't a bad idea. Work and play. Check out some chicks. Follow a tiny hit or two, just to see where they take him. Maybe like a good James Bond movie, he'd find a strong blue surge in a real, you know, real buxom young thing. Would make the fuckin' headaches worth it. Besides, he was bored stupid. Might as well go out and scan around.

No choice anyhow. In their last meeting, QT had started on a new jag. New intelligence reports indicated that they were going to lose the entangled twin photon console race with the Russians. The consequences were monumental: Sputnik was going to be a mere blip on the Space Race screen when compared to twin photon space navigation. Not to mention the implications for the Arms Race. Monumental! Not to mention everything else they might discover they could do with this new technology. Staggering!

QT was pacing and shouting, forgetting Matt and Yazzie had perfected the whole fuckin' project, and had figured out what NASA needed to make the photons work for them. Instead he was actually blaming Matt and Yazzie because the NSC and everyone else super-important were on his back. He had to produce some strong new ESP-type console engineers to replace Matt and Yazzie real soon and force whatever recruit they located to serve, willing or not. Tell 'em it's their patriotic duty. For a 'greater good.'

Forced ESP? Not what Matt had in mind. First of all, it was probably impossible. Second of all, locating candidates and convincing them to become photon console engineers was one thing. Practically impossible, especially if they're reds. Would give them much too much information. Forcing them was something else again. They'd have to be "disappeared" and detained, retrained or perhaps truly "disappeared" for good if the console work ended up frying their brains like what was happening to Yazzie.

"Force them?" he managed.

"Yeah, pay 'em something of course. Get 'em involved, but if they're unwilling, for whatever reason, slip 'em an acid tab."

"A sugar cube?" Matt already knew what QT was driving at, as he sat in QT's plush underground office in Basking Ridge and watched his agitated pacing. There he was surrounded by a multitude of beautiful plants and trees, all lit by artificial globes. Somehow they didn't croak from QT's black-market Cuban cigars.

Slipping people LSD without their knowing about it was not exactly what he had signed up for. The MK-ULTRA program had been one of the main reasons Matt had left the Company. "It'll just help people along," QT continued. "You know, subtle coercion. They won't mind. Or they won't know. Besides, they'd find out that they like it. Most of 'em drop acid anyway."

QT's cigar stench made Matt gag. Well, it wasn't only the fuckin' cigar. Maybe he should leave MPII. It was really getting out of hand.

QT's voice rose to match his agitation. "Vivian has some possible ESP console engineer candidates from Duke that she wants you to scan, and I also want you to do the prisons next. Scan every penitentiary in the country. Tell 'em it's work rehab for their country and they'll be famous, at the cusp of scientific research, something like that. Tell 'em there'll get off for good behavior. And if those recruits don't cooperate, well then we'll do a little, shall we say, enhanced prompting."

"But the paired photons won't respond right. The console engineer has to be willing, committed, and most of all not distracted by trying to escape."

"You'll find a way, Dr. Matt. You'll experiment. Slip 'em a really good high, and voila! They're a photon engineer. Maybe they don't have to sit right at the console. Maybe they don't actually have to be at the controls. We just hook up their, you know, their surges, and let a real engineer feed the surges through, like a conduit. We'll figure it out. You'll figure it out. You and Yazzie. And Charlie. You guys know more than any of us how all that stuff works."

"Better if they're willing," Matt repeated. "At least with willing engineers, they would know the risks, having signed a contract and we'd monitor for abnormal brain activity, pull them off for a while when their brain starts to fry. Besides, who knows how sensitive blue surge type people are to LSD. The combination of the console work and an acid trip might kill them right in front of our noses the first time we hook them up. That's kind of unethical, don't you think? With all due respect."

"Look, Dr. Matt, you and your team go out there and scan for the recruits, and let our lawyers worry about ethics, okay? We're talking about goddamned hippies and Duke University freaks. We're talking about lifers and death-row inmates. Not real people. So if you can't find any 'willing' blue surge candidates in New York City by the end of the summer, I want your team to start working the prisons. I probably should relocate you to the prisons right now, and forget New York altogether. Too damned liberal."

Just a few weeks. He didn't want to work with goddamned prisoners. He couldn't imagine that they had the same innate talent, anyway. Not hardened fucking psychopaths. No, it was a real big waste of time. Next it'll be loony bins? No fucking way! He had to find willing subjects. Maybe not the pair of hippies at the demonstration, but other kids who would give their eye teeth for signing on to a fabulous pure science, wave-of-the-future experiment. Some of those hippy types were essentially very ambitious, young, privileged middle class spoiled brats just sowing their oats. He had to hunt down those kids! But he only had a couple more weeks.

He plugged Charlie's battery pack into his new "nifty-jiffy" scanner and placed it gently into his knapsack. Charlie was right. It could kill him if he did the actual scanning himself, without certain safeguards. Well, he didn't' have to soak himself in the scanning. Just do it a little bit. Take a Fiorinal, and perform some of Yazzie's brief mind-building exercise. So what if it looks like a goddamn Indian ritual. It might work to lessen the impact of scanner feedback. Not exactly like zapping his brain while working on the actual console.

An hour later Matt, now ritual and Fiorinal shielded, strapped the scanner pack onto his back, inserted the tiny earphone into his ear, and stepped out into the oppressive sidewalk heat. 43rd and Broadway was abuzz with tourist husbands in their pressed Bermuda shorts and their tourist wives in their pressed sun dresses, swarming around open briefcases filled with fake Rolex watches balanced precariously on cardboard tables; swarming around men in black conductor's hats hawking bargain bus tours. If his scanning migraines didn't kill him when the shield started wearing off, goddamn crowds, impatiently honking taxis, sooty wheezing buses, and screeching sirens surely would. He pushed his way toward the subway, dreading the beggars wallowing in their own piss and the unbearable iron-on-iron screeching.

He longed for open fields, soft rhythmic crickets—and cows. Why not cows? Yes! As he descended the subway steps at Times Square, harnessing cow ESP seemed absolutely brilliant. His cows talked to him when he was a kid. Why wouldn't they talk to photon pairs? Besides, the project would put him back on the farm. Milk them, play music for them, give them a bull to screw every once and a while, and hook them to some sort of conduit to the photon consoles. They never complained about those automatic milking machines. And they'd be willing. What did they know? And what newspaper would care if their brains exploded? There's millions of cows, and besides no one would have to know.

They'd set it up in a barn on Palm Island, something like that. QT would hate his kooky idea at first, but after a while he always came around. This ESP business: they needed kooky geniuses like him. The guys on top always wanted oddballs to think up their schemes, even if they hated their guts.

Cows, hmmm. At the token booth, he thought better of his brilliant idea. He liked cows.

The D train to Coney Island roared into the Times Square station and smashed his thoughts. He wondered if everyone got so smashed by the screeching. Plus the stifling urine stench. He flinched and tried to drown out the overpowering onslaught as best he could. He popped another Fiorinal, for the cause. In spite of himself, he thought about cows all the way to Coney Island on the El.

He changed into his bathing suit in the bathhouse, scanning all the time. When he stepped onto the boardwalk, he felt completely stupid and clumsy with his heavy knapsack on his hairy back. There was some sort of breeze on the boardwalk, offering vague relief. He searched for Nathan's.

Matt savored the sting of mustard smothering his perfectly grilled frank. In his other hand a tall bubbling Coke. New York had some redeeming qualities, he thought. And he was just a couple of blocks from the Hebrew National knish stand. The Jews sure knew how to cook. He knew this boardwalk like he knew the nuances of the south quarter at home.

Between bites and sips, Matt struggled to screen out the tiny bursts of blue surge signals from the sweaty kids squealing and careening around him. Mostly they were just a steady high reading. He'd already thought about hooking up kids in his desperation. Yazzie wouldn't approve of that. Well, he wouldn't either. Imagine if they hooked up his own kids. Every time it occurred to him that kids were the perfect solution, he would flush. He imagined QT drooling with delight. "Great idea, Matt my boy," he would say. "We'll contract with orphanages and buy us some Negro kids. They have nothing to live for anyway, so why not put 'em to good use with a little ESP?"

Whenever QT got really hopped up, his queasy Cuban cigars would singe Matt's throat. And then he would think of Yazzie wheezing his last breaths on the library recliner. In spite of himself, he loved his kids. Nope, kids were out of the question.

Matt navigated his clumsy self and his knapsack onto the sand, around blankets and beer cans and old Jewish hags with huge folds of fat spilling out of really ugly bathing suits. The ocean was calm, except for tiny rhythmic waves willing the reluctant tide outward. He walked slowly along the edge of the beach, letting wet sand ooze between his toes, wanting the cool lapping surf to distract him from the incessant scanner humming and blipping in his left ear.

Just a minute or two of actual ocean on his toes. He's allowed. Coming from a landlocked town, the only water forever was a small creek, and well, if you really wanted to travel, the Mississippi River. The first time he saw ocean was off the coast of Maryland. With Emma. Both of them just fell head over heels in love with the waves, and the birds, and the salty air. Probably it was the first and last time he actually felt love for her as well. If only he had someone right now to share this ocean with. Maybe he should bring Emma and the kids for a visit. Just for a weekend. Nah, no time. Besides, he'd have to answer her billion questions. God, she doted on him so, no matter what he did to her, what he thought of her.

The only time she ever flatly refused to do something he really wanted was when he wanted to fuck her in the ass. Just once. Just to see how it felt to do it with his very own wife. He pleaded. Then he wouldn't have to get it elsewhere. Not that he told her all that. But it would be really convenient and much cheaper. She cried and cried. She shook so awful, he thought he was killing her. Just because he wanted to fuck his own wife in the ass? So he'd get it elsewhere. Not with a man. NO! Never with a man. He weren't no faggot. Once he did it with Barney, his old collie. That was different. He was 13 and on the farm. All the kids did it. Goats. Dogs. Crazy Bobby even did it with a pig. Too much. Hated when his thoughts went that way. Couldn't help it. Have to get laid real soon. Maybe tonight.

When the first blue surge hit, Matt pitched forward, awkwardly breaking his fall with his hands. Nevertheless, the weight of his knapsack pitched his face right into a little tide pool. He spit the brine out, and involuntarily snatched the earphone out of his ear. It took enormous energy and willpower to pull himself up. He forced his fingers to push the earphone back into place, and looked around to see which bikini noticed his asshole tumble.

Another burst. This time he was prepared, digging his feet into the sand and rocking into the thrust. Flashes of jagged blue and yellow lights rushed furiously from the top of his head down the small of his back, burning and violently pounding at every cell along the way. Even with Fiorinal and the stupid Indian ritual. He wheeled around in all directions. Zap again. And again. He summoned the strength he thought he had lost forever in his twenties.

Stumbling over his own feet, Matt followed the surges along the water's edge, pulled by them, repulsed by them. He lurched headlong over sand castles and buckets and protesting kids. "Hey, pal!" shouted someone's dad, "Watch where you're going, why don't-cha?"

As he careened toward the Brooklyn Aquarium, the beach and ocean coalesced into a staggering bright blue blur, flashing, blazing, searing his temples, his spine, his fingertips. He forced his eyes to stay open, groping and toppling forward, no longer caring who witnessed his myopic frenzy. At the ticket booth he pulled out wads of bills, slammed them down, and lurched through the turnstile. Another hit! He swayed precariously just at the entrance to the indoor deep sea tanks, leaned against the wall for support, and without thinking yanked out his earphone. The next surge bathed and caressed him in warm, silky luminescence. He sucked in his breath and gave into the extraordinary sensations wafting around and through him. It was as if his entire body were suddenly infused with sensuality: his skin tingled with painful and ecstatic expectation, and his manhood yearned and released in spasmodic pulses. Swooning in ecstasy, he drifted toward the underground deep-sea tank exhibit.

With blue surges ebbing and flowing through his viscera, steady, comforting, discomforting, and so intense they exceeded his wildest expectations, he found himself face-to-face, eye to eye with a dolphin.

✹ ✹ ✹

Amid the tangle of IV tubes and monitor wires, Yazzie squinted at his friend. "Why do you look like you've seen a spirit from beyond, Matthew? I haven't joined my ancestors yet." His voice was slower even than a few days ago. More hesitant than ever. But at least he was out of the ICU. His lips hovered a bit between words, thinking about how to form themselves before each sound. He'll never be the same again, Matt thought, if he makes it at all. He waited for the stupid nurse to stop fiddling. Then she scooted out, without so much as a glance. Well, he *was* out of the ICU. That's something, however they figure those things out.

He realized he was still holding the new potted plant he had purchased in the lobby for a fortune and a half, and placed it on the window with the rest of the collected works of nature. Helicopters along the east river jackhammered his already abused temples. He strained his neck to try and catch a glimpse of the culprits. "They're pretty damned loud, aren't they?" forced Yazzie.

Matt turned around to face his friend, and pulled the chair up as close as the machines and wires would allow. Good thing NASA reserved secret hospital suites. With secret guards outside and specially security cleared private duty nurses. Aren't they supposed to be prettier than the regular ones?

"I have to tell you something." Matthew glanced toward the door and went on. "You have to promise not to breathe anything to a soul, not even Charlie. Not to nobody."

"Breathing isn't one of my strong suits these days, son, and as for souls...."

Well, at least he hasn't lost his sense of humor, Matt thought.

"I'm serious, Yazzie." Another helicopter hammered. How in the hell can they build a hospital right next to a heliport? Just plain asinine. "I just got detained at the Coney Island Aquarium: seized and searched like a common druggie. Of course they didn't find anything. I'm no hippie pothead or nothing."

"So welcome to the world of the underdog, the disenfranchised, the red/black/brown man. How's it feel?"

Matt hated when Yazzie seized the opportunity to push a political point. But, it was a sign of his old irascible self returning. Okay he'd take it. Maybe the old Indian won't die after all. He moved in a little closer, looked around to see if anyone was hovering at the door, and whispered: "They caught me having a conversation with a, a dolphin. They thought I was nodding out on horse."

Yazzie crunched his eyes into a smile.

"You don't believe me!"

"Of course I believe you! I used to talk to dolphins and whales all the time in my day. Lusty characters. But you, I know you have some talent in that area, but I didn't think, I mean not yet! I mean, well congratulations, my boy! There's hope for you yet."

Matt tried in vain to tell his misadventure in a few simple paragraphs. It was real close to the end of visiting hours.

Yazzie closed his eyes as Matt talked, but Matt plunged on. Yazzie would often listen with his eyes closed. In fact he did most things with his eyes closed. He spent most of his life with his eyes closed. Just as long as he wasn't dead yet. No alarms were going off; no frantic nurses were barging into his room to fiddle with life support.

He recounted in precise detail the scan data readings and their blue surge correlations at the beach.

Yazzie jerked his eyes open. "You used that thing yourself? What are you crazy? Look at what the console did to me. No different, you hear? They can't lose both of us, Matt. Don't be so stupid! Are you okay?"

"I'm fine. I'm fine, damn it! Maybe I'm not as fuckin' sensitive as you think I am. Yeah I got hit with it, so I turned the scanner off, but then well, somebody, something else did the rest."

He told him how he was drawn irresistibly to the Aquarium.

"Okay, good, You're not dead yet. Don't do that again. Ok, but you still haven't told me what the dolphins said to you." Yazzie's voice seemed stronger now.

"I'm getting to that...." He actually wished he didn't have to tell him that part. It wasn't important what they said to him. It was important that they said something. After all....

"Look, my boy. Old Yazzie here ain't no fool. You don't have to convince me they blue surge. I coulda told you that."

"You knew all along? You gotta be kidding. All this time we're looking for how to conduit those photons, and you knew all the time!"

Yazzie shifted his weight, sending the wires rippling all around him. "Damn these contraptions! When will you white folks ever learn!"

Matthew glanced toward the door. He wasn't supposed to get the old man roused up. Keep things light, and certainly not talk about job-related stuff.

"Dolphins are too damned smart!" Yazzie continued.

"Too smart?"

"They'd catch on in a nanosecond, go on strike before you could even think of hooking them up to a console. They don't need no fame and glory, power and prestige." He stopped for a couple of breaths. "So what'd they say to you, my boy?"

"Nothing very significant."

"Always significant. They always say what they think. I'd take a dolphin for a best friend any day. They're just damned embarrassing sometimes." He chuckled.

"This one dolphin, he just kept pointing his damned eye at my eyes, and demanded that I meet him just in his eye, like he wouldn't say anymore unless I really enjoyed, that's the word he used, 'enjoyed' entering his goddamned eye. Plus, he was smiling, friendly like, although at first I thought he was making fun, assessing me, criticizing me, thinking I was a goddamned asshole. Then—well , then—" He looked to see if Yazzie was still listening. He didn't want to exhaust him. But the old man looked like someone had poured red dye right into his cheeks.

"So then what? Come on, my boy, you got me perked real good. What'd the ol' guy say, 'Come on in and give me a blow job?' Wouldn't put it past 'em, actually."

"Just about—I mean, he said I didn't know the first thing about love, but he could teach me. How dare he? What kind of—I must've been imagining it, but no! He even invited me back, demanded it. Yeah! Told me how to sneak in at night and join him and his friends in their tank. Can you imagine? Shit. What kind of stuff have we stumbled on here? And how dare he—if, if— "

"If what?" Yazzie guffawed, juggling the entire console of wires. "I shoulda thought of it in the first place. It would take a good old-fashioned dolphin to get your mind juiced. How 'bout that? Look at you. You're madder than a cornered coyote, and more ablaze than one in heat!"

"Of course I'm mad, I'm furious! Look, man, I got enough trouble with my wife and kids and stuff without a stupid old fish giving me unsolicited feedback. Next he'll be inviting my whole family to the tank for a family session."

"Not a bad idea."

"Cut it out, Yazzie!"

"Think of it as a shrink tank!" Yazzie's face was crimson from laughing so hard, the wires flew and whipped in unison. "Oh forgive me, please forgive me, Dr. Matt, but I have more hope for you now and for MPII, than ever."

"What do you mean?" Surely the old Indian wasn't serious about sneaking his family into the aquarium.

"Do what he says. No, not your whole family. Just you. Do it."

"You can't be serious!"

"You bet I am. You got a true buddy there in the making. Take advantage. It's for free, and it's not like you don't know how to sneak around. Taking the aquarium is a piece of cake for guys like you. You know that. I can't wait to see what you and he come up with next." He paused. "Sure it's a he?"

"No question about that! You shoulda seen…."

Now they were both laughing.

"What a great piece of work, Matt, my boy. I couldn't have planned it better myself. Well, this is a great turn of events. I actually think you and your new buddy went and cured me. You know, dolphins are great doctors, better than these human assholes, even better than our ancestral medicine men. Boy, I envy you. So, when you gonna go? Tonight?"

"Common, Yazzie, give me a fuckin' break. They fuckin' practically arrested me in the daytime, and now you want me to sneak in at night?"

"No, you give me a break!" Yazzie was suddenly serious, angry, pointed. "You go there tonight, you hear? We got to get this project back on the road and he just might tell us how to find ESP talent, without you telling him why you are searching. Maybe he'll tell how not to get fried in the process. Whether you bargained for it or not, in your goddamned hunt for prestige and on-the-cusp research, you got it now. Not where or how you thought you would get it. But here it is. See what your old barnyard buddies did for you? Right back to cows and bulls! I shoulda known! Go for it, and when I get the hell off these gizmos, you'll introduce me to your new friends, and we'll all swim together. Right now, you blue-surged yourself into next steps. And goddamn lucky you didn't blue-surge yourself out of existence! Did you do those rituals? Maybe they work on you better than on me. Lost their potency over the years.

"And if talking to those fiery creatures changes your infantile personality in the process, so much the better. When you think I'm sending you to your grave just because I demand you meet eye-to-eye, brain wave to brain wave with an old dolphin, remember that I love you like a son, Matthew.

"Okay, Okay, but it doesn't have to be tonight."

"Yes, damn it, tonight! Why wait? Go a-swimmin' tonight. I'll be thinking of you, like we did when we sent those photon twins out into the cosmos together. Besides, we got a deadline. Gotta get a few true blue surges for Sir Admiral QT, didn't you say? So you get me all those blue surge reports you have from upper Manhattan. So's we can tell 'em we've almost nailed new console engineers. We'll tell the Navy, NASA, the feds, and whoever else is choppin' at the bit, just what they want to hear. Not about dolphins, we won't tell them one iota about dolphins. I'll figure something out to keep 'em interested and convince them to give your MPII crew some more time. But first you just get your ass into that tank!"

"He also said I was a lousy, a lousy—"

"What? A lousy son-of-a-bitch? I coulda told you that!"

"No—a lousy—" Well, he might as well just say it. "A lousy screw."

"Well, I bet he's right on that one. Maybe he'll teach you a thing or two."

"Not on your life! Screw you, Yazzie. Awright! Awright! I'm gonna do this thing, not because of you, but because I, I...." It was all he could do to keep from screaming. That would kill the poor bastard. Yazzie's monitors must be off the scale right now. But no one was smashing through the door. A guy like Yazzie could croak to the millionth exponential and no one would come, not even to pull the sheet over his head.

"Changed your mind, huh? Can't help but race right back there, right?"

"How'd you know?"

"I've splashed about with those rascals in my day. Enjoy 'em. And now let me sleep. You've exhausted this old bull. I need to get my strength back, now's I got something to get my strength back for! Get those printouts to me first thing in the morning, you hear? AFTER you have that little chat with Flipper."

CHAPTER TWENTY-THREE

Johnny

Johnny's head was pounding. From the center of his forehead to his left temple. Pounding was not part of his practice scenario. Heat, yeah, perhaps the slight stench of burning flesh, perhaps his hair, perhaps an ozone smell like before a serious thunderstorm. But not a goddamn headache. He kept his eyes shut, or rather, his eyes were not fully reformulated yet. He had to think of them as shut so they could finish reformulating. He didn't even have a fully developed skull yet. Okay, first things first. He had to make sure his shield was intact. No matter what, he must not be detected by empath scanners, no matter how primitive they happened to be. Next, he had to listen hard. Is he in a city? A suburb? In a forest? Near an ocean? In an ocean? Did he land on a white tablecloth in an outdoor café, a scorched black pebble, perhaps still reeking of reentry? He heard no outrage or surprise, so.... Nevertheless, he should prepare to roll in pebble form to a hidden area where he could finish reformulating himself: he should be preparing to inflate the pebble-sized capsule enough to float up to the surface of the ocean. Or, is he safe just where he landed?

He hoped he could stay put. The effort of rolling like a pebble required a surge of empath energy, scant as it now was, and he would need time to let that energy build up. He knew it was still night. At least Gir and the flight engineers were able to plan for that. He also knew he was in North America, or at least he thought so. They could also plan that. The rest of the trip was in genuine free-fall. Anywhere in North America from Canada to the banks of the Rio Grande, perhaps south of there, but not likely, given the initial trajectory. Ultimately he needed to end up in New York City, so he could connect with the two other earthling monitors (finally meeting them! What would they be like? Could he work with them? Gir assured him he could). The Europa outpost engineers aimed as best they could.

First he had to reformulate the catapult capsule, now a prune-like pebble, from the outside in. Like blowing up a balloon. That's what Gir said. Just blow it up. Slowly. Think about it from the inside of your essence, not yet a formulated real body. He concentrated. If the capsule were damaged at all, air would rush inside and crush him to death. Slowly. If there were any fissures, he needed to have enough energy to seal them as they appeared. He was impatient. Did his trumpet survive the burn-in? He wouldn't know until he reformulated the capsule into a whole, then his own body and finally, however long it all took, his travel pouch. Stop impatience.

Jeez, what if he's expanding in a conspicuous place, and there's a crowd of people standing around him, watching with awe. Someone has called the militia. "At first it just looked like a sponge just filling with water, but no, look how big it's getting. Watch out! Men from outer space!" He'd step out of the capsule and be surrounded by Uzis. "Mow him down first. Ask questions later." Oh Jeez.

So he stopped reformulating the capsule. Better first figure out where the hell he had landed. Yeah, that's what Gir told him. Get enough power going to figure out where you are. Scan the area. Roll or float, if you need to, while it's still dark. Expanding to original size and shape could take three to five Earth hours. So be patient. Patient. Shit. Uh-oh, don't get pissed. Yeah. Okay. He concentrated on building back energy. His headache intensified. Okay, has to be. Need to know where he is first before he mysteriously materializes out from a mere pebble. Oh Jeez. What time is it? Does he have time to scan and roll? Is it going to be light soon? Days in the summer were long, nights short. How much nighttime did he have left? Concentrate.

Well, there was no commotion. That was a good sign. It was actually deathly quiet. Perhaps he wasn't fully in tune with his surroundings. Deadly quiet. He concentrated beyond his throbbing. How could his head throb without having a reformulated head yet? Stop trying to find logic. Maybe he was more reformulated than he thought, and just couldn't feel it yet.

Grinding, a whirring grinding. That's what he heard. It was deep purple and black, with occasional flashes of yellow. Then it stopped. Men's voices. What were they saying? Calling. Yelling? No, just talking loud. Concentrate. It hurt to concentrate. Surely if anyone is scanning, they would pick up the energy of his concentration. No matter. He had to know where he was. They surely wouldn't think to look at a stupid pebble even if their scanning actually located this very spot. Okay. At least he was alive. Oh, that's a thought. At least he's alive. Alive but not safe. Okay? Okay. Back to concentrating. Silence again.

✻ ✻ ✻

The tall grass exhilarated his skin. He rolled over and let the morning dampness soak his stomach. Just a few more moments. He pushed his head onto the ground and took in the multiple fragrances of the soil. He wept.

Funny how he hadn't wanted to be here at all. Now he was home. Wow. His very own home planet.

He sat up, still naked, and hugged his knees. He still didn't want to finish reformulating his travel sac and retrieve his clothing and trumpet. Something about being as close to the damp earth as possible. Something about what might have happened to his trumpet. Something about Gir. Something. Besides, he needed to muster a lot more empath energy to finish reformulating his travel sac. His headache intensified once again. Jeez. Something about Gir. He pulled his knees closer and rocked. He longed to send out a strong empath call. Just to tell Gir he landed, on the actual soil of his homeworld, in one piece. Yeah! In one piece! Hey, Gir, just like you said! By this time Gir was back on Europa, desperate to scan just to assure himself that the burn in free-fall worked, that Johnny was alive and well. But he wouldn't dare, not under current blackout restrictions. Hell, Johnny would find a way to let him know. Some shielded signal that eluded the goddamned earthling scanners. What was all his training for if he couldn't find a way?

He eyed his travel sac on the grass in front of him, still sealed and partially reformulated, but now expanded to the size of a cigarette pack. A long way to go. Okay, in a few moments, he would start concentrating again and push it into full form. Before the sun got too high. It would take a couple of hours. But at least he could extricate his travel suit. Yeah. Needed to cover his naked self up before someone stumbled upon him. Whoa, that would be bad news. He closed his eyes and mustered whatever energy he had left. With great effort, he willed a gelatinous substance out from his travel sac. It oozed out slowly, and then lay wobbling in a pool next to the "cigarette box," now even smaller for having given up some of its contents.

He looked around. The grass was tall, silky. In the distance a constant roar. More like a drone. Perhaps a highway, the morning rush hour already. But where? A dog barked in the distance. Black birds were cawing and complaining. Well, no roosters crowing. No seagulls either. He longed to empath scan the entire area, just to get his bearings. No, he needed to build his reserve to finish reformulating the travel pouch. And then, as planned: go into total empath shutdown, at least until he figured out what was going on since he last left his planet.

The barking was closer. Now two distinct barking voices, maybe even a third. Or more. Closer yet. Shit. One naked black dude caught cowering in the tall grass. Where? In the Mississippi Delta? Ah, cornered by bloodhounds like a runaway slave. Shit. He focused on the gelatinous blob and shaped it into his travel suit. Okay. Now the booties. Jeez, hardly the sturdy Keds he needed to outrace a bunch of bloodhounds. As if he could outrace them. He struggled into his travel suit. The familiar fabric already felt alien. It shaped itself around his muscles, adjusting itself and clinging to every slight contour of his body, like a living creature hungrily embracing each cell as if it could never get close enough. Melding. Then his travel hood. No, maybe not his hood. Too weird. But surely the suit was weird. It left nothing to the imagination. He might as well be naked. Okay. Maybe he could pass as an acrobat out for his morning exercises. Yeah, a circus dude. Yeah, leotard and tights. Something like that. Better than in his goddamn birthday suit!

The barks were louder still, ringing in the pre-dawn air, echoing, calling back and forth to each other. Maybe wolves. No, they're not howling. They're goddamn barking like fucking bloodhounds. Wait, bloodhounds bay, don't they? No, they bark. Maybe prairie dogs. Yeah, prairie dogs. So much for panicking. Just prairie dogs. Now where on Earth do those critters live?

He lifted his partially reformulated travel sac and slipped it into his sleeve. His travel suit spontaneously molded itself around it. Then he crouched and waited. Uh oh, the expanded catapult capsule. Where was it? Oh! There! Ten yards from him, partially hidden by the tall grass, black, charred, certainly not a porous rock indigenous to the area. Open on the top, like a huge walnut shell, split in two, just sitting. Two humungous walnut shells shadowy in the predawn glow, shrouded by the tall quivering grass. He had to hide the stupid capsule. Why hadn't they thought of these contingencies ahead of time? Yeah, the plan was to squeeze it back into the size of a marble and slip it into his earthling pocket, once he retrieved his earthling clothing in his travel sac. But he didn't have the reserve energy yet to reformulate the travel sac, much less to shrink the whole goddamn capsule. Why didn't he think to pull out his earthling clothing instead of his goddamned travel suit? Jeez! He didn't even have enough energy to crawl over to the capsule to force the hatch closed. At this moment he couldn't even muster enough empath energy to push over a blade of grass. Okay, just lie still and wait for replenished empath energy. He entered replenish trance. If the dogs come, they come. They'll be his wake-up call. He'll take it from there, no matter what comes. No choice. As he flattened himself into the tall grass, he wondered what he smelled like to earthling bloodhounds.

"Lester! Bustea! Come! You jus' stop that fussin' and come!" A woman's voice, no a kid's voice in a foreign accent, but somehow still English.

With tremendous effort, he rolled onto his stomach and lay still. A definite thrashing amid growls and barks. He could feel the vibrations though his chin. Shit. The voice was directly to his left, just where his capsule lay. Shit. He held his breath. Don't move an iota. He had to concentrate without risking an empath look. He wished he could lift his head. Just a little. His chin chafed against the sandpaper ground. His ears searched in the direction of the capsule, which he couldn't see without moving his head. He turned, and his cheek scraped against some pebbles. He held back a wince. The capsule lay just as he had left it. Huge, imposing, obvious. The commotion was on the other side. Now why didn't they think to send him with a weapon? Just a fucking switchblade. That would do. So much for prescient thinking.

"Come, I say! Hello, what have we here?"

"What'd cha find?"

"Oh wow. Hey, Jimmy, wouldja take a look at this." Not southern. Well, that's a small relief.

"Looks like a friggin' rock to me. What's the big deal?" A hoarser voice, cracking, like an adolescent. "Hey! Where ya think ya goin'?"

A scrambling sound. The capsule moved slightly, and then a small blonde head appeared over the top. Johnny pressed deeper into the grass.

"No look! It shines inside. Come up here. It's all shiny and smooth on the inside."

Johnny pressed himself even closer into the grass. Where was the top of the capsule now? Would they find that also?

"Shit, you get the hell down from there. We better get outta here. Maybe it's radioactive or somethin'. Maybe it'll explode or somethin'. A broken land mine or somethin'. Let's get outta here!"

"Or a UFO, Jimmy. Just think. Maybe it's a UFO! Wow! We'll be famous!" The younger voice.

"You come down now! Get down from there right this very minute, 'fore I tell pa on you. Get down, I'm tellin' ya." More scraping, and the head disappeared from the top. "Let's go get pa. He'll know what to do. Bustea! Lester! Away from that thing now. Come on! C'mon, Jess. Now, Jessie!" Scraping and scuffling, and then their voices and scampering feet faded to faint echo, the dogs panting and yelping close behind them. They'd all be back real soon. He pushed himself up on all fours, and crawled painfully toward the capsule. Even crawling slowly felt like climbing a huge mountain without enough oxygen.

Several tasks left to do: Close, seal and shrink the capsule, reformulate his travel sac, get his Earth clothing on, and get the hell out of the area. Before those boys came back with lord knows who. Prioritize. How to do it. How much time did he have? Where to get the energy. He reached the edge of the capsule looming above him, and grabbed onto a crag on its porous skin. It looked much bigger than he remembered. Had he inflated it too much? Maybe he wasn't fully formulated himself. Oh jeez, maybe he wasn't even human yet. A tiny replica of himself. Maybe the grass isn't all that tall, but instead he is that small. What would become of him if he couldn't reformulate completely? It hadn't even occurred to him to check himself out. No time now to figure that out. What if they found him in this condition?

At least his heart was pumping. It pounded the soil, and he realized it was in fact reaching down into the soil, effusing it like a frimulator. Churning it. Okay, Okay, what's happenin' now? He pulsated with the effusion rhythm, plunging and groping into the moist pulsating Earth. It reached up in spasms to envelop his entire chest, now encasing and cradling his torso, now closing in on his groin and buttocks, now capturing his legs, leaving only left arm and his fingers clutching the crag on the capsule's skin. Quicksand! NO! He's going to suffocate! He was just succumbing to, merging with the rich warm soil as if he had done it a million times before, like an earthworm, undulating its way back home.

Just as his chin began to yield to the undulation, he tightened his fingers on the crag. Perhaps he could drag the capsule down with him. It was a plan that came from outside of himself. Like when the fusion empath jazz took over his soul, and he merged with Lenx, Rico and Raygoth, their rhythmic harmonies and timbres swooping and careening without structure or forethought. But there was structure, definite structure, almost divine structure, that defied his understanding. His Imari and Pomdos musician buddies would smile knowingly, and tell him to give up figuring it out. Well, there was no figuring this one out. Except for his left arm, he now lay completely under the soil, the soil and its creatures oozing around and through him, and he took uncanny pleasure in it, almost forgetting that he had to finish dragging in the capsule. He strained. It wouldn't yield. The soil hardened around it, refusing to accept its mass. Instead, it beckoned his arm, with unrelenting force, and he reluctantly let his fingers slip from the crag, and only found completeness when the tip of his index finger finally sank beneath the surface of the soil. Well, no one could find him now. If they took the capsule, well, so they took the capsule. He couldn't remember a time he had ever been more content and unencumbered by real or imagined concerns.

Johnny finally slept. A deep sleep, no dreaming, no V.E., no trance. Just sleep. He knew he had been sleeping, because he was awakened by loud scratching somewhere above him. Muffled voices and barking, panting dogs. He restrained turning up his empath ear. The soil was moving, opening in the direction of the scratching. He lay still as the growling and scratching came closer. Steady thuds resounded from one direction and then another, syncopating in steady and then unsteady cadences with the scratching. A cool wisp of air reached his nostrils. He opened his eyes, and looked into two huge deep brown eyes, intensely searching his face.

"Hush," he empathed to the creature above him. "Don't say a word. Please." Oh Jeez, has he lost his friggin' mind? He's trying to reason with a friggin' earthling dog. One thing to discuss the history of sentient mongrels at an intergalactic forum, another to assume these earthling mutts could do much more than complain and gnaw at their prey. Oh shit!

The scratching stopped.

A deep human voice, bass with a swath of baritone, gravelly, clip: "Whatcha make eh this he-ah thing, Jacques?"

"Hey, let's jus' get the hell outta here 'fore it explodes. We gotta call the sheriff!" Another voice, panicked, trying to sound steady and authoritative.

"Whatcha got the-ah Bustea? Come Bustea. Ya jus' come he-ah."

"You keep my secret and I'll keep yours," empathed the mongrel. "Now you keep perfectly still so's you get all your energy back. I'll send you an energy surge or two, but you're almost as skilled as us. How'd you manage? You clods don't have what it takes, except when you're mere pups and then you don't know any better. Don't you say a word either. We'll talk later. I gotta know everything, you hear? Everything. Wait'll I tell my pals." The dog pulled his eyes away and covered up the hole before Johnny could process what had just happened. Nowhere in his prescient wanderings…. No wonder Gir wasn't worried. With comrades like this! Jeez.

Johnny waited for the voices to fade, and then easily pushed his way up to the surface. A miracle! He was completely energized, and within minutes he shrunk the travel capsule to the size of a marble, expanded his travel sac to size, retrieved his trumpet and earthling clothing, shrunk the travel sac back to the size of a cigarette box, and plunked it in his back pocket along with the marbelized capsule. During each maneuver, he tentatively extended his empath scans beyond the field, just to see what was what, but he didn't scan much past the rugged rocky road over the rise, for fear of detection. Then, convinced no one was within shouting distance, he went about his work with miraculous speed. That mongrel must have given him quite a surge. Beyond his wildest expectations. Of course, he would have to make contact with the mongrel again; he could point him towards New York. He hoped. Unless the dogs were so provincial, they only knew the perimeter of their immediate wanderings.

His denims and tee-shirt felt so alien against his skin that he itched all over, and wondered if he would survive the chafing. At least he looked somewhat human again. He pulled his baseball cap low down over his forehead to cover his budding cilia. What would he do when they got so long he couldn't hide them anymore? Perhaps a sweatband or a stocking cap. Yeah, in New York he could get away with a stocking cap. But right now, he had to figure out where he was and whether he, a black stranger, was in any danger. Sure as hell he was. The accents were not southern, but they sure weren't from any place he recognized. At least it was sort of English. And most likely in the United States. The dog spoke regular like him, but maybe that's because he picked up his thoughts empathetically.

It was getting dark, again, and he was beginning to feel hungry. Hungry for the first time in how many days? He reached into his pocket and fingered the currency Gir had given him. What will it fetch him? He sure as hell wasn't going to chow down with the mongrel. He crept to the edge of the field and surveyed the rocky road. The air was crisp and dry, and the fields that flanked both sides of the road as far as the eye could see were various shades of green, peppered with gray and white pebbles. The odor was almost like musk, and the little plants in the field just across from him stretched in neat rows over the flat, until they converged at a fence, beyond which lay a blue-gray weather-beaten barn.

Should he simply walk upright on the road so he wouldn't look so suspicious? No, in isolated farm areas, even in the north, anyone not white would be sure to raise alarms. Where's that damned mutt?

Without thinking, he found himself among the rows of plants, making his way upright toward the barn. He stretched his empath vision just a bit beyond the horizon in all directions, and was ready to fling himself flat in-between the rows at the slightest movement. The steady drone of farm equipment did not emanate from anywhere near the barn, which seemed abandoned, or at least only used to store old equipment. If he could make it there, he could collect his thoughts, perhaps figure out something to eat, call to that mongrel. Bustea. That's his name: Bustea.

By the time he was several yards from the barn, his hunger was overwhelming. Only then did it occur to him that the rows of plants might be edible. There was a stretch of open space between the end of the planted field and the barn. He lay down on the rocky soil between two rows and pulled at a plant. To his delight, up popped a tiny round starchy object. A potato! Holy Jeez a goddamned potato. He pulled up a few more, and gathered them in his cap. Whoever thought potatoes could sound so good? Jeez, he'd forgotten about such things. Once he found his way into the barn, he would auto-effuse a feast.

So engrossed was he in gathering his dinner, that he didn't hear the roar of trucks until they were almost upon him. On the other side of the barn, a road stretched in both directions. The dust and pebbles were flying and whipping beyond the corner of the barn, with a blaze of blinking white, blue and red lights rotating and shimmering, but in sinisterly silence, rushing toward him like a tornado or a cloud of locusts. He flattened himself out as best he could, and shielded to maximum, just as swiftly as the lights sped past, swung around the next field, and came roaring back in Johnny's direction, but now on the far side of the field. They screeched to a halt, and Johnny discerned three or four fire trucks, a brown and green jeep, and several cars with rotating flashing lights. He hadn't abandoned his landing area a moment too soon. What are those guys going to do when they find nothing there? The terrain right here was very dusty and rocky. What if they find footprints? Shit, he hadn't thought about that. So much for auto-effused potatoes. He shoved them in his pockets, smoothed the ground around him and slithered on his belly back the way he had come for several yards, churning the pebbles and dust to obscure his tracks.

Then using all the empath strength his could muster, he hover-lifted his body a couple of inches off the ground, but kept himself horizontal to it. The maneuver was empath energy expensive. It meant he'd need another night of re-energizing before he'd have enough energy to actually escape the area altogether. He hovered himself directly toward the barn, barely skimming the surface of the open field, and managed, with a last burst of energy, to glide himself into the partially opened door, almost careening headlong into a rusted old tractor parked just inside. With a heavy grunt, he lowered himself to the ground, and looked for a hiding spot. His head hurt now, and he was desperately thirsty. Well, all must wait. Barns have lofts, don't they? He searched above him, and with great effort, he found his way up a rickety ladder, and climbed like an ordinary earthling.

From a small window he could survey the field, the vehicles beyond, and at least a dozen or so uniformed people moving about. So far, nobody seemed to be interested in his potato field. Okay, it was almost sunset. Once he found his energy, he could go back and harvest more potatoes. But right now he needed to rest. Jeez, so much resting! What had happened to his youthful vigor? Maybe he would never be able to sustain a high C ever again. In this dizzying state, he swooned into a deep sleep.

A wetness on his cheek and a panting in his ear pulled him gently out of unspeakable nightmares about Gir lying in a pool of blood under the El.

"Look Mac, I brought you some dinner. It ain't much, I figgered ya must be hungry, having traveled and all. Can't do much with those raw potatoes, you know." Bustea pushed a paper bag into Johnny's blurred vision. "And I hope ya don't mind, but I brought a couple of the pals, just in case ya felt like company. You know, I told them I'd have to ask you first. They're real curious, you know. We don't see critters like you round these parts, and I told them how this dark one can even talk behind his eyes like us, so'd they're all hot to take a look. Do you mind? Nah, I thought ya wouldn't. Yeah, the grub's right here. Hold on. 'Taint much, took it off the kid's plate when he wasn't looking, and the other kid, the little pup, always hands me stuff, you know. We took up a collection." Two other mongrels, one a tiny terrier type and, the other, larger and shaggy brown like Bustea, appeared in the blur, panting and murmuring an unbearable cacophony of questions into the right side of his head.

"I actually haven't got much empath energy left," he managed through the din. He slumped against the barn wall, overwhelmed by the spirit of the little group, now calmly and quietly sitting opposite him. At the same time, he clearly perceived the rush of warm, almost golden effusions rushing through his blood and into his skull, as if each and every dog were privately injecting him with some highly charged substance, with the thickness of mercury, and the potency of the highest caliber raw and unharnessed empath energy, like he had experienced off world, and more recently on Europa before embarking on his free-fall trip to Earth. He welcomed it, but it also made him dizzy. "Too much. Wait, too much," he pleaded. And just as easily the flow stopped, as if someone had pulled a switch.

"Go ahead," empathed Bustea. "Take some people grub. We can wait a bit, can't we, fellas?" To Johnny it seemed as if Bustea enjoyed his role, as if Johnny were some sort of trophy that Bustea had rounded up for all the others to see and to admire him for finding. He was in charge, and he liked that.

Under the thoughtful calm eyes of the mongrels, Johnny scarfed down vegetables, bread slices, and some hard cheese. He gagged at the sight of some broiled meat. Hungry as he was, he couldn't push himself to eat the flesh of his brethren from off-world. "Jeez," he thought, "I've become a goddamned vegetarian! No more White Castle sliders for me!"

He pushed the slices of meat out to the group, and to his surprise, no one took them. He was now able to survey the bunch, as they sat patiently waiting for him to initiate conversation. It was like being in Journica or Galern II, or especially in Belorsha VI, where intergalactic species gathered for periodic ritual retreats. There he had met coyote-like creatures, some of whom were as mongrel as these folks were, but, of course, on Belorsha VI, they would be so wrapped up in their own issues and meditations, they would pay him no mind, even if he looked odd: yes an Imiari looking fellow, but weirdly smaller and with poorly formed cilia and stunted empath capacity.

In Belorsha VI, it wasn't until he took out his trumpet at the evening entertainment (which was why he was there in the first place) that they actually took notice of him, especially a particular group of coyotes and wolves, who howled along with his trumpet and demanded lessons, private lessons, not only on how to blow the instrument but on how they could manufacture them. Yeah, they had been fun. Never in a million years had it occurred to him that he would find some resemblance on Earth. Holy jeez.

Plus, in his memory, he had never experienced earthling dogs like this. Offer a dog a scrap of meat, and they'd fight over it. That's what he remembered, growing up with the various dogs in the alleyways (his mom, foster mothers and then his uncle never allowed dogs. Too much trouble). He had some of the alley mongrels as friends, but they never really talked to him, well, maybe in pretend, when he was five or six. Maybe it hadn't been pretend after all.

Now the silence was deafening. Yet all out of respect of his wishes.

Bustea broke the silence. "The blood has returned to your skin. It glows like coal, my friend. Where you from? We really have never met a creature like you before. Can all dark- skinned humans talk behind their eyes? Why does your fur sit like a poodle on the top of your head? And you seem to be growing soft whiskers above your eyebrows. Are you part cat? We have so many questions. And we know you're in danger, but we can't figure out why."

"First things, first. Let's get to the basic questions first," empathed Johnny. "Where am I?"

"On Scofield's farm. In glorious Athens," offered the small white and gray terrier.

"Greece? Oh shit!"

"Athens, New York!" they empathed almost in unison.

"New York!" Pretty damn good, Gir. Pretty damned accurate!

He looked at the group. "Okay. I gotta get to New York City. Do you know how far I am from New York City?"

✳ ✳ ✳

There was a chill in the air, and Johnny's earthling jacket pushed down heavy on his shoulders. So many things he had taken for granted in his travels. Like lightweight wishapthas that kept him cozy warm in the freezing cold mountains of Galern II. Now to get used to a night sky with only one moon, without constant auroras, like on Galern II, or the red/green glow on the eastern horizon on Mimnar, or the shimmering dust storms off the western limb of the rest stop asteroid between the Galern and Delray systems. The familiar and unfamiliar Earth sky cast its own kind of glow on the potato field. Just last night all he could hear was his own heartbeat, and pounding head. Now crickets and scampering critters were trading fours. He filled his lungs. He hadn't tested out his trumpet yet. Nah, wouldn't dare. Not yet.

Now to figure out directions. These earthling dogs didn't know diddly about how to get to New York City, not even which direction was which. They did know something about truck stops and small-town gas stations. Well, that's a start. He'd coalesce himself back into his capsule again and roll. That was the plan.

Now to get his bearings. He'd traveled all over the civilized universe, but getting his bearings on Earth? Not nearly as safe. Not for a dark person. Not on this part of the planet. The potato field was quiet and comforting. Oh, the Big Dipper, his uncle's mom used to say, "follow the drinking gourd." Yeah, there it is. Turn your back on that drinking gourd. That outta do it. Assuming he's north of New York City. He had to be. The city was as south as you could get in New York. Running away in reverse.

He turned slowly and faced a huge lantern in the sky. Oh Jeez, Jupiter. Sure as he's standing there in the potato field. It's Jupiter alright. So it's setting in the west? Rising in the east? Off to the south. Sort of south. Not quite as far south as it would be in New York City.

Okay! Getting it down. Turn your back on the drinking gourd. Follow the lantern. At least Gir's there on the Galilean moon. He tried to relax his eyes, and let the tiny dots of Jupiter's moons come into focus. Imagining them? He never remembered Jupiter being that bright before, before he traveled off world, or even that obvious. He swayed a little, not sure if he was falling upward into the lantern or downward into a cluster of potato plants.

He re-coalesced himself into a non-corporeal entity, willed himself into his pebble-sized capsule, and rolled away from the drinking gourd.

CHAPTER TWENTY-FOUR

Telmx

Telmx winced and writhed on her mat. At moments the spasms were so
sharp she feared she would pass out and never awaken.

"Hold on there, Tel!" empath-shouted Winstx from the helm. "I can't di-
vide my energies right this second. Just hold on!"

"I will. I'm sorry. I can't even shield my spasms from you. I'm alright. Just
don't listen to me!" She twisted in anticipation of the next one. Spasm after
spasm. No end to them. And between spasms, endless worry. Try to control
the spasms so Winstx doesn't get distracted.

Winstx was maneuvering their ship out of Grjimbe's gravitational pull as
rapidly as she could. Fortunately things moved slowly on the Ursine planet
when it came to wanton violence. Their medical response teams were well organized for accidents, but there was no forensic system. They were practically
unheard of in modern times, major apathy and ignorance: fewer and fewer
planets believed that treachery was possible. Some planets didn't even have
words for it in their species' vocabulary any more.

The Ursine medics had performed emergency surgery, but time had been
short. They needed to get her back to her ship before any Council representative detained her for using the deadly take-out.

She would require many weeks of quiet concentration to recover from
her wounds and burns and to regain her strength. If she lived. Dark purple ooze was slowing growing from a corner of her inner eye. Death. "Oh
no you don't," she thought. She forced her inner eye away from the ooze
and searched her inner chambers. At last she located a scant crimson ember
of raw empath energy. But the glow ebbed and retracted without growing.
Replenishing was much more difficult than it should be. Her wounds were
depleting her energies as fast as she replenished them.

"Tel, the gel tubes are on your right side. Can you find them? Hold on,
girl, we're almost out of the system. No one is following us. Just a few more
minutes here."

Telmx groped for the tubes. She pushed thought into a corner and slowly, painfully applied various potions to the wounds and burns she could reach, twisting and turning to maneuver her hands, and to brace for the next inevitable spasm.

She lay down on her back again, struggling to visit each wound in her mind, calling upon fluids and organs, rerouting resources. The salves would aid the process, but she had to guide them in their work. The undulating purple ooze sat patiently, like an oysigot lying in wait for its prey, its advance thwarted for the moment. She had to trust.

She had never experienced a synergistic empath drain. How does she replenish empath energy from such a dry place? Her reserves were all but empty. What had happened?

"Tel, stop it! I mean it! Thinking, worrying and raging are killing you! Please! Push thought away! I'm boosting the ship *and* you. Gotcha! Let me do it, Tel. I gotcha."

From some far away place, Winstx's gentle massage joined her own. Gentle breezes. Gentle let-go. Gentle darkness.

✻ ✻ ✻

Winstx squatted opposite Telmx under an omblhgatr tree. Its leaves were broad and comforting, emitting a soft, smoothing aroma. She lowered her head, inviting her comrade to do the same. Their cilia touched. That morning, before primary sunrise, they had made love, long delayed while Telmx's wounds healed. Sweet fragrances of lovemaking lingered.

Telmx inhaled deeply, uncomfortable with Winstx's silent entreaty to wait just a bit longer before delving into the crisis. The network of rogues and thugs was growing at an alarming pace, even reaching into their secure and vigilant Imari homeworld.

So far their secret rendezvous spot on the fifth moon of gas giant Uthitks was still safe. Perhaps not for long. Years ago they had picked wisely, and the tiny paradise they had constructed deep in one of the many crosshatches of canyons offered comfort and shelter, while positioned for a rapid response strategy should they ever be detected.

Telmx was grateful to Goshing for originally suggesting that Winstx complete the then- fledgling triad: "Old Gir for salty wisdom; Winstx for patience, warmth and practical ingenuity." Winstx could also rise to the occasion of hardy, gusty guffaws, especially when Telmx and Gir got going over several goblets of bot. Winstx could also tell an uproariously wicked joke like the rest of them, having let her guard down. Because her jokes were essentially out of character, they were all the funnier.

Like all the Imari, she was thin and tall (not as tall as Telmx, who seemed to tower above even the tallest of their species), and although she spent a good deal of her "down" time working out on a set of hover counter-balances she had designed and constructed herself, one wouldn't know, to look at her, how strong she actually was. Quiet, unassuming strength. Telmx adored the way her full and voluptuous mouth pursed in thoughtful musings of imagined scenarios. If she hadn't been an Imari Travel Scout, she would have devoted her life to working out and writing fantasy tales and self-spun treatises on scientific "what-if's." "In my next life," Winstx would quip, when urgent responsibilities interrupted one of her scenario weavings. She half believed that there was a real-world next life, far different from residing after death in an inner chamber of her primary student. "Well, maybe your Scotty will become the next great American novelist, and at last sci-fi will find its rightful place in American literature," Telmx would quip back, and there it would sit, Telmx wishing in one of her most shielded places that Winstx could indeed devote her life to what she loved best. But they were living in dangerous times. And she desperately needed Winstx in this life, and so did Scotty, her trainee, for that matter.

Now Telmx was an outlaw, and Winstx her accomplice. It happened so quickly. Certainly the encounter with Raymond had initially disoriented and drained her energies, which could not have helped her judgment when she confronted the two renegade Imaris. She had obliterated them by instinct, by methods she had never summoned except in student simulations, without forethought and strategy. It had just happened. Fortunately the Ursine medics were quick to understand, and not turn her in to the Council rep. But how would she ever explain it to the Intergalactic Council?

Imari scouts were supposed to solve danger, impending, and clear and present, by more civilized methods: anticipating and averting, stunning if absolutely necessary, or even fleeing, disappearing from a dangerous situation brilliantly and completely in order to consult with triad comrades, or with an elder supervisor, or with the Council. She trembled. An outlaw. Gir not in shouting distance, and Goshing unavailable. In this case, they might never forgive her for disobeying the Code of the Order of Empath Travel Scouts. And the Pomdos block would use any excuse it could to discredit her and her triad team at the Council.

"I tell you what," empathed Winstx. "Let's take a hover climb to the top of the canyon and back. I think you can mange that now. We'll work up a hardy appetite, maybe even pick some vifdyhth spices, suffuse ourselves a fabulous taste sequence, and then we can analyze what happened and figure out what to do next."

The gas giant was beginning to set as they reached the top of the ridge, and two sister moons glowed red and orange on the southeast horizon. It was Telmx's favorite time of day on Uthitks-sub5.

"It's difficult to know who to trust anymore," empathed Telmx. They were squatting on the canyon rim. "My run-in with Raymond and the attacks at the space port really are mind-boggling. Most disturbing, I didn't pick up the depth of Raymond's sinister." Winstx wanted to delay this discussion until after they had made love yet again, but Telmx was anxious not to put off the inevitable any further.

"Well, I guess duty calls." Winstx sighed. And without waiting a beat, "In spite of me, I've been thinking a lot about what we need to do. First off, we need to study that woven V.E.-tapestry the Oglassis gave you, perhaps rooting around your chamber libraries to catch a glimpse of anything you happened to pick up from it."

"I hardly entered it."

"Yes, but you know, even brief entry might have lingered in a library. Especially those that weave a V.E.-tale."

"True enough."

"So—"

"So somehow—"

"You're fearful of delving."

"It strikes a strong uneasy."

Another moon had risen. A rare synchronization of moon orbits cast triple shadows on the canyon walls.

"It would be better if we found Orja and Beja. Maybe I can remember where they said they were going." Telmx closed her eyes and tried to reconstruct the moment when Orja and Beja had given her their gift. Then she was going to have dinner with them. She was late....

The stench. Rounding the side of the warehouse. Charred feathers and flesh. "Oh Winnie! They're dead! I can't believe I forgot! They didn't want to get involved. Just felt they had to. They made an exception." Telmx collapsed into Winstx's firm grip and allowed grief and horror to overtake her.

"Take it easy, Tel. I'm right here."

"I almost said that we should find them, as if they were still alive! Have them describe the tapestry's V.E.-tale. Then I remembered the stench. I remembered the charred stench first. I completely forgot about that until this moment! I went completely berserk that day, didn't I?"

"From what I'm picking up, the problem started in the relay station."

"I was on my way to break froth with the Oglassis on their ship. I knew I needed to go there, but I was a whole day late. Then discovering them like that. But I didn't remember until now. How eerie. Do you think—?"

"Raymond."

"The T'cha box!"

"A kind of retro-sweep, a selective and incomplete." Winstx leaped away from their empath connection. "You know what?" she stumbled over her out-loud words. Her agitation was so uncharacteristic, it startled them both. "It's too brilliant, it could only be conceived by a turned Imari Level VI, someone who could understand and wield the power of partial retro-sweep to his advantage. Of course you lost control of your empath powers."

"I almost took him out. He knew I could do it because he had already retro-swept my capacity for good judgment in the cube. He let me go once he tested his dirty work. He knew I wouldn't go for the take-back proc. He didn't want me to, and manipulated me into making the decision to forgo it and just get away from him. Then he just let me go!"

"And then you responded at the terminal port out of instinctual response. Your energies were bottled by Raymond's retro-sweep, so you were ready to fire like an old-fashioned cocked laser. When you unleashed them on those creeps, they never knew what hit them."

"Raymond set them up, just like he set me up, knowing what would happen when they tried to go after me. In effect, he concocted a scenario that would force me to become an outlaw to the Imari Order, perhaps even to Goshing and the elders."

"And to yourself."

Understanding why she unleashed such empath force was partial relief.

But who were those attackers? And why did they want to destroy the Oglassis? How is Raymond involved? Is he part of a new organization? Perhaps that's what Goshing was warning her against. How did the Pomdos fit in? If at all. The Pomdos didn't believe in violence. They believed all could be solved with words and reasoning. "Peaceful Reconciliation," they called it, even assuming they could reconcile with the most backward and determinedly violent elements, like those she had discovered on Earth. The closest the Pomdos and their block ever came to reading and understanding The Books of Kro'an'ot was to gloss over secondary school summaries which they then quoted out of context and criticized contemptuously as so much ancient and outdated fear-mongering. Those days have long since passed, they argued, completely irrelevant in today's enlightened universe.

Winstx wrapped her arms, legs and cilia tightly around her comrade's rage and grief. "Time for a swig of bot and a good old-fashioned taste sequence," she empath-whispered.

"We haven't finished figuring all this out. Besides, I don't know if I can break the froth right now, or even if I should."

"Look, I'm not talking about shoving things into oblivion. Just making stuff a little more bearable. Besides, a bit of bot will help us figure out that tapestry tale. I have a strong feeling about that."

They hovered slowly down the side of the canyon, with triple moon shadows mimicking their decent. By the time they had auto-effused the dipping sauces and set the bot goblet between them, night critters were calling for their lovers. Echoes. A hutio howled nearby. Another answered further off.

※ ※ ※

Telmx crouched at the edge of a small clearing in the forest. From the forest beyond the clearing, the faint scent of bot'ime. In the blue-green patch of grass, an adolescent giontha turned her head in Telmx's direction and sniffed the air. It was a small sinewy creature, about the size of an Imari child, but infinitely stronger. If frightened, it would ask no questions. Gionthas were formidable protectors of the Kiolanthe, whose nests, she knew it without knowing, were less than 20 meters into the forest beyond the other side of the clearing. If there was one giontha, there must be others nearby. Its elders, for sure. But Telmx could not discern them.

She held her breath. Slowly and tenderly she reached for the giontha's sophisticated olfactory chamber. Surely her empathed message would penetrate its powerful field of stenches. "Here in peace, in solidarity, in friendship. Please inform the Kiolanthe that we have finally come." A fiery blast of stenches rushed through her nostrils and she withdrew. Telmx shook off momentary dizziness. The giontha shifted weight and suddenly crouched so low, she seemed to meld with the grass. Telmx held her uneasy in check. There had to be a way to penetrate this creature's tenacious. She closed her eyes and tried talking to it again. A multitude of blasts hurled her backward into the grass. Howls rushed into her head from all directions. Claws ripped at her arms, neck, and face. The stench of blood, her own screams filling her chambers. She instinctively curled herself into a ball and struggled to hover away instead. Her mind wrapped around the take-out. Not again! Not now! All in an instant. Telmx heaved herself upwards, beyond the claws, but something was grabbing at her, pulling violently at her shoulders. Wrestling with her take-out.

"I'm here, dearest! Hush, they're gone!"

"No! No! The howls! Get them off!"

"Come, Tel, come with me. Right here. See? We found them. Look! Just for a second. Then we'll wake up from our dream. C'mon, we have been informed. We know exactly what we have to do. We're on our way. We know exactly what we have to do."

Telmx heard Winstx's words through the howls. They were strong, excited. She suddenly wasn't hurting. Howls now in the distance. Calling and answering, calling and answering.

"Let's finish our dream! Look!"

The bot'ime roots were already laid out in a circle, a small mound smoldering gently in front of each Kiolanthe. Winstx, squatting opposite Telmx in the circle, lifted her neck to reveal her throbbing veins in silent support. In the center, a very pregnant female was propped up on a bed of leaves and crushed flowers. Around her were four females, who chattered and sang. The outer circle blended, as if in chorus, clicking, chirping and beating the ground with their paws in a steady rhythm, in cadences so loud that the Imari were sure the vigilant pack of gionthas would hear them and investigate. But none came, because the loud was mostly in their heads. The birthing ritual was long and joyous, and when the minuscule baby cub was finally passed around the outer circle, still covered in his milky amniotic fluid, Winstx and Telmx each took her turn, like the others, licking the babe clean, sucking in the sweet aqueous nectar, and reeling from an intense energy rush.

Telmx awakened still quivering. Winstx's eyes met hers, her arms and legs holding her in reassuring embrace. "You figured it out, Tel," Winstx empathed softly.

Without empathing another word, the two Imari rolled up their mats, packed their gear and hiked down the canyon to the shuttlecraft. Telmx marveled at her renewed energy. By sunrise, they were in the starship, breaking though the crisscross of Uthitks and plotting coordinates for the mythic planet Kiol.

Winstx broke the silence a few hours later: "I never thought I would ever meet the Kiolanthe in my lifetime."

"Me neither." Telmx smiled. "Thanks for jumping into my dream. Those gionthas are fearsome."

"Are they real?"

"I have no idea. I guess we'll find out soon enough." She paused. "I seem to have known the tapestry's message all along. I even dreamed about Kro'an'ot in Grjimbe City. I wonder if the Kiolanthe know we are coming. I wonder if they sent the Oglassis to find us."

And later, from her uneasy: "Winnie, I am very worried about how readily I still pull for my take-out."

"I know. Perhaps the Kiolanthe will help with that too."

"I really need Goshing."

"Well, we don't have her right now, so I guess the rest of us will have to do for a while."

CHAPTER TWENTY-FIVE

J

Making love glowed in the dark. J already knew that, but this was different. This glowing shimmered over the meadow, its bouquet incredibly sweet, like lilac. Maybe it was just very different with earthlings. With Telmx the afterglow was intense: reverberations and echoes. J's whole body would be swelling and undulating, often for hours afterward, almost too much. Sometimes it would be several days before she could let Telmx touch her like that again. And then she was wanting her so bad, the pain of wanting would drive her to distraction. With Scotty, the after-sensations wafted around her, gently, almost imperceptibly, a fine filament mist, and just so sweet. And then she wanted her so bad within minutes. Not better or worse. Just different.

Scotty's fingers were searching for hers. She shifted her own and they touched. Her body tingled. She pushed her thigh next to Scotty's. She knew Scotty was smiling, having heard J's thoughts, but not wishing to break the silence. Not even break the empath silence. Scotty placed her hand over J's.

Their families were very different. Scotty's dad, a high school history teacher, doted on her, and treated his wife and children with kindness and compassion. But he died when she was thirteen, and her mom "kind of lost it." Out of embarrassment, Scotty dropped her friends, squirreled herself in her room away from her mom's demons, and filled mind with her dad's books. "We lived in a very small town, Pinewood, Michigan, and I was trapped, miserable and dying to see for myself all the places I read about. That's how Winstx found me. My baby brother just got more and more bitter, dropped out of high school and hung in bars and shooting ranges with the town rednecks. Maybe if I hadn't followed Winstx into the universe, I could've helped him find his way. Dunno."

That night was the peak of the Perseid meteors. "Did ya see that one?" They traded squeals, like little kids who had never traveled anywhere in the universe, or seen incredible celestial phenomena.

Jupiter inched above the trees.

"I wish we had a telescope," empathed J. "We could see its moons, maybe even find the Europa outpost."

"I'll try and find the right one," empathed Scotty. "Just for fun." She was excited and playful. "Maybe I can even get Europa's light to come our way. You know, kind of give us some added strength for enduring those wretched scanners. Even a tiny dot'll do for us, don'tcha think? Just to make that tiny kind of connection."

J wished they could really make an empath connection. Even if they happened to have empath boosters that could reach Europa, it would be intensely reckless because of the sophisticated scanners dogging them. But just to look at the tiny speck of light where the Empath Scouts watched over things and waited for their messages…. Wow. It would just feel real good.

Telmx wouldn't be there, of course. She was off on some incredible adventure in a newly discovered system. J worried about her. She was reckless, often unnecessarily so, and didn't take care of herself the way she took care of others. The Council wouldn't let old Gir go on that particular trip because he was too fragile to survive the new but expected rigors of an unknown star system. Instead Gir was supposed to come to Europa, and then eventually find a way to circumvent the earthling scanners to join them on Earth, or send some new booster technology that avoided the scanners altogether. Imagine seeing Gir again. Maybe he would have news of Telmx: how she was faring in the most precarious Mission she had taken on so far. She could talk to him about Telmx's devil-may-care attitude.

She imagined Telmx in lusty conversation with Gir and Winstx, squatting out there on some faraway asteroid rest stop, swilling her favorite bot blend, and gazing fondly from way up there into J's eyes gazing into hers from way down there in the meadow. How excited Telmx would be that Scotty and J were finally together. "Ah," she would wink wickedly, "it was meant to be. See? Didn't I tell you? Loving more than one person is downright fun, right? You earthling pups have so much to learn!" And she would let forth a particularly delighted guffaw just to punctuate her point.

"Wait, Wait! I'm getting it in focus." Scotty closed her eyes and became serious and serene. J raised herself up on one elbow and watched her new lover sink into a soft reverie. She dared not follow lest she distract her. J watched Scotty's cilia waft lazily in the chilly meadow breeze, and her cheeks flush crimson in the starlight, her soft round breasts rising and falling slightly in even cadence. J resisted leaning over to kiss each small erect nipple.

What a beautiful woman! How incredibly lucky she was. Scotty serious and playful, smart and yet completely unpretentious. When she took delight in something J would say or think, she would squint her eyes and savor the thought like good vintage bot. And, to think, she had endured the same doubts about the Mission, but was more convinced than ever that it was urgent to stick with it.

Well, with the two of them together? More than simply bearable. It was even downright fun, even with horrible prescient inklings of what was to come. Scotty felt them more. She knew more. Saw possible futures. She wasn't secretive, just cautious about how much J could take in at any one time.

"Shh," empathed Scotty. "I just about have Europa in my inner vision. There. There it is. Close your eyes. C'mon J, come here and close your eyes."

J lay down on her back and closed her eyes just as Scotty's hand found hers again. Jupiter's striated red-orange disk emerged behind the backdrop of her eyelids. "It's the second one to the right. The moons go out in a row. See 'em? The second one. Yeah, that one. Isn't that just the best?"

The lovers lay on their backs, thigh to thigh and followed Jupiter westward in their minds. They followed Europa as it migrated across the huge planet.

Just after the transit, J perceived a thin sudden stream of effervescent light shoot out from Europa. It faded even as she shouted in her mind, "Ohmygod, Scotty did you see that? That wasn't just a shooting star!"

"Wow! And there's another one!"

At the same instant Scotty's hand, now suddenly cold and clammy, tightened around J's. "Something really awful and fabulous just happened," she empath-whispered. The image of Europa blinked out and Scotty and J jumped to standing, very still, facing south-west as Jupiter faded to daylight. Two upright prairie dogs, immobile, listening. Normally J would be the more self-conscious of the two, fearful of early morning hikers wandering into the meadow, or a trooper pulling up out of nowhere to arrest them for indecent exposure. But this morning, it didn't even occur to her to be careful, except to be careful not to break their concentration.

Scotty was shaking. "Ohmygod, J, it's Gir. He's in trouble! Oh J, we gotta figure this out really quick, or we'll lose him. We're going to lose Gir!"

J had no idea how Scotty knew this. Her certainty was overwhelming. J held onto Scotty's cold, shaking hand. How could Gir be lost? It made no sense. But Scotty was so much better at this. She couldn't see or feel Gir, just her certainty.

Her own fathoming revealed something more metallic, not Imari, not anything really living, but not inert either. Tiny and heavy. Careening to Earth. Already in the stratosphere. Then bouncing onto Earthen terrain like a Spaulding ball, rolling and stopping. Silence. Silence so long, she thought her heart would stop for waiting. Then a glimmer of someone or something searching. Vague, pulsating flickers of searching. Like a small sailing craft whose electronic equipment has died, lost in a fog with a very dim searchlight rotating plaintively in all directions.

"J, I don't know how you did that. You made me see it too. You don't even have cilia and you just did that! J, you're incredible! Wait, we gotta think. Just keep with me, think with me. Ohmygod, whatta team we are. I love you so, so very much."

"Whatever it is has just enough energy to send out a very faint distress song," J empathed slowly, pulling vague images and tones (actual tones, musical tones) from a place in her chambers she didn't know existed. "But I can't really locate the source except to know that it's not terribly far away. I mean maybe a hundred miles as opposed to thousands."

"Okay J. I got it. I see it. I hear it. Ohmygod, will you listen to that? It's singing. I can't believe it's actually singing. It's moving on its own, very slowly, like it's rolling or something. Like a ball. Yeah, like a ball. But with great painful effort. Wounded, or at least its empath energy is almost gone."

"I still can't tell if it's sentient or some kind of space pod."

"Maybe both. Let's just bring it to us. I have an idea. Bear with me, J. I'm gonna formulate a towline, like an empath pulley. And then we're gonna pull it to us. We gotta do this together. Gently, but quickly. I'll show you how. I think I know how. I have to know how. I only have a textbook understanding of this, but together we can do it."

✳ ✳ ✳

They were driven. Instinctively they knew exactly what to do. For the next several days, they sent out this guiding/pulling empath signal, not worrying at all about whether earthling scanners might track them down, only stopping occasionally to replenish themselves with bot and some vegetation Scotty suffused from the surrounding woods. "For empath energy," she said.

It was nippy, and they lay on their backs over and under several Imari blankets, heads touching, sometimes J's on Scotty's shoulder, sometimes Scotty's on hers. Sleeping was not an option, although sometimes they felt like they were toiling in their sleep, or in a merged semi-dream state: They were pulling and rolling a boulder together. Over and over, forever like Prometheus, pulling and rolling it over mountains and valleys, through farms and over country roads and highways. Though they were thoroughly exhausted, somehow they mustered the empath energy to empath and empath.

✳ ✳ ✳

At some point J had the thought that whatever or whoever it was they were pulling had somehow found a way to latch onto a moving vehicle.

"You're right," Scotty empathed closing down the pulley. "If we pull it any more, it'll crumble. It's almost here. It's not rolling anymore. So do you know where it is now? I think, I know you do. You know what it is, too."

* * *

I actually did know. I was amazing myself at every point. It was as if I could feel my cilia growing as the days went by. But that was impossible. It was absolutely my most passionate wish forever, but I was convinced cilia were never meant for me, especially since Telmx never offered to help me grow them. In fact, I was actually budding them on my own, but I didn't know that yet. Now my cilia are so long and thick, I need really thick bangs to cover them. I'm real proud of them too. Not that what happened next that summer isn't incredibly important. Our lives changed forever. But whenever the Perseids arrive in August, I celebrate my cilia. For me their birth is even more important than my Name Day. —J

* * *

"Somewhere on the road into town from the north," J said as if she were talking on autopilot. "And it's a *he*."

"How do you know that?"

At that instant, a bus formed in J's mind. Whoever they were there to meet was actually outside of it, somehow clinging to the ridges of a tire, or lodged within the treads. "Impossible," she thought. "This whole thing's just too far-out."

"Don't you feel him? He's actually on a bus. In the tire treads of a bus. He's almost here. Don't you feel him?"

"What if it's Gir? Ohmygod! We gotta get to him. C'mon J, we gotta hurry! The bus to New York is due at the oval in a half hour!"

Somehow they mustered the energy to do the impossible. They scrambled into clothing, rolled up the blankets, stuffed everything else into knapsacks, and "broke camp" within seconds.

Mead's Mountain Road is long and winding, and at some places careens almost straight downward. Weighted down by her backpack, and drained from the days of empath effort, J kept on falling behind as they ran. Some early morning bikers whisked past them, rounding a curve beneath. J wondered how they didn't smash into the forest that reached hungrily into the road. Other bikers were huffing up the sharp incline. Some had given up and were walking their wheels up the last stretch of road leading to the monastery at the top. Scotty was in great shape. She carried her knapsack and her blanket roll as if they were floating feathers. "Just go on ahead," J empathed, "I can catch up at the bottom. I don't want to be a drag."

"Cut it out! We gotta do this together," yelled Scotty in her head. "All's I'm doing is hovering stuff. Hold on, I'll hover the loads for both of us." In the same instant, J's load lifted from her shoulders. She surged ahead, almost falling over her own feet, her load flying millimeters from her back down the slope. "Far-out!" she squealed. Energized, she filled her lungs with the brisk air. They whooped in harmony, merging and merging again with their own echoes, and reached the bottom much too soon for J. "Far-out!" she yelled. It was such a relief to be moving, alive and moving. With energy! To hell with the cramp in her side.

"Think up some cold ice to your right side," empathed Scotty. "Oh, of course," thought J. They trotted on side by side.

By the time they arrived at Tinker Street, the town was abuzz with diffuse empath noise. Sleepy flower children staggered through the streets, or sprawled on the sidewalks, or clustered in small groups at the oval at the village center. A girl, fourteen or so, in tie-dye, beads and barefoot, sat lotus style trying to commune with the morning sun. She sent immature wafting messages upwards, but they had no focus, and, of course, they needed an empath booster and probably some good strong bot to make it all work. But then you don't empath with a million degrees of heat, even if it's 93 million miles away, if you don't want to fry your brains out.

"Wow," empathed Scotty. "How close they are to harnessing their energies, and yet how far." Bongos and bells and chants wafted throughout the streets. J knew this scene. Washington Square Park, or vice versa. She loved and hated their primitive attempts, a foreshadowing of the future, because she could not really join in without giving herself away. To Scotty it was completely new. When they had first ambled through Washington Square Park, she had become terrified. "In the wrong hands, you know, their experimentation can be lethal to all of us. Let's just hope we fix things up before someone gets too good at this stuff." J could feel Scotty's mind racing. "Imagine just taking these earthlings into a kind of circle, yeah an empath circle of some sort." Could that be really possible, or safe, J wondered.

J wished they could recruit some of these folks to join the Mission, if they could be trained to focus their energies. "Wow, whatta thought."

The bus was about to arrive, and J doubted that she had anywhere near the amount of energy they would they need in the next few minutes. They were tired, their focus slipping.

"Okay, okay. Hold it! Guess what? We got a reprieve!" Scotty empathed. "The bus is late. It's not out of Arkville yet. In fact, it's going to be another hour or so. I wish we'd thought to empath-check before we raced away from the meadow so quick. We're not thinking so good, J. We let the emergency and everything distract us big time. But it means we can rest a little. Not much we can do now, anyway. Let's not waste any empath energy. We need our Imari stuff when the bus arrives. In the meantime, let's be earthlings and get a real earthling breakfast."

They ordered breakfast at the Tinker Street Café, and devoured it in empath silence. Scotty had gone into an inner shielded chamber, needing to "replenish herself for a few minutes." Deep repose. J was scared. What if Scotty lost some of her skills? Even though she insisted they were a team, Scotty knew so much more, could do practically everything, a Level VI empath. She listened for the bus, trying in vain to listen and watch like an earthling and not worry about her lover. So difficult.

Woodstock empath noise was harsh, with spikes, occasionally softened by soft blue-green pastel intonations that briefly drowned out the noise and offered some needed respite. These kids were actually helping her replenish. "Great skill here," she thought. She wondered which one of the many young faces wandering by possessed the capacity to intone so deliciously, with such powers to heal her frazzled head. Perhaps it was the woman at the next table who sat cross-legged on her chair staring at her teacup? It certainly wasn't the fellow on the sidewalk just outside the café dragging on a joint. She resisted looking into each mind as she glanced around her. A talented one could figure them out.

She had long ago learned to shield herself from the sweet lure of weed. It clouded her focus and, she was sure, made it impossible for empath energy to really do its thing. She guessed weed was good for some things. But Telmx had warned her early on to avoid it, even if it meant jeopardizing her connection with people she needed to connect with. "It saps the blue levels big time," Telmx explained. "Besides, your shield will weaken, and someone might just happen to find you out." Occasionally J had gotten a contact high, hating and loving it. Bot was far better, and it enhanced rather than diminished her energy. She wondered what would happen if people around here got their hands on some bot.

Careful not to intrude, she looked at Scotty. What would happen if she and Scotty ever split? Well, she would never, never ever involve herself with another. That was certain. Too much pain. If this perfection didn't last, nothing would. Whenever Scotty entered her own inner place she felt alone. Gone. Like longing for Telmx during years of absence. Could Scotty be reading her thoughts right now? No, she was far too inward, deep within herself. Each one in her private place. How unnerving to be with her and not be with her, not have their thoughts blend. There had hardly been a moment, even in dreaming, when their thoughts didn't meld. Often they couldn't peel them apart. It was joyous. Even with Telmx, she never felt such true companionship. Of course, she always knew that Telmx would leave almost as quickly as she arrived. The most time she had spent with her was actually off-world, for the several two and three week visits to Galern II and its various neighboring systems. Besides, Telmx and J were hardly peers or partners like she and Scotty. Yes, J and Telmx really loved each other. Deeply. But there was no way to compare the two relationships. Different. That's all. Just different. Somehow.

The street was filling up. And it was getting hotter. Dusty dog days of August. Not so up the mountain. Suddenly, a surge of dust and diesel filled her lungs. Ohmygod, it's here. The roar and the stench from far up the road invaded her temples. "Scotty!" she empath yelled. Scotty was immobile. She turned back to the street just as the New York City bound bus rolled past the cafe, kicking up pebbles and dust. It wheezed to a stop several hundred yards up the street. "Scotty! It's here!"

A frail blue-green light flickered into her left temple. It wavered and dimmed out and then flickered again. It was mournful, somehow. Was that from Scotty? No, couldn't be. It had an entirely different timbre, a new, yet familiar vibration. One of the flower children? It pulsated with her, pleaded, like a child crying for its mother.

"Scotty! The bus!" Diesel and pleading competed for her attention. "Scotty!" She grabbed her friend's shoulders and desperately shook her. What if they missed the connection altogether. Scotty would know how to read the signals. "Scotty! The bus!"

Scotty jerked her eyes open and J welcomed the sudden melding. "Oh jeez, it's here," empathed Scotty. "Jeez, what a stench. Let me see. Okay I got it. It's tough with all this shit in the way. Wait. Here, read the energy this way." As if J's brain were a kaleidoscope, the light changed positions. Different angles, same light. Diesel stench and wheezing faded, and the blue-green light coalesced into a tiny effervescent point. J was suddenly bathed in calm, a mournful calm, like a soulful cry, but steady, almost sweet.

"It's not Gir, but it's definitely a 'him,'" empath whispered J.

"Yeah. You're right. It's definitely not Gir. Actually it's not quite human, I mean, he's not in full human form. He's—It's so odd, I can't read it exactly. Let's just walk to the bus stop, you know, slowly. Don't open up too much, just in case. We can't be exactly sure what we got here. I think it's okay, but jeez, J, he's human and not human, almost mineral, I think.

"Maybe you think, maybe they sent us an empath booster?" ventured J. "Maybe since it's not Gir, it's actually a strong signal from him to look for the booster. What do you think? And maybe it's sitting right there in the street, in a suitcase, or something, just waiting for us to pick it up."

J and Scotty got up from the table simultaneously, slowly pulling on their knapsacks, in one motion, as if in a well-coordinated and synchronized dance. Moving like they were attached at the hip, they quickly walked up the steps from the sunken terrace of the café onto the street. Anyone watching them would think they were on some awesome acid trip. They glided up the street toward the Village Green, where the uniformed driver (alien and stilted among the flowing colors of the street) was throwing duffels and suitcases into the hold. By the time they reached the bus, a small cluster of long skirts and sandals and bare feet, bandannas, amulets and crystals were clambering on, and whoever had gotten off had since melted into the town. No luggage remained on the sidewalk, and the driver was revving his engine. No empath booster. No almost sentient being.

"Did we miss it?" empathed J. "Shit! I don't know whether to call it a 'he' or an 'it'!"

"Shh, it's here somewhere; don't you see it?"

The light was more diffuse now, mingling with the errant and unformed empath energies streaming from the guitars, bongos and incense in the Village Green oval. "I can't keep it centered," J empathed.

"Okay, hold tight. It's actually not right here. It's back a-ways. I don't know, I think it's back the way the bus just came. I think it got kicked out of the tire tread or something. This way. I can't believe it's not really Gir. It's so much like him, but it's definitely not him. But it's human, sort of, no I think definitely human—a *he*." They turned around and walked slowly back toward the café in silence, concentrating. The blue-green light coalesced again, this time a bit larger in diameter, sharper now, and then fading out and then sharper yet again. J followed Scotty's concentration. The pulsating was engaging. It merged with their breathing. Scotty's hand found J's. It was warm and wet, and pulsated with J's, palm to palm. They walked slowly past the café and continued along the road, past the hardware store and the Twin Gables Guest House. As they approached the Tinker Street Cinema, three energies pulsated in harmony.

The synchronized pulses reached maximum on the right side of the road several yards past the theater. "There's no one here," J empathed. Nevertheless, the mournful weight in each pulse surged through her toes. A resigned mournful. Whoever he was, he was bearing a heavy load. Behind her eyelids she discerned a small boy, not older than eight or nine, crouched in a thicket, shivering and crying, as if his heart were broken. His head was buried in his arms and his body heaved in heavy rhythmic sobs, in sync with the pulses. "I found him! I found him!" empathed J. Letting go of Scotty's hand, she closed her eyes, drawn irresistibly into the tufts of tall grass and shrubbery toward the wooded area beyond. She stopped several paces beyond the tree line, expecting to stumble right onto the slight lad, fearful she would hurt him in her stumble. Nothing in sight. "I don't get it," she called to Scotty out loud. "He's right here, but he isn't. So weird."

Scotty was by her side. "I think you're right on top of him now. I followed you in, I mean, in your mind's eye, and I almost stumbled with you onto this lad. You resonate with his mournful. It's so painful. Oh, how painful. We must get to him right away. He's hurting a lot." Scotty took both her hands. "Let's just squat. You know, in ceremonial Imari style. It will inform us, I'm sure of it. Let's just do that and see what happens. I just have a feeling, you know."

The two women squatted face to face over a small tuft of grass. Except when a car momentarily drowned the sounds from the woods, the mournful pulses now blended in magnificent harmony with the rhythmic chirping of the birds, the furtive whooshing from nearby bushes, the rustling of the trees. The grieving child filled their hearts, and resonated in some depth of their beings. J hadn't tapped into such grief in a very long time. So familiar and so overwhelming. All alone, she would be at a loss, actually terrified to go deeper. "Okay," she empathed, "what do we do next?"

"I know this sounds really weird." Scotty delved her hands into the tuft of grass, and spread the strands apart. "Look. That's what I thought."

Nestled in the tuft was an oblong, smooth white stone, about the size of a parakeet's egg. "It's coming from right here," she empathed almost inaudibly.

J already knew. As she gazed at it, it seemed to her as if it wobbled a bit, even caught the sunlight a little bit brighter than stones do. "What do we do now?" J empathed, formulating exactly what had to be done. Scotty was cupping her hands around it, pushing the tufts of grass aside with the back of her hands. J put her palms together like Scotty's and surrounded the stone from the other side to meet her fingers. She immediately felt the heat pulsating from the stone. "Go ahead into him," empathed Scotty. "I'll be right here."

J had a terrible premonition. It smelled like sulfur. Like the sulfur storm on Galern II while Telmx was out getting provisions.

"I don't know—"

"Go ahead in, I'm right here. I got you, like that towline. I really have you. I won't lose you, I promise."

J closed her eyes, reluctantly and with urgency. She pushed herself toward the center of the pulses. Like entering a V.E. without V.E.-goggles, but okay, Scotty's right there. Like a V.E.-towline. Okay. Okay, must find this boy.

Suddenly a yellow billowing mass sucked her into a whirling vortex. Sulfur! Scotty! She jolted awake into Scotty's arms, flailing and choking, her tongue, her throat, her mouth and cheeks seared raw.

"Oh shit, J! J? are you all right?" Scotty from very far away. But ohmygod, in her arms. Oh definitely in her arms.

"I have you. I'm right here! Okay. Okay, stop screaming. I have you. Okay, hold real still. Here. Let me in a minute. That's it. Here now."

The stench and burning faded into smooth silky aloe. "Okay now, sweetheart. There. Okay? Okay?"

"I thought we were all going to die. He's dying Scotty, ohmygod, he's actually dying in there, whirling in some sort of a sulfuric storm. Scotty, I'm scared. What do we do now? We have to go back and get him. Scotty, he's gonna die!"

"I know, I know, sweetheart. Hold on, we'll get him out. Take a few more breaths, long ones. That's it, long and even, long and even. I'm so sorry. I just didn't know how bad it was in there. Now I know. I really, really do."

J struggled between terror and urgent passion for this stranger boy who was no longer a stranger. She raised her head and met Scotty's deep azure eyes, shining. Just above them, her cilia wafted. They seemed longer, definitely longer, and silvery. Scotty was in a deep place with her eyes wide open. A kind of rapture. They were depending upon each other, lovers in deep surrendering trust. That and much, much more. Each deep breath they took, an elixir of energy, familiar and unfamiliar.

"C'mon," Scotty softly empathed. Her words brushed against J's eyelids like a tiny puff of air. "Together, now. Take a few more breaths. I'll take care of the storm. You know what to do."

J entered Scotty's eyes. Without thinking, she again cupped her hands around the stone and met Scotty's fingers. A warmer, firmer surge. Aloe and lilac. She lowered her head and allowed her forehead to accept the brush strokes of Scotty's cilia. She again entered this boy's mournful, but this time with her eyes wide open, transfixed on the outer shell of the stone, while plumbing its depths where the child was writhing in his storm. At the same time, she gazed at the outer shell of the stone, nestled in the parted tuft of grass, surrounded by their hands, their fingertips pulsating in warm synchronization with the new modulations. Painful and sweet. She, Scotty, and the boy, in painful and sweet unison.

The stone was swaying slightly. Then it lifted ever so slowly. Their hands rose with it, following and urging, until it hovered and rocked just over the strands of grass. "Okay," empath-whispered Scotty. "Let's see. The outer shell first, just a little. We don't want to break it apart. If you sense a crack, heat it sealed again. Like blowing up a fragile balloon. Yeah, that's it. Jeez, I think we're doing it right. Careful, careful. Help me, J. I actually don't know how to do this. I only saw a reformulation once." Though J had never seen one, she knew what to do, and silently followed and led Scotty through the sensitive expansion. Riding deftly with Scotty's apprehension and calm and deliberate focus on the stone, she pushed away wave after wave of dizziness and nausea, hers and Scotty's, and simultaneously fused with Scotty's measured puffs of energy. The stone, now hovering above their cupped hands, inflated slowly to fragile thinness. As it grew, the two women inched backward their palms now facing a swelling oblong boulder hovering between them and slowly obscuring each from the other. J was sweating and puffing with exhaustion and exhilaration.

He was alive. He was and was not a mere child, a man and a child, grieving, pulling at their last gasps of strength, but gently, as if he, boy and man, knew how to borrow and give back. He was also very fragile and injured, still flailing in his grief and in physical pain. "We must hurry slowly," she empathed to Scotty, knowing she already knew, but wishing to reaffirm her own desperate knowledge, and temper her urge to abruptly snatch him out and breathe life and energy into his failing body.

Scotty was now behind her, holding firmly onto her shoulders. "Okay, just a few more puffs," she empathed softly, "Breath into his pain slowly. We have him now."

The rock, now swollen to the size of a hovercraft, shuddered slightly and slowly settled back onto its original tuft of grass. Exhausted, J fell back onto Scotty's chest. Shivering and dizzy, she welcomed Scotty's arms and legs gently and firmly embracing her own.

"What now?" she empath-whispered, resisting her compelling urge to succumb to a deep restorative slumber.

"Enter his V.E.-travel dream," empathed Scotty. "Go there. He's retro-traveling." J sucked in her breath. Of course. That's why he was simultaneously man and boy. He was traveling to his younger self, and reliving a horror.

Scotty held her tighter. "I have you. I won't let go. And just in case you hadn't picked it up, I love you."

J desperately did not want to go back into that storm. No choice. Telmx would do it. Be driven like Telmx! Bravely reckless. "Okay. Against my better judgment. You hold onto me and I'll hold onto him. He's in one hell of a childhood nightmare. Here I go."

No sulfur storm. Worse.

The El at Lake and Wells was a hubbub of sirens, flashing lights and silhouettes of uniforms milling about. She saw a frail youth, no more than ten or eleven, careening into the chaos toward the crumpled body of an old man.

Now the boy was screaming, kicking and biting the medics who struggled to pull him away from the body, shouting, "Hey you! Get offa him! Get him outta here!"

For a moment, J stood helpless, a mere observer of this child heaving in flailing devastation over the man, who was as rigid as the reddening concrete beneath him, his smashed eye sockets spewing spasms of blood. In the next instant J and the boy were one, wailing and heaving over the body. "Gir! It's Gir. No, it can't be you. Ohmygosh!" Rage and disbelief. They pressed their mouths on the old Imari's mouth, desperately trying to force him back into life, their lips slipping from their mark in the streaming blood.

"Leave the boy alone! That's his uncle! Leave the child alone!" The shrieking seemed to emerge from J's own blood-soaked mouth, but it actually came from an elderly black woman arching and struggling in the grip of a uniformed hulk somewhere in the shadows of the urban elevated subway track.

"Johnny!" Miss Jenny screamed. "Hey! That's his nephew!" She flung herself at the medics and grabbed J and the boy into her bosom, wheeling them away from the body. "My baby, oh Johnny baby. Shh, hush hush, Johnny baby. They killed your Uncle Wally just like you told him they would from your dreams, Johnny. Oh, Johnny. Johnny knows who did it. Don't you, baby? Ask him. He knows exactly who did it, don't you Johnny?" They sunk to the sidewalk, clinging to each other, Jenny rocking Johnny and J in the rain.

"Whatdya know about this? Whatcha doing here in this here storm? Whatdidya see? Who shot him? Who is he? How'd you just happen to come running out here in this storm to just this place tonight, eh? Speak up!" Johnny and J felt the cop tugging roughly at their jackets. "You get the hell offa him!"

"Hey! Let him go! He didn't do anything! He's just a poor orphan boy! Let him be, you motha fuckas!" Miss Jenny was wailing again.

"Don't you go mouthin' off at me!"

J and Johnny were suddenly wrenched from Miss Jenny's embrace. The huge white cops dragged Johnny away, kicking and screaming, like after they smashed down the door and shot Johnny's parents dead. "Mamma! Papa! Miss Jenny! Uncle Wally!"

"Don't say anything, Johnny," a faint echo, like when Uncle Wally used to whisper to Johnny in his head, but this time it wasn't his uncle. "Just be quiet! And when I tell you to, you run like a bat outta hell. Don't worry, Johnny, just run like hell. Ol' Gir won't let anything happen to you."

Even now as the cops heaved Johnny and J against a squad car and forced their legs and arms apart into a spread-eagle, even now, as they grabbed at their pockets, his balls, her privates, laughing and cursing, Johnny and J were suddenly mysteriously calmed by that voice in their heads.

"Now!" Gir screamed. Johnny and J wiggled out of the goons' clutches and ran outta hell. "Halt or I'll shoot!" Firecrackers popped and zinged. "Halt!"

Then Scotty's voice echoed Gir's through the swirling confusion. "When I shout 'run' I want you guys to run outta hell! Johnny! J! Listen! Don't squirm. I'm right here, you two. I got you both. Don't worry, I'll catch you! Johnny? J? Are you listening? Are you ready? Now!"

J found strength in Scotty's call. She revved her strength to run, her own strength and Johnny's, a slip of a boy, whose strength was all but gone. When Scotty's command finally came, she wrestled herself free from the officers' grip and ran for their lives, hers and Johnny's.

"I have your trumpet, young Johnny. That's alright; you can shiver and cry all you want. You're safe now. Here take some of this." A cup of strong aromatic liquid touched his lips, and Johnny drank the elixir without thinking. "That's it, my fine young man." It was strangely quiet. And the voice talking to him was still inside his head, but he didn't feel terrified any more. He opened his eyes and held his breath. A huge crinkly black man was smiling back at him while he fussed with the blanket and babbled about the best tea in the universe, bar none. He wore a multicolored cloak that reached up to his wrinkled ebony face. The top of his head was wrapped with a maroon cloth that covered his forehead and ears. "See?" said the old man. "See? Here's your trumpet and everything. Just stick with me, young fellow. Old Gir will take care of everything. Good running, there, young Johnny. Good running, my brave young man."

It was no longer raining, and someone was wrapping J in a large warm blanket. How did they get on Gir's ship? Wait, is he dead? "Ohmygosh, Gir, are you okay?"

"C'mon J, open your eyes. We're here. In the meadow. He's okay. He's not Gir. He's Johnny, another monitor recruit. Gir's recruit. It's me, Scotty. Now then, look at us, babe."

J forced her eyes open. Two pairs of eyes met hers, close in, familiar and kind, their cilia wafting gently above her forehead in the twilight. Somehow they were back in the meadow, all the way up Meads Mountain Road. It was getting dark, and two earthling empath monitor friends were taking real good care of her, Imari style.

"Hey, there, J. Welcome back. We did it!" empathed Scotty.

"Hi, J. My name is Johnny," empathed the other softly. "Scotty told me what you did. Thank you for guiding me to this place, for finding me, and for pulling me out of my V.E.-travel-horror." An Imari: same ebony, chiseled features; elegant wide nostrils; full sensuous lips, pursed in a manner that exuded wisdom and intensity in the promise of fabulous music. Young, no more than twenty-five or so, definitely male, and, she intuited, a tiny bit shorter than towering Imaris, although by no means short by earthling standards, maybe six-five. Not Imari! Of course! Scotty just said it! Another earthling empath traveler! Another one! "Oh, Scotty! He's our third monitor!"

"I am," he empathed. "Gir and Telmx sent me here to find you two. Just lay still. You absorbed my reformulation shock big time. We're doing some of that good ol' fashioned Imari healing stuff. I'm so, so sorry you had to V.E.-travel-merge into my nightmare past. That's exactly what happened when I was a boy. Gir saved my life the day my Uncle Wally was murdered under the El. He was a union organizer, you know. I'll tell you about him some time."

J closed her eyes. She felt safe now.

CHAPTER TWENTY-SIX

J

J, Johnny and Scotty squatted on Imari mats around the auto-effuse.

"I can hardly believe you didn't see Johnny until I did," empathed J. "Or hear him, you know. You're a Level VI, Scotty. I can't believe you relied on me to find him."

"Well you're one extraordinary woman, J," empathed Johnny. "No formal training, and you just went right in there and did what you had to do, like you'd been doing it forever." He handed J the bot goblet.

"There's no explaining it, J," empathed Scotty. "You just got the touch. I knew you did. See? We're one hell of a team. And with Johnny here. Mr. Techie. Lookout, you evil scanners! Here we come! Away with all headaches!"

J suddenly felt cold, the memory of Johnny's nightmare shattering their levity. "Is Gir okay? I saw him in your nightmare. Was that just a nightmare?" The thought of losing Telmx! Beyond comprehension. Life would not be bearable, even with Scotty. But Johnny's empath mood did not read devastation. Rather, his aroma and hue slowly dissolved her grief. Inside he was singing, constantly singing, fusing melodies upon melodies. Harmonies of familiar and unfamiliar symphonies, playful and serious, all somehow delightfully reinforcing each other.

"No, he... I don't know. I don't think so. At least I hope not. I just brought a lot of him with me. I mean, I think he's okay. He's no fool. He wouldn't take chances. I lost my uncle, you know. And before him my parents. A long, long time ago. I think I'm just afraid of losing Gir too. He's, well, he's so special I couldn't bear to lose him. No, it was just a nightmare, and you saved me from it. Both of you. Anyway, look. Look here. What d'ya see?" He brought his face up close to J's. His eyes, wise way beyond his twenty-five years, playful and bawdy, philosophic and scientific, moistened as she gazed. His lips trembled. Sure enough, Gir had kept his promise about sending them new technology after all. He sent Johnny!

She desperately wanted to know about Telmx.

"She's off on some secret, highly sensitive mission in Andromeda. We have no word yet," Johnny empathed. J instinctively focused her gaze on the vaguely shimmering nebula in the northeastern sky.

"I know where she went," she said. "It's just hard not knowing more."

"When I build that new shielded booster, we'll ask Gir," he empathed.

That dreadful feeling tugged at J again.

"But it's not only Telmx, J," intoned Scotty. "There's something else bothering you."

"Yeah, something else. I can't quite get at it." High up on Meads Mountain Road, with the huge swatch of the Milky Way and the ephemeral Andromeda apparition casting their magical glow on the triumphant trio, J tasted sanguine, but also disquiet that eluded her friends. A nondescript something tugged relentlessly.

✳ ✳ ✳

That night, the three empath earthlings, wrapped in layers of Imari blankets squatted around a soft hoverglow in a corner of the meadow, passing a goblet from one to the other, and auto-suffusing Imari powders and mountain vegetation. The glow resembled a small campfire, multicolored, shimmering several inches above the tenderly cleared center of their circle, and emitting an almost imperceptible and pleasing hum.

After they had reformulated Johnny in town, her friends were so fragile that Scotty had ended up hitching a ride up Meads Mountain Road. She had shielded all three to protect them from stray empath hits and to conserve whatever was left of their energies. Now they sat still in silence, while Scotty sent wave after wave of nourishing pulses into Johnny's temples. Even after Scotty warned him not to revisit his nightmare, Johnny was unable to ward off images, filling him with nauseous dread. He was scared. What if he never regained his former empath strength? What would happen to him and Lenx? What would happen to his empath fusion jazz? He couldn't help thinking about it all, even though these two strangers, yet not so strange white earthling women could read everything he was thinking. But he was too tired to shield. Nor should he use up precious energy building a shield strong enough to shut them out. From what? Just stupid embarrassing thoughts.

"You have to curb those images on your own," Scotty reiterated. "I can't do that for you. The healing is not going to work if you keep going there. It's like filling a bucket with a hole in it."

"I can't help it. I really can't. It's so strong. I feel so compelled to go back there and find if that was a prescient V.E.-dream." Deep sobs entered his chest and began working their way to the open air. Cadence upon cadence. He tried to gulp them back down. No matter how intergalactic and otherworldly he had become, no matter how much empath training he had absorbed, he still was self-conscious sobbing before females, especially white females. Of course these women knew everything he thought anyway. Jeez.

J's arms were around him now. Her slight, still weakened body and her blanket entwined around his shoulders and back. "Do you really want to go back into that nightmare? I'll go there with you, if you really want to go there, but I honestly don't know if I can stand it."

"Neither of you can stand it," said Scotty. And I can't promise I can pull you out again. We're all spent. Golly guys. Can't you just leave things be for one night? Just one measly night?"

Cadences of cacophony wrapped around his sobs, swelling upward through his throat and into his forehead. A clarion call, one he recognized: the distant series of tones, deep horn arpeggios calling, a deep strong bass voice echoing, weaving in and around the arpeggios, mournful and strong, beckoning and reassuring. And dreadful.

"*Requiem*," he murmured.

J's arms tightened around him.

"What is that?" she empathed. "It's utterly beautiful."

"You hear it too?" Now his sobs were unfettered. A blended duet of French horn and bass voice of solemn beckoning and rejoicing reverberated in his head and around the meadow.

Now Scotty was squatting in front of him. "What is that Johnny?"

"Off-er-tor-i-um," Johnny squeezed the word out a syllable at a time, fearful that naming it would somehow make it all go away. Talking would break it all up; it would never return. But instead, his voice, and Scotty's and J's, rising and falling, moved gracefully inside the blended tones.

"I know what I need to do," he empathed softly. "I need to go there alone." His gut was endeavoring to escape his body, as if pulled by a huge magnet. He felt Scotty's demur, and J's determination to accompany him, no matter what.

"I need to go there alone," he repeated, irritated by their responses. "Now! Alone!"

"You don't need to be back in that nightmare," Scotty insisted.

"No, trust me! Not to the nightmare—it's, it's somewhere else. Just inside, like to a V.E.-chamber, yeah to a V.E.-chamber. I can't explain it. I don't need any help going there, I actually must go there alone. Not tonight, I promise you. Not tonight. When I'm stronger. I gotta go there alone. Okay? I'm going to sleep now. Over there by the hoverglow. Don't bother with me, okay? I'm fine."

Afterward J watched Scotty auto-infuse another batch of hot toddies. She marveled at her focused concentration, her cilia occasionally catching the light of the hoverglow, as they touched each goblet in turn, and the way her tousled auburn hair threw off bursts of red and orange. She wondered what it would be like to do that, to have cilia. But it was actually happening to her too. The buds were there. Her own very own cilia. They itched like mosquito bites. Just since the arrival of Johnny. How utterly amazing. A dream come true. Of course she'd have to hide them, wear headbands and bandannas, and have to deal with Katie's incessant curiosity.

She wondered if Telmx knew about Johnny and Scotty, but of course she knew, planned it, hinted at it, in fact. Probably planned it with Gir and Winstx. Not the details, just the overall fact. If only Telmx were here with them now. She would know how to pull Johnny through his struggle. She was not sure they could.

"If we don't go to sleep soon, it'll be morning and we won't be in any shape to help Johnny, whatever it is he's going through," Scotty said.

CHAPTER TWENTY-SEVEN

Meads Mountain

J and Scotty were asleep, probably dream sharing. Johnny wasn't about to check. They had invited him to merge with their dreams, anytime he chose, but in his still weakened condition, that merging would actually be a drain. It was their own private experience. Even though they both insisted he would have a blast if he entered there, and perhaps with the three of them meandering together, they would figure things out even better. Well, they don't know a thing about his nightmares, awake or asleep. They did pull him out of that retro-V.E.-dream. That's different. They wouldn't want to know about it's really like to be him on this planet.

The sun wasn't up yet, but the birds were beginning to warble. An overcast pre-dawn.

He had to make a decision.

He was a black man hanging out with two white women in an isolated meadow in America, on Earth. Familiar. Like when his uncle sent him to deliver a package to the peculiar-smelling white area of Chicago, on Lake Shore Drive. He dreaded facing the wary doormen; then some white woman would be answering the doorbell. They would eye each other with mutual dread and distrust.

Hanging out with these two, not such a good idea. Gir and the Imari didn't know what it was like to be a black man hanging out with two white women in this country. They didn't know about Emmitt Till. He had to think about this some more before he made a true commitment with them in the Mission. Perhaps it would be better if he worked alone.

He was certainly drawn to the notion of being close friends with J and Scotty. In some important way they were like older sisters, or even mothers, but that was what was wrong with the whole arrangement. He could easily fall into being a good son. People were always saving him. First his brother, then his uncle, then Gir. And now J and Scotty. No! Enough!

Plus: what if he got real close to them? What if they just upped and died? No use getting close to anyone. See? Now he didn't have Lenx, probably never see him again either. That was the truth he always forgot. Now he was about to forget again. Uh uh, not this time, no way. If they want to pursue the Mission with him, it would have to be on his terms. No promises of "friendship forever; you can always count on me." None of that shit. Just everyone be their own person, and then see what happens in this and that situation. First and foremost, he had to be a technician, a strategist, and sleuth. If he really wanted to take on this next phase of the Mission.

Well, he needed time to think. Alone.

✸ ✸ ✸

Johnny took halting steps down Meads Mountain Road. He was quite unsure of his energy, but somehow, he felt a bit renewed. And enraged. Harmonies of "Offertorium," confusing and exalting, taunted his determined rage. What the hell was going on?

The Keds Gir had packed for him were awkward, cutting into his ankles, and the jeans didn't quite fit, pushing his balls, ass and thighs in all the wrong ways. He'd have to get some stuff that fit, as soon as he could. He rounded the bend in the road and stopped.

Off to the left, opposite the monastery was a small clearing, and beyond it a narrow dirt path leading around and up the mountainside. Yeah, he knew he had seen it vaguely in his mind several nights before. There were no cars in the tiny parking area. A good sign.

He gripped his travel sac tighter, wishing he had a real knapsack. He was still too weak to hover the burden, horn and all. He paused to catch his breath, leaning against a tree trunk at the beginning of the path, but out of sight of the main road. If he could just get to the top and find a place to hide, far enough from humanity, maybe even find refuge off the path along the way, some place, just to be private, with no empaths listening in. It was ecstasy traveling around the galaxies, the friends he made, the sounds they made together, Lenx. Making love with Lenx. And with Gir, different but, oh so tender. Now Lenx was far away. Unreachable.

He felt so good merged with the tree trunk. He leaned his head back, just for a moment. Just to tone down dizziness and nausea. Someday he would take up Mozart in earnest. Imagine empath-fusion Mozart with his off-world ensemble. Mozart would love it. He knew he would. If he were living today, would Mozart be a raw empath talent ready to be plucked for the Mission? What magnificent symphonies might have been lost to the Mission? There it was. What great heights of music would he, John W. Jefferson, have attained if he had not been sidetracked by the Mission. There. Now he said it.

It was truly daylight now. He pushed himself away from the tree and put one foot in front of the other on the gravel path, in spite of nausea and exhaustion. One foot in front of the other. That's how you climb a mountain. That's what Gir always told him. Well, here it is. A real mountain.

He had to stop and catch his breath many times along the way. If he weren't a horn player, he wouldn't have made it at all. An easy climb, but not now. He met no one coming up or down. Too early. Had to hurry. Soon hikers would be swarming. And not long before J and Scotty send out empath waves. Frantically searching. Especially J. She was something else. He wanted to be settled in his mind exactly what he wanted to do for the Mission, if anything, way before they located him. Or perhaps he would elude them altogether, if he could figure out how. If he had the strength.

Actually it was lucky they had located him when he landed, and towed him in. He could never have found his way to their rendezvous without them. Now that they had found him, he just wasn't sure anymore that he was happy about it. Yeah, he did need to carry on the Mission, construct the new empath booster, team up with these white earthlings. But what happens to Johnny, the empath fusion jazz horn blower? What happens to him and Lenx? Maybe, just maybe he wasn't cut out for all this. It was so incredible what he and his horn had going out there in the cosmos.

I'm really pissed off. And miserable.

It took him an hour and a half to reach an eerie carcass of what seemed to be an abandoned hotel. He eased onto the bottom step of the entranceway. Cicadas? No, rattlers. Can't stretch out here. Crumpled beer cans, dusty clumps of marijuana roaches, and a blackened hash pipe. Yeah, not here.

He trudged on. The path led to a rickety fire tower. Nope. Too popular. People actually try climbing that thing. He turned around and walked back to another path he had noticed just below. He followed it to a rocky ledge and peered into the huge expanse, a hazy morning vista. Beneath the ledge, a sheer drop to a narrow rocky cliff, and to his left a series of shallow footholds that led to a small crevice, no, actually more than a crevice, perhaps an actual cave. A true cutout in the wall of the cliff, with a small ledge at its entrance.

There was ice in there, he noticed with his mind's eye, though it was summer. So it had to be real cold. Still, it was a place to hide and shield. The cliff was steep. He was no rock climber, but with only a moment's hesitation, he summoned some kind of sputtering energy and started hovering down. The ledge at the mouth of the cave was just wide enough to stand on comfortably. He peered inside. The cave was actually larger and deeper than he thought, and once he had squeezed through the narrow opening it was easy to stand upright, even for him. Perfect. A great place to hide while figuring things out.

The somber and exalted chorus still reverberated in his temples. Now in the walls of the cave, syncopated counterpoint by some distant crows calling to each other, subtly reshaped the "Kyrie." Empath-fusion jazz. Pleasing. He knelt to open his travel sac, and with a slight quiver, took out his glistening silver horn, still hermetically sealed, but apparently fully reconstituted within its puffy transparent wrap. He gently turned the package around and around in his trembling hands, searching for the tiny blue-green pressure valve. Holding his breath, he pulled gently on the tab. The sac came alive in his palms, breathing in and out with a passionate purring, like Lenx savoring soft wonderful pleasures.

Then the sac slowly melted into the air, and cool silver metal lay gently in his hands. He turned the horn around, and his pouch of special valve grease he had discovered on Emtileya's second moon, tumbled into his palm. Wow, he thought, Gir didn't miss a trick! I love you, man. He pursed his lips, and, still trembling, pressed the mouthpiece to his mouth. The first several tries were sputters, but he was dog-tired, out of breath and out of practice. No chops! He tried not to panic. Then with the French horn and bassoon now ringing in his ears, as if the *Requiem* had started over again, just for his benefit, he reached for the D, found it and softly merged with the obbligato sotto. Obbligato sotto, bassoon and clarinet, cellos in soft pulses underneath, and anticipating, he intoned the small punch, softly, gently, and then in crescendo, he reached full blend, and stopped for weeping.

The "Introitus" continued, the "Kyrie," the "Sequentia." He didn't pick up until the "Offertorium" drew him in once again, irresistibly without effort, trumpet and French horn arpeggio, now in grand support of "ex lux perpetua luceat eis…." Mozart wouldn't mind at all. He'd dig it big time. Yeah. And on and on for almost an hour, resting at times to catch his breath and to savor the rich tones, before picking up again, him, Mozart and the crows improvising in exquisite collaboration.

Suddenly he was swimming in thickness. The *Requiem* was gone, replaced by the roar of thick churning, viscous substance. He swam with one arm, holding his horn way above his head with the other, compelled into making each stroke. The thick mixture parted in front of him, as if expecting each stroke. No choice but to follow its lead. And yet, in actuality, it followed his. He swam in apprehension and calm. No one, not even Level VI's entered a V.E. without V.E.-goggles. Oh Jeez, not how he'd ever imagine dying, trapped in V.E. But it wasn't an ordinary V.E. He thought about turning around. It was too daunting. He was compelled to swim onward, no matter what.

Then, as if reading his vague impulse to turn around, the viscous mixture closed around him from behind, firmly and resolutely, pushing him onward, without any possibility of changing course.

"You made it, my boy!"

"Gir! You came with me! I knew it! Are you okay?"

"Hush! Conserve your energy."

He could vaguely make him out in the thickness ahead, shimmering and floating, rolling and writhing. He struggled to reach him. "Slow down, Johnny. Leave me be and listen. Just listen hard. And be brave. Above all, you must be brave."

"What's happening? Oh good Jesus, tell me what's happening?"

"Just listen. By the time you enter this V.E., there'll be nothing you can do but listen. All's in the past now. Please understand, Johnny. It had to be this way."

Panic filled Johnny's throat and rushed headlong into his eyes. "You *are* dead. You went and died on me didn't you. Why? What'd you do that for? I told you. You knew you wouldn't make it. I told you to stay behind! I knew it! Oh good Jesus!"

"*You* knew, you see. That's the point. You have mastered prescient. You're ready to take it all on, Johnny, and you can do it a million times better than I could possibly do in my weakened condition. Yes, you knew and I knew what had to be. I wouldn't send you if I doubted your strength. Now you're a master empath, and a master technician. All you need lies within your inner chamber. Don't look now. I just want you to listen. Remember when you searched that chamber, you know the one we entered together in the old city on Galern II, in Irabi Proper? Well everything's ready. Use it selectively, only when necessary. Don't be tempted to go there now. You need all your energy to train Scotty and J, for the three of you to train each other."

"But you went and died on me!" Johnny fought the viscous pool to get to the old Imari. "I can still save you, can't I? Tell me how. Please tell me how. Oh God, Gir, you promised!"

"This is only a V.E., my Johnny. You're simply reading a V.E. I prepared months ago. It's over. I knew I wouldn't make it through the crisscross—"

"Oh shit, I killed you 'cuz I'm a goddamned sissy. I just went and killed you. You didn't have to come with me. I told you not to come with me. You wouldn't listen!"

"Johnny! I didn't even get to the crisscross. You crossed it on your own. I turned back long before you even reached the outer edges of the stratosphere. You didn't need me. You just thought you did. I made it look like I was with you. But you did it alone, completely on your own strength. On your own high C, just like you said you would."

"You were too there! You encouraged and smiled. I heard you! I saw you!" He thrashed at the thickness, now even more gelatinous and unyielding.

"I never left Jupiter's orbit. I circled back. All the rest was illusion. I circled back and landed safely on Europa. I came back to die, because my time was up. My time was up Johnny. That dust storm accident I told you about finally caught up with me. It took 'bout 150 years, but it finally caught up with me."

"Naw, you're just saying this. You're lying!" But he knew otherwise. "Oh shit, Gir! I really, really need you! Don't you understand? I love you."

"Now banish that frightened orphan boy voice of yours and listen. You, you and Scotty and J have been conferred. The three of you need to enter even more rigorous training as soon as possible."

Conferred? The word had special meaning. Where had he heard it before? Conferred. Conferred. Confirmed? His mind flung backward, Baptized? Something like that? It had that kind of strength. Something about that.

"Conferred. You and your new friends. Listen! Ask Scotty about an Imari conferral. She probably has already figured it out. But bring her my words. It's all up to your team. It's dangerous, extremely difficult, but not impossible."

"I don't understand. What do we have to do?"

"No time to explain. Accept the conferral, the highest honor and privilege empaths can obtain after Ascension, but also a serious obligation. Scotty will know how to start." Gir's voice was fading, his image slipping into a dim shadow of itself.

"Wait! Wait! Don't go yet! Don't you know about being a black guy on this planet? Wait, Gir! Just for another minute."

"I know everything there is to know about being a black guy on your planet. That's the point! The Mission is the Mission for a reason. Imagine Jim Crow across the entire universe?

"Now then, get the hell out of this V.E., while you still have the strength. You don't have goggles, and too much of this V.E. stuff will mush your brain big time. I'll be here when you need me, so for what it's worth, your team will never be without me. That's of comfort to me. I hope it is for you too. So leave now! Remember, the inner chamber. It's safe there, even from the most powerful scanners. Even Galern II scanners can't penetrate it. You know how to enter. Bring your team to the chamber. It's your refuge and contains your training libraries. Now get the hell out of here before I kick you out, and that won't be any fun, I promise you. Now git!"

The thick mixture suddenly became unbearably hot, and started to churn furiously. In an instant, Johnny was saturated in a sticky sweat. He jerked awake and found himself drenched, flat on his stomach, thrashing at the thickness that was no longer there.

He writhed in grief. The crowing seemed right on top of him. Alone, more alone than ever. The gravel on the floor of the cave writhed with him, relentlessly scraping his cheeks, raw from crying.

✳ ✳ ✳

J was startled awake by a sudden emptiness on the other side of the hoverglow. Silence. No Johnny. Clearly no Johnny. Not even an internal whisper. Scotty was also stirring. She felt it too. The sun was already up, but it was overcast and grey. How could he have left without their knowing about it?

They both sat up.

"He can't have gone far. He's too weak," said Scotty.

"Well, he took his travel sac, earthling duds and his trumpet and just went and disappeared to silence. I don't even know how long he's been gone. Could be hours by now. I can't believe we didn't notice him leave. I was hardly asleep, I thought. He's got some shielding we don't have a clue about. Like you think he's here right by your side but he's really not. Then nothing. Total silence. It's eerie. Actually, do you think he's done something asinine?"

"I'm such an asshole! I shoulda listened to you. We coulda figured it out. Stopped him before he went berserk. We had all the clues. *You* knew. Jeez, you knew and I didn't listen."

"Holy shit, Scotty, stop already! You didn't listen and I didn't insist."

"Jeez, it's almost 8 a.m. He could've been gone for hours. Can you locate him?"

"Not yet." J was already searching. She'd done it before. But that's when he was desperately calling for help, an extremely weak but open searching. Looking for their towline. This time, dead silence. If he's hurt himself.... And now Scotty was busy feeling sorry for herself when she should be helping. She wondered if Telmx, the Imari, were so, so human.

Scotty silently apologized by joining the searching.

"I'm right here," Johnny called out loud. "No need for fancy stuff. Just look across the goddamn meadow!"

There he was, loping along, completely energized, and laden with packages. "Hey, look at what they got in that town! Organic bread, great coffee, and chi, steaming hot green chi, just like you like it, J. Oh, and some bitter marmalade. It's a trip and a half down there. And there's enough unharnessed empath energy hanging out to fuel six trips to Galern II and back."

J was not fooled. Scotty was a nanosecond behind.

"Oh, Johnny," J empathed. "It's Gir." Tears welled. "Your nightmare. Oh I am so, so sorry. I knew Gir. How could you not love him to pieces? I mean, I think of what'd it be like to lose Telmx."

Scotty's hand found his shoulder, one finger pressing gently, the others barely caressing, hovering. Her other hand found J's. She wept softly.

"It's alright now, really, you two," he said. "He's here. We, Gir and me, we're here to help! These Imari have a million tricks tucked away in their wishaptha and travel hoods."

"And you're writing a symphonic poem about him," J managed. "With, with, an absolutely extraordinary trumpet aria. It's, it's exquisite."

"It's Mozart."

"No, it's you *and* Mozart. He's kind of there with you too."

"Okay, okay. C'mon, help me lay these treats out. I'm famished. Then I have a shit-load to tell you guys."

****

"Conferred?" Scotty was beside herself. "We're conferred? You gotta be kidding!"

"What are you talking about?" J read Scotty's excitement and Johnny's jumbled messages from the V.E. Somehow Telmx was mixed up in all this.

Johnny sat with his knees pulled up to his chest. Still grieving, but mostly excited.

"Ohmygosh," J empathed. "We have to go through a Triad Conferral Rite, don't we?" Telmx's words were on top of her, now. From the past, the future, as a little girl? On Galern II during her first visit? After she and Telmx made love for the first time? "When you are ready," Telmx had whispered, "you will assume your travel hood in earnest. Be patient."

"And I have to auto-mold some new travel hoods for the occasion." Scotty was composed now. "Where are your duds from that capsule, Johnny?"

"I dunno right now." He just wanted to sleep again. Without any dreams, no nightmares. Just a calm, blissful sleep. Deal with everything later. Much later. J handed him a goblet. "Here, it's Scotty's concoction. She calls it a 'Ki-olanthe hot toddy.' You've been through a lot."

CHAPTER TWENTY-EIGHT

Meads Mountain Cave

"You're actually going to be able to do that?" J's empath enthusiasm bounced around the walls of the cave.

"That's what I was trained to do. That's why I'm here." Johnny was serious, monotonic.

"Ohmygosh, how utterly fab." empathed J. "A real honest-to-god empath booster, right here on Earth. Will it work from the cave? Won't we be detected? What about the scanners?"

"Whoa, first things first. We need to get it built. Then we'll figure out a way to get it running without being detected. Ultimately we need it to reach to the Imari Outpost team on Europa without being picked up by the boys here on Earth."

"Do you hear that Scotty?" Scotty was at the mouth of the cave, looking out at the vista. Her shield was impenetrable. "Scotty?"

Scotty turned around. Her eyes were steel, piercing. "Johnny, you still really haven't come clean with us. I mean you really don't want to be doing this. You need to talk about that, damn it, before we make all these amazing plans. How can you truly concentrate on this thing with all that static going on?"

"Wait a minute, Scotty. He doesn't need to talk about anything he doesn't want to talk about. You don't need to talk about it, Johnny. So there's static. I got conflicts about this project too. Don't you think I'd rather be hanging around drinking bot and listening to the Beatles and Herbie Hancock? I mean, hanging out with you guys, and Katie and everybody, without all this intrigue and freaking 'do or die' Mission. You know how hard it is to keep everything from Katie, my best friend Katie, who knows more about making a revolution and Marx and Fidel and stuff, more than almost anyone. And *my* clarinet, what about that? Don't you think I'd rather—"

"There's another thing, guys, I got to get a job," continued Johnny. He seemed unfazed, meditative. "I've been thinking about that too. I probably should try out for some local bands up here and see what happens. Then I can stay here and build this thing, kind of get the whole cave organized. I have some ideas. And, yeah, you're right, Scotty, we all need to talk about this static stuff. You got all that writing you want to do. You're more shielded than both of us put together. We don't have a goddamned clue what's going on with you. You're the most control freak empath I've ever met. It makes it real hard, you know. How we going to work together with your huge control stuff?"

"Touché," empathed Scotty.

The three stood staring at each other in silence. J suddenly noticed that the cave was damp and cold. In truth, they hardly knew each other. Even as empaths. She was madly in love with Scotty, but knew her less than two weeks, and Johnny, just a couple of days. And now they were supposed to be a Conferred Triad Team. How long did it take Telmx, Gir and Winstx to work organically as a triad team, she wondered. And they were Imari Level VI's? "I guess we got a lot of work to do," she said aloud.

Water was dripping somewhere in the recesses of the cave. Deep and far. The three listened and probed the depth of the cave in silence. "Okay," empathed Scotty. "At the risk of being accused of taking charge, I would like to suggest we spend the next several days exploring this cave and getting to know each other. No secrets, no yes-buts, letting it all hang out. Doesn't have to be a what-cha-ma-call-it group, T-group, nothing like that. Just plain sharing. Merge our library chambers, all the various chambers, but not just that: really talking. I for one would prefer to do all of that over huge quantities of bot."

"And suffused ch'em root," added J. She took her comrades' hands and pulled them into a tight circle. They bent their heads to touching.

"Wow! A Conferred Triad Team!" whispered Scotty. "I can hardly believe it. Johnny, you must have all the training manuals in that chamber library of yours. Gives me a headache and a real surge, just thinking about it. Plus the unabridged *Books of Kro'an'ot* right here! Right in your very own brain, just itching to be studied."

"Before we go and get stoned silly on bot and ch'em," empathed Johnny, "we have to camouflage this cave, so no one else finds it. It's hard to find, but you know, there are rock climbers in these parts. Actually hide it so that even those who've been here before can't find even a tiny trace."

"How we going to do that?" asked Scotty, and before she could finish, they knew exactly what they had to do.

CHAPTER TWENTY-NINE

Telmx

The city of Gimot, erected by the first Imari families at the foot of the Mythic Mitharri Mountains on the planet Kiol, was the oldest Imari city in the galaxies. Even Galern II was modern in comparison, although the central part of the western hub of Galern had attempted to replicate the old byways and architecture. To make a pilgrimage back to Imari roots was a privilege few Imari Scouts had the time to indulge in. Plus it took huge amounts of empath energy to reach the planet. However, occasionally their missions required them to visit the dense forest of Kiol in order to consult with the legendary Kiolanthe, the little ones.

Gimot sat quietly in the valley, surrounded by the forest and the very mountains Kro'an'ot and Gimot (as the epic recounts) had traveled with their families in search of a permanent site to build their new civilization. In the center of the city hovered the Founders Monument, marking the very spot where Kro'an'ot found her cousin Gimot's partially decomposed body after she had led her clan through the perilous trek down the mountain with the empath powers she and her cousin had recently absorbed from their secret relationship with the tiny Kiolanthe. On the plaque were etched some of the most moving verses of the original epic. Hermetically encased within was the entire unabridged chronicle and the sacred *Books of Kro'an'ot*, the original parchment leaves penned by the founding elders as dictated by Kro'an'ot herself.

The streets leading away from the center in all directions were winding and narrow, with high swaying hujnaut trees every few meters, and hundreds of flower-filled baskets hanging from balconies, so that the trees and the flowers intermingled in a splendid canopy of colors and aromas. Wind whistles and occasional wind pipettes dangled from windows and gently arched entrances, signaling their presence, for they were difficult to discern otherwise, so much did they blend with arrays of ferns and shrubs that lined the narrow roadways. Jungle and city together. Silent save for the wind music and forest chatter. Out-loud silent, for the Imari had no need here for out-loud communication, except for the occasional travelers hostel that serviced non-empath tourists. For Winstx and Telmx, it was teeming with empath aliveness and endless discussion, and empathed poetry, recited or in the making. Telmx had never heard so much recited and communicative poetry, even on her home planet.

Their travel hoods were neatly tucked in their pouches, and they joyfully took in the familiar aromas of the auto-suffusing frimulators. It had been months, no probably years, since Telmx had felt so safe, so at home. She yearned for the simple pleasures of home-cooked empah root and dipping sauces. And Gimot was famed for its bot, brewed from the original bot'ime root, farmed in the foothills and occasionally shipped to Galern and other Imari settlements, but primarily for the locals, who had no need to engage in import and export.

Winstx was a few paces ahead, navigating toward a particular set of steps that would bring them to an Imari compound that lay just at the bottom of the foothills. Her navigational instincts were impeccable. Telmx hung back, taking in the city. Occasionally an Imari would pass by, nodding in formal greeting. But for the most part the streets were empty, the traditional preparatory time for Imari dinner ritual. Telmx was particularly thrilled by the snatches of empath-recited poetry primarily from the children, who were working and reworking their lessons into rhymes as they prepared for breaking the evening froth.

"It's just ahead," empathed Winstx. She stopped to let Telmx catch up, and took her hand. The roadway led to a narrow set of stone steps. They silently climbed. The steps were cut through lush amber and lavender vines which were themselves entwined with clusters of aqua sunburst glories that swayed gently as if to proffer a silent formal Imari greeting as the Scouts climbed past each grouping. Their natural aromas mingled with the distinctive Imari cooking oils. Telmx savored the anticipated feast. It had been a long time.

Telmx didn't believe in magic, or mysticism, and had a hard time allowing herself the shadowy reaches into unreality that Winstx reveled in when time allowed, or mission demanded. However, when Winstx delved into serenity, Telmx was compelled to follow her. As they mounted the narrow steps, Winstx's serenity traveled through her hand to hers. They were about to enter a very special place. Of course, there were some Imari on this planet that enjoyed close and intimate communication with the forest-protected Kiolanthe, but few off-world Imari knew where to find their compound. Winstx knew who had access to the Kiolanthe. Telmx felt privileged, humbled, and exhilarated.

✳ ✳ ✳

After a huge and boisterous feast, which included a hilarious mini-musical performed by the children of the compound, Uiolx announced that it was time to offer his story. It was not unusual in traditional Imari feasts, especially ones that hosted special guests, for the elder in the compound to entertain in such manner. However, Telmx's uneasy flooded her chambers, and seconds later Winstx's trembling hand took hers. Uiolx stood up and began to pace. He fell silent and bent over the frimulator. He ladled out a new batch of warm bot, and hovered a huge frothy goblet to the circle of mats. He hesitated to rejoin them. He finally squatted opposite Telmx and Winstx and took a deep silent breath. Even the children's empath chatter went silent, attentive. Babies, snuggled in the arms of various adults, slipped into easy slumber.

"Much has happened since we discerned you were on your way," he empathed. "We almost pleaded with you to turn back, but Iol convinced us that it was unsafe to send you a relay, for fear of interception. And turning you around would actually put you much more in harm's way because you need to know what we know. We did set your minds completely at ease, to dull your uneasy in case your chambers were penetrated. It was crucial that no one discern, as you approached our planet, that you were anticipating what you are about to hear.

"Several weeks ago, a small group of Imari entered the forest from the molten ocean side. As you well know, no one has ever attempted that before. Even with solidly shielded hovercraft, it is uncanny that the group managed to survive the blistering radiation, But they did. They did not open themselves up to us, or to any of the other Imari compounds. They were so well shielded that we only found out after the Kiolanthe sent an urgent V.E.-message to us through the miniature felines who roam these foothills, after it was all over.

"The Kiolanthe, of course, had discerned their arrival, long before the group navigated the crisscross. They were ready. But they could not fathom why the Imari group entered stealthily, without making contact with one of our Imari compounds here in the city, as is usual custom. The Kiolanthe smelled sour bot on their breath, and their energies were jagged and arrogant, and enhanced in unnatural ways. For the first time ever, the Kiolanthe went into deep hiding, leaving several brave families behind in their usual encampments of nests, just enough groupings to forestall suspicion that they knew something was very wrong with these particular Imari visitors. Taking every precaution, they also mustered their protectors, the gionthas, a very unusual move, because those creatures are intractable, dull, and very unpredictable. And they called in a scouting party of miniature felines from the foothills to observe unobtrusively and report by foot, to us and to the Kiolanthe in hiding.

"For the entire time these impostor Imari scouts were there, the volume of Kiolanthe empath chatter went down several decibels, not completely silent, for that would have alerted the visitors' uneasy, but quiet enough to give us, who are blessed to hear their perpetual array of empath music, strong foreboding that something was very wrong in the forest. We decided to send a group out to check on them, but for reasons we now understand, we thought better of the plan. Instead, we pushed our uneasy to our inner most shielded chambers, and waited. The felines arrived a few days later to confirm our worst fears.

"As you know, never in the recorded history of the galaxies has there even been a stealth intrusion of these forests. The Kiolanthe have lived eternally in peace and tranquility. That Imari Travel Scouts, apparently on an official mission, should so arouse their uneasy was unheard of and distressing. No one has ever dared bring our petty political squabbles to the little creatures of our sacred Legends, not even during that brief era of roving Olioth renegades. Even then it would never have crossed their evil minds to be that arrogant.

"Of course, Imari shielding is usually no match for the Kiolanthe's powers of discerning, and the arrogance of this band was almost laughable to them. But the Kiolanthe took no chances, and used the opportunity to discern as much as they could. They did not discern enough. This band of imposter Imari Scouts had managed to shield sinister aspects of themselves from the staggering powers of the Kiolanthe.

"The band visited several nest compounds, breaking the froth and making idle talk. They claimed they were on a secret mission to a very distant renegade planet. They said the newly discovered planet was developing forces that would ultimately shatter all our lives in unimaginable ways. They could not risk petitioning the Intergalactic Council for the amount of empath energy they required to intervene, because, they claimed, there were infiltrators in the Intergalactic Council who would warn the earthlings, as they were called. They were forced to petition secretly the Kiolanthe for assistance, even bypassing the Imari compounds here in Gimot. Their requirements were simple. They said they needed several vats of their most potent bot and several infusions of their most powerful empath energy through participation in their traditional Kiolanthe birthing circles. Not unusual. Many of us are privileged to join the circles, especially during this time of year when there are so many. But we must be invited. We cannot just show up and make a request, even if we are concerned that our energies require a supplemental boosting. That's what was so unusual about this request. So arrogant. So disrespectful.

"The Kiolanthe graciously delayed answering, saying they had to consult among the elders. Then they graciously refused."

Uiolx paused. His trembling hands accepted the bot goblet.

In the next instant the entire circle of Imari, his compound grouping, even the children (each one wrapped securely in the arms and legs of an adult), Telmx and Winstx, everyone, followed Uiolx into the feline V.E.-message. There was Raymond (Telmx knew it had to be Raymond), along with perhaps twenty Imari in traditional scouting travel hoods. The imposter Imari Scouts were huddled in a circle, passing to each other something, she could not immediately discern, afraid what she thought it to be, but could not be.

On the ground just outside the circle lay a female Kiolanthe, her belly slit, her entrails splayed and oozing globules of thick maroon blood. Telmx's inner eyes clouded, but she forced herself to enter Raymond's circle, to witness a gruesome version of her and Winstx's most recent dream, now retold in the feline V.E.-message.

Raymond and his group were passing a limp, slightly squirming fetus around their circle, each one of his group taking a turn licking the dying fetus clean, glutinously sucking in its energy-rich amniotic fluid with insatiable thirst, reluctant to give the tiny, dying unborn up to the next one in their circle. Telmx reached for the unborn, desperately and futilely trying to save it from their clutches. Screaming out loud, she wrenched herself from the V.E., flung herself out on to the verandah, and vomited. Someone handed her some chi and after a few moments, Winstx led her back to Uiolx's circle, gently placed her in front of her and wrapped her strong arms and legs around her. Telmx laid her head back on Winstx's breast like the children of the compound.

"They are on their way to that tiny star system you've been monitoring," Uiolx finally empath-whispered. "For what purpose, we could not discern."

"How could these Imari do all that?" managed Winstx.

"We do not know, and frankly we're terrified."

A flurry of activity interrupted. Many of the adults had begun to herd sleepily protesting children to their separate quarters. Others were discreetly fading back into their areas within the compound, leaving Uiolx to strategize with Telmx and Winstx.

They squatted silently on the verandah that opened into the foothills. The feline-V.E. felt unreal. If she hadn't experienced Raymond's treachery herself, Telmx would have been tempted to call the V.E. a fabrication (as if anyone could or would fabricate such a nightmare). Now more than ever they needed Goshing and Gir. But Raymond's group had apparently even made Goshing unavailable to her. Now they were on their way to attack Gir and the outpost team on Europa. Of course they would compromise the outpost station before heading to Earth.

"We have to leave for the Earth system right away!" empathed Telmx. "We have absolutely no time to waste."

"I know, but we need to rest, Tel," empathed Winstx. "Plus we need to formulate a plan. We don't have the people or the empath energy to deal with this on our own."

"We thought you would report this to the Intergalactic Council. If you hadn't been on your way here, we would have already sent a delegation. Perhaps we should have anyway. You're right. You cannot deal with this imposter Scout group on your own, two Imari empath scouts against power even the Kiolanthe and the gionthas couldn't tackle. You'll need many scouts and a staggering amount of empath energy. The Council has the Order of Empath Travel Scouts and the necessary empath reserves at its disposal."

Winstx looked at Telmx, who nodded in silent agreement. "We cannot go to the Council, Uiolx," empathed Winstx hesitantly. "By now we are probably considered outlaws."

He looked at them with some alarm. "We had not been forewarned about you." Telmx felt him gently surface searching without intruding. "And we have discerned nothing to make us uneasy about you. What do you refer to?"

Telmx sent him a brief V.E. of the encounter with Raymond at the relay center and the spaceport incident.

"The Council needs to know you were manipulated," empathed Uiolx. "We should send our own delegation. Perhaps some felines as well."

"No," empathed Winstx. "There are now infiltrators in the Council. They cannot know that we know. They'll warn Raymond."

"Things weren't supposed to happen this quickly," empathed Telmx. "Not according to my predictive V.E.-scans. Things are very wrong."

"I wish you could run some more scans," empathed Winstx.

"It would take too long, and besides my apparatus isn't with me. I need Goshing."

"We *will* have to do without her, Tel."

"I would feel better if we could somehow reach the Kiolanthe," empathed Telmx. "But why should they even trust us after what happened?" She paused, trying to reach out to the forest, trying to merge with its song and their chatter. "Perhaps there's a way."

"At least we know that the gionthas are real," whispered Winstx, "as intractable and ferocious as we fathomed in our dream."

"What do we do next?" A chilling wind was picking up from the west. Winstx pulled her travel hood around her head. Uliox passed her a goblet of warm graftac malt.

"Time is crucial. We have to intercept Raymond and his mercenaries," said Telmx.

"But we don't know what they're up to," said Winstx.

"Well we at least know where they're headed, and the sooner we figure out what they're planning, the sooner we can stop them."

"I suspect the Kiolanthe know their plans," said Uiolx.

"Do you think the Kiolanthe will also know what to do?" asked Winstx.

"No time to try," said Telmx. "Even if they could help me control my runaway take-out."

"You might need your take-out just as it is," said Winstx.

"Look what happened at the terminal. Ever since Raymond somehow provoked it, I can't manage it the way I had been trained. I need my own control back."

"Even if you did have the time, The Kiolanthes are still heavily guarded by the gionthas," warned Uiolx. "We have not dared enter the forest since then. Even the felines won't take us."

"Can you communicate with them through the felines?" Telmx accepted the goblet from Winstx, and inhaled its soothing aroma.

"With time." He closed his eyes and seemed to reach out into the night air. "It will take more than a day," he empathed. "The rogues have at least three days lead. I agree with you. There should be no delay."

"Have you talked to the felines at all since then?" asked Telmx

"No."

"I can't think about it anymore," empathed Telmx. "Perhaps we should just take off for Earth's star system tonight, and on the way figure out a plan."

"Perhaps we should rest for the night here at the compound, and take on some supplies," said Winstx. "If we follow them directly to the Earth star system, we'll probably not be able to stop off anywhere. As it is, we'll have to take a somewhat circuitous route. Besides, we need a staggering amount of empath energy, just like Raymond's group required. We have to figure that out."

"I think we can figure that part out," empathed Uiolx. "Leave that project to us."

"Alright. We'll leave at daybreak," empathed Telmx. "Even if the felines could take us there in the morning, there is no more time. We just need to be on our way."

Telmx was exhausted. Winstx was right. They desperately needed to sleep. The journey had been very draining, and now they needed to replenish personal energies. Besides, she wasn't completely recovered from her wounds. Uiolx already had a plan for the larger pool of empath energies they would need for the journey and to deal with Raymond's group. He wouldn't let them in on what he had in mind, but she trusted he would be successful. But what about needing more Imari Scouts? Would there be possible recruits here on Gimot? The young ones were too young, even though they were the most promising. Perhaps some older adolescents, but wouldn't the best of them already be off-world in training at the Imari Scout universities? Even if they could find some recruits, it would take time to train them. And besides, there wouldn't be room for them on their tiny vessel.

"Like children who fight sleep, you will want to stay up and figure things out tonight," empathed Uiolx as he led them to the guest quarters, shrouded among large ferns and ernith't trees. A small suffusing frimulator, medicinal bot nightcaps and snacks had been tastefully prepared for them. "Please do allow your strategizing and forebodings to take a rest. As you know, they are a useless drain of precious energies. The recipes for the nightcap and the various nocturnal calming snacks are traditional. The Kiolanthe themselves introduced them to our ancestors. Please be in comfort and repose until the light of day." Then he was gone.

Winstx hardly needed the Kiolanthe soporifics. She was asleep before the hoverglows retreated into the ferns. Even after several draughts, and a good number of confections, Telmx continued to struggle. She remembered how much she and the other compound children used to want to stay up and play way past their bedtime. Sleeping mats were pulled out into clusters no later than two hours past final sundown, except on special occasions. Tonight was such an occasion. Four hours later, she could still hear some of them sleepily protesting. Some still needed to perform their final recitation rituals for their lessons the next day. Others were pleading for one more song before retiring.

The adults had surely soothed the children's uneasy, but not so much as to make them naive and unschooled in the ways of the universe. The parents seem much less protective here than at home, she thought. The children mingle with all the adults, as if all are their parents, yet not ever losing the loving tenderness of their birth parents. It was emulated on her birth world, but not as successfully as here. She recalled her mother's pride at her achievements mingled with desperate envy and clinging. Some of the children here had a much easier time leaving home to train for the Order of Empath Travel Scouts. The children seemed to achieve at least Level IV without schooling. And some of the elders were natural Level VI's, even without having studied the *Books of Kro'an'ot* in their entirety.

Empathed verses of one of her favorite nighttime rhymes drifted through the compound. And wind pipettes and small cymbalies. The forest seemed to listen as well. Such a perfectly calm night after such a tumultuous V.E. The forest was hushed, but not completely silent. Nevertheless, funereal. The distant subdued chatter of the Kiolanthe was distinct. The faint odor of the gionthas. Telmx smiled, finally giving in to the soporific tonics.

While the two scouts slept, the compound organized. By second sunrise they had already gathered several vats of supplies and all the boosters that they could from the neighboring compounds. All through the night, a long procession of young and old silently hovered bin upon bin of supplies through the central square to the port.

When the Scouts were awakened, scores of adolescents were already lined up to touch their cilia, emptying their vibrantly enhanced energies into the Scouts' inner chambers. Although their donations would temporarily deplete cherished libidos of the recently ascended teens, they did so willingly and proudly. Several pleaded to be allowed to join the mission, and one even seemed like he could readily take on crucial responsibilities of a well trained Imari Scout, not a disciplined Level VI yet, but potentially able to achieve that level of proficiency within a relatively short period, with the proper mentoring.

"Gilliac would make an excellent Scout," Telmx told his parents. "Perhaps he should apply to the Order. He is very talented and he clearly wants to travel."

"He will travel," said his mother. "It is planned. However, he is still young, and the Kiolanthe have already designated him as one of the few Imari on Gimot to join their training rituals in the Fall. He will be going there for an extended stay, once this current crisis is behind us. After his training, he will travel. Perhaps to Galern II, perhaps to become a Scout. We will see what he wants. He is young and impatient. He must learn patience."

Telmx turned to Gilliac. "I too had to learn patience. I'm still arrogant at times. It's my failing. Learn well from Kiolanthe. I'm jealous of your opportunity. Don't ever think of throwing it away."

The youth raised his neck in silent assent. "If you would consent to become my mentor," he empathed finally, "I would travel anywhere to find you."

Telmx was flustered and flattered. She had trouble shielding such feelings from the strong empath of this boy. "In time," she whispered. "When you go to Galern II, find my mentor Goshing, and seek her guidance. Besides, I may not survive this challenge we face. You must look to the masters." She paused. "When you find Goshing, relay my opha to her, only once you have joined her in her most inner shielded chambers, for your protection and hers. She will know to bring you there when she meets you. I have no doubt. "

She turned away to avoid revealing her tears. His knowledge of her foreboding grief was profound, in spite of her confident advice. She felt comforted by him, in spite of her shielding.

Telmx felt Gilliac tugging at her and at his own shyness battling with his urgency to speak more.

"I have something I need to tell you," he finally empathed respectfully to Telmx as they loaded supplies into the hold. "If you might listen to me, just for a moment. I see that you have fathomed my potential. I am simply very lucky. But with this luck comes responsibility. I must speak to you in private."

These were words beyond his years.

"If you would allow me to enter an inner chamber—just for a few minutes, I really do need to speak to you," he repeated.

Telmx felt him reaching from a depth she thought was only reserved for those of Goshing's capacities. It stirred misgivings. In this new realm of intrigue, anything was possible. Raymond had made her intensely wary. She hated her wariness. It was unwelcoming and restrictive. There was already an indescribable bond developing between Gilliac and herself. Then again, she hadn't even questioned the excitement she felt upon meeting her Raymond, going all the way back to their dorm days. How do you trust?

"I invite you to enter *my* inner chamber, as undeveloped as it is," he added. "Whichever way you are most comfortable. I sense and thoroughly understand your uneasy."

Indeed, this child was way beyond his years. Her feeling was mixed: wary because of Raymond and intrigued by Gilliac's precocious. She remembered how upset she had been at how quickly J had exponentially advanced as a child, just by her contact with her. His precocious was similar, but not from contact with her, but from the Kiolanathe. He was indeed special.

Winstx came back to the cargo bay with another load. "Go ahead, Tel," she empathed. "I think it's alright. I'll be close by, in any event. He needs to speak to you. Desperately. So I'll be here but not listening. He needs privacy."

Gilliac stood patiently on the side. He was thin and gangly, not more than 13 or so, and his young cilia shimmered in the new light of the morning. "I am sorry to cause you anxiety," he empathed after another long and hesitant silence. "I have been waiting for the right moment, but the right moment did not manifest, so now you are about to depart and I must overcome my shyness and, and—"

"It's alright, Gilliac. Where shall we go?"

"If it is comfortable for you, there is a clearing right on the other side of the trees toward the foothills, about five minutes from here. What I have to say will not take very long, but we must not be disturbed at all, not even by my family. If you don't mind, I have shielded from them, from everyone except you, but left a slight opening for Winstx so that you and she can feel comfortable. It's important that you both feel comfortable. But I'm not yet capable of bringing more than one person at a time fully into my inner chamber. Perhaps by next year—"

"Come Gilliac, we haven't much time."

He broke the silence when they reached the clearing. "There is no one on Gimot to trust." They squatted in the shadow of an umbraht tree at the far side, bordering the thickened tangle of the forest. He was clearly anxious, and didn't want to presume to take the lead. Telmx bent her head toward his. His inner chamber was newly formed. Its tapestry walls were freshly woven, and undulated with the fervent energy of youth. But they were secure, as secure as Goshing's had ever been. "Thank you for consenting to visit," he empath-whispered.

His vibrant chamber tapestries quivered, restive and serene. His responsibilities were beyond his years, and he felt their weight. He wanted her to know that, and she did.

"No one, not even my family must know what I know. As much as I love them. I even had to make sure you were you. The Kiolanthe and the felines assisted me."

"What do you mean no one to trust?"

"I honestly think everyone in our village can be trusted. But Raymond's powers are profound. The felines gave me the skills to figure out whether you were under his influence. You are, kind of, but not in the way they fear. You are still you. You are strong. You are special. There is much Uiolx does not know. Because the full story could not be told. You need the full story. Then you need to figure out how to proceed. Uiolx and the others have some ideas. But…."

"You talk in riddles, Gilliac, and I can't fathom. You are so well shielded, even as we meet within your deepest chamber, and I don't want to insult you by trying."

"I apologize. I am unschooled in this kind of communication. Please forgive me. Through me the Kiolanthe elders have sent formal invitation to break the froth with them in their nesting compound."

It had been Telmx's lifelong dream to meet the Kiolanthe, ever since she had learned about Kro'an'ot and Gimot, in her earliest nursery rhymes. Indeed, it was somehow the messages from the tapestry and, in a way, from Goshing, that had brought them here to meet the little people. But they needed to leave for Europa immediately and waylay Raymond and his armada. There was no way to accept this incredible invitation.

"I am honored, and you should convey our deepest regrets to the elders. But as you well know, there is no time to waste. The urgency of the situation leaves us no luxury of time to enjoy Kiolanthe hospitality and to immerse ourselves in their gentle customs. Perhaps there will be another opportunity, when our responsibilities do not prevail. Please fathom and transmit my disappointment, for we must decline their invitation."

"I apologize for my disrespectful insistence. I cannot myself pass on to you the full account of Raymond's intentions. There is more to be told, and the Kiolanthe elders wish to tell you themselves. They have insisted that they speak to you in person, to infuse orientation and energies you require before you leave Kiol.

"They said you will understand if I informed you that the Oglassis visited them earlier this year and were sent to summon you. I am entrusted to guide you to their nesting compound. To that end, you must act as if you are taking me with you to Earth, even though my parents will object. You must convince them that I am worthy and ready to join your mission, although I am in truth poorly prepared to go. In fact, I will probably stay with the Kiolanthe for further training, unless you and the Kiolanthe elders feel I should in fact accompany you to intercept Raymond's regiment. They absolutely must be intercepted. But since I am not trained, my inexperience and youth will surely be hazardous and disruptive.

"I am most anxious to come with you, but I await your decision after you confer with the Kiolanthe elders. In no way can I return to my village, because even the little bit I know might leak out. For their protection, and my family's, should Raymond come back, or if one or more of the Imari here become turned without our fathoming. I am not fully skilled at powerful shielding and stealth, and some of the Imari elders are, should I say, curious when an adolescent is as secretive and as shielded as I must be. As you know, I am struggling and in pain. My parents know something is wrong, and it also pains me to lie to them."

In spite of his attempts at respectful formality, his emotions reverberated in his chamber. He desperately did not want to show Telmx how terrified he actually was to leave home before he felt he was ready. In the safety of his chamber his emotions were raw and unfettered. How very excruciating it was for him to keep his turmoil under strict control in everyday life. He didn't even have time to be a gangling, confused adolescent.

"My parents will allow me to guide you to the Kiolanthe. I have illegally used some slight mind urging on them, imperceptible, I am hoping, to all. They will be easily persuaded." His tapestries suddenly turned crimson, and Telmx tasted tears of profound shame.

"You did what you had to do."

"Indeed, we have no time for my irrational and immature regrets." He was already recovering. "If you and Winstx agree, I will travel with you to the hidden Kiolanthe nesting compound. They have cleared away a landing space for your ship. It is well hidden and safe. As you know, we cannot go by land right now, because the gionthas have been stirred up and will not discriminate friend from foe. Not even the felines have been able to calm them. Plus there is so little time."

"Gilliac, you are too young to have all of this on your shoulders. I am truly sorry."

"I am honored to have been designated."

"No need to explain further, Gilliac," Telmx empathed gently, withdrawing from his chamber. Gilliac's message from the Kiolanthe made total sense. Not only would they orient them to the task ahead, but they would probably be able to modulate her still unwieldy take-out powers. "I must not make this decision alone. We must ask Winstx to join us here, and then talk to your parents. "

"The invitation makes total sense," said Winstx after she listened to Telmx and Gilliac. "We are already several days behind, so we can't overtake Raymond and his armada before they attack the Europa Outpost. And even if we could, we are but two. At best the Kiolanthe might help us send subtle warnings to the earthling monitors. Raymond assumes you were compromised at the Grjimbe port, and by now either dead or retro-swept by the Council for unauthorized and unfettered take-out of seemingly innocent people. He wouldn't necessarily know that you had absorbed the tapestry message bidding us to visit Kiol, and probably would never have foreseen that we would have the opportunity to consult with them. We might have all this on our side as we figure out how to stop his treachery."

✳ ✳ ✳

Gilliac guided their ship effortlessly to a clearing deep in the Kiol forest. Although Telmx could hear and smell the gionthas in the distance, she felt no uneasy. The peaceful forest dominated.

Two Kiolanthe, one female and one male, met them as they disembarked. They bowed their heads in silent formal greeting, Imari style, immediately empath-chattering about the urgency of the situation. They were even smaller than Telmx had envisioned. Child-sized sapiens no more than two and a half or three feet tall, but clearly adults, probably elders. They were unclad, except for exquisitely crafted wooden and stone adornments tastefully distributed around their necks, arms and legs. Their blue and gold fur was short, except where long silvery strands of cilia wafted in tufts, on their foreheads, chins, chests, and genitalia.

"We are honored to break the froth with you," Y'rk empathed. Without further discussion, she and M'rk hovered the Scouts across the landing strip back into the forest, taking care that the travelers expend no empath energy of their own, because they required every iota for the tasks ahead.

Gilliac, clearly ecstatic to be a pivotal part of the proceedings, nevertheless hovered a respectful distance on his own behind them, until Y'rk playfully and kindly reprimanded him not to hover separately, as if an inferior being.

Their nest compound was in another huge clearing, surrounded by thick forest and foliage. At least a hundred nests of various sizes surrounded a small natural pool of rushing mountain water. On one side, in a cordoned-off field, even tinier Kiolanthe children played a kind of team-tag game with a set of colorful hovering woven spheres. Their squeals of delight aloud and empathed, in themselves seemed to have special meanings to the several teams.

Their guides did not allow them to linger, ushering them into the center of a small cluster of nests on the far side of the pool, where seven adults were squatting on mats arrayed in a circle, three of which were designated for Winstx, Telmx, and Gilliac.

Then, to Telmx's dismay, Y'rk insisted they break the froth with them in traditional protocol reserved for consultations and deliberations. "Yes, you must depart as quickly as possible, but you must be prepared properly for your journey. Please have patience."

To Telmx, even the most elaborate and formal Imari feast was a pale imitation of the Kiolanthe's repast and ceremony they enjoyed that morning. The infused bot was so freshly brewed, it rushed through Telmx's body as if it couldn't wait to fuse with her cells. Each root, each dipping sauce they passed around the circle, brought the Scouts closer to a sense of well-being and energy than the one previous.

"We regret we cannot go ourselves to deal with Raymond and his throng," O'ot, the eldest of the elders began, as soon as the first goblet of bot had been passed around. "As you know, we have never left Kiol. We are far too fragile and unwarlike to handle the treacheries that your Order of Empath Travel Scouts have been trained to carry out. All we can do, having fathomed in ways we cannot share, that Earth does pose threat dangers to all of us, just as you and Telmx Discerned. We were forced to break with tradition and sent the Oglassis to bring you here to receive the plan we have forged.

"We have yet to analyze why we didn't fully anticipate Raymond's wretched invasion here to empath-boost himself and his renegades for his trip to Earth. He has developed some unusual powers and must be subdued."

They briefly apologized for being among the recipients of the Imari's generous and courageous willingness to take on the dangerous task of protecting the civilized planets. The division of labor had been forged several millennia ago, and no one needed to spend time revisiting the arrangement. It was as it always had been.

There was not a lot of time to spend on formalities. But in their very informal manner, they were in fact formal and with traditional protocol.

They then moved to their proposal. Gilliac, whose empath reserve was ample for the trip, would navigate the Imari ship. Telmx and Winstx would be put in stasis until they were within two light years from Earth's solar system, in order to reserve their energies for the confrontation with Raymond and his throng, should it be required. "The empath energies we are infusing in you at this moment, combined with the Imari youths' donations earlier this morning, should be more than enough to prevail over the rogues. The three of you should be able to take back the Europa Outpost, with the element of surprise as your most potent weapon.

"That, plus the enhanced and focused take-out capacity we are generating within your inner tapestries, in case you are required to wield that level of weaponry against the regiment. We have restored your capacity to control your take-out, Telmx. Your training was clearly well hewn. We are not at all concerned.

"Three felines will accompany you to one of the moons on an outer gas giant, and then solo-condense pod down to Earth to organize their earthling counterparts. They have the main task of confronting and battling Raymond himself, who, we discerned from his crudely shielded mind, is the only one who will actually solo-condense pod to Earth. As you know, the earthlings have developed such a potent defense shield of their skies, because of their primitive wars, that no intergalactic ship can orbit there unobserved any more.

"As far as we can fathom, minimal retro-sweep will be required of specified earthlings. The felines and their earthling feline recruits should be able to take care of those immediately involved in the planet's rapid movement toward an unfettered Empath Era, and the planet's own more evolved elements of its population should be able to take care of the rest. Do not concern yourself right now about the Intergalactic Council. There is no time to obtain their approval. Nor would they necessarily grant it. As you know, evolution is full of contradictions. Together we will solve this one over time.

"We cannot promise that our plan will succeed, or that you will be there soon enough to save your beloved earthling monitors, or even that you will survive this mission, with such monumental implications for all. We sorely wish we could manipulate timing and culminations, but we cannot. We can only trust in our *Books of Kro'an'ot*, that our reasoning is sound: 'Where paranoia rules, conquest is ephemeral. Where perception rules, outcomes are unfailing.'"

Another apology. Winstx and Telmx tried in vain to shield the Kiolanthe from their anxieties about the fate of Earth and their three young monitors. And the Kiolanthe in response apologized even more vigorously, gently chiding them for trying to protect them from the inevitable distress the Imari felt for those they loved.

Without lingering on farewell formalities, the Kiolanthe rapidly hovered the Imari back to their ship, where three longhaired grey and white felines were patiently waiting permission to board.

Gilliac was ecstatic and terrified. He was not only entrusted to pilot the Imari Scout ship to Earth's solar system, but he was now an honorary triad team member, with much more responsibility than he ever imagined he could handle.

CHAPTER THIRTY

Matt

Matt desperately needed a pint. He was starving and Charlie was late. The hotel room was unbearable. He quickly shaved, put on his other suit, and tacked a scribbled a note to Charlie on his door to meet him at McSorley's. He would wait for him there and order a sizzling chicken pot pie. Just so much he could take of this! He was, he thought, going completely bananas. Couldn't have Charlie see him like that. Good thing he was late.

It was still light out at eight something, but hardly. The Times Square hustle and bustle was just plain infuriating. No, not just today. He was a farm boy and it always got to him, except when he wanted some excitement and perhaps a hot Korean lay. Not tonight. Not the kind of thing Charlie was into. He wondered about Charlie. What did he do to get some? Maybe just jerked off. Maybe he was a fucking faggot. No way. Matt could smell faggots a mile away.

The summer was almost gone, and MPII was batting zero. Those amazing blue surges during August were gone, completely silent. The best spikes were from infants and Coney Island dolphins. Well, how about hooking up the consoles to infants, he thought as he fought his way through the infuriating street. Infants were better than a couple of beatniks. Lots of spiked surges with them. But how would you exploit infants without creating a massive hullabaloo? Perhaps they could start an infant farm. No, that's the stuff stupid sci-fi movies were made of, and it wouldn't go over big with anybody, not even Dawes, certainly not Yazzie, and well, it didn't exactly go over big with himself either. Maybe post-birth embryonic fluid? Boy, now that was incredibly asinine. Where was his stupid head? Incredibly desperate.

He wished the dolphins hadn't been so fucking smart and self-righteous. Well maybe back to the cow machine idea. Hey, what was he thinking? That episode with the dolphins. It was a fucking dream, a nightmare. Even Yazzie had wondered at first if he wasn't seeing things. Coo-coo. Well he did tell him to go back and find out some more. Shit, he wouldn't dare do that. They'd put him away for sure. Lose whatever clout he had left with the Company, and with NASA. They might tolerate those kooky things with half-breeds like

Yazzie, singing with whales, etc., but not with Dr. Matthew. Even though he did, actually did, talk to cows as a kid. Maybe he had imagined that stuff too. Jeez, a complete psycho.

It was only a matter of time before Dawes called off the search. They desperately needed a new proposal. Charlie had some ideas about an ESP mining and transfer machine using dolphins. It was useless to keep on looking for raw talent among the various beatniks and hippies, and besides, even if they were to locate them, they would probably be so rebellious, they would sell the entire project to the reds, and blow up the whole damn MPII. Jeez, he needed that pint.

"Excuse me." He felt the stranger's sheer size before he turned to look. Really tall, basketball-and-then-some tall, and really thin, really, really dark, obviously really strong too. Better give him some coins. He dipped into his pocket.

"I'm not asking for a handout. I just want to talk to you for a bit of your time."

"I'm busy, gotta be somewhere. Could'ja maybe pick someone else this time?" He'd better be civil.

"Actually, I was specifically looking to talk to you. Can I buy you a pint?"

Matt was suddenly drawn to him in a very distressing, uncanny way. And repelled. What in God's name did he think he was? He sped up. Somehow he wasn't afraid of him anymore. A fucking fruit. "Sorry, buddy, I ain't that kind of guy. You just go and find someone else. I'm in a hurry to meet someone and I'm in no mood to deal with this kind of stuff right now. You got me pegged all wrong, buddy, and if you don't move on, I'll have to call a cop. Cops are all over the place you know. In plain clothes too. C'mon, buddy, could'ja just—"

"You and your friend will really want to hear what I have to say. Also I don't have a whole lot of time to waste on your primitive phobias. I have some information for you and your NASA crony about those blue surges that's going to change your life forever, Dr. Matthew. So you better let me buy you and Charlie a pint or two."

Matt stopped and turned to faced him, his mind flying in all directions. "Who the fuck are you and who sent you?" Wary and calm, but logic and training immediately put him on the wary side. A spy? A Russian spy? A Company man? A black Company man? Was the Company testing him in some back-assed way? "I said who are you and who sent you?"

"Listen, Dr. Matthew, I'll tell you everything you want to know, but not in the middle of the sidewalk. There's that McSorley's you were heading for, and Charlie has already ordered your chicken pot pie, so why don't we just take a walk over there and I promise you, you and your friend won't be sorry in the least. I'm about to save your MPII and you're about to be a superhero, winning the cold war, and everything. Of course, if you call the cops—"

Matt's fingers tuned to sand. His head was spinning. He wanted to run, just disappear. But the guy was riveting. "How the hell do you know so fucking much? Listen buddy, have you been tailing and bugging us the whole fucking summer? Whose payroll are you on? Oh shit, it's a goddamned grade-B spy movie. Okay, Mr. Bond, I'll listen to what you have to say, but don't expect anything from me. I'm not about to tell you shit. Besides, if you're so much in the know, you know more than I can possibly tell you."

Suspicion and calm wouldn't quit. It was as if the guy were leading *him* to McSorley's, and when they got there, Charlie was already spreading out his sketches and stats in a back booth, and the waiter was already slapping down three pints, two chicken pot pies and a huge green salad. Matt decided he was having another lunatic nightmare, and wished to hell he would wake up in a hurry.

"Thought you'd never show up," said Charlie. "I don't know how I knew you'd be here, but I went straight here from Penn Station, as if we'd planned it all along. Did you tell me to meet you here? Or did I imagine it and just guessed right? I must be losing it. I didn't get a whole lot of sleep 'cause I was figuring out the fine-tuning of this gizmo I want to show you. I have all the specs here. Holy moley, Matt, I even ordered your dinner, though I don't know how in the hell I knew what you wanted. Seemed the waiter sort of knew too. Chris sake, Matt, have you been, you know, ESP-ing me all the way to Parsippany? You got something going I need to know about? Maybe we don't need no goddamned ESP gizmo."

"Shut the fuck up, Charlie!" Matt gestured behind him, and Charlie abruptly started scooping up all his papers.

"Please, calm down, both of you. Thank you for the greens, and the dressing on the side, Charlie. Just the way I like it. And the froth. Let's just drink to friendship, and, no, hey, let me. Let's do it my way. One pint at a time. I'll take the first sip and pass it on to you, and then you pass it on to Charlie. It's the way of my people. Let's do that first, and then if you don't mind, I'd like to do all the talking for starters." The stranger climbed up on top of the seat opposite Matt and Charlie, folded his long legs into a kind of squat, and calmly broke the froth.

"Now, what if I told you that I could locate those blue surges for you, that I actually know who they are? And what's more, what if I could get them to do exactly what you need them to do with your consoles and gizmos? And, after a bit of subtle influence, the same kind of subtle influence that brought you here to McSorley's, what if I could assure you that your blue surges won't even think of putting up the slightest fuss, and certainly won't let any of your little enemies in on our little secrets? All that I ask in return is a bit of collaboration that would help my people. What if I told you that those blue surges of yours are actually spies, sent here to monitor your progress with your twin photon teleportation experiments, and that they're actually in the service of terrorists who aim to scuttle your research and your country's objective to win the cold war and the space race? So you see, with my help, you can capture these spies with impunity, and, with my help, get them to do exactly what you want them to do. By the way, they'll never be the wiser, because they'll never know that they're being manipulated. What if I told you all that?"

He stopped.

Matt measured the silence. He and Charlie just stared at the man and Matt could feel, actually feel the man digging around in his brain, somehow. His imagination. Maybe. Maybe not.

"I'd say you're out of your fucking mind." Charlie broke the silence. He pushed the mug away from him, and got up. "And what's more, you're a goddamned fool, to think we'd believe this horseshit. You might be big, and all that, but there's two of us and one of you. So I'm just gonna pay the tab, and you're gonna walk out of here with us. I mean between us. And don't think you can just get away from us. I may look like a geek, but you just try me buddy. You're fucking with the wrong people here. Get up Matt. I mean it. "

Charlie was between Matt and the wall. Matt would have to get up to let him out, and he wasn't moving.

"Just a minute, Charlie. Let's hear him out. We got nothing to lose. We're not telling him anything. Listen buddy, you're making some heavy-duty assumptions here, and I want to hear exactly how you come to think what you think and, and what's behind all this stuff."

"What in the fuck are you talking about?" said Charlie. "Have you gone completely bonkers? Let me out of the fucking booth, or I'll fucking climb over you. Get the fuck up, Matthew."

Meanwhile the creep just sat there, dipping lettuce leaves into the dressing, one leaf at a time, and slowly placing them in his mouth.

"Hold on, Charlie. Calm down. You can bail out if you want to, but I want to hear what this guy's gonna say."

He found himself willing Charlie to sit the fuck down. Charlie sat down.

Matt took another gulp of beer and passed it to Charlie, now wide-eyed and fidgeting.

"How the fuck—" Charlie started.

"Yeah, how the fuck—" Matt said to the man.

"We'll finish eating and drinking here, and then we'll take a walk to your little hotel room. Sorry, fellas, there's so little time, so I had to coerce your cooperation a bit. Just so you know: kind of a mini-demonstration of what I can do for you. Now drink up. We've got much to discuss."

CHAPTER THIRTY-ONE

Meads Mountain Cave

J, Scotty, and Johnny were squatting at the mouth of the cave, sipping bot and munching on roots and berries they had harvested on the mountain. Beneath them the Hudson Valley expanse had long since lost its burgundy hue, and coyotes were revving up. They were practicing enforced empath silence, deeply shielded and relying on real, out-loud earthling conversation.

"We must learn not to panic," said Johnny. "Strategy lesson number one. When we panic we empath without realizing it and they pick it up and try to hone in."

He got up and started pacing. J wished he would just sit down. Poor Johnny, he always thinks that people will only believe him if he paces. "The surveillance is real," he went on. "It's not just in our paranoid conspiracy-minded heads. If we clean our minds enough, maybe they'll give up, though I doubt it. They're surely on to us. They just can't locate us. Not yet."

"What do we do next?" asked Scotty.

"I've been working on advanced, one-way empath connections," said Johnny. "Like tapping a phone without being detected. I can do it for short spurts of time. Then I weaken, and the path begins to open the other way. I think if we get together I can train all of us to do it at the same time with my new boosters."

"Do you think we can send out a one-way undetectable narrow burst toward the group on Europa?" J squeezed out the question and tried not to sound desperate. Telmx was so close and so far. If only just a tiny split second of something, just to know she was there. And safe.

"I don't know if that's cool yet," said Johnny. "I can't figure out whether they have actually discovered our Europa outpost, or they've simply perfected their anti-Soviet radar. They may in fact have gotten farther than we think. I just can't tell."

"But who's the 'they'? What kind of experiments?" asked Scotty.

"I don't know who, exactly. Probably the military. Perhaps for missiles, or space travel. I think it's NASA. No, I know it's NASA!"

"Space travel! That's it!" said J. "NASA's getting ready to conquer outer space before the Russians. Sputnik was their wakeup call. They're going after bigger game. It's what Telmx said would happen. It's why we're here. It's why you had to come back, Johnny! It all makes sense. Our Mission was right smack in front of our noses. They're looking to get spaceships out into the solar system and then beyond. They must've figured out how to use empath, and they must need to gather and store empath energy the only way they know how, siphoning it from human guinea pigs rather than properly titrating it in small bursts from bot-enhanced donors. They're experimenting with technology that requires empath for fuel. They probably call it ESP, but they don't know what they're fooling around with. Trouble is, harvesting empath their way will suck cerebral synapses dry. They're scanning for disposable donors."

"Well, that explains our headaches. We possess more empath energy than they ever dreamed possible," said Scotty. "Especially clustered together. No wonder they zeroed in on us. We're the disposable donors."

"Good thing they don't go after pregnant black women and infants," said Johnny. "Oh shit! They probably do."

"Why pregnant black women?" J was getting nauseous.

"Because the most potent empath juice is found in the embryonic fluid, and in infants."

"C'mon, Johnny. You really think they'd stoop that low?"

"Jesus, J, haven't you ever heard of Jim Crow? Lynching? I bet if I could access government research, I'd find a shit-load of scientific experiments on blacks. They're probably siphoning embryonic juices from poor pregnant black women from the Mississippi Delta as we speak. Might even be paying them some desperately needed pennies to be part of their experiment, killing them off in the process. What makes you think this country's government is any different from the Nazis? It's just the victim's color that's different!"

J felt shitty. Johnny was always catching her on some deeply embedded racism. She needed him to call her on her insensitivity, her ignorance, but she sure as hell didn't like it. It was a wonder he stuck around.

"It's really okay, J," he said. He didn't need fancy empath to read her mood. "You're brought up where you're brought up. I don't hate you. I mean it." He pulled her to him, and they held onto each other for a long time. "Those who work to change things can themselves be victims of the things they're working to change," he whispered. "When Gir first came on to me, I almost puked. No, I did puke. I would've rather died than make love to a man. Not where I come from. No way!" He paused. "Now look at me," he forced through his tears. "Jesus, oh Good Jesus, I miss him so!"

Scotty joined their embrace. "Here we are," she whispered, "three empath earthlings hiding out in a cave only accessible by hovering, tinkering with technology from another galaxy, embroiled in universe-class intrigue. What would earthlings say if they could see us now?"

"I'd be lynched at sunset," said Johnny. And you guys would be busted for bad-assed LSD shit, which they would desperately search for because they'd want some too, and you'd be locked up tight in a loony bin, if they wanted to be kind, that is, for hanging around a black guy, not to mention for being lesbians. We have all the strikes against us, big time."

Johnny broke from their embrace. "Listen, if this disposable donor theory is right, we need to research it out, locate the bad guys, and crank up my communication contraption really soon so we can let the team on the Europa outpost know what's happening. But we better be sure about our information. I don't have a whole lot of booster power in that baby. I don't even know if it'll reach the outpost, and if it does, our message better be short and information-packed. Besides, Jupiter isn't gong to be on this side of the sun forever."

"If they're even still at the outpost," said Scotty.

"Well, it wasn't that long ago that I jumped away from Europa, and they didn't look like they were planning to pack up any time soon."

"So Telmx's V.E.-scans were off by several decades, maybe," said J. "But hell, she couldn't really know precisely."

"Well they knew something was up, or they wouldn't have called Scotty and me back to Earth so soon," said Johnny. "I haven't really told you how upsetting it was to leave my band, and especially to be separated from Lenx. They wouldn't have done that to me if it weren't really really crucial."

"We need to try your single channel burst," said Scotty.

"Right!" said Johnny. "And quickly. And we should continue figuring out the source of the scanning from the city, exactly the spot where your headaches become loudest."

It was the first time in a while that J felt the importance and urgency of their work. A pivotal place in time. All these years she had been told about the weight of responsibility that she had to bear, she thought she was alone. Well, she had her earthling friends, and she helped as best she could with the struggle. She endured the pain she had to live with for knowing too much or feeling too much. But it had remained very personal, private. Even when she finally was able to share it with Scotty and then with Johnny, it still felt as if each of them were dealing with their own personal journey and struggle.

But now—

She tried to find memories of having V.E.-traveled in the immediate future. Yes, she had read books from the future, V.E. versions of them. But she actu-

ally had never tried to look at her own future, not that V.E.-future-travel was
under her own volition. And scanning for possible futures was way beyond
her training. And would be very confusing. A million different future you's.

"Have you guys ever V.E.-future-traveled just to know exactly what was
going to happen to you?" she asked.

No one answered.

"Well?"

"I've never felt the need to," said Scotty. "Actually I don't know how to
make it happen."

"And you?" J to Johnny.

"Nope."

Silence

"We gotta stop it, you guys!" yelled Johnny. "Nobody can look for personal
outcomes. Not even the highest level Imari Empath can do that. It's actually
considered self-centered. We gotta cut this out. Our panic will stop us from
collaborating on that short empath burst and from thinking clearly about
how we can get the information we need for the message we'll finally send to
the Europa team."

"I just meant that it's really scary that we don't have the power to go into
controlled V.E.-future-travel," J said. "In order to check things out. You
know, be prepared for stuff that might happen in the next hour, or in a few
days. That's all." She didn't think she was being self-centered, just frightened.
Why does she always have to be so sensitive to what others think about her?
It's about time she got over that stuff. She shook off her dread, and looked at
each friend in turn.

"Okay, comrades," J said. Her mind careened toward the inevitable. "I
have to somehow infiltrate NASA, don't I?" "I have to get a job there so I
can get us the information. Perhaps a tech-writing job. I bet they have a lab
somewhere in New York. It's where they're scanning."

"We don't have time for you to get enough resume clout and references to
qualify for a job there," said Scotty. "Assuming we can locate their labs in the
first place. Besides, I don't think you'd exactly get A-1 security clearance."

"Oh Jeez, guys. I have to move back to the city, drop all shields, let them
scan me down and capture me, don't I?"

"Wait a minute, why should it be, you, J?" said Johnny. "Why not Scotty
or me? Okay, okay, I know it can't be me because I have to do the tech work
right here in the cave so we can send that single empath burst to Europa. But
I'd do it, just to see for myself what they're up to. Wait, no I wouldn't. I don't
think so. They'd harness me for my empath juices and kill me before I could
even begin to fiddle with their tiny minds."

This is it, J thought. The day I've been dreading. The next phase of the Mission. Why now, when she finally had empath friends on Earth? Especially Scotty, who would certainly not want to be with her any more if she chickened out? She'll probably even lose all her earthling friends because the Council will sure as hell retro-sweep her for punking out and knowing too much. Then, of course, what would Telmx think?

"It has to be me," she said. "It's what Telmx's been training me for all these years. I've known it and not known it all along. You and Scotty are here for your particular skills. But I'm the designated spy-monitor. Shit on ice, I don't want to do this. Big time!"

"Take it easy J," said Scotty. "Let's figure this out. Together."

"Yes! Together. That's the point! I've never felt more together! We're just getting to know each other, and we're already an incredible team." J started pacing at the mouth of the cave. "I've never been happier. Okay, I'm really pissed off. All I wanted was Telmx's loving, and what I got was a bargain from hell. I never fully embraced the Mission, and here I am, about to walk with my eyes wide open into the thick of it, with others just jumping around on the sidelines like a cheerleading squad while I get trammeled, the running back clutching the goddamned football. Well, that's why I'm getting captured in the first place. To find out what's going on. Okay, okay, I'll try and remember the Mission.

"But I want more for me. I'm really kind of selfish, in case you hadn't figured that out. And terrified. I've never even been arrested. Katie and her comrades get busted on purpose. They can do it. I just don't know if I can. Katie said they search your cunt for drugs. No way are they getting into my cunt! What would I be arrested for? For loving women? For having Johnny as a friend? For being an empath? For allowing them to see I'm an empath? How can that threaten them, unless they know more about us than we think they do? Do they think we're spies for the Russians? We haven't done anything to make them even think that. We do research, or rather I did research, on ESP technology, and dolphin and bat communication. Stuff like that. How's that a crime?"

"Take it easy, J," Scotty repeated. "You've forgotten why they're looking for us. First of all, you're not going to be arrested. They're out to recruit. They're going to want your cooperation so they can use your empath juices. They can't coerce that. You gotta be willing to join their experiment. So they find you, and boom, you enthusiastically agree, and they plunk you right into their secret labs, where you can easily empath-scan all their secrets. Get the essential data and then mindshift them a micro-bit, just enough to make them let you quit the operation (in case they feel you have too much secret information and don't want you to leave), and we'll have the information to send to Europa. You just need to assess how far they've gotten. Where they're at. If they do try to hook you to one of their devices, so much the better. Just shield up so they don't tinker with your synapses. They're probably closer to the technology than we thought, however primitive it may be."

"I'll have to devise a tracking system for you," said Johnny. "We need to know where they take you, just in case. And you need to have an emergency distress call. No! Don't worry! Just in case, you know, worst-case scenario, I know exactly how to do it. I'll use Jupiter as a global positioning device. It'll be so cool. You'll see."

"Great," said Scotty. "Then you won't be alone even for a nano-sec, J. Hopefully we won't need to pull you out of their clutches. You'll waltz out of there on your own with all the info, and they won't even know you bent their minds in order to escape. We don't want to make it more dramatic than we have to. And we don't want them hurt in the process either. There can't be any traces of our meddling. If we need to interfere, it'll be just enough to get the information and get you out."

"Well, all I gotta tell you, oh fuck it, you already know! I'm no hero. Never was, and don't want to be. I feel vulnerable enough. And haunted. I do and I don't need to do this. There you have it. That's what I really think. That's the big, honest-to-god fight I have with Telmx every time we get together. But what do I do now? If I want to keep you guys in my life I have to let these NASA goons pick me up. Then I might lose you anyway. Just when I fucking found you! I hate this!" Her tears raged.

Scotty's arms enveloped her. Fighting the impulse to shake her off, J wept into her shoulder.

"Okay, you two." She heard Johnny walking back into the cave. "I'm going to jury-rig that tracking device."

"Look," Scotty whispered. "There's Orion. They're all depending on us. We can do this."

"I didn't say I wasn't going to do it. I just don't fucking want to."

✳ ✳ ✳

The three held hands in a circle, squatting in Mead's Mountain Meadow. "Isn't a phone communication code a bit much? Like grade-B spy movies?" J had been dubious of getting so carried away, Nancy Drew style. And now one more complication: she had to memorize Johnny's intricate coding system, when she was a terrible memorizer.

"Just in case," empathed Johnny. "File it in one of your inner chambers."

"But they don't even know who they're looking for yet. They can't tap every goddamned phone in New York City."

"Humor me," he empathed.

"I agree," empathed Scotty. She was leaving for the city on the morning bus to find a place to live. Too dangerous for the two empaths to be together in the city right now. They would be separated for the first time since they had met. J would follow in a week. Johnny had brought in provisions to set up housekeeping in the cave, on 24/7 tracking duty.

J was miserable. "How we going to do this? I'm addicted to you guys. I don't want us to separate."

"It's only temporary." Scotty was confident, calm.

The Hunter hovered between the Unicorn's hoofs and horns of the Bull. Off to the west, Pegasus kept watch. J was riveted on the Hunter's sword, searching desperately into the invisible Horsehead Nebula for Telmx.

"She's probably on Europa by now waiting for our messages," empathed Scotty.

"We're just making all that up," empathed J. "I haven't felt her in our solar system. Not even a scintilla. And, you know, I can always tell when she's on her way. But there's not even a peep. I bet something terrible's happened to her."

"You forgot that we are all on empath communication blackout with them. Nothing in and nothing out until we have the information they need. That's what Johnny's new device is all about."

"Right! Where's my mind? I told you I'm not up to all the new demands of the Mission!"

CHAPTER THIRTY-TWO

J

The bus ride from Woodstock had been long and hot and J desperately had to pee. The Port Authority announcements pounded relentlessly. Where were the bathrooms? No, better just get herself uptown.

She was shielded Scotty-style. Except for the intermittent minuscule bursts that Johnny had set up to track her, so imperceptible, nothing would detect them, not even a heavy-duty scanner, not even a Level VI. Maybe Scotty came to meet her. No. Forget it. She wouldn't do that, couldn't, not with their shieldings so vulnerable to each other. Love was funny like that: ruptured their shielding, and leaked out empath, in spite of deepest Level VI shielding.

Almost full empath silence allowed the discordant din of the terminal to dominate. She was already brewing a headache. But so far not the headache she and Scotty had escaped from no more than five weeks earlier. Only five weeks? So much in five weeks. She bumped along, searching for the AA train, pushing past rushing commuters, confused tourists and soporific, desperate homeless. Everybody's rhythms were alien, contradictory, so much did she usually depend upon empath cues to navigate her life.

Scotty, already settled in her new digs on the Lower East Side, was probably out looking for a job or sipping cappuccino at Figaro's. She so much wanted to send an empath call to her, just one tiny message. But discipline was discipline. Near and not near. Silence. Big time silence. But coded phone calls were okay. Far-out! When she gets home, she'll call her. Maybe she'll be home. Even hearing her voice on her answering machine would help.

She conjured up Johnny, squatting deep in their cave, tracking her with global positioning bursts. He couldn't empath-enter her mind, but he knew exactly where she was at any given moment. And she could signal him in an emergency. Their Triad Team. It bathed her like a hoverglow. Okay, okay, she could do this.

She couldn't wait to be home, her sanctuary. But alone? Shit. Couldn't she just spend one more night with Scotty before she opened herself up to NASA's scanners? Just one night. Just to give her more strength, to boost her bravery. No way. Too dangerous. One dream merge, one orgasm. No, they couldn't risk even the slightest empath leak. They both would be snatched in a nanosec.

Scotty had to be free to help if something went wrong after NASA tracked her down. Okay, she had endured long years between visits from Telmx. She could wait a few more days to see Scotty. Not if she dies in captivity. No, that's not going to happen! Johnny and Scotty will know exactly where she's being held. With his amazing global positioning gizmo, it was no-risk activism. What kind of bravery does that take? Okay, Soweto kids! I'll do it. My little risky maneuver doesn't hold a candle to what you guys did.

Well, why wait? She could open fully and just let herself be scanned and snatched right there in suffocating subway stench. No, not the plan. She had to be at home, out of public view. Triad Team discipline. Besides, she had to pee (as usual!), and she needed her dungarees, sneakers, and knapsack. Nope. She was wearing all that. Perhaps a tiny swig of bot would calm her. She hadn't felt this frightened since fire escape goblins. And then she had her hugging lady. Oh, dearest Tel, you'd definitely not be proud of me now. I'm so, so terrified.

What would Katie think if she backed out? Katie had been arrested dozens of times. Each time, she said, she learned something new. Not that Katie knew anything about the Mission, but what if she could know, or learned later on what a wimp she was. Perhaps she could call her. Just to talk to a friend. Would she be in town? Would she be free? What boyfriend would she be shacking up with now? Would she break away long enough to have a glass of Chianti? Can't just empath-search her out to see what's she up to and up for. She'll have to call her on the phone, like a regular earthling. God, if only she could discuss her real life with Katie. "Outta sight! I knew you possessed some far-out ESP!" Katie would say. "Whoa! This is bad, real bad!" It was goddamned shitty not being able to share stuff with her best friend.

Actually she was lucky: her earthling friends simply enjoyed her for who she was to them: a spacey, uptight little Jewish girl with a lousy childhood and some hopes to change the world a little bit, by moving it along, with others who were trying to move it along. Like Katie, who didn't need empath or bot or a special power to mind-poke. Katie didn't need to travel to another planet to figure out her politics. Just some Marx, Lenin, sit-ins, and committed comrades. If Katie and her comrades were in her shoes, they'd be doing exactly the same thing.

Sure, J now had some really wonderful comrades too. Empath earthlings she couldn't imagine having in her life just two months ago (although she vaguely remembered Telmx mentioning something about not being alone in the Mission. Funny how she had forgotten that over the years.) Scotty and Johnny knew exactly what she was all about and how she got there, and who Telmx is, and Gir and the Mission. So what was she whining about?

Plus, she had Scotty now, loved her with passion she had only reserved for Telmx. Happiness she'd never thought possible except with Telmx. But hell's bells, now that she also has a lover right here on Earth, she suddenly becomes an idiotic sacrificial lamb in some cockamamie intrigue.

Scotty and Johnny were more into the Mission than she, although Johnny sure had his moments. And they had spent a lot more time out there in Telmx's universe. Actually, it wasn't Scotty's involvement with the Mission or her Level VI training that made her so fabulous. It was the way she smiled, and made love, and, most of all, even more than the way she made love, it was her spunkiness. Her energy. And how much she cared about J. That mattered a whole lot. Much more than the Mission. She just wanted to be back with Scotty in Mead's Mountain Meadow snuggling under their Imari blankets. No complications. No Triad Team. No special cave for hiding Johnny's empath communication and tracking gizmos. Scotty, Johnny, and Katie, for that matter, were much more mature than she. She was still a kind of self-centered, really really frightened kid in a grown-up body, still a terrified squirt thinking she was about to be gobbled or raped or beaten up, or thrown into a dark hole, to die a slow and painful death. Miserable. Self-centered miserable. Boy, why can't I get me out of me? Now I'm hating myself for being too much into myself. Fuck-a-duck!

The AA train screeched and clanked heavily into the station. Somehow she found herself sitting (so awkward not to be squatting), her knapsack clutched between her legs. She closed her eyes and lurched backward with the train's forward heave. If Johnny's using Jupiter as a positioning guide, how the hell could he locate her so far underground? If she got taken now, Scotty and Johnny wouldn't have a clue. What's more, when the NASA boys grab her, they might take her to some exotic sub-subbasement holding cell, torture chamber where Johnny couldn't trace her. No, Johnny must have included underground tracking. Of course he had. But they'd certainly know exactly how to torture her. They'll lock her up in Orwell's Room 101. Ever since she was ten, that dreaded torture room had haunted her. Worse than those goddamn goblins. What would her J-tailored torture be? Rats? Roaches? Lightening bolts? Rapists? Rapists! Could she hold out? Keep the Mission a secret? Not reveal anything about Scotty or Johnny, or the Imari? Of course she could. Well, maybe not. Stop! Don't think like that! They just want to siphon your empath energies. They need your cooperation. That's what Scotty said. But she couldn't help it.

She almost missed her stop. She shoved her knapsack between the closing doors and got a lot of people pissed off. Okay, number-one pariah on the AA train. Anything for the Mission. She hated everyone and everything. She could just trot right into NASA headquarters and say, "You've been scanning for me, so here I am. What do you want?" Maybe that wasn't such a bad idea. If they didn't find her in her apartment after a few days, perhaps she should actually go down to Bethesda and offer her services.

When she got into her apartment the phone was ringing.

"I have a strong feeling you need mouth-to-mouth resuscitation just about now," Scotty opened in code.

"How'd you know? We're on ridiculous stone silence mode."

"C'mon, J, you think I need special Level VI to know what you're feeling right now? You're not about to be thrown to the wolves. Take a few days to get yourself organized. And, J? You don't have to be a fully evolved Level Seventy-thousand empath to be ready to do your part. You're going to do just great. All of us have our doubts and nightmares."

"Hold on, I gotta pee something fierce. Don't go away." She came back to the phone with a goblet of bot. "I'm breaking the froth for both of us. Holy shit, I so much want to be with you tonight." She forgot to code. Well, that part didn't need coding. It was just a lovers' conversation. (not quite safe, she thought: a lesbian conversation) "I know we can't. But just the same," J resumed in code, "I'd like to postpone this spy stuff for a month or two, just a month or two, and cuddle with you somewhere far away. Like in a cabin in the woods on a planetoid in another star system. You know, get to know your doubts and nightmares a little better, where nothing can touch us. What do you think? Don't say anything. I'm just kidding. Sort of. Did I ever tell you that I love you?"

"I have a vague recollection—"

They were silent for a few minutes. J was aching. She assumed Scotty was also. "My apartment is real spooky. It's a tomb without you. My front door creaks, my sleeping mat is empty, it's ridiculously hot, and I won't even dare open the fuckin' fridge. I need you right here next to me breaking the froth. I can't possibly lie on my mat alone even for one night listening for psychopath NASA boys sneaking around on my fire escape like goblins. I won't be able to sleep!"

"Just shield up tight for tonight, get a good night's sleep, and open up in the morning."

"No, I have a better idea. I'm going down by the river tonight and wait for them."

"No way! That's not how we planned it. You have to stay in your apartment and wait for them. They won't take you if you're out in the street for others to see."

"But I'll be alone. No one'll be out there at three in the morning."

"Three in the morning? On Riverside Drive? What are you thinking? Are you out of your mind? You'll be mugged or raped, or even killed!" Scotty's coded phone voice was desperate. "You go down by the river alone tonight and we're aborting the whole plan. You're freaking me out, J!"

"I'd rather be anywhere else but in my apartment. I just don't want my domain invaded. That's it. If a psycho rapist comes along while I'm wandering down by the river, he won't know what hit him. Trust me! I'll just tweak his mind a bit, and he'll take me out for a drink, chide me for being out alone so late at night, and see me safely home in a cab. I think I can tell the difference between a government goon and a killer. One gives you a nasty migraine and the other takes your life away. Well, maybe they both do, but you know what I mean."

"Don't make a joke out of this, J. I'm big-time not kidding. You're being self-destructive and indulgent, not to mention selfish! What about me?"

"And I'm big-time not joking. Sort of. I'm fucking terrified. I'm getting the hell out of this apartment tonight, going to huddle on a park bench, take down my shield, and scream for NASA to find me. Let me do it my way. I'll have some strong swigs of bot before I go. I'll be okay. Just tell Johnny what I'm doing and stand by. Okay? Ok? I love you!" She hung up before Scotty could protest.

CHAPTER THIRTY-THREE

J

J often went down to Riverside Drive to get away from urban static, but never after dark. Now buoyed by some inner strength (probably from the bot, she thought), she was calmer. What will be, will be. She squatted on her park bench and pretended she was by a stream in the mountains: the Hudson River lapped on the rocks not many yards away, crickets chirped, and thick fog obscured city lights just up the embankment on the other side of the drive. Occasionally a distant siren jarred her resolve. Maybe Scotty was right. Maybe she was being reckless.

In full open empath, the miniscule pings of Johnny's tracking bursts (actually, he was not that many miles up the river), causing tiny pinches in her right temple, comforted, in spite of the terrible knowledge that opening this wide could finally lead to the dreaded capture. So far, though, no headache, which meant no NASA scanners. Maybe they'd given up, went recruiting at Duke, or in the Mississippi Delta, like Johnny said. Please let it be tonight. The sooner she got this over with, the sooner she and Scotty would be together again. If she lived through it all.

The humming of an approaching car. Was it them? She turned around so she could see the driver. And probed. No, just a solitary worker coming home from his shift. His headlights morphed the haze into swirling smoke. Then the rhythmic drone whizzed by, leaving behind an iridescent burgundy nebula. J wondered if drivers spotted her squatting on her bench. Probably not.

After a while she began counting the seconds from the oncoming motor drone, to the lights, to the receding taillights. She calculated the speed of each car and created a portrait of its driver, then checked out her fantasy with the actual driver by briefly entering, non-intrusively, just to be connected to someone.

CHAPTER THIRTY-FOUR

Matt

Charlie was jabbering a mile a minute about everything and nothing: about aliens, men from Mars, kidnapping, UFOs. "I know what I know! It all makes sense to me now! Einstein was right!" He started quoting formulas, space warp, time travel, stuff Matt had learned in graduate school, that he had thought about all the time, stuff that sort of made sense in the NASA MPII work, but it was as if Charlie had suddenly put the whole package together and couldn't spit it out fast enough. "Listen, listen! You gotta listen! It's all right here in front of our noses. Let's get Dawson here immediately. I've figured the whole thing out. We don't need no fucking bright blue surges, or whatever we've been calling these kooks we're after. Don't need them at all. There's a whole other technology. Wait, wait! I got all the formulas in my head. I need a computer. I need—hey, what'cha doin'? Shit!" Then he was silent.

"He's too high-strung," said Raymond. "I went in and slowed down his mind a bit. It'll give him some time to breathe, and us too." Charlie was in a trance, right there in the back seat of the van on Riverside Drive. Like he had dropped some powerful acid and was nowhere on this planet. How had this guy done that?

Matt looked at Raymond, whose voice was muted, as if Matt's ears were stuffed with fuzzy cotton. "He's almost right, you know, but his mind moves too quickly. We do need these blue surges. At least for a while. I'll explain why later. But here she comes. Just like I said. See? There she is now, on 163rd Street and Riverside Drive. No, you don't see. How could you?"

No, Matt couldn't see. They were parked by the entrance to the George Washington Bridge, and Raymond claimed she was maybe a mile south. What a friggin' asshole. He expects him to believe he can see what's not in front of him.

"Whoa, she's scared. She knows something's up. We'll take it all very slow. You just stay here. I'm going to talk to her first. No, don't turn on the scanner. She'd know we're here. Trust me, Dr. Matthew. She has more technology and power in that tiny earthling head of hers than you can ever imagine."

Everything was happening too quickly, for Charlie, and for himself. And look at poor Charlie. This space creature can do really powerful things to a guy's mind. He sure didn't want Raymond fucking around with his mind. He probably already has. Sure he has. Wait a minute! Is he kidding himself? He's under the same spell. Shit. They'd been scanning for these blue surges for months, and this dude coolly plucks one out of the night air, and now he's going to just trot down the road to chat with their prized blue surge like it's two in the afternoon and say, "Hi, wanna go for a drink?" or offer her a joint, or something hokey like that.

Wait one nano-sec. He didn't care who this chick was, he wasn't leaving her alone with this creep. It's actually an elaborate alien plan to rape some innocent white girl on Riverside Drive. And he was falling for it. He was a full-blooded American, a Company man, a flag-waving white Christian citizen. "No, I'll drive you down," Matt said. "We'll do this thing together. I've gotten too far into this without letting you out of my sight. So you listen here—"

"No, Dr. Matthew, you just stay put. Toss out your infantile racism and stay put until I tell you to come."

With that he got out of the van and slammed the door behind him, as if to say, "You better listen or you'll end up like Charlie." Even if he had wanted to follow him, Matt's foot suddenly couldn't reach the gas pedal. "Okay, okay," he said to no one.

Raymond had already disappeared into the haze. "Thanks, Dr. Matthew," Raymond said through the fuzz in his ears.

Charlie was still in his trance, but not him! Matt certainly knew what was going on. Just couldn't fuckin' move.

CHAPTER THIRTY-FIVE

J

There were other vague, undefined empath presences, perhaps down by the river, perhaps on the Drive, other maniacs like herself, wandering around at three in the morning. If rapists sent out empath resonances, wouldn't they be jagged, like her father's? Perhaps they were just desperate homeless guys looking for the perfect park bench.

She still didn't feel even the slightest migraine twinge. Soon it would be sunrise, and the early joggers would be loping by. Maybe Scotty was right. She should go home, shield up tight, and get some sleep. Tomorrow she'd try again. They could come for her in the daytime at her house. That might be okay.

No. Someone or something was hovering (actually hovering!) toward her from maybe a half mile uptown. A strong, very skilled empath signal, but with an extraordinary jagged edge. Overwhelming. Sinister. Her body felt like rushing sand. She kept her head wrapped in her flannel hoody as she empath-scanned the presence through the haze. A male. Extremely tall. Like Imari tall. Wait! He was calling to her as if he knew her. He did know her. Calling her by name! He was partially shielded, like modified Imari shielding. And he was trying to pry his way into her inner chambers, slowly, with unskilled stealth.

Why hadn't she sensed him earlier?

Holy shit! It couldn't be possible. He wasn't earthling. He was stronger, uncanny, terrifying. She had to shield herself. She certainly wasn't going to let him invade her inner chambers, even if he were an Imari, which was impossible, because she had never met an Imari disrespectful of empath privacy. Something was terribly wrong. Only NASA was supposed to seize her, and no way was this creature from NASA. Her shielding wavered. He was wearing her down! On purpose!

Should she press Johnny's panic button? No, this alien presence would detect it. It would give him away. Why hadn't they anticipated this? She had to flee, but not to her apartment. No, definitely not there. She should rapid-

ly hover to an all-night tavern on Broadway, where she could be safely surrounded by people, anybody. But she was riveted to the bench, weakened by
her futile struggle to move into hover mode.

He was now a few feet away. She kept her head down, as if in a depression,
secretly preparing to defend herself as best she could. He could see though
her act. He couldn't be Imari. An Imari wouldn't elicit such a mixed feeling
of comfort and dread.

"Please don't be afraid, J." He emerged from the shadows. "I'm so pleased
I reached you before NASA did. I've come to warn you." Though his empath
was smooth, Imari like, friendly, she knew not to look at him, not to give him
even more power over her. In spite of herself, she raised her head. He was
indeed Imari, tall and thin, as dark as Telmx, and one of the most striking
Imaris she had ever seen, chiseled like Gir, but without the countenance of
wisdom. His travel hood was down, and his cilia flickered in the streetlamp
glow.

Now he was going for her inner chambers again. She could feel the tug, his
effort to push apart the tapestries. No way. Not even an Imari would do that.
Not without her permission. Unless they broke sacred protocol. What kind
of an Imari would try to break protocol?

"I'm not breaking protocol," he empathed. "I am racing for time. Please
don't try to shield from me anymore. We haven't got time for your primitive
paranoia. You must listen to what I have to say before the others get here.
And I must communicate with you in the complete security of your inner
chambers. Quickly. NASA is far more advanced than you think. Your life is
in danger. All three of you are in danger. Fortunately NASA doesn't know
where your two friends are hiding. I must speak to all three of you before it's
too late. The NASA team means to drain you of your empath energies and
leave you for dead. There is no way you can bend their minds. You have a
false sense of safety in your plan. But I'm saying too much without shielding.
Please, I must speak to you in private, so they can't overhear us. They're here.
Just up the road. Quickly, J! Let me in!"

He squatted in front of her and bowed his head toward hers. She involuntarily lowered her head and abruptly recoiled before her budding sprouts
could touch his cilia. What was she doing? It was like being under a sorcerer's
spell. She fought it. "Sorry," he empath-whispered.

"My name is Raymond. I come with loving greetings from Telmx. She was
my friend, my best friend. My oldest Imari Training Institute buddy."

She gasped for air. He was lying. She must stay with her perceptions. But
wait a minute! What was that he said?

"What do you mean 'was'? What's happened to her? Where is she?"

"I'm so sorry. I come with her instructions, her message for your inner chamber, the one you keep just for you and her."

"What do you mean? No way is she dead. You can't force me to open any inner chamber to you, no matter what you claim."

"She told me to tell you to be brave and carry on the Mission no matter what. I can understand your not wanting to open your chamber to me. You don't know me yet. You're wise. She trained you well. How do I convince you to give up your uneasy? I have a t'cha box, if you wish. I could help you get there. Retrieve her love for you the only way she would want you to. I can do that for you. She asked me to do that for you. She told me how hesitant you are about every new thing. But—"

"Just tell me what happened to her!" J willed herself to stand up. He stood up and recoiled. For all his bravado, he was suddenly fearful of her. An incomplete Imari. She froze. Suddenly she had the power to grind him into little bits, pulverize him before her eyes, just with a thought, a killing force. Where'd that come from? She struggled to control it.

"Whoa, little one," he empathed. "She taught you that too? You better control that rage of yours. It could get you into a heap of trouble. That's exactly why she's no longer with us."

Her powerful force melted as quickly as it emerged, not entirely of her own volition. She was his to manipulate. Almost. Well, he couldn't control her tears. "Please! Please don't speak in riddles. I can't read your innermost thoughts. Nor would I try. I honor the Imari code. Though you apparently do not. Please tell me what's happened to her. You don't need to enter my innermost chambers to tell me that."

"Alright. She was arrested by the Council for murder, for wielding that force you suddenly found in yourself. She, Winstx and Goshing have been summarily retro-swept by Consular decree. They're no longer the same people. I met with her just before their arrest. She had a premonition. As you know, she could future-scan with amazing accuracy. She gave me her chamber message to bring to you. Just in case. She asked me to take her place as your mentor.

"I know I cannot be Telmx for you. Although I wish, I deeply wish I could. There's no one like her. But she'll live in you as she was meant to. As is the Imari way. I carry her with me to convey that to you. J, it's urgent that you make yourself ready to receive her."

Now she knew he was lying. "She has enemies in the Council, but it's all stupid political haggling. She wouldn't kill anyone, even in self-defense, even if someone tried to assassinate her. Hell, they don't do that kind of thing out there in the civilized universe. You know that. Or do you? There's no Kennedy-type assassinations where Telmx comes from. She doesn't have those kinds of enemies."

"No, my dear one, she didn't kill intentionally. For reasons we do not understand, she suddenly could not modulate that 'take-out' force, an unfortunate byproduct of our powers that you seem to have absorbed without formal training. You're young and inexperienced. I will teach you to modulate that force. She'd want me to do so."

J shielded to maximum, and this time he didn't stop her. She didn't want to hear another thing. He was devious. Disarming. Nothing rang true. But yet again, she almost believed him. Though he did respect her sudden empath silence this time, he could probably dissolve her shields if he wanted to. "I need to be alone," she said out loud. "Please leave me alone! You obviously know how to find, me. I need time."

CHAPTER THIRTY-SIX

Matt

Matt was "summoned." He abruptly got his foot back, and was rolling three miles an hour downtown. Riverside Drive was his, except for an occasional car speeding uptown in the other direction. Devil's eyes coming after him through the fog. He was a kid again, seeing spooks in the dark. Like his little brother who would sit up in his sleep and scream holy murder at the top of his lungs out of nowhere. Of course, back then, his father would storm in and beat the shit out of Matt for committing the most outrageously deviant sex crimes. Maybe he did do them after all. Perhaps he had actually been in a blackout trance sodomizing his poor little brother like his father claimed.

Perhaps he was in a nightmare. He'd better wake up from it real soon. He had work to do.

What was he about to save? This blue surge from an alien? Or the world from the reds? Or some hokum about the universe that this guy kept yapping about. Collaboration with him that would change the course of history, for all creatures everywhere in the universe. Grandiose thoughts like that. Making the universe safe for democracy, it sounded like. He practically used those words.

These blue surge hippies were earthling spies hired by communist aliens, Raymond had explained. They were recruited to help these creatures from outer space conquer all the world's humans and take it over for their own demagogic ambitions, just like the Russians. Matt and Raymond needed to capture the spies before they contacted the aliens and told them about NASA's new MPII technology. If the aliens found out what NASA was doing, they'd attack Earth immediately. Earthlings wouldn't know what hit them, and the aliens would erect a Communist dictatorship, with earthlings as their slaves.

Not only could NASA silence these spies, MPII could make use of them for their entangled twin photon consoles, although Raymond promised to show them a more sophisticated way to harness earthling energies for the consoles. That was the bargain. Allow Raymond and his small band of heroes (he called them "freedom fighters") to set up base camp at NASA in exchange for his advanced alien technology. Imagine, bargaining with a so-called space dude for superior technology. No one in the Pentagon'll buy that story. They'll lock Matt up and throw away the key. Raymond told him not to worry. "I can change people's minds one person at a time." Like he did him and Charlie. Make them see the truth.

There were three true blue surges, three spies. He claimed they were monitoring NASA because they were earthling stooges recruited to help the aliens conquer the civilized universe with a kind of silent terrorism. It seemed to make sense, somehow. They were like fifth-column Communists, crazy peaceniks working for the reds, or Jewish undercover agents like the Rosenbergs. They had to be stopped. But Raymond could only locate this one chick on Riverside Drive. So much for his fancy alien powers. "Be patient," he said. "They have advanced techniques of hiding. But we'll ferret them out. We need just one spy to begin with. She'll lead us to the others." Matt inched down the Drive. Finally he was going to lay eyes on this true blue surge alien-lover, Commie spy for himself.

✹ ✹ ✹

Raymond towered above J, but somehow she was not afraid anymore, just determined to walk away from him, one step at a time. He was stronger in stature. But she was stronger in will. He seemed to know that. She had powers she hadn't possessed even fifteen minutes earlier. She didn't know if she could control that lethal force, but his wariness of it made him gentler, extremely careful.

"I can't let you go," he said out loud. "You're in grave danger. There's a crisis on this planet. That's why I'm here. The Mission is upon us."

As J turned to walk away, a huge van materialized through the fog and blocked her way.

CHAPTER THIRTY-SEVEN

Matt

Matt looked at J through the one-way mirror as she squatted like Yazzie in the detention room waiting and wondering what was going to happen to her. The hippie was tiny, like his wife, but very Jewish: her nose, her hair, her ass, the smart way she pushed her bangs out of her eyes, her shyness and her cockiness, her New York accent, all Jewish. She was in jeans and a tee shirt, a tee shirt that was way too big for her body, so he couldn't tell what her tits were like. He was positive she wasn't wearing a bra. Even so, she was probably not very busty. And sneakers, certainly not feminine. Yet she was very feminine, also boyish. He was intrigued and disgusted.

Had Raymond caught the right person? He wanted to use the scanner on her, but Raymond claimed her reverse surge would crunch his brains out at such close range. "Just like the dolphins at Coney Island," he had said. "Trust me."

"How can I trust you? You fuck with my mind."

"Well if you think I can fuck around with your mind, Dr. Matthew, and make you do things you just wouldn't have thought of doing a moment ago, imagine what this little lady can do. She doesn't even know how powerful she is. But you can exploit that power of hers. That's my promise to you, because I can bend her mind better than she can bend mine. Oh I know, you don't trust me, but you'd be wise to let me at her before you hook her up to your primitive consoles. All I'm going to do is neutralize that part of her that can read and bend your minds, so you can do what you need to do with her. I need to make some minor adjustments of her powers before you come in any more contact with her. So don't try to secretly gawk at her with your one-way mirror thing. Mark my words; she'll know you're there behind the mirror doing what cops do in your movies. And definitely don't try to deal with her until I return. Don't worry you'll get plenty of ESP juices from her for your consoles. In the long term, I actually have a more efficient way for you to harness this ESP energy, if you give me more time. For now, she'll have to do, so you can get credit for your search.

"I know, you have looming deadlines. But if you act in haste you could shatter her brain into little bits, even more than what the consoles are doing to your friend Yazzie, who by the way, is also more powerful than you know. I'll deal with him later. You'd be better off doing things my way."

Raymond had actually taken charge! Kept telling him what he could and couldn't do. "Oh, and one more thing, don't think you can fuck her, I mean actually fuck her, because she won't have any part of it, even if you play the really good cop and let her know what a great guy you are underneath all that bravado and bullshit. She's not that happy fucking with men. Now, wait a minute. Don't go getting all high and moral with her or me. She is just not into men, that's all. So don't get any bright ideas. And I'm not about to bend her mind in that direction. That wasn't part of our deal."

To hell with Raymond's demands! He wasn't in charge. And besides, the alien seemed to have shrunken since they had captured the hippie kike, as if his powers had suddenly stopped working. Though the change was subtle. Matt could tell. He was no longer worried about what the creature might do to him. Besides, he had suddenly disappeared. AWOL. He'd said he'd be back right away. That was more than an hour ago.

All Matt could think of when he saw J behind the mirror was that this little lesbo just didn't know what a good hard cock was all about. She didn't know and he would show her, simply let her feel it once and she'd be transformed. He canned that thought, the more he observed her. Mr. Alien could be right. Maybe she would turn him into mincemeat if he got on her bad side. Raymond had also warned him that she could probably read his mind. "She'll break the Richter scale on your ESP scanners," he had warned. How the hell could he get her to sign up for ESP duty on the consoles if she could already read his mind? "Not to worry," Raymond had promised. "She'll do what you want after I get through with her. Just don't approach her until I get back." But he didn't come back. So he got her and himself some coffee and donuts from the library pantry (can't let her starve!) and took matters into his own hands, check her out first before actually entering the room.

Perhaps as she's sitting there looking all innocent and fragile, she's plotting her escape. Well he won't let her out of his sight. If she's as powerful as Raymond claims, she could probably pick locks or walk through walls. Hell, she could probably pick him apart in an instant.

Still she definitely looked terrified. Like his wife looked when he insisted on fucking her in the ass. But he never did fuck his wife in the ass. Wouldn't risk her hating him forever. He was alone enough already in this dangerous world, where you couldn't trust anybody. Nah, he loved her for stopping him. Loved her? Yeah, he'd have to admit it, deep down he actually loved his wife and kid.

What just happened? Was this little lesbo already bending his mind from behind the mirror? Raymond said she could do that. Shit. He had never really thought about actually loving his wife until then. She worshipped him, so he married her. She would raise his kids to be good God-fearing Americans.

Mr. Alien must be right. The lesbo kike had powers that were tinkering with his mind even as he sat on the other side of a one-way mirror. That's where this loving stuff coming from. That's big-time ESP. So she's already reading his mind. She knows what's going on. He'll have to wait until Raymond gets at her, like he said he would.

He watched the little Jewess, now serene and dignified, meditating like Yazzie. Don't you worry your little Yid head. That dude's going to fix you up for MPII no matter what you think you can do to outwit us. But where the hell was he? Said something about needing to replenish himself. So what if he didn't return? He didn't need Raymond's so-called help to manage this recruitment. He was a Company Man, an A-plus-plus in Psychological Warfare Man. He sure as hell knew how to get anyone to do exactly what he wanted, no matter what. He'd tackle her alone.

CHAPTER THIRTY-EIGHT

J

As best as J could tell, now that her blindfold was off, she was locked in some kind of interview or small conference room in a huge underground complex in New Jersey. Although they had blindfolded her for the trip, she had recognized the rhythms of the George Washington Bridge. Johnny was still keeping her in his tracking beam, even though she was several stories underground. She could occasionally discern the ping. But he wouldn't know about Raymond. Where was Raymond now? He had to be very well shielded, because from the moment they locked her in this room, she could no longer read him.

She squatted on a large swivel chair facing a long table in the middle of the room and breathed deeply, her palms turned up. On the other side of the table was a huge mirror. It didn't take incredible empath to figure out its purpose. Her Orwellian Room 101?

When a smartly tailored stiff walked into the room behind the one-way mirror, she was immediately aware of his jagged edges. It felt familiar. Like the headaches. But not exactly. Large swaths of anti-Semitism. Shit! Johnny was so on target about these creeps. Like "all Jews were reds," and worse, they were "freaks," "queers," "disposable," like concentration-camp disposable. She and this NASA goon were alone together, with only a peeping-tom mirror between them.

Right away she knew he wanted to rape her. She sucked in her breath, and kept herself very very still. It was too familiar. Worse than Room 101. Johnny's panic button: All she had to do was send a slight empath ping into Johnny's pinging. Yes, she had to do that. Rape? No, no way, she couldn't, wouldn't deal with that. Not now! Not in a million years! Abort this plan! Push the panic button. Scotty would be there in a nano-second. She waited forever for Johnny's next ping, so she could panic-ping back to him. Forever. They were actually about ten minutes apart, and the last one had just happened. Nausea welled.

I have to hold on, she thought. I can't fink out that quickly. I'll mind-bend this creep if he tries anything. Ever so slightly. I'll be that brave. She let the next ping go by without tapping into it.

She remained in meditative repose, trying to appear as calm as she could. Faint traces of music, like wisps of whale song, were leaking from some inner place in this creep's brain. He possessed a bit of raw empath himself, but had no idea about how to use it. He was actually an intriguing combination. He loved kids, animals, cows and dolphins, it seemed. He was also a bit scared of them, and of humans. He was the quintessential nerd and a macho frat boy. All of the above. But somehow, he also respected her. She began caressing that perception to calm herself down.

He knew her empath was special. He was the one with those horrid scanners. She probed his mind further. He was worrying that he had breached security like a greenhorn by bringing Raymond and her into NASA's deepest, top-security labs. So he wasn't about to ask for help from anybody. Except perhaps from someone who pulsed in and out of his mind. A friend! This psycho-nerd turned macho man has a friend! He seems to call him "Yazzie," very sophisticated earthling empath, whose mind was almost fried by their research. She pushed for greater calm, struggling to modulate nausea. She needed to get to this Yazzie person. If she could only convince this guy to send for him. If Yazzie was well enough to come.

She also gleaned from his thoughts that he was waiting for Raymond to come back, that the rogue Imari was "replenishing," and that he had been gone much too long. Like her captor, she was terrified of Raymond's replenished powers. Where was he?

Raymond and this guy were somewhat at odds with each other. She could use that. Along with that whale song he had tucked somewhere behind all his putrid, jagged bursts of yellow spikes behind her eyes. Yes, she had to get to Yazzie. He was special. She hoped he wasn't too far gone. Perhaps with his help, she could get back to the NASA man's whale song.

Okay, she would mind-bend her captor just a jot. Just to get Yazzie in the room. Could she do that without giving her powers away? Just a jot. Perhaps with Yazzie and whatever decency this character still had left in him, she could deal with Raymond. Maybe. Better than answering Johnny's ping and sending Scotty running to mind-blast her way in and blow the whole Mission. Perhaps Raymond had already found Scotty and Johnny. Picked them out of J's brain, when she wasn't looking. Or on his own. After all, he located J almost immediately. But J had dropped her shielding on purpose, making it real easy, and he probably already knew where to find her from Telmx. And Scotty and Johnny were masters at shielding.

Okay, okay, don't call for help. Besides, Scotty knows nothing about Raymond, and wouldn't be prepared for his powers. Was love clouding her mind? No, she just had to think this though calmly. Damn, she wasn't good at this spy stuff. Never even read those pulp spy thrillers. Not even Ludlum. Wait, he wasn't published yet. Well, she hadn't ever been the least bit interested, even in her V.E.-literature explorations. That was one genre she almost compulsively ignored. Now she wished she hadn't, just to prepare! Too much thinking! The room was spinning.

She sensed the man standing up to come into the room, and decided to remain in her meditative pose, while ever so slightly accessing that whale song, perhaps harmonizing with it a bit. Just a tiny bit.

His whale song stopped abruptly as soon as he entered the room. She was female, and he was horny. She didn't need empath to figure that one out. She struggled to concentrate, so difficult with his lust bobbing there like a lost puppy. Nausea dominated, but perhaps she could conquer that also, use his weakness to her advantage. He certainly didn't look like a villain. Nothing about him seemed anything other than a frightened little boy in grownup clothing with a huge swatch of macho. She heard his mind loud and clear. She had to be careful, hear what he had to say without giving away that she also knew what he wasn't saying.

"My name is Dr. Matthew Hobbs," he said, pleasantly enough, setting donuts and coffee down on the table. He pulled up a swivel chair on the other side of the table, ignoring her obvious meditative state. "Help yourself to some breakfast. I'm so sorry we had to be so inconsiderate of you initially. It's a matter of national security. Uh, you can call me Matt. I believe you call yourself J?"

"No thanks, I'm not exactly hungry, and I could have done without the manhandling and the blindfold."

"I know, J. I am so sorry. As I said, it was a matter of national security. But let me get right to the point."

J listened to his mind struggling to find the right, soft-touch approach: Raymond had told him too much. Matt knew, but didn't quite believe, that she could read his mind, and he didn't know how to proceed.

"So you have pretty powerful ESP."

"I do?"

"Please don't play me for a fool, J. Raymond told me everything. He'll be back very soon. But I want to talk before he gets back."

He doesn't trust Raymond either, but it's based on racism.

"We've been searching for talent like yours. We have a very special deal to offer you in exchange for us not pressing charges."

"Charges?"

"For spying."

Well, he knew and didn't know. He didn't believe Raymond's extraterrestrial claims, she knew that, but he was enraged and terrified the Imari could play with his mind. Plus, with all those national security protocols, people could still spy on his sacred project. The hunter was hunted.

"We want to cut a deal with you. You can trust me. How much do you know? We'll start off with that. And who's paying you? You give us what we need to know, names, addresses, for starters, and we won't press charges. In fact, we'll allow you to be part of history. We need your ESP talents. You do for us and we'll do for you."

He was going to let her in on their research really quickly. Maybe even show her the labs. Already giving up his secrets without realizing it.

"What do you mean spying? Who for? I don't understand. What kind of use could you have for me? What kind of talent do you think I have? ESP? I really doubt it."

"We need names and addresses first, J. Who are the spies working with you? Who are you working for?"

He rolled his chair a little closer. J reeled from the intensity of his lust and briefly lost her concentration. His breath stunk, his sweat sour. He clearly hadn't been sleeping for a while. In fact, he was really exhausted. Okay, okay. Calm down. She would have an easy time pushing his thoughts. But not yet.

He had not reported his quarry to the government. He was worried they wouldn't believe him, especially about the creature from another planet. He did have to strike a deal with her so he could use her for this project he was calling MPII. That was top priority. "I don't have any names and addresses. I'm not a spy. I'm not paid by anyone. I'm a graduate student at CUNY, getting my degree in psychology. I was on vacation until yesterday and came back to start my classes."

"You belong to SDS, and some other secret Communist front organization. I know you hang out with radicals on campus and that you go to Communist demonstrations. Anti-war, anti-American, subversive activities. I also know that you're spying on our research for the Russians, and who knows who else. You can't deny that."

A Russian spy! Katie would get a kick out of that one. Well, it's a great cover story.

He's definitely CIA. No, actually, a combination of NASA and CIA, or some deeper more secretive security group. Well, CIA trained, but his "intelligence" was actually from Raymond. She slowly probed into the stuff he was struggling to keep secret. His mind unraveled easily into hers. Raymond had told him almost everything about her, but had deliberately distorted the Mission. The Imari were, in Matt's eyes, as ruthless as he thought the Russians were. Out to conquer this world, and brainwash every earthling to serve them in their exploits, and exterminate anyone who balked. At the same time, he could hardly believe Raymond's extraordinary extraterrestrial claims. As far as he was concerned, the alien stuff was probably an elaborate ruse of some sort, perhaps concocted by the Russians themselves, and he was double-thinking himself all over the place. He also had fallen victim to Raymond's extraordinary extraterrestrial powers, which terrified and humbled him a bit.

"There's no law against who I hang out with and what I do. I don't know what you think I'm up to and who my secret connections are. You already seem to have spied on me. Like there's a secret HUAC file on me, something like that. But going to demos and having political convictions are my rights as an American citizen. No matter what Hoover thinks up. I don't know what kind of deal you want to strike with me. But I could sure use some money for grad school, if you want to show me how you can use the ESP you seem to think I have. That sounds really cool. Although I don't know why you wouldn't just go to Duke, or some place like that."

Matt was getting impatient, fidgety, and Raymond would be back real soon. She had to act quickly.

CHAPTER THIRTY-NINE

Scotty

When I came back from Woodstock, I found a garden apartment in a huge, ramshackle Victorian brownstone off 2ⁿᵈ Avenue. It was part of the Gramercy Women's Commune, which I joined because it was cheap, peopled, but not intrusively so, and most like the off-world compounds I was used to. Shelly, my garden-floor roommate was busy, political, and a livewire.

The upstairs women, two single mothers and three graduate students, were fun, available to socialize, but also respectful of privacy. Plus I loved the inquisitive little kids, three of them, who were currently scampering and jumping around upstairs, restless before dinner. The thumping usually didn't bother me. This time it did. Occasionally, when Shelly shacked up with her boyfriend for the weekend, I had to feed her two cats, a bit weird, because I wasn't used to treating animals like pets, having met so many species off-world.

It wasn't sundown yet, but September shadows were closing in on the half-window that opened into the concrete area beneath the brownstone steps. I was in my bedroom, hunched in front of the little console Johnny had constructed, exchanging messages with him as he, safely ensconced within our Shawangunk cave, monitored J.

J had really pissed me off the night before by jumping into the capture immediately. I wanted a few more days. Perhaps see her one more time before we did this thing. Now she had been detained for more than fifteen hours, and something was very wrong. I had a terrible premonition, which Johnny wouldn't buy into. As far as he was concerned, our plan seemed to be working.

We were on strict empath silence, except for the occasional miniscule bursts Johnny sent out, required to track J and to keep the instant communication going between Johnny's and my consoles. Out of this deep silence, I slowly became aware of a vague humming, increasing in volume, from outside the cave, not from outside my bedroom. "Johnny, something's going down out there. Something or someone is approaching the entrance to the cave. Do you hear it?" I typed.

"No way, Scotty!" His letters, unfolding on my screen, echoed his words in my head. Then, "Wait, I hear something too," he empathed as he typed, apparently unaware that we were now empathing to each other up and down the Hudson Valley, in spite of our enforced empath silence. "I'll be right back." The display abruptly blanked to solid green, except for the blinking white cursor dot, taunting, silent.

Now I was at the mouth of the cave, crouched low, as if I were suddenly within Johnny's body. I recoiled backward from a deafening, pulsating roar as two huge primitive hovering crafts rapidly approached the mouth of the cave. Suddenly my mat began to tilt, and abruptly lifted several inches off my bedroom floor. As Johnny, I was roughly dragged from the mouth of our cave off the cliff by some unseen force. Then I was falling, rocking, dipping, like a kite on a windy day, at the same time speeding south in mid-air, way above the Hudson River. Dizzy and nauseous, I struggled against my automatic impulse to shield from the sensation. I had to stay connected, to follow what was happening to him, just in case it was real.

Stunned and terrified, I lay on my back where I had fallen, several feet from my mat, struggling to shield to maximum.

At first I thought it might be a V.E.-premonition. I pulled myself up on all fours, and crawled to my mat, now perfectly still on the floor. I reached over and pressed the connect key on the console. Nothing but the taunting cursor.

I hadn't meant to empath to him like that. We were simply texting to each other. A miniscule amount of empath booster energy was required, but he had rigged the process to be impenetrable, imperceptible to the earthling scanners. I certainly didn't intentionally bypass the console to empath-connect directly with him. In our panic, it simply happened in spite of our shields. In that brief burst of empath, all the way from Gramercy to the Shawangunks, maybe we had inadvertently given ourselves away. But it didn't make any sense. Our direct empath connection had happened after the helicopters arrived. For sure Johnny was captured, and I was next. But I didn't have that telltale headache, which would warn me of approaching scanners.

I thought of calling J's best friend Katie. Finally let her in on what was going on, because I couldn't handle this alone. If I got caught, how could I help J and Johnny? Someone had to be on the outside. NASA had found Johnny even in deep empath silence. Even if the three of us had more power than all those earthling NASA boys could muster, even with their Uzis, and scanners, and any foolhardy secret gizmos they thought were so state-of-the-art, something or someone else was a bit more sophisticated than we figured.

I had to think. Quietly and calmly. Johnny had followed J with his tracker, filling me in every few minutes, so I vaguely knew where they had taken her:

to Bell Labs, somewhere in New Jersey, off Route 78. So I debated if I should just go there, take the NASA boys by surprise, and hover J and Johnny (if he was there too) to safety before the creeps could fry their brains. Certainly by then, I figured, J had gathered enough information for Johnny to send to the Europa team.

Then I decided we couldn't just give ourselves away. Besides, in spite of my panic about my foolish lover's safety, she could handle those psychopaths by herself. So could Johnny. I took long, deep breaths, and closed my eyes. Securely shielded, I caressed my inner tapestries, one layer at a time. Not to search out solutions. Just to put myself in the calmest place I could possibly find, so solutions could come.

A scratching at the window almost imperceptibly blended with the silence, forcing itself into my repose and willing my reluctant eyes open. I didn't break my empath shield. Somehow I wasn't frightened, just curious, but given what had just happened, I was intensely cautious.

Two luminous eyes emerged at the window. Now I was scared. "Please do not be alarmed, Scotty," it empathed straight through my deepest shielding. "Could you open the window and let me in, please. It is urgent." I thought I was hallucinating. What had pierced my shielding? In any event, no way would I open my window! What was going on? Anything was possible. Reinforcing my shielding didn't work. "Please, we are almost out of time. Just open the window. I have a message from Winstx and Telmx. It is urgent. My empath is strong, but on a frequency that cannot be tapped by those human scanners."

As if on automatic, I found myself opening my window against my will, and a silky angora squeezed between the security bars and leapt lightly down onto my sleeping mat. Within seconds, she was snuggling up against me, rubbing and purring, as if she had been living with me forever. Then she moved slowly away, and lay down facing me. "My name is Gum. Please listen to what I have to say," she empathed.

Gum's eyes were penetrating and reassuring. I wanted to scoop her up in my arms and cradle her, to feel the vibrations of her purring on my chest, but I had learned from my travels that it was absolutely not cool to pet other species. It is insulting, like meeting another human being and immediately cooing and stroking her.

"We have come to help. We have a plan. It will require reinforcements. So we need to train earthling felines to join the Mission. You must follow our instructions, even if they feel dangerous and counter-intuitive."

Utterly bizarre. I was deeply suspicious. Too many unknowns. Too many surprises. Maybe the goons, the NASA boys, had been able to fashion robot puppets that could break though my shielding. I had a million scenarios in my head. I had met felines off-world, incredible varieties of brilliant empaths, none of them resembling any particular earthling breeds. The most contact I'd had with some felines had been at the university. Most of them were music majors, and a few of my closest feline friends were into philosophical physics. But I was here on Earth. I was intensely curious, frantic, suspicious, and most of all, unable to penetrate whatever shield this feline had erected.

Again, as if on autopilot, I peered out my window. Sure enough, there was another angora huddled against the stairs. And another one by the tree in front. For reasons I can't explain, I decided to trust.

"Telmx and Winstx? Where are they? Are they okay?"

"Lingering on the other side of Venus, but not able to land safely on Earth the way we can."

"Ohmygosh! How—? What happened? Listen, Johnny and J are captured. We gotta do something!"

"We figured. Winstx and Telmx are fine. We have concluded that an Imari rogue has contacted the earthling scientists and has given the three of you away. You are probably going to be apprehended within several Earth hours or days. So you have to set up some things. Do not worry! It is part of our strategy. We think, we hope, we have things under control. This rogue Imari is sharp, so it will be a struggle. But, no one, not even this rogue, expects us felines to have followed him and his team to this star system. Our feline triad team, with some help from some of our earthling counterparts, should be able to take care of things. If we can manage it in time. Somehow we will overcome this unpredicted development.

"We need more help. Most of our time here has to be devoted to winning over your compound-mate's felines, Mushka and Koshka. So you have to leave me alone with them. They are going to be organizers and trainers. They will not be the ones who actually do the pivotal jobs. We'll leave those tasks to the freer ones, the felines who do not live as pets. But they are harder for us to contact and organize in the limited amount of time we have. So Mushka and Koshka will need to go out to work the neighborhoods, so to speak."

"How do you know earthling felines will cooperate, would understand?"

"It will take time. But we should be able to do it. Be patient."

"Patient! You just said we are out of time! Johnny and J are captured, and now you say that I will be too!"

"Now, how much do your compound-mates know about the Mission?"

Gum was accusing me of giving away the Mission. Were they actually here to retro-sweep us? Do a blink-out of the entire planet? No. Too soon to do something so drastic. They hadn't given us time to do our work. Maybe they were actually the rogues.

"Your paranoia is slowing us down, Scotty," Gum empathed with a slight edge to her serenity.

"My compound-mates think I write science fiction," I empathed, still defensive and frantic.

Gum waited calmly (I could sense her wisdom and tolerance) while this confused humanoid let this all sink in.

"Telmx and Winstx trust you, implicitly and without reserve. They said you would have some habobot. Might we have some? Warmed up just a bit?"

I rushed to auto-effuse several saucers of bot-laced warm milk for Gum and her two comrades, placing one of them right by my mat, and the others outside under the stairs.

After quickly emptying her saucer, Gum started empathing to Mushka and Koshka, who sat bolt upright and listened. I wasn't sure I liked this idea. I had trouble with Shelly's cats. They scratched my furniture and my new Persian rug and woke me up in the night with their complaints. Now I would have to have conversations with them, depend upon them, collaborate and cooperate with them like they were co-eds at the university. Now they would give me feedback for all the times I had not so kindly thrown them out of my bedroom. Funny, though, for all the times I wanted them to stop bothering me, they always forgave me. They would purr and rub and serenely watch me think and work. Still, it always comes back at you, I thought. Maybe roaches will be next. Let these cats work the neighborhood? I wanted to tell everyone the joke. Pussycats crucial to the survival of Earth, the universe? Amazing.

Actually, I was convinced I was hallucinating. It was too comical, like a Walt Disney cartoon! It couldn't be real. As much as I had learned to respect all species of animals from my trainings and travels, as much as felines were my buddies at the university, this was more than my training could handle. Shelly was always finding ways to let her cats outside to romp. No problem there. Nothing would change. Work the neighborhood? I wanted to giggle, to bring my compound-mates in on the scheme. Shelly would love it to pieces if she could know it. Even with all my off-world experience, Shelly had a mutual understanding with cats that went far beyond mine.

I ran outside to check on the lookouts. The saucers were empty. One angora was calmly stretched out on top of a Ma Bell repair truck, the other still at her station beneath the steps. I tried not to stare as I brought the saucers in to brew more habobot. I was now thinking slowly and deliberately, like the felines.

When I came back in, Mushka and Koshka appeared to be asleep on my mat and Gum was so deeply empathing to them, she didn't notice me at all.

I also was developing one of those nagging low-roar headaches, and from my headache I suspected the Ma Bell truck wasn't there to repair phone wires.

Shelly was away for the weekend. Would she notice something different about her cats when she got back? God she would be so proud! I always knew that Shelly's cats were smarter than anyone gave them credit for. I was sure Shelly would pick up the difference when she got home. She was so in tune with them.

I wanted to sleep, desperately wanted to be relieved of the pounding on the back of my neck.

The silence was unbearable. I sat on the rug and waited. Mushka and Koshka were still in a stupor. Koshka was on his back-paws spread out, head to one side, as if he would be damned if he ever had to bother with being awake. Maybe it was too much for them.

Gum didn't seem concerned. Finally without a word she scratched to get out. Then she sat by the open door and stared at me. Silence. Then she suddenly licked my hand and scampered out the door. I watched her run down the block toward the truck, then past it without a hint of hesitation. I was too obvious. Watching a fucking cat run down the block as if it mattered.

I had no idea what Mushka and Koshka now knew. Were they going to empath with me? What kind of a relationship was this going to be? Would they act differently? Mushka had moved to the back of my reclining chair and, in her usual fashion, was perched on top, staring at me with lidded, dreamy eyes. Koshka had not moved and I bent over him to see if he was breathing. Breathing, purring, now twitching.

I decided to wait another half hour and call Katie. Plus I had an overwhelming desire to sleep. Drown out the headache. Well, maybe for a half hour. Set an alarm and sleep. With Shelly's cats, now feline recruits waiting for orders. In my own bedroom. Amazing.

I stretched out on my mat, and was immediately dreaming: I was riding on the back of a dolphin, desperately holding on to his dorsal fin. We were riding in the air as if the dolphin were a spaceship. Jet planes were shooting at us from all sides, and up he soared. I was wounded, and bleeding, his back and sides red and dripping with my hemorrhage. I clung tightly, for fear of falling off or fainting. If I fainted I would fall. And the buzzing of the missiles. He dodged and pitched and I held on.

Then there were dolphins all over the sky, each one with an earthling empath Monitor (as if we had hundreds of earthling recruits) riding their backs like the water babies in a children's book I once read. They soared higher into the sky and left the bombers and missiles flailing below. But my dolphin was tiring. He couldn't keep up, and I knew he was hit. Now our blood. We fell into the whining missiles as the other dolphins soared out of sight.

The buzzing was deafening. I heard the drones of the jets as I lay on my mat, eyes closed, waiting for what? The drone of the jets. I opened my eyes, trying to shake the roar.

I kept the light off and gingerly approached my now darkened window. Not jet planes. Helicopters. Dozens of them with spotlights scanning the street, back and forth. Something had happened. My headache pounded.

I turned on WINS. Nothing on the news. Gramercy bombarded with helicopters and no one cared.

My phone rang. Carla was calling from upstairs: "Do you know what's going on? The whole street is full of soldiers and helicopters and commotion."

"I know. I don't know. Whatdaya think?"

"Feels like an invasion. I expect to hear shooting next. What do you suppose? I can't keep the kids away from the windows. Can you come up and help? Nobody else is home."

"Give me a sec. Keep them away from the windows and don't open the door!" I pushed my shoes on my feet, and raced upstairs. Why the fuck had I gone to sleep? Of all the asinine....

Jackie and Naomi were crying because they wanted to see the helicopters. "Carla, you take the kids into the parlor."

There was a sharp knocking on the door. "Okay, I'll talk to the soldiers. You take the kids into the parlor." I repeated it so emphatically that Jackie and Naomi just whirled around and marched into the parlor. Carla followed, with Tommy squirming to get out of her arms.

I opened the door to three awkward young soldiers trying to act officious. "Hi, what's happening?"

Now my headache moved into my neck and back, pulsating in spasms.

"Sorry to bother you ma'am. We have to search every house on this block. We have reason to believe that terrorists are hiding somewhere in one of the buildings."

They were carrying scanners! I was sure of it! I pushed away spasms and panic, pushed away thoughts, desperately forcing my shielding tighter and tighter.

"Okay, don't scare the kids. Okay? They're in the other room with their mother. Please close the door. It's cold. I'm sure no one is here, but certainly look around. Just close the door. Thank you."

If I fainted, I didn't know what they'd discover in my weakened state. I desperately needed to get away from their scanners.

The next thing I knew, I was bound and gagged in the back of a speeding vehicle.

CHAPTER FORTY

Matt and J

Matt was mesmerized. This chick rested on the swivel chair Yazzie-style, palms out, still talking slowly with him, with such incredible tranquility, like when Yazzie did his prayers, yet incisive, and to the point. Something so alike about the two of them. He found himself wondering how the old Indian was doing. Yazzie was back with the research team in the underground compound, ensconced in his own medical setup, just in case he had a sudden relapse, ready for technical consultation, but adamantly refusing to allow himself or Matt to be hooked up to the photon consoles.

Yazzie had no idea what had transpired in the last twenty-four hours. Would he be horrified? Probably. But Matt needed his help now. He was the only one he could confide in. Certainly Dawes would have to know they had located a blue surge with their scanners. But bringing her here without security clearance? Matt had disobeyed orders, big time. How to do this. Lord knows where Charlie was, poor jerk. Down for the count? Raymond said Charlie would not be in the way until they needed his expertise. So let him sleep, wherever Raymond had taken him. Christ! One minute he believed the dude, and the next minute he felt he was being played the fool. He desperately needed Yazzie to help him sort things out, because J and Raymond were Yazzie's type of people.

"There's someone I'd like you to meet," he said to J as calmly as he could muster. He was practically whispering, almost as if he hadn't said anything at all. She looked at him, hesitated, and said, "I'm sorry, I didn't quite hear you."

"I said there's a fellow here you'd like. You should meet him as we prepare for you to do your ESP stuff. We can cut a deal with you. Of course we'll pay you. We'll waive the spy charges if you cut a deal. We'll prepare a contract. You'll see. It'll all be legal, on the up and up. Not to worry. Let me introduce you to the head technician. Then we can go to next steps."

She might freak out being alone with two men. After all, he bet this lesbo could tell how much he wanted to get into her pants. On the other hand, maybe she'd be relieved not to be alone with him. Can't get into figuring that out.

Just get Yazzie here. Talk to him alone first? Or just call him on the intercom? Yeah, just call him. Shouldn't leave J alone now, not even for a minute. Didn't trust her. With all the so-called powers Raymond claimed she had, who knew whether she'd even be here when he returned. If for no other reason, he needed Yazzie here to protect him. Oh Christ! What? Has my brain turned to corn mush? He picked up the intercom, as if his hand were not his own.

✸ ✸ ✸

Matt's whole demeanor changed when Yazzie entered the room. The faint whale song was in the air. Everywhere. Did they hear it?

"J, this is Yazzie. He's the head technician for our research. Uh, Yazzie, we have located our first blue surge, and she's thinking about whether to work with us."

Yazzie reminded J of Gir. He was tall, incredibly handsome, with deep wisdom etched into his face. Except he was very very sick. She gently probed. His brain synapses were struggling to fire, and his corpus colossi were almost completely fused. His synapses struggled painfully. It had been worse. He was struggling to heal himself. Slowly and painstakingly. And he was brilliant, the way dolphins and whales were brilliant.

She nodded at his nod, when Matt introduced them, and heard his dismay, as if he had been secretly hoping against hope that no blue surges would be located.

"So I see. Ma'am, welcome. I am honored to meet someone who is already a talented ESP. But there is fear under your serenity. Dr. Matthew, what has happened? Or do I ask the young lady directly? Ma'am, did I hear your name is J? How did you get the name J? That's a very interesting name. Is it your birth name? Has Dr. Matthew been treating you with dignity? He has lapses in judgment sometimes, but he's really a good guy, when all is gathered at the end of the day."

An ally. Yes, Yazzie was an ally. Maybe she had no reason to fear Matt. He was clearly Matt's mentor.

Only then did she realize she hadn't discerned Johnny's pings in a long time. Scotty! Does Raymond have Scotty too? She sent out her scanners as far as she could, to call for Scotty and discern Raymond's whereabouts. Yazzie was listening to her struggling to listen.

"You can hear me, can't you?" she empathed.

She looked straight at him. His eyes were now closed. She climbed off the chair and moved to the carpet. She empathed him to squat opposite her, aware that Matt was watching them with suspicious awe. No matter.

Yazzie moved very slowly, wincing out loud as he attempted to fold himself into lotus position opposite her. "I am honored and humbled to make your acquaintance," he empathed.

His empath voice was halting and barely audible. He was ill, quite ill, struggling with enormous compassion to connect to her struggle. Each empath word they exchanged weakened him even further. How to talk to him without draining him even more. She must strengthen him. If only Telmx were here, she'd know how to massage his chambers into health.

"He wants me to learn how to operate your system."

"You cannot. They will fry your brain as they have fried mine."

"I will not let them.You will help me not let them. We are in grave danger here, Yazzie. The alien is an evil creature, traveling an enormous distance with no good intent. I am not sure he knows about you. Probably he does. Matthew is caught in his spell."

"I have sensed him. A yellow, jagged presence. He has a wall, similar to yours, but you are beckoning me within."

"He calls himself Raymond. He has almost killed your hardware engineer. I think he only keeps Charlie alive to use his technical skills."

"I fear for Matthew, for you, for me as well, but so far, I am too weakened to do battle with the creature. Perhaps together..."

Matthew shifted, folding and unfolding his arms. "I see you two are simpatico. I kind of figured that would happen," he said. "Listen, you want me to leave you alone? Do I trust she won't bend your mind? She can do that, you know. Raymond told me she can enter people's minds, make them do things they didn't think they wanted to do, just by focusing on you. Like he did Charlie, like he did me. He hasn't gotten to you yet, Yazzie, but he will. She will, I mean. What the fuck's going on here? Why won't you fuckin' answer me?"

"Matthew, Matthew, slow down, my young friend. She is trying to communicate with her ESP, not to harm me. I actually feel empowered by her. I can't explain it." Yazzie looked back at J and smiled. "You're trying to give me back my strength, aren't you? I think so. Matthew, this young lady is your blue surge for good reason. She is indeed very special. You must not harm her in any way. You can join us, by sitting here with us, or you can leave. I would prefer that you join us to make a true circle. We can change our tactics later. But right now, I think it is the wise thing to do."

"She has already bent your mind, Yazzie. I can feel it."

"Of course you can feel it. She has, in fact, entered my mind. As a healer. Her quiet meditation sends out potions. You send out potions, don't you J?"

"Poisons! Poisons!! Don't you see?"

"It is you who has been poisoned, Matthew. Please, slow down, and listen to me. Before that devil in human skin comes back to mix things up all over again. Where has he gone, anyway?"

"He said he had to replenish. He said he would be back in an hour. But it's almost seven hours later. I don't know. Any minute now, I guess."

"Then we have no time to lose."

"If you don't mind, Yazzie, I will lull Matt into a trance for a few moments so we can figure things out, without his confusing interference," empathed J. "Our struggle to communicate is draining you. I can't possibly replenish you with so much confusion and rage in the air. I hope that won't make you uneasy about me. May I silence Matt for a while?"

"I trust you will not harm him. He's ignorant about people, but under all those jagged rocks he has potential. He speaks to cows and dolphins, even to planets."

"I know."

"Of course you know."

She was now about to do what the directives said she should never do. She had learned through hard experience and strenuous warnings from Telmx, never to intrude in another's functioning. Not even altruistically. But this was different. She had to. In a little while they would have to confront Raymond, who was already mind-bending everyone he came in contact with. She had to fight back. And she needed Yazzie's alliance. So many times had she wanted to enter Katie's mind, to ease her from herself, and from the cops at demos. Yes, she sometimes entered their ragged rages and strategies, but just to know what was going on, not to alter their minds in any way. Really difficult, especially when her comrades were endangered. Hell, she and Scotty had mind-shifted an entire demo. It's okay now. The Mission was upon them, It was everything she had been trained for. She had to go ahead. It was strange and easy at the same time. Well, if her judgment ended up being faulty, she would be retro-swept, as soon as Telmx arrived, a chance she had to take.

"You ponder long and hard. I see you are a young woman with years of wisdom. You do not suddenly leap with your eyes shut."

"Not completely," she thought, in the inner reaches of her chambers. The new "take-out" force she and Raymond had discerned was not fully in her control. It had terrified Raymond. Probably made him leave to "replenish." No, more likely to capture her friends. Oh Jeez, Scotty! Johnny!

"Just don't harm him," Yazzie repeated.

"I won't." But if he made a sudden hostile move, she had no idea what she might do. Her powers were beyond her. She would have to work very slowly and deliberately, so Matt didn't catch on.

"You are frightened," Yazzie empathed. "You are so powerful in your mind, and yet you cower."

"He must not move suddenly toward me. Maybe it would be better if I just let him show me the console. Get me started on the task."

Matt was fidgeting. "You know I would like to introduce you to the project before Raymond and my boss comes back. They could pose complications, especially Raymond."

"Dr. Matt, it would be important to protect the young lady from harm."

Matt flashed him a disgusted glance.

"Stop being such a mush, Yazzie. We won't hook her up just yet. Let her see what we are offering, and then between the three of us, we can figure out a way to test it out. One hit won't hurt her. It didn't you. Constant hits are dangerous, and debilitating. We'll be spreading the task around, once you tell us where your friends are, there'll be more than enough people so that no one will get the full brunt of it. Yazzie here was the only really talented one. Now there are more. No one has to take the brunt of its kickback. Besides, according to Raymond, you're stronger and more protected from its effects. Let us just do a tiny experiment."

J knew he was lying. Raymond had told him the console would fry her brains out in a nano-sec. "I would like to see what it is all about. Without making any commitments."

"Don't make any commitments, J," empathed Yazzie.

J could hardly control her emotions. She so much wanted to take the bastard Matthew out. His movement toward her, just to show her the console, made her cringe. His lust was strangely attractive and repulsive. Had he more loving in him, perhaps she might have even allowed herself to get intrigued. But his lust was out of frustration and a strong desire to be all-powerful. She listened to Yazzie listening to her struggle. "He is a pussycat, J. Do not be upset with him. He had a very hard upbringing."

"A hard life does not take away from his menace to others. It is his hard life that makes him who he is, a menace to others."

"You are of great wisdom. I did not know such wisdom existed in ones so young. Please forgive my assumptions."

"First things first. I'm putting him in a semi-trance, just for a few minutes, so I can try to give you more strength. You're going to die if you continue the way you are, sir. Will you let me enter your cellular structure? I must make him oblivious to the proceedings. It would infuriate Matt if he saw me do this, because it means I must touch you. Once you are a little stronger, we can work together to deal with him and Raymond. I do need your help, but not in your current state."

"I understand."

She didn't know if she could do this. Telmx had taught her some rudimentary cellular techniques. She allowed her to practice on her. She had performed some brief Gn'ike on Scotty, and she on her to alleviate their headaches, but Yazzie was actually dying. The electrical connectivity between his synapses were failing, almost as if they were feeding back on themselves, in small spurts, rather than leaping across the space between nerve endings. It was a wonder that he still had the capacity to empath much stronger signals between much larger spaces. She held on to this, because if he had the capacity to redirect his energies back to the synapses.... It was only a hypothesis, with little to go on. She was arrogant or desperate. Telmx had taught her that arrogance can be a way of announcing to oneself and others what one wants to become. It wasn't always a bad thing. A person can live up to her own arrogance. That's a wonderful thing. Like making a dream come true.

There was one hitch to all of this: If she used her energies to heal, would she be strong enough to deal with Raymond when he returned? If she succeeded with Yazzie, there would be two of them. But if she didn't, she'd be in much worse shape, with no ally. Not to mention that she'd have a much harder time dealing with Matt, and whoever else he called in to help him.

"It is quite amazing," Yazzie empathed. "You know the basic healing techniques of my people, yet you have acquired them from the same species of the evil one. Perhaps if we work together, our combined efforts will do more than what each of us could do alone. I am ready."

CHAPTER FORTY-ONE

Johnny

The helicopter drone finally quit. Johnny was no longer free-falling. On the contrary, he was lying prone in the back of a large speeding vehicle, precariously bumping and skidding.

Someone was frantically organizing his shielding. "Can you hear me?" Scotty! It was Scotty! "Keep your empath energy focused within a space no larger than 20 centimeters."

"I hear you," he empathed. But it was with struggle. His energies were failing him. "Where are we? What happened? How did you—," he managed.

"I watched you, felt you, snatched from the mouth of the cave. And then within the hour, that same helicopter rooted me out. Take it very slow, Johnny. We are drained of practically all our empath. It's uncanny. The person driving like a maniac seems to have extraordinary empath powers. I can't figure out who he is. He's Imari, but not Imari. And he's definitely not earthling. His capacities are confusing. He's at least a Level V, maybe even a Level VI, but I don't know. There are friendly and serene elements about him, yet he's sharp-edged, conniving. He mustn't know we have awakened. I don't think he can penetrate our low empath."

"He doesn't seem to hear us," empathed Johnny.

"He thinks he's drained us completely, and that only he has the power to revive us," empathed Scotty. "He seems incomplete. That's it! an incomplete Level VI. I don't know how else to describe it."

They were speeding so fast that it was a wonder they hadn't been pulled over yet.

"Whoever he is, he sure knows how to disable radar and squad cars," empathed Johnny.

Scotty told him about the felines.

CHAPTER FORTY-TWO

Matt and J

Matt stood behind Yazzie and J on adjacent chairs at the console. Yazzie murmured directions, like an incantation. He insisted J name each photon, absolutely required for successfully sending a series of behavior commands to its entangled twin, a mile or so away in another lab. Most of the time, the distant twin photon behaved exactly the opposite of the one he manipulated at close range, he explained. But only he and Matt could get what he called a reliable "hit" (a successful manipulation of the distant twin) but only after they had given each photon a name, essentially after making friends with it. J marveled that Matt could be that empathic. A hopeful sign.

Now she had to hurry up and get at least one photon communicating with its entangled twin, in order to prove to them she was, in fact, a reliable "blue surge," and to buy more time to absorb the entire system documentation into her inner chamber.

"Would you guys stop staring at the console and get going!" Matt was frantic. The silent connection between J and Yazzie was upsetting him. Jealousy, a human emotion. Another hopeful sign, thought J.

"Patience, my young friend. First things first. We must meditate, in the tradition of my people. As I had taught you. The process with J is no different."

"So they decided to fry the brains of others," empathed J.

"Yes, they desperately need talented ESPs like you. Matt convinced them he could find new ESP talents to replace me. So in fact the entire project has been on hold, until now. I was hoping they wouldn't find anyone. Although I knew they would. I was hoping that young Matthew would back away from such an evil quest, but he did not. He almost did. Perhaps with your assistance—"

For his own safety, Yazzie dared not demonstrate a successful "hit," but he patiently and reluctantly talked J through each step, warning her every thirty seconds that her synapses could be fried. "I feel, I hope, you have enough power to resist the ill effects. It would be good if you did prove to Matthew and to the MPII team that he has finally located his "blue surge." Otherwise I fear you will be disposed of because you now know too much."

Matt's pacing brought him intermittently to the back of their chairs, where he frantically backseat-drove J's key strokes. He couldn't wait to boast to Dawes that his scanners had finally worked, that he had located a "blue surge," which would absolve him of his security breach and make him a national hero. He didn't know what he'd do with her if she couldn't get a "hit." He had compromised top-secret information. He could always "disappear" her. Cleanly. No one would know. Dawes wouldn't be the wiser.

J couldn't concentrate. There was so much at risk. For Raymond, it didn't matter whether she got a "hit." He had no reason to keep her alive. She was just a pawn to get NASA to trust him. In spite of Matt's desperation, Raymond had the sophisticated empath technology that didn't require "blue surges." Why was he so interested in collaborating with MPII? Had Telmx missed him entirely in her V.E.-future-scans, for reasons only Raymond knew?

And if Telmx and Winstx couldn't get there, it would be up to Scotty, Johnny and her to push back the technology. Tweaking minds here and there was one thing, but retro-sweep an entire lab?

Johnny's pings had stopped. Perhaps Raymond had already captured him and Scotty. Their entire plan wasn't working! Well, she possessed this new "take-out" force. But Raymond might come back replenished, with a "take-out" force of his own. Where had that force in her come from? How could she use it safely? Could she overpower him again? Surely he'd be more prepared this time. What if she suddenly summoned it, as she had done on Riverside Drive, and demolished the entire lab, or for that matter, all of Piscataway? Why hadn't Telmx warned her about such powers?

Her mind flew in frantic circles. Too much responsibility for mere earthlings. The Mission was way over their heads now.

J's first ten tries failed miserably. Johnny would know how to do this.

"Ok, so much for all your empath talents," said Matt, breathing hard over her shoulder. "Yazzie, can't you get her to do this thing right? Perhaps she's a fucking dud."

"Give her a chance, Matthew," said Yazzie. "You are distracting her with your impatience. Successes have never been built on impatience."

"No! You don't fucking understand! Dawes is somewhere in the lab ready to pull the plug on MPII, and I can't tell him we found a 'blue surge' unless she performs like a 'blue surge.'"

"You have twisted your head into an impossible loop. Come with me for a cup of coffee. We will leave you alone now, J. I will take my poor mad scientist back into the library."

"She'll escape, you fool!"

"Okay, we'll lock the door here."

"She can walk though walls, I tell you!"

"Leave her be!"

J looked at Yazzie, and silently they agreed to put Matt back into a semi-trance. This time they worked on him together. Yazzie had learned the Imari ways very quickly. He smiled inwardly. Back in her innermost chamber she worried that he would know too much. Telmx would have to retro-sweep him. If she ever saw her again. She recoiled. She couldn't go there just now. Matt sat upright on a swivel chair in the corner, his eyes lidded, his jaw soaked in drool.

With Matt back in a stupor, J relaxed.

The technology was alarmingly similar to the empath booster technology the Imari used on their intergalactic ships. NASA had no idea how close they had come to wielding extraordinary powers, with dire implications for the entire civilized intergalactic universe. Telmx's future V.E.-scans were ultimately accurate, even if they were off by a few years. Well, that's why they were monitoring. Telmx's scans only predicted with a .01 level of confidence. That's a .01 percent chance she was off by some smidgen of time.

J was more interested in recording the technology than in actually succeeding, but she also needed to keep up the charade so she could garner as much information as she could. There were many technicians and other researchers in the lab. She needed to probe each mind and discern what they knew about the project. She needed to locate every bit of code, every shred of documentation. No guarantees that Telmx and Winstx would be able to actually land on Earth to perform a precise retro-sweep of the project. Worse case, the three earthling monitors would have to retro-sweep without the help of the Imari. There was no question that this technology had to be obliterated.

Learning the prototype empath technology was fascinating. Perhaps it was how all planets moved from Electronic to Empath Eras. There was a certain elegance about the technology, in spite of its primitive architecture.

She was comforted by Yazzie, even though Matt was only a few yards away. When she tuned in for a second, he was in such a horrible nightmare, she had to pull away in order to stay focused.

She also had to listen for Raymond.

"Do not worry, young gentle one. I will smell his stench the moment he's within ten miles of us. I haven't met this creature, but I know his every crag and crevice. In the submarines, I learned to discern the difference between whale song, and Nazi rant. You concentrate on my photons, and I will listen for the enemy." She listened anyway.

When she got her first "hit" she was jubilant. She directed a right turn to her photon, and its entangled twin turned left more than a mile away. She couldn't believe it, so she did it again. She had to make sure it wasn't because she was simply using empath to move the distant twin photon. It had to come from her maneuvering the one right there in the lab. Could she maneuver a distant photon without maneuvering this one? Was that really how empath technology worked? Maybe it had nothing to do with this elegant software at all.

"You mean you can maneuver the distant photon without instructing the one right here?"

"I don't know."

"Well, that would be totally extraordinary."

She wished Johnny were there. He knew all about booster technology, and empath relays. Then again, she didn't want to give Yazzie any more information than he already had. Maybe there was a way to save him from the retro-sweep. Wait, she was assuming the Mission would succeed. What about Raymond?

Her head was beginning to ache. The beginning of synaptic failure. If she drained her empath by continuing the photon work, she would not be able to fight off Raymond.

"I have to stop. I have made distant entangled photons turn to the left and right in their chambers, whether I did it by 'making friends' with them, or by simply empathing a directive to the distant one. We must now prepare for Raymond's return."

"He is returning. Don't you feel him? His negative energies make my eyes spin."

It was uncanny. She couldn't hear a thing. Her scanning only drained her further. She had to reserve whatever energy she had left to hide what she'd accomplished so far.

"I am about to build a shield for us," she said wearily out loud.

"A what?"

"A way for Raymond not to know exactly what has happened here. He is able to tap our memories and thoughts if we are not properly shielded."

"Where have you learned all this? I want to learn everything you know."

"You have it in you already, sir. I'm just bringing it to the forefront of your mind. You were surrounded by it in the womb. You were born with it. All of us were. Most people lose touch with it as they grow older."

She wanted to explain more. She really enjoyed being with this old man and didn't want their connection to stop. She wanted to teach him and have him teach her his traditional ways. She raised his shielding as rapidly as she could, and then modulated it so he could keep track of Raymond, leaving him open to empath-scan, hoping that Raymond would hardly expect anyone but her to have that capacity.

She was drained. She had no capacity for multitasking. It was frustrating, but she had to work methodically without panicking.

"Uh oh, he's parking near the lab," Yazzie empathed.

She completed the shielding, and couldn't move. "I will have to rely on your capacities, Yazzie. This work has exhausted me."

"I was afraid of that. I warned you. I am so distressed."

"How much time do I have before he finds us?"

"He has to pass the security guards. Ah, he has two more gentle ones with him. I can't hear them, but I can hear Raymond talking harshly to them out loud. Don't you hear them?"

Scotty and Johnny! If only she could scan for them.

"I'm afraid I can't hear them at all, sir. I'm completely drained. Can you tell me if they're okay?" Tears were imminent. She had to pull them back. They were a luxury right now.

"His jagged evil is so overwhelming, J. I regret that I can't discern their wellbeing. You love them deeply. I fear for them, J."

"I'm going to try and replenish myself in the few moments I have left."

"Perhaps they can be detained at the security checkpoint."

"Like before, Raymond'll get past them without difficulty." She shifted as far away from the console as she could, squatted, and closed her eyes. No matter how hard she concentrated, she couldn't replenish fast enough. She was too anxious and angry. It never worked like that.

Yazzie approached her and squatted opposite. "Useful power never comes from haste and rage," he whispered. They bent heads until they were touching, and he started transferring some of his energies back to her.

CHAPTER FORTY-THREE

Johnny

Raymond opened the back door of the van. "Welcome to the end of your lofty Mission! Get yourself looking as normal as you possibly can," he commanded out loud, handing Scotty and Johnny official looking Bell Lab Photo IDs. He didn't seem to detect that they were communicating with each other in close empath.

"I'm delivering you guys as part of a bargain. But don't think you can get away with anything. They think they need you to drive their primitive empath system. They don't. I'm going to show them they don't need any human ESP talents to drive their machines. Not that I am such a nice guy. I don't care one iota if they fry earthling brains. Once they discover they don't need your ESP, they'll have to get rid of you because you're now a dangerous security leak."

"He's confident and not confident," Scotty empathed.

"Just listen," empathed Johnny. "He's about to boast away his objectives."

"And, if the Intergalactic Council finds out just how far the Earth has managed to get, and that my regiment has established a base here, the Intergalactic Council will send other Scouts to retro-sweep NASA's technology. But don't get your hopes up. With my enhancement of your government's Missile Defense System, not even a tiny meteorite-sized object will penetrate Earth's stratosphere. Right now those shrunken solo-pods that mimic meteorites are their System's only weakness. Not for long. In collaboration with your government's military, we'll permanently shield Earth from Travel Scout interference. Your government'll love it. No Russian, no Cuban, no off-world enemy, will get past our collaborative shields. And just for added enticement, I'll promise them technology to enhance their first-strike capacity. They will be so sophisticated, they'll be dizzy with power.

"There'll be plenty of time to implement our new merged technology because that so-called egalitarian Council will deliberate forever before authorizing a retro-sweep of a planet's technology. Their scruples are their weakness. I have my people securely situated in the Council. I'll have ample warning. So no matter what, you see, you have no options.

"I don't need or want you three either. You're thorns, like Telmx, Winstx, and their entire elitist Order of Empath Travel Scouts. But for the time being I have to keep my end of the bargain, in order to obtain the cooperation of your government. I'm compelling you to play along. So, you see, I'm stronger than all three of you. I have my ways. I may be an 'unfinished' Imari, unworthy of membership in the Order of Empath Travel Scouts, but my 'unworthiness' is my power. I'm not bound by any Scout codes. I even recruited my regiment from un-evolved planets, just like I am doing here. I'm free to do as I please, with no scruples that you can negotiate with. I moved past all that years ago.

"And by the way, don't think that Telmx and Winstx can help you. The Council retro-swept them beyond recognition.

"That's not possible!" Johnny was spinning.

"He's lying," empathed Scotty. "It's a distraction. If we get worked up, we won't be able to resist him. Hold on. Once we're with J, the three of us together can out-empath him. We must hold on."

"We don't know he's lying! See? People just fuckin' get disappeared on you! Again and again and again."

"Johnny! Sweetheart! Don't use up your energy on this crap! J's depending on us!" She was yelling into his head to drown out his terror.

"Enough, you two!" Raymond empath yelled even louder than Scotty. "You're more skilled than I gave you credit for! That's all! No more!"

Johnny suddenly realized he was relying completely on out-loud cues. The Imari creep had completely neutralized their empath. He looked at Scotty. She was glazed and stony. He couldn't even read Raymond's inner moods anymore.

They were parked on the edge of a huge lot, on the side of a two- or three-story building that sprawled in all directions forever. They hardly looked like people who visit the lab for a top-secret conference, each of them with different get-ups to cover their cilia. Raymond with his travel hood pulled tightly around his head like a do-rag, Scotty with her sandals and long auburn bangs that practically covered her glassy eyes, and Johnny with his inverted Woodstock baseball cap, looking no more with it than she. They moved through the parking lot like computerized robots on a singular mission.

Raymond led them up an obscure path off to one side of the building, at the end of which was a small security door that required a punched-in code. He willed it open, and they continued down a long dimly lit hallway to a bunch of security guards armed with Uzis in a glassed-in area. Raymond stared hard at them, and they immediately slumped into a trance.

In spite of his outward demeanor of control and bravado, Raymond was agitated. Johnny didn't need empath to know that.

The underground lab was buzzing with people, mostly male technicians in open cubicles, very intent on their little computer screens, and oblivious to their passage.

Raymond's agitation and rage intensified as they neared a cordoned-off area of the complex. He stopped abruptly at another set of security doors.

"Telmx's beloved little trainee is in here, but all three of you combined have about as much empath energy as an earthling worm. As you know, I can increase and decrease your capacities at will. J's energies are so low, she's desperately trying to borrow them from an earthling. It's pathetic and impossible."

He opened the door to a large lab, filled with a myriad of electronic equipment. Johnny saw J, squatting in a corner opposite a tall, elderly man, oblivious to their entry. They were bent forward so that their foreheads touched, in empath exchange mode. She was clearly in deep physical and emotional trouble. A starched honky was sitting stiffly, upright on a swivel chair across the lab, his wide-open eyes glazed, his dropped jaw drooling. A console in the middle of the room was "asleep," with the letters "Welcome to NASA" glowing white against a primitive green screen.

No one moved. No one knew they had entered. Raymond had frozen everyone into an eerie tableau, including Scotty and Johnny.

Johnny was paralyzed. He had no way to maneuver. Even his strategizing capacity had been drained. Nothing was working, except raw, human emotion. Raymond didn't seem to be able to touch that, or didn't know it existed. Johnny's earthling, human "sixth sense" knew that. Like him, Scotty was frantic, terrified and frustrated. As for J, she seemed alive, but completely incapacitated as well.

CHAPTER FORTY-FOUR

Matt

Pa's face was crimson. His beer belly heaved as he pulled down the horse-whip from its hook next to the barn door. "Yer gonna git the whooping of yer life, you little sissy faggot squirt! I'll learn ya ta hold yer brother's hand, jus' 'cause he's a sissy cry baby like you. I'm gonna learn him ta be a man. An' ya ain't gonna git in my way. I'm gonna tan you but good, and then break every little finger in you faggot hands." Matt woke up abruptly, screams stuck in his throat. Raymond was towering above him.

"You were supposed to wait until I got back! She put you in a trance, you asshole! I warned you. Her powers are not of this world."

"No, No! It's not like that! You were gone so long, I was afraid Dawes would discover us. I had to get her succeeding at the console before he arrived back from his conference. I broke security protocol. She shouldn't be here. You don't understand. I convinced her to work with us. She's intrigued. But slow to perform."

"You're just lucky, because her console work drained her ESP energies, quicker than Yazzie's. Look at the two of them. They stupidly think they can energize each other."

Matt looked over at Yazzie and J bent toward each other like lovers, and he found himself yearning to connect with them, not to be left out. Yazzie was his closest friend, his only friend. He could resent J for taking him away, or he could find a way to be united with them. He was surprised at his own careening and conflicting thoughts.

But they weren't moving. They were eerily still. As were two other new-comers. A young hippie chick with long red hair, and a Negro boy with a backward baseball cap pulled over his forehead.

"Your two other blue surges, delivered as promised," said Raymond. "Right now, you're the only one here who's not in the same state as Charlie. Here's what I want you to do. Dawes will arrive real soon. It would be better if you called him here before he just barges in. So get your story together."

"Well, he certainly can't come into a scene like this!"

"Don't worry, he won't. Here's what you should tell him. You located three blue surges. That's it. They're signing a contract. Kudos to you!

"In truth, you don't need them for anything. They're simply in the way, and you should get rid of them. I mean, really get rid of them. I'm going to teach you a technology that far surpasses using and depleting earthling brains for photon communication. In the long run, you can't depend upon finding and depleting ESP talents. But I'll only teach you the advanced technology if you do something for me.

"My regiment requires a safe base here on Earth from which to operate. Together we'll protect your planet from extraterrestrial Communists and with our combined technology we'll conquer other planets before they conquer you. You'll be keeping your planet (how do you put it?) 'safe for democracy.' And bringing democracy, at long last to other civilized worlds. You'll be a worldwide, ultimately a universal, hero."

"I don't understand. You have an entire regiment? Where are they?"

"On Europa. We conquered the extraterrestrial Communist base there. They were preparing to attack and conquer your planet. They were worried about your ESP/photon experiments and had targeted this very lab for obliteration, based on the information obtained from these three spies you see here before you. It was the alien's first-strike strategy. We didn't get to Europa a moment too soon. They're no longer a threat. You can thank us for that. It's a down payment (as you say) for what we can give you if you forge an alliance with us.

"In return we demand a major share of the prize. The power and wealth from your colonization of other species must be generously shared with us, or your hegemony will fail. I promise you that. It will fail, if you do not give us what we want.

"As for these three, they are dispensable. Either you fry their brains using your primitive technology, or you get rid of them as common spies. I'll leave that up to you. Or I'll do it myself. They're dangerous the longer they stay alive. They know much too much. And that includes Yazzie. He needs to go too. He now knows much too much."

Not Yazzie! With him Matt felt things he hadn't experienced with anyone else, including his wife, except maybe for his Uncle Donny, who had died several years previously, and well, perhaps his younger brother.

So he had become a fucking mush? Well, okay, What of it? He had never felt quite human like everyone else. Always bugged him. With Yazzie, something different. It took a long time, but the old sailor filled an emptiness he didn't know he'd been living with.

"Don't go getting soft and stupid on me, Dr. Matt," said Raymond. "Besides there's a lot of glory and prestige in this for you. Keep your wits about you. Remember, you're dispensable too if you don't do as I say."

"Can't I have one fucking thought without you reading my fucking mind? Maybe I'd rather be dead than be tangled with the likes of you. Ever think of that? I don't have to play along."

"You will play along. I'm waking them all up now. Go get Dawes on the intercom, and let's get this thing over with."

Matt looked at Yazzie and J huddled together and suddenly hated their guts. He hated everyone and everything. If he were a better person, he thought, he'd put up a better fight. His head hurt and he was very tired.

"How do I convince Dawes to build a base for your regiment?" he whispered.

"I'll take care of that part. Just get him here so I can have him pull the proper strings with the proper authorities."

Yazzie and J moved in slow motion back to the console and sat down. J started punching in another set of commands. The two newcomers robotically took their places behind them, and began watching intently. Matt wanted to speak to them, to tell them what was going on, warn them. Raymond was setting a goddamned stage. Instead, he dully punched Dawes' extension.

"We've located four blue surges, sir," said Matt.

When Dawes arrived, he was furious, but Matt forged ahead. "Admiral Dawes, Sir, this is J. She's gotten a bunch of long distance hits already! And this is Scotty and John. And this is Raymond. All talented blue surge ESPs. We finally located them. We had to grab them while we could, and you were away, so—"

Matt wanted everything to work smoothly. Just introduce them and boast about his success. The rest would follow, just as Raymond had promised.

"Excuse me, folks," said Dawes, without looking at Matt. "I'm glad Matt found some ESP talents, but I'm sorry. I have to call security. You need clearance before you can enter this area. I know it seems like bureaucratic nonsense, but it's protocol around here." Matt knew that Raymond was playing with the admiral's mind. Making him feel like he was in charge. Okay, Raymond'll do it in his own alien way.

CHAPTER FORTY-FIVE

Katie

It was in the middle of September, and we were walking on University Place at about one-thirty in the morning, after a long, grueling meeting about a huge Fall action at the Pentagon. My comrades' excited voices echoed in the quiet street. I hung back, watching Nance, BJ. Larry, Beth and Sandy and Joe, analyzing, complaining, strategizing. There were many factions within the MOBE, each with different agendas and strategies. We had to merge them, find common ground. It was going to be dangerous and significant. And we had a lot of big names behind us: Spock, Coffin, Mailer. A very exciting time. But there were so many factions, undermining tactics, FBI maneuvers. Very thorny.

We were on our way to The Cedar Tavern, our regular watering hole, to cool down and debrief, before going our separate ways. Joe was beside himself. In addition to all the Pentagon planning, there was stuff going on between me and him. I was having major problems with his macho. I was questioning our relationship big time, finding myself more attracted to the women in our cadre. He was devastated by my shift in attention, protecting himself by acting cool and distant. I was crying myself to sleep at night, what little time we all did have to sleep before the action. I would think, oh stop freaking out, it's only September, and the Pentagon isn't 'til late October, actually on J's birthday.

J wasn't around. I needed her calm council. She was AWOL again. This time with her new girlfriend. It happens, I thought. You start shacking up with someone and all your friends drop off the radar. I was pissed. But, hell, I did the same thing. Not to her, though. She was a constant. Not fair.

So I was very focused on J. More so than any other time she had disappeared, sometimes for months at a time. She would be quite mysterious about where she went. It was her way. She was kind of out there, a space cadet, in a good way, like how she could suss out maneuvers in the street, finger an undercover agent before any of us, know when something really bad was about to happen. I trusted her sixth sense. Like she had incredible ESP or something. She would joke with me about that. She claimed she was enthralled by aliens, and that she had studied their incredible psychic powers, was actually gallivanting around the galaxies learning deeper ESP. One fantastic sci-fi scenario after another. Our running banter.

Joe decided she was really a double agent. No way. Not her. He didn't especially like her. Though he could never put his finger on why. He felt she disapproved of him. "She's a penis- hating dyke!" He was sort of accurate, not about the double agent, or dyke hatred of penises. She just despised his macho. Not only J: comrades were increasingly impatient with the way he treated the women in our cadre.

I didn't want to be with him that night. Maybe Beth would need a place to crash, rather than go all the way back to Elmhurst in the middle of the night. Sometimes she stayed, and I would shrug apologetically at Joe, but I secretly preferred that arrangement.

Beth slowed down to walk with me. I was a little taken by her. When she stayed over, we would crash on my futon, and she would be out as soon as her head hit the pillow. I would lay awake wondering what it would be like to make love to her, to make love to a woman. Repulsive and utterly exhilarating. Plus Beth was super phobic too. And seductive. J's incredible sixth sense said so too. But you really didn't need six senses to know. Beth was Beth. So when she'd slept over, I'd lay on my side of the futon, super still, extremely alone and deprived. Especially if she rolled over and forgot where she was, and our arms touched, or her thigh glanced against mine. God, the cadre didn't need me to be sleepless. Or distracted by the impossible.

I was fighting with myself over my Beth stuff as we entered The Cedar. We squeezed into a large wooden booth toward the back and ordered a mess of fries, onion rings, and several pitchers of Millers. Beth maneuvered to squeeze in next to me. Joe was across. Sullen.

J certainly was a vanguard about sex with women. Her preference was no secret. My canary in the mine. We would discuss my embarrassed curiosity, and she always said, if she and I shacked up, it would threaten our friendship. As a kind of joke she would add something about getting so carried away, she might give away her "alien secrets" and she would end up out of synch with me, in a kind of weird time warp. She should really write sci-fi. We stayed best friends.

No, I decided, that night I wouldn't offer to share my futon with Beth, even though she kind of assumed that I would. In all our efforts as comrades, it was essential that we be open and clear with each other. And here we were, mired in all sorts of un-saids and what-ifs. Like maybe Beth actually wanted to stay with me, not only because it was so late, but also because just maybe she was secretly curious too. J always insisted Beth's phobia trumps all. I desperately needed sleep, so….

Also, I could tell Joe I had a headache and needed to be alone. Then I could sleep in the raw. The air was sultry. It wasn't cooling down at night and I couldn't afford air conditioning. I had jury-rigged a bunch of fans with pots of water, summer maneuvers for railroad flats with windows at either end. Besides, I did need to be alone.

All of this was going through my mind, when J suddenly called to me from the booth behind us across the aisle: "Katie, can you hear me? Please listen. There's big trouble. Please, can you hear me? I need your help! We need your help." I remember her exact words. And her echo-like voice, like a bad phone connection.

I whipped my head around, but instead, I was staring at a pair of angora cats who, I assumed, belonged to the restaurant for catching mice. They were squatting stony still under the booth across the isle. Someone said, "What's the matter, Katie, see a ghost?" and went back to arguing about some tactic.

I freaked again. Hearing voices, like some nutcase. Finally gone off the deep end. Oh how I needed J now! Well, she was there. Somehow she was talking to me. Okay, okay, just chill, I said to myself. As Jackie, our true and feisty late-night waitress, slid the pitchers and frosty steins onto our table, one of the cats slowly crawled under our table and started rubbing against my leg, and I swear, J's plea got even louder.

I poured myself a draught without looking, and it foamed up and spilled over. Beth asked if I was okay. I didn't answer. Just took a long one, hoping everything would fucking go away. It had finally happened. Too much weed. I was a raving schizoid.

I still can't believe what happened next: It as if I were being led by the nose, as if I were a marionette being manipulated by invisible strings, like being powered by remote control.

"I have to make a phone call."

"What? At two be-fucking o'clock in the morning?" Joe looked at me with that suspicious gleam he could muster with his incredible steely blue-green eyes.

"I have to call J. Something I forgot to tell her, and she's up tonight. If she's gone to bed, she won't answer."

"I bet she won't," said Joe. "She's in bed alright, busy eating pussy with no time to stoop to the mundane, like sleep, phone calls, and the anti-war movement."

Larry yelled at Joe to shut the fuck up, and stop being such an asshole. Like a robot, I squeezed out of the booth and headed to the street to find a pay phone. Several years previous, I had been on an acid trip, the only one I ever took. Our cadre finally decided it was counter-revolutionary to dabble in "tune in and drop out," that Leary was a sinister tool of the CIA. Well, I don't know if he was or not, but that night I sure thought an agent had slipped a sugar cube into my beer.

CHAPTER FORTY-SIX

Bell Labs

Jupiter and Venus glowed like searchlights, persistent in their vigilance in the mid-September sky, though somewhat paled by the uncompromising lamps that dimly lit the sparsely populated Bell Labs parking lot in Piscataway, off Route 78.

Little by little the cars and minivans pulled into the lot, some with four or five people, others with as many as ten or twelve. They arrived in rhythm with the trickle of Bell Labs traffic, mostly cleaning ladies on their way out and young, determined programmers on their way in, starched and proper, even though it was several hours before the "normal" workers arrived. The cars and minivans parked in disparate areas, within eye contact, but not in clusters. Headlights off. Just sitting. Waiting. Patient.

Within a half hour, more than a hundred silent vehicles sat in the stillness. The wheezing of several Greyhound buses parking just outside the entrance signaled the arrival of more. Women and men, multi-racial and intergenerational, silently poured out of the buses and retrieved their cardboard placards from the cargo hatches. As the buses rolled away, the new arrivals silently lined up outside the parking lot entrance and sat down. Shortly afterwards, two dilapidated yellow school buses also wheezed to a stop, this time several feet to the left of the very pathway that led to the secret underground lab. The occupants, twenty or thirty of them, uniformly clad in black tee shirts with clenched raised fists etched in white, and variously hued bandannas, efficiently and swiftly loaded out instruments and amps, along with several gasoline generators.

One would think that security guards would have been alerted to the unusual activity. But without interference the musicians were able to set up their array of equipment on a makeshift riser, including two full sets of drums, several microphones, a huge PA system and soundboard.

Katie stepped up to the center mike, and tapped it. The tapping echoed throughout the area. "Free the NASA Three!" she shouted. "Free the NASA

Three!" came the simultaneous response. Within seconds, car trunks slammed as others retrieved their placards. Tiny gleams of candlelight revealed a smattering of determined faces around the lot. Then a few more. The sultry night suddenly cracked alive with music and chants. Hundreds began marching toward the bandstand from the parking lot entrance, in one hand a placard and in the other a lit candle.

CHAPTER FORTY-SEVEN

Matt

Matt was relieved that the alien and his quarry had been taken to a holding area. Raymond didn't even put up a fuss. Nor did he try and freeze anybody. He simply looked sternly at Matt, as if to say, it's in your hands now. If you don't do what I am bidding, I'll do it for you, and I'll take you out in a most unpleasant manner. Then he followed the MPs.

Matt desperately wanted to tell Dawes the entire truth, but his tongue stuck in his mouth.

Dawes wasn't polite when he found Matt pacing in the lab some four hours later. He chewed him out like he was a lowly foot soldier who had been caught humping a chick in his bunk bed.

"Well, Mister, what do they know so far? How do you know they are secure? You were supposed to inform me if and when you actually located a blue surge, not bring them in without my consent. I told you I would interview them first. You just can't recruit as I—I mean, you're a Company Man. Don't you friggin' know better? You've broken every protocol rule in the goddamned book. Have you gone completely bonkers?"

"Well, sir, you were out of town, and, well, it's a long story, but once we found them, we were anxious to test them out right away. They don't know anything, really. Once they learned how much money they would get paid to play a vital part in our national defense, they simply agreed. We're drawing up a contract. Everything's on the up and up. I really don't think we've breached anything, sir."

Dawes was calming down. Perhaps Raymond was working on him from the holding area.

"But there are some other issues we need to work out," Matt continued. This was going to be the hard part.

Dawes' beeper went off. He picked up the intercom.

"What do you mean? Here? How many? You're sure? They're yelling what? I'll be right there. No I won't. Call the public relations crew and get them up here right away."

Dawes slammed the receiver down, his eyes scrunched into steamy slits.

"What the blazes is going on, Matthew? There's hundreds of hippies and beatniks out in the parking lot about to start a friggin' riot. What kind of a mess have you made?"

"In the parking lot? Here? What do they want?"

"Who the hell are the 'NASA Three?' No one knows NASA works out of Bell Labs. What in blazes has happened here? 'Free the NASA Three!' What's that all about? How in God's name did the most top-secret project in the universe suddenly get blown?"

"For the life of me I don't know how anyone in the world would find out that these kids are here."

"Well, everything might be on the up and up, but MPII has been breached because now we have a mob out there demanding their release, as if they had been captured instead of recruited, like you claimed. As far as that mob is concerned, they were detained illegally.

"You better have answers for me in the next thirty seconds. We've got a major security breach on our hands! How they found out that NASA is even in Piscataway is utterly beyond me, and I'm sure as hell not going to take the blame!"

CHAPTER FORTY-EIGHT

J

I sort of missed all the excitement. From out of nothingness, tiny bursts of energy from distant chanting slowly pulled me into fuzzy consciousness, and I struggled to figure out who the "NASA Three" were. Then it was five-thirty in the morning. Yazzie and Matt led Scotty, Johnny and me out to the parking lot ablaze with tiny candle lights. Overhead, helicopter beams crisscrossed hundreds of chanting demonstrators. Squadrons of dazed security forces lazed at the edge of the parking lot, Uzis in their laps.

The crowd roared. An amplified band started playing a song I had never heard before. I particularly remember these lyrics: "...and the killers ride around in limousines. We gotta stop 'em before they kill us all!"

Later I learned from Katie that she and a small team of comrades negotiated with a squinty old fart, and some stiffly suited publicists. She claimed that NBC and CBS were on their way; she suggested NASA and Ma Bell end the embarrassing standoff without publicity.

I never learned how the Imari could retro-sweep the documentation and the NASA special research team.

But here's the rumor: Right after we left the lab, hundreds of cats, mostly scrungy feral ones, along with some gorgeous purebred angoras, emerged from out of nowhere, and ran amok around the underground lab for about thirty minutes. They squatted on keyboards, peed on documents, tangled up cables, chewed on connectors, batted around computer mice, and converted the huge control boards into scratching posts. By 8:30 AM, the NASA team wondered why they were bunked in Piscataway rather than at home with their families. Bookcases were toppled and empty. Tops of cubicles were swept clean, except for mugs, photos and other mementos. Entire programs were missing from

the mainframes, causing massive system failures. We think the
cats went a little overboard in their zeal to wipe everything
clean.

Also gone from anyone's memory was the unexplained
mid-September meteor storm, a month after the Perseids, which
had camouflaged the felines' luminous compressed solo-pod entry into Earth's atmosphere.

When Scotty, Johnny and I finally met up with Telmx and Winstx on the now-liberated Europa, our jubilance was tempered by
Raymond's disappearance.

Oh, one more thing. Just before the three of us squeezed
into Katie's little Volkswagen Bug, I noticed Matt standing alone
watching elated and exhausted musicians breaking down their
equipment. He was weeping. I actually walked over and hugged
him. A warm embrace. Not sexual or anything, just a warm
moment. In my mind I felt Yazzie's smile. He was nearby, maybe with the marauding cats. I don't know. Later I asked Telmx
if Yazzie could be a new recruit. The Mission had to continue its
work. We could always use a bit more help.

Today

I am traveling to Galern II, where I will spend a few days with Telmx. Then we will hop to the fifth moon of the gas giant Uthitks, where Winstx and Scotty will join us. I am on vacation (I am a life counselor in New York City. I promise, I don't use my empath powers to read minds. Never even tempted. I do have strong empathic connections with people, however. Really helps my work.)

Johnny and Lenx reconstituted the inter-species fusion jazz group. Maybe they'll stop by between gigs. Johnny is on-call to the Mission. He comes back, I think, more than we know, for secret organizing, particularly in prisons and schools. Probably violates all sorts of Council restrictions about interference. No matter. He's right.

Scotty and I continue the monitoring Mission on Earth. In addition to Telmx and Winstx, some of our other lovers are off-world, along with other earthlings. Rather than diminish our love for each other, our multiple intimate experiences have enhanced our relationship, just as Telmx had promised. Quite incredible. We're in love with our lives.

Back in the day, we had to resist spontaneous impulses to use our powers. For a brief moment, we even considered helping Abbie Hoffman levitate the Pentagon. Now we mind-bend here and there. But the struggle, as always, belongs to the people.

Right now, among other issues, we are confronting the horrendous wars on Iraq and Afghanistan, the collapse of Earth's eco-system, and saving the life of Mumia Abu-Jamal, the voice of the voiceless. I wish I could just mesmerize his guards and set him free. No, also a task for the people. We do our small part: We occasionally use our "sixth sense" to anticipate or warn, nothing that calls attention to us, or alters the inevitable, painfully slow progress toward the egalitarian world we now truly know is possible.

Telmx invited Katie to be trained off-world as an empath monitor. But she chose to remain an earthling revolutionary. "In fighting for improving conditions on Earth, empath energy will develop. We will liberate people to feel for each other," she promised. After much deliberation, Telmx and Winstx decided she was trustworthy: no need to retro-sweep her involvement with us in the sixties. She will keep our Mission secret. Her knowledge about the civilized universe enhances her resolve, and she's there when we need her. I love her. She and her comrades, our comrades, do incredible political work.

Yazzie traveled off-world for healing and training. He became a very astute scholar of the **Books of Kro'an'ot**, and ultimately replaced Gir, completing Telmx's and Winstx's Triad Team. His cilia are resplendent, long silvery clusters radiating his craggy chestnut face. He's still a fabulous storyteller, and over the next several years, when he would visit Scotty and me, he would immediately corral our three little boys and keep them entranced for hours. Our kids are grown now and off doing their own thing. Only one, the youngest, applied to be an Empath Travel Scout.

Egalitarianism, or Communism, is still not how most people live on Earth. I have stopped being impatient and self-righteous about it. I now respect the struggle, the contradictions, the frustrating setbacks, the incredible leaps forward. We are very hopeful that developments in South America and the immigrant movement in the States will accelerate things.

I refrain from looking ahead with V.E.-scans. Examining possible futures to the .01 level of confidence is like taking my blood pressure every ten minutes. We have to live our lives.

Scotty and I are particularly involved in the case of the Cuban Five. Their mission was so much like ours: warning against terrorist threats to their egalitarian country, but, of course, the plight of the Cuban Five is much worse than ours ever was.

I occasionally get together with K'dasti (the s/he on the asteroid). S/he's a farmer and a sculptor. Not interested in politics. One day I hope s/he will visit Earth, to learn what the struggle is all about. But it's okay. S/he's very serene, and aware that those who protect her/his serenity must employ all the incredible technology *that s/he refuses to have anything to do with. S/he is one of the reasons we struggle to maintain universal serenity.*

Raymond and his band are still out there. He recruits mercenaries from un-evolved planets. Universal monitoring goes on. So far, we have not sensed his presence on Earth. He fears our collective powers, and can no longer surprise us. Johnny, Scotty and I have become very skilled Level VI monitors. I've grown a fine set of cilia (not as fine as Yazzie's!), and can control my fearsome "take-out" capacity. That struggle is another story.

Scotty will write Matt's story next. His struggles are compelling, and inevitable, given who he was and who he was to become.

When Scotty visits our lunar hide-away, she will open her empath chamber so we may enter her science fiction manuscript (Beyond the Horse's Eye). It's almost finished, and she needs our comments. She had plumbed every scintilla from the V.E.-dream-memories of Telmx, Johnny, Matt, Katie and myself to put this work together. No chance of revealing anything: her book is so outlandish, no one will believe it.

*Why should it be written? The struggles in the universe must be chronicled, even if the book reads like science fiction. As an allegory, it might do some good, maybe tweak Earth's development toward egalitarianism (without our risking retro-sweep). It's my compromise with my urge to get on a megaphone in Union Square and shout "truths" about the inevitable development of civilizations in the universe. I do speak out: the people (the 99 percent!) are collectively stronger than the few at the top; workers and disenfranchised will always win out. But can't prove my convictions using the **Books of Kro'an'ot** and the history of the civilized sentient universe. The left would dismiss me as a psychotic fanatic, although I might attract absolutely useless fringe elements. And no one would come to me for life counseling.*

Goshing died just before the Pentagon action. Given the political atmosphere, her compound couldn't go through its proper molting sequence and lost its ability to protect itself from Raymond's band. Without strong Imari wisdom from her grouping, the Intergalactic Council went through strenuous upheavals, caused by the expansion and interference of compliancy factions spearheaded by the Pomdos, and by Raymond's group, which exploited the complacency and confusion.

It was difficult and delicate for Telmx to update the Council. Her triad group had broken protocols. Had she timed presentations poorly, we would have been summarily retro-swept. Her V.E.-depictions, particularly of Raymond's grizzly massacre of the Kiolanthe on Kiol, finally convinced the delegates. Raymond's faction resigned, and even the complacent Pomdos awakened to the necessity for vigilance. Another precarious period.

As long as no secret project tries to harness empath energy to subjugate on-world and off-world beings, the struggle on Earth continues without extra-terrestrial or impatient earthling empath monitor interference.

Exploitation of the many by the few is why we struggle. Telmx's Triad Group keeps us hopeful, patient and relentless by quoting from the **Books of Kro'an'ot** *and from those whose teachings are informed by the Books: "Egalitarian serenity is inevitable." "Dialectical materialism is a scientific given, perpetually confirmed by the history of developing civilizations in the sentient universe." "Those with vision must have patience, and yet be intractable and ever prepared to seize the moment." "Change happens slower than civilization desires, and swifter than it is comfortable with." Marx, Lenin, Marcy, Kelly-Broone, and all the bygone, current and future visionary revolutionaries would have loved hanging out with the Imari and the Kiolanthes. Maybe they do.*

Glossary

Age of Empath

A period of time in a planet's history in which the distinctive characteristic is the dependence on empath energy. If an ethically immature species, one organized for conquering and exploitation, discovers how to harness and wield empath energy for space travel, weapons, and ultimately time travel, intergalactic species would be endangered. The Intergalactic Council oversees and mandates the Order of Empath Travel Scouts to identify and monitor planets that are entering the Age of Empath prematurely. Since the peaceful Age of Empath has been in existence on member planets for so many millennia, a growing number of Council delegates have become complaisant and question the need for continued monitoring.

Auto-effuse

A method of heating food and drink by effusing personal empath energy directly into the container. To auto-effuse, bend your head until your cilia are directly over the container, and transmit your empath energy. Works best on vegan stews, dipping sauces and teas. Most efficient if used with a frimulator. It is also possible to use an ordinary container, earthling or otherwise, but the result will be far less satisfying.

Books of Kro'an'ot

A tome of many volumes that formulates and explains the philosophy of the ancient legendary Imari, whose wisdom was originally empathically gleaned from the Kiolanthe, the little people on the planet Kiol. The Books must be studied by all who apply to the Order of Empath Travel Scouts, with full mastery attained after three grueling Galern II years of training at the Institute.

Bot

A beverage brewed from the bot'ime root, originally discovered on the planet Kiol, where the Kiolanthe cultivated and harvested it in their sprawling forests. The most delicious vintage varieties of bot are from Kiol, but bot'ime is now cultivated throughout the known sentient universe, and excellent varieties of the brew are abundant and readily available. As people mature beyond the rich natural empath capabilities of infancy and childhood (with a strong resurgence in adolescence), natural personal empath energy must be boosted and maintained by bot.

Cilia

Clusters of long silvery wafting filaments emanating from sentients who possess advanced empath energy powers. In sapient species the cilia grow directly above the eyes, replacing eyebrows. But on other species they can be found in various places. For example, on elephant-like species, they cluster at the edge of their nostrils. On certain dolphin-like species they completely cover the body like soft fur.

Empath energy

A powerful form of energy generated by all living beings as they interact with each other. Infants, in their in utero connection with their biological parent, possess the most empath energy, which is then assimilated by the embryonic fluid (Kiolanthe birthing ritual includes drinking the embryonic fluid to enhance empath energy, especially among those who will be caretaking the infant). Infants depend on empath energy to communicate with the primary parenting one(s), sending that energy out to their caretaker(s). At any given moment, the primary caretaker absorbs the empathically borne communication in order to meet the infant's needs, and in the process, having been so empathically enhanced by the interaction, communicates directly back to the infant his or her moods, positive and negative, which the infant absorbs like a sponge. The back-and-forth communication is seamless and profound, and is the primary early influence on the infant's personality development.

Communal interaction, as well as interaction between two people, or even imagined interaction between two people, all enhance empath. Even drinking bot alone works to enhance empath. Ceremonial communal practices of "breaking the froth" and sharing a goblet of bot further synergistically enhance empath.

To keep in touch with and enhance one's empath capacities past childhood requires discipline. As recorded in the *Legend of Kro'an'ot*, the Imari species was the first to develop high levels of connection with birth-given empath capacities. Eventually the Imari trained other species. The most disciplined reach high levels of skill in harnessing and wielding inherent empath capabilities.

The chemistry of empath energy enhancement is only understood by the most sophisticated scientists. In order to supplement solar energy and maintain the energy grids and fuel required for all modes of travel (including interstellar), all sentients possessing empath energy donate their energy on a regular schedule to booster generating plants.

Frimulator

An Imari "samovar" that has absorbed empath energy from users over the millennia. A large Imari ornate metallic device that receives empath energy via cilia (see auto-effuse), and auto-effuses or heats powders, liquids and solid food. The top looks like a narrow chimney with a flared opening. The steamy liquid can be poured using a spigot on the bottom side; heated foods can be accessed via a sliding tray. The older the frimulator, the more succulent the brew.

Galern II

The second planet from the sun in the Galern star system. Home to the Imari species, populated by the descendents of the original Imari who were nomads on the planet Kiol in the Gilophir star system.

Imari

Originally a nomadic sapient socialist species living on the planet Kiol. The first species in the known universe to harness empath energy for peaceful practical use, including space travel. A major grouping ultimately settled on Galern II.

Kiolanthe

Highly empathic sentients indigenous to the planet Kiol, who, according to legend, first communicated with the Imari nomads and warned them about the misuse of empath energy in the universe.

Legend of Kro'an'ot

The story of the Imari Kro'an'ot and her best friend, Gimot, who first encountered the Kiolanthe. She is the author of the *Books of Kro'an'ot*.

Mindshift

A slight tweaking of someone else's mind. Forbidden by the Intergalactic Council except in extraordinary circumstances. Level VI Empaths are endowed with controlled mindshift but are only allowed to exercise this power when mandated by the Council. Untrained empaths, particularly children of planets not yet in the Age of Empath, might discover mindshifting and inadvertently use it on others to obtain what they want or need.

Order of Empath Travel Scouts

Originally only qualified Imari were trained at the Institute, but the Ki-olanthe mandate was for all ethically mature sentients in the universe to have the opportunity to apply for training and attain Level VI status. The Kiolanthe knew there were multitudes of sentient species in the universe, and trained the original Imari children with the explicit mandate that when they located a sentient species whose planet was entering the Age of Empath, they would train appropriate children on that planet to enter the Order. In each case, the Mission of the Travel Scouts is to assess whether or not the sentients on the discovered planet are ethically ready to use empath energy peacefully or for enthrallment of others within their own planet or of species on other planets. When necessary, the Travel Scouts must select and train empath talented indigenous children to monitor the situation on their planet if, when analyzed, that planet appears to be emerging prematurely into the Age of Empath.

Paired photons or "quantum entanglement"

Michio Kaku, in *Physics of the Impossible:* "If two electrons are initially vibrating in unison (a state called coherence) they can remain in wavelike synchronization even if they are separated by a large distance.... If something happens to one electron, then some of that information is immediately transmitted to the other.... Einstein derisively called this 'spooky-action-at distance,'..." (p. 60).[1] In 1967, NASA scientists were beginning to discover that a primitive form of empath connection with the photons (they called it ESP) allowed them to manipulate the "spooky action" at will (a precursor to intergalactic space travel), which meant they were prematurely entering the Age of Empath.

Pomdos

Panda-like sentients who vigorously question the Mission of the Order of Empath Travel Scouts. The Pomdos and their allies form a powerful faction in the Intergalactic Council.

---

[1] Kaku, Michio. *Physics of the Impossible.* New York: Doubleday, 2008.

Retro-sweep

A very rarely used process which brings an individual, grouping or entire planet back to an earlier period in development. It is authorized by the Intergalactic Council in very rare instances on those who would harness empath energy, wittingly or unwittingly, for purposes that threaten the tranquility of the universe.

Virtual Empath (V.E.)

A dream-like state that allows users to access from their inner chambers mini-dramas of events acquired from various sources:

1) A dramatized message empathically sent by one or more people to another person's inner chamber. V.E.-dreamers can actually have a conversation with the person or people who have placed a V.E.-message in their inner chamber, but only to ask questions and obtain clarity. They might object to what the other person has sent them , but they can't change the content. Such messages are often sent by people who are about to die to someone they are extremely close to, only to be accessed in that person's inner chamber posthumously.

2) A dramatized message, accessible by a V.E.-viewer, generally sent by one person at a console to a group of people, each sitting in front of an individual viewer. Often used in meetings to efficiently convey complicated information. If the mini-drama is downloaded from a person's inner chamber to a V.E.-chip, minimal empath energy is required. First the energy is used to perform the download from a person's inner chamber to the chip. Then, the chip is inserted into a master console, which sends the V.E.-experience to the other viewers. The only other energy required is from each receiving user to absorb the V.E. that has been sent. If viewers and chips are not available, a person can send the V.E.-mini-drama to the inner-mind chambers of those in close proximity, but this requires much more empath energy from the sender and the receivers.

3) A V.E.-time-travel-mini-drama, in which a person with very advanced empath powers can access past and future events without the aid of consoles or messages conveyed by others. The event is accessible simply because it exists on the time/space continuum. Sometimes an extremely talented but untrained child with exponentially enhanced empath powers, will fall into a V.E.-time-travel dream. These are sometimes experienced as intensely horrible nightmares.

In some instances people in a V.E.-state may feel as if they are actually participating in the mini-drama, but they cannot alter anything through action or thought. Inexperienced individuals are often convinced they can have an impact upon what they are viewing. Trained empaths can consciously or unconsciously absorb V.E.-messages from objects that have been immersed with V.E.

People can V.E.-travel to their inner chambers at will, but sometimes they simply find themselves there.

Because V.E.-states are intensely vibrant, adult users are cautioned to wear V.E.-goggles, which not only protect them from the staggering sensations associated with the mini-drama, but also help minimize their empath energy drain. In certain instances not wearing goggles can be permanently damaging or even lethal because of the intensity of the V.E.-experience, so adults usually carry goggles with them at all times. Because children are naturally endowed with empath energy and consciously or unconsciously communicate using empath anyway, their bodies intuitively control the intensity of the V.E.-experience, i.e., they do not require goggles.

Save the Children:

A Brief Record of their Sufferings and Bravery

by J

SUFFERINGS

Hiroshima, 1945:

A Japanese schoolgirl... saw a B-29 fly by, then a flash. She put her hands up and "my hands went right through my face." She saw "a man without feet walking on his ankles." She passed out. "By the time I wake up, black rain was falling.... I thought I was blind, but I got my eyes open and I saw a beautiful blue sky and the dead city. Nobody is standing up. Nobody is walking around.... I wanted to go home to my mother." (Zinn 1995)

Vietnam, 1964:

By this time Conti could see that only a few children were left standing. Mothers had thrown themselves on top of the young ones in a last desperate bid to protect them from the bullets raining down on them. The children were trying to stand up. Calley opened fire again, killing them one by one. (Bilton and Sim 1992, 120-121)

Louisiana, 1838:

A shaman led the line of measle-sick children into the river, and after bathing in the cold water they did seem to be better, somewhat better. An hour or so later, most of them began to shiver and chatter and quake. (Ehle 1988, 356)

Birmingham 1963:

From: "Ballad of Birmingham"

The mother smiled to know her child
Was in a sacred place,
But that smile was the last smile
To come upon her face.
For when she heard the explosion,
Her eyes grew wet and wild.
She raced through the streets of Birmingham
Calling for her child. (Randall 2009, 105-106)

From "Birmingham Sunday"
Four little girls
Who went to Sunday School that day
And never came back home at all
But left instead
Their blood upon the wall
With spattered flesh
And bloodied Sunday dresses
Torn to shreds by dynamite (Hughes 1994, 557)

Jackson State, 1970:

The police opened fire at approximately 12:05 a.m., May 15, and continued firing for more than 30 seconds. The students scattered, some running for the trees in front of the library, but most scrambling for the Alexander Hall west end door. (Anonymous)

New York City, April 28, 1973:

From "**Power**"

The policeman who shot down a 10-year-old in Queens stood over the boy with his cop shoes in childish blood and a voice said "die you little motherfucker" and there are tapes to prove that. At his trial the policeman said in his own defense"I didn't notice the size or nothing else only the color." And there are tapes to prove that, too. (Lorde 1997, 215)

Guatemala, 1970s and 1980s:

   The next day I was in my small green house
when I heard the screams and shouts begin. A
young girl, bleeding from a blow to the mouth
ran up the hill to me, sobbing. The army had
come with the stranger. It was, after all, a
trick. They were rounding up all of the co-op
members and loading them into a truck. I must
hide--they were looking for me. I ran into the
tall corn plants and up a slope where I could
see what was happening in the center of the
village. The co-op building that we had all
built together was burning. The army vehicle was
there, the back opened up like a cattle truck.
The soldiers were screaming obscenities and
dragging the people inside. The other villagers
were begging and pleading for their relatives.
An old woman hung onto her son and was clubbed
to the ground. My uncle reached out for his
daughter, and a soldier slashed his face with a
bayonet. None of our people had guns, only their
voices to plead for mercy, to beg for the lives
of their family. I saw Mariella then, bending
over the old man. The soldiers fell on her, dragging her to the truck. It took three of them to
drag her, she fought so hard. She looked once towards where I was hiding. Could she have known
I was there? Her beautiful face was covered with
blood from a blow to her head. I started to run
to her, but the village girl next to me pulled
me down and held my face against her shoulder,
so I couldn't see anything else. Two other villagers who had hidden with us held my arms. When
I looked up again he truck was gone, with nine-
teen of our people. (Harbury 1994, 62)

May 15, 1970: Kent State Massacre:

Mary Ann Vecchio with Jeffrey Miller, one of the four students killed in the Kent State University Massacre [photo credit: John Paul Filo, *Valley Daily News,* 1970.]

Philadelphia: Attack on MOVE, 1978:

Dilbert Africa, during a police attack on a MOVE home in Philadelphia [from police footage, reprinted in The Philadelphia Daily News, *August 8, 1978]*

Warsaw Jewish Ghetto Uprising, April-May 1943:

"German storm troopers force Warsaw ghetto dwellers of all ages to move, hands up, during the Jewish Ghetto Uprising in April-May 1943." [from Main Commission for the Investigation of Nazi War Crimes (http://fcit.usf.edu/holocaust/gallery/46199.htm). By permission of the United States Holocaust Memorial Museum. Credit: National Archives and Records Administration, College Park Instytut Pamieci Narodowej Panstwowe Muzeum Auschwitz-Birkenau w Oswiecimiu]

BRAVERY

Soweto, June 16, 1976:

Early on 16 June 1976, pupils marched from various assembly points around Soweto towards a meeting point in Orlando West from where they were going to march together to Orlando Stadium for a rally. The march was peaceful and disciplined; pupils sang freedom songs and chanted slogans as they walked. They arrived with placards bearing phrases such as, "Down with Afrikaans" and "Bantu Education—To Hell with IT".

Just as the demonstrators converged, the police appeared, armed with automatic rifles, and formed up facing them. As the crowd sang Morena Boloka (the Sotho version of the African national anthem), a white policeman threw a tear-gas canister. The police then opened fire, killing 13-year-old Hector Peterson and at least three others. The crowd reacted by picking up stones, bricks and bottles and pelting the police, who were forced to retreat despite their weapons and the fact that the pupils suffered more causalities. Thus began an uprising which was to continue through to the end of 1977 and lead to the loss of over a thousand lives, most as a result of police action. (Pampallis 1991, 256-7)

Mbuyisa Makhubu carrying the body of Hector Pieterson, one of the first casualties. [Photo credit: Sam Nzima; http://en.wikipedia.org/wiki/Apartheid]

Guatemala, 1970s and 1980s:

But now I was beginning to think about the poverty of our people, the wages we were paid for hard labor, the inequalities. Thing were beginning to fit together, to make sense to me.

In the end I ran off to join the guerrilla movement. I was still very young, and didn't know exactly what I was getting myself into. But I knew that these people were good and decent, and I knew that what they were saying about conditions in our country was the truth. I wanted things to get better, not just for me, for everyone, and I wanted to be part of the change. Really, I was very thrilled about all of this. So I rolled up a blanket and packed some corn tortillas with black beans, and left in the darkness with a young couple I had barely met. (Harbury 1994, 73)

Holland: June 4, 1940:

The Nazis are trying all their tricks to win over the schoolchildren. They have given us sweets, which most of us have put down the drain, and they have allowed the top class to matriculate without passing the exams.

Our teacher says, "Be brave, Hold your head up."

...

June 9, 1940:

I have decided that we must do all we can to make life unpleasant for the Nazis. We have formed a Secret Society—me, Piet, Jos and Henricjk. But Charlotees, Piet's twin sister, has found out about us, and insists on joining. I told her that this isn't a job for girls. "Don't be so superior," she said.

I explained that we're not being superior. There may be danger, and the Nazis don't care whom they torture. Charlotte then threatened that if we don't take her in with us, she would work on her own. A girl can do things that a boy can't.

So now we are the Secret Society Five, the SS5, we call ourselves for fun.... (Cowan 1976, 137)

Mumia Abu-Jamal:

Still, many of these children don't give up. Perhaps the best thing we can do for them is to nurture their hope--give them reason for new hopes and feed the hope already within them so it can grow into something strong that will sustain them through life....Children do not only have an innate hope; they are hope....They carry their hope with them to a future we can't see. (Abu-Jamal 2003, 83)

**Fidel Castro in a 1953 speech
quoting Jose Marti:**

To those who would call me a dreamer, I quote the words of Marti: "A true man does not seek the path where advantage lies, and this is the only practical man, whose dream of today will be the law of tomorrow, because he who has looked back on the essential course of history and has seen flaming and bleeding peoples seethe in the cauldron of the ages, knows that, without a single exception, the future lies on the side of duty." (Castro 1975, 95)

The "International":

Arise, you children* of starvation!
Arise, you wretched of the earth!
For justice thunders condemnation:
A better world's in birth!
No more tradition's chains shall bind us,
Arise you slaves, no more in thrall!
The earth shall rise on new foundations:
We have been naught, we shall be all!

*[*Line changed from the original:
"Arise, you prisoners of starvation!"]*

Bibliography

Abu-Jamal, Mumia. "Children." In *Death Blossoms; Reflections from a Prisoner of Conscience*, 83. Cambridge: South End Press, 2003.

Anonymous. *Jackson State -- May 1970; "Lest We Forget."* www.may41970.com/Jackson%20State/jackson_state_may_1970.htm.

Bilton, Michael, and Kevin Sim. *Four Hours in My Lai.* New York: Viking Penguin, 1992.

Castro, Fidel. *History Will Absolve Me.* Translated by Pedro Alverez Tabio and Andred Paul Booth. La Habana: Politicas Editorial de Ciencias Sociales, 1975.

Cowan, Lore. *Children of the Resistance.* New York: Archway Paperback, 1976.

Ehle, John. *Trail of Tears: The Rise and Fall of the Cherokee Nation.* New York: AnchorDoubleday, 1988.

Harbury, Jennifer. *Bridge of Courage.* Monroe: Common Courage Press, 1994.

Hughes, Langston. "Birmingham Sunday." In *Collected Poems of Langston Hughes*, by Arnold Rampersad, 557. New York: Alfred A. Knopf, 1994.

Lorde, Audre. "Power." In *The Collected Works of Audre Lorde*, by Audre Lorde, 215. New York: W.W. Norton, 1997.

Main Commission for the Investigation of Nazi
War Crimes (http://fcit.usf.edu/holocaust/
gallery/46199.htm). By permission of the United
States Holocaust Memorial Museum. The views or
opinions expressed in this book, and the con-
text in which the image is used, do not neces-
sarily reflect the views or policy of, nor imply
approval or endorsement by, the United States
Holocaust Memorial Museum. Credit: National
Archives and Records Administration, College
Park Instytut Pamieci Narodowej Panstwowe
Muzeum Auschwitz-Birkenau w Oswiecimiu

Pampallis, John. *Foundations of the New South
Africa*. London: Zed Books Ltd., 1991.

Randall, Dudley. "Ballad of Birmingham." In
*Roses and Revolutions; The Selected Writings of
Dudley Randall*, by Ed. Melba Jones Boyd, 105-106.
Detroit: Wayne State University Press, 2009.

Zinn, Howard. "Hiroshima; Breaking the Silence."
Open Magazine Pamphlet Series, 1995.

Acknowledgments

When you write a novel on scattered weekends and vacations, it takes a very long time (even if you can write more steadily, it takes a very long time!). So there are so many people to thank for their support over so many years.* Without their encouragement, patient listening, toleration of my whining and self-doubts, these pages would have remained in closets and drawers (literally!). Not to mention that I feared "retro-sweep" (literally!). I'm sure I've left some people out. Not on purpose.

So, my most grateful thanks to: My Prose Writing Group: Josephine Diamond, Loretta Goldberg, Jeri Hilderley, Siobhan May and Caroline Thomas. My fellow classmates in Emily Hanlon's writing class: Jean Busatti, Susan Elizabeth Davis, Judith Dupre, Vallerie Huyghue and Terry Purinton. Patient listeners and encouraging supporters: Joanne Brown, Carol Buck, Shelley Ettinger, Linda Gould, Robert Hayden, Imani Henry, Jeanner Jacobson, Ralph Klein, Joan Klein, Marilyn Miller, and Stanley Siegel. And Richard Voloshen, Project Director, Overlook Fire Tower, Woodstock, New York.

Then special thanks to: those who read or listened to various iterations of the manuscript and give me such cogent and valuable critiques: Rain Bengis, Pat Cox, Susan Elizabeth Davis, LeiLani Dowell, Kathy Durkin, Sara Flounders, Lisa Freedman, Sue Harris, Jeri Hilderley, Sita Jag, Siobhan May, Manuel Posada, Lallan Schoenstein, and Gary Wilson.

And to Felix Serrano, for his inspiring first iteration of the cover.

There also can be no words to express my appreciation to:

Lallan Schoenstein, for her exquisite final cover, book designs, and website;

LeiLani Dowell for her patient and utterly accurate copyediting;

Patricia Cox (PL Cox Communications), for her pithy plot descriptions, unending encouragement, and brilliant publicist's sensibility;

Emily Hanlon, whose down-the-rabbit-hole class pulled the best out of me, although I rewrote each passage kicking and screaming;

Hannelore Hahn and The International Women's Writing Guild for the many summers of inspiration and encouragement; and the dedicated activists in the International Action Center and Workers World, whose political analyses, publications, actions, and determined optimism for the triumph of the 99 percent, helped me form the essential political thesis of *Beyond the Horse's Eye*.

Finally (notice how many time her name appears!), thank you to my loving partner, Jeri Hilderley, without whom I couldn't have survived each neurotic bout of impending "retro-sweep." She read and reread, listened and re-listened; validated and critiqued; and suffered with me though every bit of writing and rewriting. Whew, Jeri! Here we are.

*Acknowledgement of people and organizations is not meant to imply that they endorse or in any way agree with assumptions put forth in my book. Those are entirely mine.

The Author

Born a "red diaper baby" next to the George Washington Bridge in New York City, Janet Rose came of age in the sixties. While earning her master's degree in English Literature at the University of California at Berkeley, she participated in the Free Speech Movement and co-edited the *Vietnam Day Newsletter* with Jerry Rubin. She remained active in the anti-war, civil rights, LGBTQ and women's movements. In the last two decades, her political home has been the International Action Center, founded by Ramsey Clark.

At nine, having developed an avid interest in astronomy, but too poor to buy binoculars and a telescope, Janet decided that once she was over forty, she would be too old to appreciate Halley's Comet. As soon as she could make money, she purchased her own equipment in anticipation of the comet and, of course, is still (at seventy) not too old to appreciate all the wonders of the universe.

The younger Janet was a fan of all the comic book superheroes, her first introduction to science fiction. Although *War of the Worlds* and *The Thing* terrified the youngster, the older Janet couldn't get enough of *Star Trek* and *Star Wars*. She also gobbled up Isaac Asimov, Ursula Le Guin, Samuel Delany (among many others) and, of course, her favorite, Octavia Butler. All profoundly inspired her own science fiction. From them she learned that science fiction is one of the most versatile genres for political expression.

Janet didn't write *Beyond the Horse's Eye* for publication, but friends (especially her partner, Jeri Hilderley, author of *Mari* and *Rune Seeker*) and enthusiastic feedback at public readings convinced her to send out queries. After two years of trying, it was time to found WordSpace Publications and self-publish, which does, in the long run, give Janet more control over every aspect of her book, especially as our political climate veers further to the right!

Beyond the Horse's Eye is for the ninety-nine percent.

Made in the USA
Charleston, SC
21 March 2013